Generation VI
The Underworld

Jeff Wimperis

Maquari Press

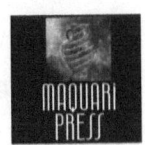

In memory of Jeanne Burd.

INTRODUCTION

I started this project seven years ago following a conversation with my mom. A close friend of hers had just passed away, who was also the mother of a close friend of mine. This lady's passing, unfortunately, had not been quick and easy. As my mom and I reflected on this, she went further to note that this had often been the way with her friend. My mom added simply, "she had a hard life." From those few words came the idea for what would eventually become an entire novel. At that moment I thought of my friend. I thought of how unfair his mother's life was. Then I thought to myself, "what if my friend could go into the Underworld, plead his case to the gods. Maybe they would let her come back."

I've never told my friend about any of this. It was always my plan to have him find out this way. In the spirit of remembering a great lady, therefore, I am happy to dedicate this novel to her and the Burd family. I hope they, and all readers, will enjoy.

PROLOGUE

A bright virtecran flashes the latest new post from the *Time's Current*: "Three Missing Bodies in the Eulimnos Section of Prometheum."

Elegant fingers scroll to reveal the image of the investigation scene, ornamented by the signature lakes of Eulimnos. The article follows:

"Dozens of mourners gathered to witness the funeral games of Pandora Maquari, daughter of renowned General the late Alexander Maquari. Events were a mix of excitement and emotion as participants and spectators rallied the contests.

Leonidas Maquari, more commonly known as The Maurileho, was slated to deliver a eulogy speech following the games. At the point of doing so, however, the 21-year-old and son of the deceased shocked the crowd by turning from the podium and running headfirst into the lake. He did not resurface.

Even more tragic was the attempt of his childhood friend, Anastasia Wildyn, 20, to rescue him, which resulted in her apparent drowning as well.

The corpse of Pandora Maquari remains unfound.

Eulimnos, Prometheum: 14:22."

The hand stays positioned as if posing for a portrait. Pristine, the skin is interrupted only by a dark, marble textured ring imprinted with the character "v."

After a pause, the browser is commanded closed.

The wallpaper displays an elevated panoramic of a series of islands along a coast.

At the bottom of the screen the time reads: 14:33.

The date: 13/16.

Year: 2080.

PROTASIS: THE DESCENT

CHAPTER 1 – THE EAGLE OVER THE ELM

Thunder and fire pour from the hands of Leonidas Maquari as he moves through his cardio rounds on Shadow Fighter. Each carefully placed strike delivered by his toned, muscular frame sends droplets of sweat scattering off his dark curls. His vigorous opponent might react the same, were he not a virtual form of low-A.I.

How did I get here.

Landed punches sound through the lonely basement that has always served as his refuge. They create a beat of sorts when taken as a whole: a pattern of music leading to anywhere.

Nowhere.

The combinations form a rhythmic array that transforms the shadow fighter into a moving drum set. The timing runs current with the blows: one, one two, one two three four.

This should be my time.

Dark, chestnut eyes demonstrate the intensity of his groove. Deep within shows an intensity of strife and burden. There is weight he means to lose besides that of the body.

But Mom...

A pang of guilt breaks his focus. He quickens his pace as punishment. Over what he's not sure.

Pound and weave. Pound and weave.

The flurry costs him more than he anticipated in energy but he soon feels lighter. Taking deep breaths he settles into lazy hooks and guarded counter shots. The virtual opponent also slows to simulate the recovery needed following a forceful exchange. Its back and forth motion soon gives it the impression of swaying like a pendulum. Leo's eyes follow, then his mind. Little by little he drifts off altogether.

He finds himself cast into a wooded area. A narrow rural road splits the trees to both sides. The place is nowhere he has gone, but somewhere he has seen.

Odd cries and smells tickle his senses. They savor of pain, despair, decay. Although he cannot locate the source, he feels their effect pressing on him.

He accelerates through the woods until his surroundings blur. He blinks hard to gain clarity. After several blinks he closes his eyes and shakes his head back and forth. When he looks again he finds himself motionless.

He stands alone in bleak silence.

He looks down to see his feet planted on a gravel pull-off.

Before him, a familiar tree.

Only now the tree carries an unfamiliar mark at the base of its trunk.

"K."

What the hell...

He searches his mind for any recollection or significance of the symbol.

Finding none, he kneels cautiously. He recognizes the tree as the elm from Lake Maquari. On this one though, the pattern of the bark tends toward the "K" as if some dominating force were luring it in.

Indeed, Leo begins to feel the pull himself. The cries and smells he sensed from earlier return. Then, as if from obedience to something in the unconscious, he extends a pair of fingertips toward the base.

At the point of contact though, everything disappears.

His pupils refocus and the next thing he sees is the Shadow Fighter. It is still: as is his body. His oily skin glistens, but only a few beads of sweat remain on his brow.

One falls like a tear over his left eye. It changes course when it meets the rugged terrain of his scars: one along the eyebrow intersecting with another running to the cheekbone. The sensation rouses him.

Damn.

He removes the glove from his right hand and runs his thumb over his fingertips.

I got to get a grip.

No feeling of tree or bark rise to the surface of his skin. The scenes, however, replay vividly in his mind. Nonetheless, he continues rubbing.

"Pound and weave," says a soft voice from behind, "doesn't mean stand around."

Smiling at his fingers, he lazily raises his head.

"That so?" he says.

In the doorway stands a blonde of modest features. Straight hair parted at the center draped over a fair skinned face wearing little to no makeup. She meets the coaxing of her childhood friend with a glitter in her blue eyes.

"Hey, you."

Leo regards her half-surprised half amused, conveniently forgoing the ancient custom of a hug.

"Well look who's back," he says, "Anastasia Wildyn." He's always found her last name ironic compared with her personality.

Her glitter fades. "Staj, in case you forgot."

"Right," says Leo, removing the glove from his other hand.

Anastasia moves into the room. She is dressed in white, loose fit trousers with a shoulderless red top. She seems to deliberately pause where nothing impedes his view, her face slightly afraid.

Leo obliges her effort then chortles, "look at you, all grown up."

Her face drops. "Hey, you're like a year older than me," she states.

Mathematically, this is true. Though compared to the fresh faced Academian, Leo feels as though it were ten.

He notes how the Academy must have let out for Yuletide if Anastasia is home. Never one to keep up on dates, he wouldn't have suspected it if she weren't standing right in front of him. Nonetheless, he wishes he could stand before her in the same capacity, and be at the start of his own break from the real world.

"So how's the Academy?" he says, doing his best to sound interested. "They teaching you your civic duty? Or just how to dress to catch a guy?"

"You're such a jerk."

He trusts she knows him better than to think he meant more than teasing; if only he could trust himself to think the same. Breathing deep, he swallows down the slight twinge of bitterness he also hopes she overlooks. His own situation – not being able to study.

He lowers his eyes from Anastasia's. For a moment he starts finagling with the gloves by clapping them together. The sound at least breaks the verbal silence.

"So you're doing pankration again?" says Anastasia, stepping forward rather quickly. Snatching a glove from Leo, she playfully jabs at the idle Shadow Fighter. She hesitates when she feels them tangibly landing on its faceless jaw. The virtual combatant, however, does not seem to care much.

Anastasia stops nonetheless and turns to Leo. Waiting for his response she inadvertently glances at his scar.

Leo catches her eye as though it were the fist that left the nasty cut. He shirks away. That she witnessed that memorable pugilist bout, he understands why she would concern herself over his taking up gloves again.

"Nah," he says. He raises his arm to wipe his brow but brings it down over his scar. "Just keeping off the gut."

She looks down through his saturated gym shirt at the rock-hard abs he calls a gut.

"You know," she says tapping him in the stomach, "it doesn't seem fair it can't hit you back." She refers to the Shadow Fighter standing at attention in front of them. It's placed to "skeleton" mode where only the outline of a body appears in neon red and the gloves in black.

"It can, don't worry," says Leo lightly jabbing her back. "It's all sensory. You need the pads."

Leo gets closer to show her the sensors on his head gear when Anastasia taps the shadow fighter a little harder than before. This provokes a sucker punch to the back of Leo's head.

"Damn, what the hell."

"Sorry!" says Anastasia, genuinely affected.

"I'll take those, thanks." Leo shuts down the program. Removing the headgear, he pours some water over his face and dabs with a towel.

"I thought you'd be getting ready for Prometheus?" says Anastasia.

Leo flicks some water at her before answering, "What, the festival? Yeah, well, guess I could stop in."

"How thoughtful," she says, taking the towel.

"How bout you?"

"I AM ready."

"Oh, right. So you're probably here to get me."

"Yeah."

"So I probably shouldn't leave you waiting then, huh?"

"YES! I mean, no! I...just get ready."

"Haha, alright alright, be back in a bit."

Leo races up the stairs and out of sight, leaving Anastasia to his domain.

The basement looks the same as ever. Next to the doorway sits the old silver couch. A multi-purpose piece, ranging from crash spot, to dining room table, to entertaining the occasional overnight guest. The latter purpose not including Anastasia, who takes a seat pretending it never included anyone.

Left of the virtecran platform the memorable music center remains intact. So often would Anastasia come over as a child and listen to Leo's father play. The renegade musician with his vintage red and white Hollis's guitar synched with a Devers stack. From Anastasia's position she sees Leo the boy imitating his father's movements on his imitation guitar: later playing alongside: until finally playing on his own as a teenager.

The area by the stairs where Leo does his training was once a recreation area of sorts. Percussion instruments, sporting balls, 4DGamer, polymer blades; until one day that was all replaced by gloves and steel. The day Leo the boy became a man too young.

A frown crosses Anastasia's lips. She stands to distract her thoughts. She then turns back toward the music center and moseys over.

On a guitar stand rests Leo's maple colored Reynolds acoustic. The depth of its resonance often reflects the state of his mind when he plucks its strings. At such times he tends to produce his most beautiful music.

She notices the guitar's electronic equalizer still illuminated. Nearby an assortment of annotated music and studio gear clutter his Devers amplifier, with about fifty different signs of having quite recently been used.

He must have been practicing for the festival.

"Oh Leo, like you didn't care to go," she says.

One item, however, contrasts with the general array.

Tucked behind the effects coordinator, the corner of a worn paper photo peaks out. Anastasia lightly pinches the exposed part, hesitating to pull: physical photos such a rarity in 2080. This photo, though old, remains sturdy, and slides out intact: just the opposite of the family therein.

To the far left poses a middle aged man who never left his 20's. Long dark hair over a V-neck T-shirt, making an effort to conceal a smirk; Leo's father, Aeschylus Serelin.

All the good that did Leo changing to his mother's paternal name.

To the right stands Leo's deceased older brother, Alexi. Such a keen physical resemblance to the mother. Though in terms of character, neither Leo nor Anastasia had been alive long enough to learn.

Below the men with a hand on either shoulder sits Khloe, the middle child of the family. A bit high strung, yet generally fair-humored, she always tended to preoccupy herself with her own life.

In the final section of the picture, a lovely woman sits with her baby. Pandora Maquari wears a neon red headband pulling back strawberry blonde hair. Her face reveals a nature both tender and strong. Both baby and mother look in prime condition: no scars, in or out.

Leo and Mom.

The contrast of such purity to what her best friend and surrogate mother have become unsettles Anastasia. The relative frailty of the human body and its effect on the soul. How life passes.

Her own father.

The photo nearly falls from her hand. She sits on Leo's practice stool to sustain her body. For the rest she relies on her faith: faith in the infinity of the soul; faith in the afterlife; trust in the words of her mentor Alexander Maquari, Leo's grandfather.

After a few deep breaths, she carefully replaces the photo how she found it.

The Screenscore next to the Devers offers a pleasant distraction. This too, she sees, was left on; in particular, to "Pre-Reckoning Favorites."

The sheet music program will enter hibernation mode if left unattended for more than ten minutes. Anastasia guesses at the password, then draws a long face in saying it.

"Thais." Leo's ex-girlfriend.

The song that displays is "November Rain," by Guns N' Roses. A band from Pre-Reckoning times, they enjoyed a cult following well beyond their years. The neo-rock movement of the 2050's reintroduced them to mainstream culture through bands such as Sirens, HellHound, and Sophie's Delight. Lyricism, melody, and musicianship started taking precedence over power and electronic effects. Its influence continues today.

That particular song is Pandora Maquari's favorite. Leo, however, has no love for preReck tunes.

The transcription on the Screenscore contains a full orchestration of the piece: strings, drums, bass, piano, and electric guitar. Only Leo's acoustic is present, however.

"It's packed away," says Leo from his seat on the stairs. The unannounced comment startles his childhood friend.

"Jerk," says Anastasia under her breath.

"Haven't had a band in a while," he continues hopping down, "so I mostly play acoustic."

Leo enters the room with his steady, deliberate walk. He wears a white wide-neck that exposes the indent between his pecs. Dark form fitting jeans complete the simple outfit.

Though Anastasia makes no comment, her eyes roll over his undeniably aesthetic features. Face of fair yet hard complexion: skin smooth and tinted the color of light caramel. She quickly looks back down on the music score.

"I didn't think you'd be playing that song," she notes, still looking down.

"That song's ancient. I was just messin' around with it."

Anastasia's expression takes on a sad and pensive tone. "It's Mom's favorite."

Leo's takes on much the same. "I know."

The sound of Anastasia referring to his mother as "Mom" has always made her feel like more of a sister than a friend. Indeed, given her age, personality, and all the time spent together growing up, she had occupied that role much more than his real sister, Khloe. He also understands Anastasia likely doesn't use the word much with her own mother at home.

He glances at the Screenscore. Something about it, however, seems off. He then remarks the corner of the photo protruding a little further than in his photographic mind.

All thoughts of sisterly love quickly vanish. His gaze bores into Anastasia who doesn't seem to need eye contact to feel it. She folds her arms and keeps her eyes fixed on the sheet music.

"Let's just go," says Leo. He glances once more at the photo, reminding himself he meant to burn it several times over. He then turns and goes.

Anastasia discreetly nudges the distended corner deeper into place, then follows him out the basement door.

Although halfway through the month of Meton, nature still breathes life's warmth. The blades of grass dry just slightly and begin to shrivel with the weight of their age. Asphodel patches line the sidewalk having lost only the white of their pink grey flowers.

Anastasia stops to admire them, but as usual Leo is rushing towards nowhere.

He turns his head impatiently, accentuating his neck and upper back muscles,

"You coming?"

"Ugh, yeah."

Leo does not watch her approach. He waits on the sidewalk looking off in the distance. When Anastasia comes within a few steps, he moves off into the yard.

"Hey, the festival's THAT way," Anastasia points at his back.

Leo pays no mind. He continues towards the edge of the family's lakefront share.

"I think they have enough fennel already," says Anastasia.

Fennel stalks serve as torches at the Festival of Prometheus, and are common to Eulimnos. They typically grow near fresh bodies of water. As Leo makes his way to the water, he doesn't go anywhere near them.

A flutter in the wind moves over the lake. He follows the sound. Scanning the area, he searches for the source he thinks he recognizes.

Anastasia reaches him unimpressed. She is about to deliver some gentle remonstrance when Leo puts his finger in the air.

"Look, Staj, it's back," he says, more reflective than observant.

She follows the direction he points.

Her lips part, "Oh!"

Perched on a small boulder in the middle of the lake, the Torment of Prometheus folds its powerful wings. Predatory eyes mark its authority over the area. A symbol of the Pre-Reckoning world, the stately bald eagle settles under the painted sky.

"That's so weird," says Anastasia, "after all this time. Maybe he's back to play."

The eagle would often come during their childhood. At first they would gawk at it, then run along the lakeshore calling out. Once they learned to swim better, it became a game to race to the boulder and try to catch the iconic creature.

Leo does not react to the comment but keeps looking on. He starts slowly,

"Do you ever think about the tree?"

Anastasia's arms immediately fold.

"The tree?" she says.

She searches the ground for an answer, checking to see if he's watching.

"Um, yeah, sometimes." She tries stuffing her hands in her pockets, but her pants don't have any. "Why do you ask?"

Leo again ignores her comment. The slight brings Anastasia's arms up as she leans on her back foot.

"You were having visions again, weren't you?" she states.

Leo snaps his head away from the boulder. "What are you talking about?"

His eyes again bore into her. Her body relaxes, and nearly closes into a guard. "I saw you...with the shadow game."

Leo opens his mouth to deny the claim. He then stops, knowing better than to lie to someone who likely knows him better than himself.

"I was just...daydreaming, and the tree popped up." Eerie images flicker in his mind: shadows, cries. They move faster until forming a continuous motion picture of road, hill, and gravel; then, the "к."

The "K."

Anastasia watches his eyes as though they were projecting a film. She doesn't pose another question.

Leo shakes off the unnerving sensation of the "daydream" and seizes the silence his interrogator's allowed.

"You remember when we found that tree? Swimming around the boulder, chasing that damn bird, then all of sudden I can't move cause my foot gets caught on something underneath."

She acknowledges with a hand over a giggle. Her trifling quenches the giggle he might've made over himself.

Leo shoves his hands in his pockets. His sore sense of humor only exacerbates the memory. It then exacerbates himself by bringing Anastasia to a full laugh.

"Whatever," says Leo. He purses his lips. "I was legit caught. Like some sea monster trying to pull me down."

"Sea monsters in a lake?" says Anastasia now covering her mouth with both hands.

"You know what I mean."

"You squirmed like it was the Ketos."

"How would I know?"

"The Ketos was killed by Heracles."

"Funny, Staj. It was just a branch anyway."

The insignificant branch led to an extraordinary discovery: an elm tree, fully preserved, extending 40 yards to the lake bed. The oval, serrated leaves swelled green like none ever seen on land, as if drawing simultaneously from lake and sky.

Leo and Anastasia would explore its boughs as long as their breath would allow. It was magic at an age when you've only just recently stopped believing in magic.

"Too bad no one believed us," says Leo looking back on the lake.

Anastasia looks on him. "I really wasn't going to tell anyone anyway."

"Really?"

Out on the boulder, the eagle ruffles its long brown feathers. Its body faces the direction of the festival. Its neck, however, rotates in the direction of Leo and Anastasia.

"There was that one kid though," Leo goes on, "remember? He made it to the rock. Then tries to say there was nothing under it. Little flib. I'm glad he almost drowned on the way back." Leo spits on the ground.

Anastasia looks away a moment. "Well," she says, "he didn't. He was saved, then told everybody we made up a story to get him to swim outside the shallow area. He got us in trouble and turned us into liars."

Leo's aspect grows dark at the mention of the incident.

"He paid for that mistake," he whispers.

Anastasia lowers her head and wraps her body as though fending off a chilly breeze.

Many remember hearing about the wrestling training where Leo partnered with the boy who slandered him. During a sparring session, Leo maneuvered him into a submission, then snapped the boy's arm before he could yield. People say the sound pierced the entire room.

Leo senses her discomfort. "Nobody talked about us again, did they?" he says a bit aggressively. "Besides, if I went after him outside training the tranqs would have nabbed me."

The times Leo talks this way are the times Anastasia regards him with fear. The darkness, the ferocity: two traits which likely earned him the name of The Maurileho. Nonetheless, she reluctantly nods to both his points.

After a few seconds, her head quickly raises. "But he wasn't the only one who believed us," she says, "there was..."

"Mom," Leo cuts in. "I know." His expression lightens. "It's funny too."

"What?" says Anastasia.

"I remember telling her, and her believing me so easily. At the time I thought she was just treating me like a kid. But the more I think about it, it was like she wasn't even surprised, almost like she expected it."

Anastasia doesn't immediately respond. "Maybe she did."

"What?"

She scrambles for an explanation when a soft thump behind Leo steals his attention.

He turns toward an apple tree a few dozen yards away. Under its branches lies the source of the noise. Walking over, he picks the piece of fruit up off the ground.

"I was wondering when you'd finally drop," he says directly to the apple. He holds it up in front of his face.

He glances at Anastasia. "Here," he says. He chucks it at her with no further warning. She catches it just before it pegs her in the forehead.

She eyes Leo. The "jerk" on her lips, however, doesn't vocalize. Leo's amusement dissipates completely when she follows with a smile.

"So you award me the Golden Apple?"

Leo takes note of the orangish hue typical of late season apples. He smirks recalling the tale.

In the Judgment of Paris, the young prince must bestow the Golden Apple to one of the old goddesses in a divine contest of beauty. His choices were Aphrodite, Hera, and Athena. He favors Aphrodite, which would eventually bring about the ruin of Troy.

"Yeah, sure," says Leo chuckling. "Hang it up on your wall."

Anastasia scoffs then moves to the old red bench on the other side of the tree.

Leo runs a finger, then a nail, along the bark.

"This tree was a gift: a wedding gift from Mom to my Dad," he says.

"Yeah, I've heard."

Leo stops. His body tenses a bit. "Yeah, well, she could've picked a better recipient."

"Mom likes it," Anastasia hastily notes, "and she's always loved sitting out here."

Leo bites his tongue. Thinking of his father makes him want to bite harder. Nonetheless, he concedes Anastasia's point by calmly joining her on the bench.

Situated on the north-west corner of the land share, their position affords them an open view of the lakes, fields, and mountains of that immediate part of Eulimnos. The water at their feet stretches far to the right. It borders with a small mountain patched with the brisk colors of late autumn. Lake Maquari itself takes its name from the man who discovered it: Alexander Maquari.

Opposite and to the left, grassy fields offset a series of other heights and bodies of water. A beauty to admire, no matter how long one has lived there. The two of them take time to do so before again speaking.

"My grandfather told my Mom that when he was younger the sky was just blue," says Leo reclining his head, "and that it would only get like this when the sun went down." He waves his finger like a paint brush across the rainbow sky.

"I was there when *she* told *you*," says Anastasia dryly.

"Oh, right...weird though, huh? I wonder what gives it its color anyway."

"I read once it was the ocean," says Anastasia.

"The ocean? Last time I went to Pronoia the water was still blue."

Anastasia turns the apple over several times in her hand. "Then maybe you didn't look close enough," she says, keeping her head down.

Leo swings his arms to the side, palms up. "What? These eyes work, you know." He makes the statement with just enough force to justify his own sanity.

A flap ripples across the surface of Lake Maquari. It reaches Leo and Anastasia like a breeze of moving energy. When the two of them look up, they see the majestic eagle stretching its wings.

A second flap follows, even stronger than the first. Leo swears he feels a wave of power shooting across the water directly into his chest. The sensation buries deep and takes hold. Though it doesn't hurt, it demands an indisputable audience.

Once the effect wears off a bit, the eagle rests its wings slowly against its body. Leo also releases the tension that has built up inside and around. Once settled, however, the mighty bird directs its attention to the two sitting on the bench.

It immediately catches their eyes. Intense, oval slits above a sharp, stern beak. Its gaze bears into them like hot coals.

Leo finds himself unable to break from it. Something of an imperious force unwilling to release him. All he manages is to adjust restlessly in his seat.

The eagle begins wading air but doesn't move its neck. The pressure again mounts inside Leo's chest. Then, with one culminating screech, it kicks off from the boulder and takes to flight.

Leo exhales at the great bird's departure. A series of light tremors follow that keep him held in position. Anastasia also stays put, and a silence ensues between them.

He eventually sneaks a glance at his old friend and finds she's already watching for his reaction.

"Look, you scared him away," he says. He moves quickly to regain his composure. "All your talk of colored oceans."

Anastasia throws him a non-threatening glare. Her eyes read curious yet placid. She hesitates a few moments before looking away.

Over the next few seconds Leo makes quick reflection of the sensations lingering in his nerves. The eagle's forceful command of attention leaves him with the feeling he's somehow missed something along the way. This notion leads to a sense of reprimand, and even ill-boding.

Another screech marks the bird soaring high west. It passes over the festival grounds bordering the Maquari share. In the distance the first torch bearers stand at attention for the festival itself.

Leo follows its flight with his eyes but not his head. Having never felt such a thing in its presence before, a part of him would like to dismiss it to his unconscious imagination again running wild. He likely would, were it not for the near certainty Anastasia felt something too.

"Come on, we're going to miss the procession," says his friend standing up briskly.

Leo rises, but takes a few moments to acknowledge her urging. When he finally reacts he does so with an uninterested turn of his head.

"I got a Cammo of it at home. It's always the same shit."

"Your Mom's already there with your sister."

"Khloe," Leo mutters. His face grows dark and frustrated. "Let her do something for once."

Anastasia crosses her arms.

Her lack of retort weighs heavier on Leo than any scolding she might have made. As such he avoids her stare for as long as he can. Eventually though, he runs out of places to look.

Her face shows a myriad of emotions. He's unsure which to interpret. What he notices most is the slight frown forming at the side of her mouth: direct, yet soft. The center of her brow moves the opposite way, raising gently to reveal the sweet infinite blue underneath.

Leo sighs.

"Yeah alright, let's go."

CHAPTER 2 – THE FESTIVAL OF PROMETHEUS

A poignant screech blares from high above the west bank of Lake Maquari. In its southeastern wake, the lakes of Eulimnos array like drops from a painter's brush. To the north the fields of the Orgon Vale ebb their fertile waves in vast array. Their greens entwine with the rounded peaks of Appalachia.

Prometheum Proper follows the mountain region as the urban center. At its summit the Tower of Winds serves as the symbolic head. The Gifted Flame burns continuously atop the great structure and can be seen from all parts of Prometheum.

Another screech sounds as the eagle dips slightly over the festival grounds. It glides to the shape the unlit torches have been set to form: п; the classic letter Pi. Leo and Anastasia arrive as it finishes its final course over the grand stage at the opening of the п.

"Well there it goes," says Leo. He salutes the air with a lazy arm. "See yah in another ten years." After the experience from earlier, he hopes it turns out to be much more.

Anastasia lifts her head and glimpses it flying toward the mountains.

Unlit fennel-stalk torches line the shape of the Pi. Outside, the crowd swells heavier and heavier in anticipation of entering. A spectator knocks into Leo's shoulder trying to get closer to the front.

"Hey, watc..." a stout man in classical dress starts to say. Leo invites him to say more by taking a step closer.

The man, sporting the common hairstyle of 2-inch locks with braids in the front, does not accept that invitation.

"Maurileho," he says in a cautious tone.

The diminutive coined by a local sportscaster for Leo's victories in the combat sport of Kladimo. It was often thought to characterize his fierce and poignant style. The name in lingua franca translates to "The Black Lion."

Leo presses his invitation once more when Anastasia takes his arm. "No, Leo."

Leo hesitates only a split second. He then shakes off Anastasia's hand and addresses the man who's trying in earnest to retain his last shred of masculinity.

"Go," he says. This time the man accepts.

Leo avoids the "was that really necessary?" look he knows Anastasia's giving him. Finally unable to resist, he turns with a grimace.

"Well I don't know why we just can't go to our tables before the flame's lit," he says. "Wouldn't have a problem then."

Tradition dictates the arrival of the torch race victor to mark the beginning of the festival. Until then, no one may enter the banquet area located inside the ceremonial п.

Anastasia just shakes her head.

Hundreds occupy the surrounding areas. From atop shoulders, houses, and nearby hills, all eyes tend north toward the Gifted Flame. From here the race originates and all torches are lit.

Many of the younger generation, like Leo and Anastasia, come to pay homage in the comfort of casual dress. Others, however, as the unfortunate tough guy, opt for classical garb. White and red are the common colors of dress to honor their major deity.

Leo spots faces who, despite living in the same corner of Eulimnos, he hasn't seen since last year's festival. Most he wouldn't mind missing until next festival either. He finds the "how have you beens" an irksome business, especially under the pretense of being judged and having no greater conquest to report than when he was last asked.

"We won't find Mom and Khloe anywhere in all this," says Anastasia. She fights to see over the wall of people mostly taller than her. "Just ping Khloe to see where they are."

"Yeah, alright," says Leo. Touching a small sensor on the back of his ear, a red light appears under this thumb. He then proceeds to whisper his message. Once the J.T device finishes its interpretation, the light goes out.

A rustle in the crowd brings their attention back to the chaos. The stage, until now dark and idle, comes to life in a burst of energy. Chatter elevates to excitement while people vie for higher ground. Leo waits calmly, then moves behind a group of teenage Lyceans to check out all the fuss.

Not far in the distance, a small torch rounds the pattern of the lake. A tall light-haired individual runs sure and swift with no other competitors following. All eyes follow the flame.

Up on stage, the Festival Artist kicks off its annual rendition of Johann Wolfgang Von Goethe's poem "Prometheus."

This year's old but legendary Scars of Bourbon assume the task:

"Now you (Zeus) must leave me alone
My Earth for Me
And my hut, which you did not build.
And my hearth
The glowing whereof
You envy me."

"Not so bad with an amp behind it," says Leo of the rock band's spin on the typically ceremonial piece.

The Festival Artist may be of any artistic inclination ranging from dancers to painters. For the festival they must apply their craft to the national hymn and any other spectacles asked of them.

Lead singer/guitarist Paul Vangar adds a tasteful edge with his heavy riffs and raspy vocals.

"Should I honor you (Zeus)? Why?
Have you softened the sufferings,
Ever, of the burdened?
Have you stilled the tears.
Ever, of the anguished?
Was I not forged as a Man
By almighty Time
And Eternal Fate
My masters and yours?"

Vangar's playing has always inspired Leo to add greater vitality to his chord progressions instead of entrenching himself in technical soloing. Even singing a hymn, Vangar's fingers create a blend definitely classic though not compromising the song's integrity.

Leo's been well acquainted with the style, and Vangar, for several years: his only regret becoming so through his father.

The heightened cheers of the crowd indicate the torch bearer in sight.

Leo, still immersed in the music, feels a gentle pull on the back of his shoulder.

"Look! Look who's holding the torch," says Anastasia pointing toward the finish line.

Leo follows the direction of her finger until he spots who everyone is already shouting for.

His lips curl into a grin.

"Son of a bitch."

Crossing the line with an air of humble smugness, Bereniko Braun lifts the torch to a roar of thunder.

Leo's best friend next to Anastasia, Beren filled the gap of the brother he never knew. Since childhood they have shared in everything from laughs to sorrows and bruises to beers. His fierce loyalty and temperate humor always bring a welcome relief to those in his company.

Scars of Bourbon signals the end of the race with an increase of volume and tempo. The crowd follows suit, swelling energy levels over the Festival Grounds to new highs. Beren acknowledges all with a finger in the air and loud whoop.

The hymn is about to move into its final verse when a distinguished older man takes the stage. Wearing a white robe with red slash, his regard is as sharp as the hair slicked back on his head. He waves his hand but once and the grounds go silent.

"Allow me," he speaks with patient command. "After all, it's not every day my son wins the Torch Race of the Prometheia."

The crowd hollers, and Statesman Boukoletes Braun embraces his son fondly. His usually measured face glistens with pride as he motions to address the crowd.

"And so to conclude," he begins.

"Here I sit, forming humans
In my image;
A people to be like me,
To suffer, to weep,
To enjoy and to delight themselves,
And to not attend to you (Zeus)-

As I!"

The crowd erupts on the final syllable. Shuttles arrive street side with competitors from earlier legs of the relay. This only compounds the excitement. Statesman Braun then takes the hand of his son, and together they raise the torch for all to see.

"Light the flame, light the flame," the crowd starts chanting. Many take inspiration from the spirit of Prometheus, and others...

"I'm starving," says Leo. "Let's go buddy." He wills his last statement toward Beren.

Anastasia ignores the obnoxious comment and rejoins the chanting in temperate fervor.

Statesman Braun appeases the call by directing Beren up toward the rear of the stage. There sits a giant elevated cauldron. Beren mounts and pauses next to it, awaiting his father's signal.

"The Gifted Flame," Statesman Braun begins, "serves as a reminder of our great patron's sacrifice." He pauses for calmness and effect. "It is at once a pillar of history, and beacon of hope. And so long as it burns in the hearts of Prometheans, it can never be extinguished."

A round of sincere applause follows. Statesman Braun allows them a minute, then nods the go-ahead to his son. Beren suppresses a smile as he lowers the torch.

A whisk of flame reaches all ears on the festival grounds. The stage lights are dimmed and the people awe in sight of the great centerpiece. Some stare, some embrace, and others gently close their eyes to let the spirit flow deep within. Even Leo forgets his hunger in his appreciation for its beauty.

After a long interval, Statesman Braun reclaims attention. "And now for the Pi torches," he announces, "designed with the fennel of our dear Eulimnos." He signals again to his son.

Beren proceeds to turn a lever connected to the cauldron by pipe. Gas hisses, then flows to the base of each torch atop the Π.

Its pressure mounts simultaneously with the suspense of the people. When it seems there can be no more on either part, the fennel stalks burst aflame all at once. A blinding wave of heat moves over the area as if the sun decided to blink.

A murmur spreads through the crowd followed by a round of contented clapping. They continue in the few seconds the flames take to stabilize. They then waste no time in filing into the banquet area.

"Finally," says Leo.

"Did they respond?" says Anastasia.

Leo touches his ear, likely having missed the ping in all the commotion. "Yeah," he says, listening carefully. "We're up front to the right."

Anastasia makes no motion to move. Leo frowns as he realizes she wishes him to go first. Sagging his powerful shoulders, he plunges once more into the melee.

Families on all sides take eagerly to their seats. Chatter ensues amongst tables and glasses are filled with wine in preparation for the toast. Many looks follow Leo as he passes by, but he doesn't return any of them.

Yellow bouquets of fennel adorn each table. The vases tell a story with their depictions of antiquity: Prometheus bound to a post; Heracles killing the Caucasian Eagle with an arrow, that same hero releasing the tortured Titan.

Leo finds he actually appreciates the art despite only accepting those tales as stories. His eyes indeed end up lingering a little too long on them and he nearly collides with a little girl running across his path. A beautiful girl, wearing a relaxed yellow dress with a smile to rival the sun. Her strawberry blond hair whips when she turns her head and giggles at another child chasing her.

"Hey," says a female voice distracting him away. An older girl of similar features stares and waits: Anastasia. "Lose your step?" she says.

Leo finds his friend's resemblance to the little girl remarkable.

"No, I jus..." he says looking off.

The girl is gone, nor are there any children in the direction she went.

Anastasia continues waiting.

"Let's just go," he says gruffly, refocusing his attention on his empty stomach.

The beauty and mysterious familiarity of the moment rests with him, however. Something distant and present at once: something primal whispering through a far off breeze.

He nonetheless pinpoints something very valuable in the girl: the light, carefree innocence bursting with life. It is an ideal he's long since known.

He is reminded of this fact as they reach the front.

Alone in a rotochair, a woman bobs a head too heavy for her shoulders. Background music sets the beat to which she still bounces her amputated leg. Age has not diminished the quality of her natural strawberry blonde, though the chalky pallor of her skin would indicate otherwise.

A strand falls over her glossy eyes. When she makes to push it back, only one hand obeys, and only two fingers grasp. Nonetheless, she resettles into the band and all else disappears.

"Mom," says Leo. Seeing her alone, he rushes over. "Where the hell is Khloe?"

Pandora Maquari turns slowly to her beloved son.

"Oh honey, she'll be back," she replies in a feeble yet spirited voice.

Leo's worry disguised as anger shifts towards his absent sister. He begins intently scanning the immediate area.

Anastasia brushes past him with the bright face that squints her eyes. "Hi, Mom."

"Annie," Pandora whispers. She speaks her name with the fondness of a child returned.

Anastasia kisses her surrogate mother affectionately on the forehead.

Pandora takes a moment to regard her. "Look at you sweetie, so beautiful." Her comment rings with pride, causing the recipient to blush and squint.

"Don't you think, Leo?" Pandora brightens as she poses the question. She even makes the labored effort to turn her torso for his answer.

"What?" says Leo, still searching for Khloe. "Uh, yeah, sure."

Anastasia forces a smile as Leo reassumes his task. Pandora frowns.

"You always look the wrong way," she says to Leo's back.

Leo checks his retort to the sound of irksome footsteps.

"Hi, everyone," Khloe greets civilly.

Seven years Leo's senior, Khloe shares the long pale cheeks of a younger Pandora. Her hair, however, is slightly darker than her mother's, and her hips wider to an equal degree.

"Nice of you to swing back around," says Leo in a sharp glare.

"I had to call my husband," Khloe states even sharper.

"And was it really too noisy here? You had to walk off and leave Mom al..."

"Leonidas," Pandora cuts in, "it's fine. Anastasia, honey, would you help Leo with the cups?"

"Khloe can get her own cup," says Leo before setting to his charge.

Statesman Braun retakes the stage a short time later. He holds his own cup in the form of a small goblet. It seems to reflect the colors of the sky depending on what angle the sunlight hits. He raises it in the air, and once again there is silence.

"Citizens. I welcome you all to the 40th annual Festival of Prometheus." He pauses for the inevitable applause.

"Each year we gather to honor our great benefactor," he continues, "to commemorate the noble deeds done for our sake. Beginning with the sacrificial share," he says motioning to the roasting ox to the side of the stage, "the theft of fire," he adds tilting his head toward the torches, "and, through the providence of General Maquari, another chance," he concludes surveying the people and bowing his head slightly to the Maquari family.

Pandora does her best to return the gesture. Leo has his eyes on the food.

"And now let us tilt our cups," says Statesmen Braun. He lifts his goblet to arm's height, "that the Lord of the omegas be ever our champion, and the 5th Generation of mankind always endure."

With that, Statesman Braun spills a sip of wine. The rest follow suit, staining the grass red with their libations.

Leo considers blowing off the ritual until he catches his mother's reproof.

He stares back a moment then sags his shoulders. "What a waste of wine," he says as it splashes the ground, "rather have a Lager Top anyway."

At the next tilt, however, all inclined drink heartily. The liquid warmth insulates the body and all is good.

Chatter builds amongst spots of hoots and hollers. The Scars of Bourbon drummer taps out the intro to "Dreamer," one of their most recognizable tunes from their early days post-Reckoning.

"Enjoy," Statesman Braun wishes to all. "Within your means."

The stage lights flash on, and the Festival Artist springs into action with as much spring as senior citizenry will allow.

Service staff appears towing an enormous rotisserie on wheels. Inside, under the open lid, the oxen of the sacrificial share: the traditional platter of the Prometheia. The aroma from the cooked meat trickles to all parts of the Pi.

"Finally," says Leo, salivating.

"Is that all you think of?" says Anastasia.

"Hey, don't mess with a man's stomach." Leo ogles the food as more passes by.

For the first serving, servers roll the oxen and side dishes down the center aisle. They all wear the common ceremonial robe aside from an added headpiece to wrap their hair. And, to Leo's great content, they start at the front. The food is afterwards left on a buffet should anyone want seconds.

Leo savors the sight of the plate before him: a large slab of tender meat with a side of buttered corn and mashed potatoes: a staple of the festival and the weather turning cooler. He applies a generous helping of dressing and digs in.

The banquet proceeds in good form until all have had their fill. Children who've eaten half their food turn the Pi into their playground. A group of teenagers and young adults convene in front of the stage for a less tamed experience with the band. More settled guests who lack the vocal range to talk over the racket show their dismay through pursed lips and deeper swigs of their wine cups.

The Maquari table, of the more settled yet not dismayed, raises their heads to a tall figure approaching. Smiles cross each set of lips including Leo's. He even condescends to lay down his spork.

"Well, the torch-race winner himself," Leo says in an overly stately manner, "gracing us with his presence,"

Bereniko Braun holds his fingernails out then rubs them on his shirt. "I just finished my interviews," he says, "figured you might feel left out."

The two hold serious faces for a moment, then break into a hearty laugh followed by a heartier guy hug.

"Good to see you, man," says Leo. "Didn't know you got leave from the Guard."

"They knew someone had to win the race," says Beren.

Leo grins. "And since I wasn't there I guess that left you," he says.

Beren tilts his head back for another laugh. "Keep dreaming, buddy. Running was quicker than a tram anyway. And besides, I couldn't leave Ms. Maquari here alone to rely on your sweet company."

Beren rounds the table and tenderly enfolds Pandora in his long, coiled arms.

"Beren, how are you?" says Pandora. She rests her head into his chest. "It looks like the Guard suits you well."

The added mass and tone to Beren's physique has improved a great deal during his service. His tall stature to boot makes for a commanding presence.

Beren accepts the compliment graciously.

"It sure hasn't suited his hairline though," Leo cuts in. "Damn buddy, I can almost see my reflection on your forehead."

Beren's pale cheeks color a bit at the insult. Though not to the extent of Leo's exaggeration, his once full head of long golden hair has undeniably receded.

"Jerk," Anastasia directs at Leo as she slides over toward Beren. She greets him with a light hug.

"Hey, Staj. Glad this one hasn't rubbed off on you."

"It's too bad she hasn't rubbed off on him," says Khloe chiming in on the opportunity Beren so nicely offered.

"Drop dead."

"Leonidas," his mother reproaches through feeble breath.

Leo avoids her look, for although terribly debilitated still carries effect. All the more so when she can barely lift her head to give it. That he can imagine this is enough to soften his reaction without turning.

"The band's version of the hymn was really neat, huh?" says Anastasia.

"Yeah it was a lot better set to post-rec rock," says Beren. "Remember last year they had that opera singer?" He turns his head toward Leo. "I'm surprised you didn't join Scars on stage," he says.

"I'm all about jamming with Scars of Bourbon, but not to that freakin' hymn."

"It's a poem about Prometheus, Leo," says Khloe indignantly.

"It's an allegory about the enlightened man, Khloe."

"Here we go again," Beren mutters under his breath.

"You and your interpretations. It's about Prometheus' defiance of Zeus and the old gods. About his role of creating man in his image."

Leo squares his shoulders. "Prometheus IS the man here," he says with a sharp finger pointing down, "the enlightened man who goes beyond the need for belief in superstitions and gods you'll never see."

"Prometheus isn't a man, in allegory or anything else."

"Says who? Goethe?"

"Says our own grandfather!" Khloe snaps. "Or maybe you've forg..."

"I haven't forgotten anything!" Leo hesitates at the risk of insulting his grandfather's memory, especially around his mother and Anastasia.

Not willing to lose face, however, he tactfully shifts the focus back to the poem. "Come to think of it, not only does this hymn not praise a god, or omega, or whatever, it actually encourages us not to!"

All eyes turn on Leo at this declaration. All except his mother, whose eyes shut and body cringes.

"It speaks of a man in the real world, seeing the tough realities of it: and instead of running away by drugging ourselves with delusions, we embrace and create order of it. Masters of our domain; we become the gods."

A silence ensues not even Khloe ventures to break. Leo remains pondering his final thought.

"We are the gods, the omegas," he whispers, then laughs. "You're right, buddy," he says patting Beren roughly on the back, "I don't know why I didn't join them on stage either. It's the perfect national hymn."

Khloe seethes at his smugness. This only adds fuel to his gloating.

Anastasia cringes as though hearing a dissonant chord. She then conscientiously glances at Pandora whose face shows much more than just dissonance.

"Mom?" she says, eliciting no response. "Mom!" She rises to her feet. Smirks and glares vanish at seeing Pandora clutching her stomach in pain.

"Mom," says Leo, dashing to his knees.

Pandora sways her head from side to side as if trying to ward off the nausea associated with her diabetes. Leo is all too used to this drill, and already has a plastic bag on standby.

At each movement of his mother's head, though, Leo feels a wave of pain bite at his core. The skeptic rests as he grabs her arm, believing somehow he can absorb her suffering through the strength of his touch. The skeptic sleeps as he pleads with an inner voice.

After a short time, the swaying stops. Deep breaths flow into the nose and out the mouth until Pandora regains composure. Leo exhales.

"It's ok, honey," Pandora consoles her son in a feeble voice.

Anastasia places her hand on the one Leo set on his mother's arm. Leo meets his friend's eyes slowly.

"It's time for her medicine," she says.

Leo makes no reply but to release his grip. For a second his hand remains held by Anastasia's. Pandora catches the moment from the corner of her eye and appears more relieved than ever. She regards them with renewed spirit, from an inner place of reassurance.

The queer look on Pandora's face startles Leo back to awareness. He abruptly, though not harshly, breaks from Anastasia and meekly searches for the medicine.

Anastasia lowers her eyes. She then casually reaches into a tiny sac on the back of the wheelchair and pulls out several plastic bottles. By the time Leo hears the shaking of the pills Khloe is already assisting Anastasia in administering the doses while Beren prepares the water. Leo sinks back into his seat.

He watches as the woman who raised him is cared for like a baby. Pill after pill pumping into what little body she has left: loading her up to compensate for what she's lost.

Is that even living?

Each swallow scratches a wound of her life's injustice in Leo's mind. Each pill an insult. By the time she finishes the last of her medicine, Leo's memory bleeds raw.

Omegas my ass. How much can you take from someone? How can you destroy someone who loves you?

Leo takes a long look around the festival: the outfits, food, torches. He stops on the Gifted Flame in the cauldron behind the stage. The heat touches his cheeks even through the wall of bodies mixing to the music.

He thinks of the reason for such faith and fervor: Prometheus.

I'd destroy you if I had the chance...

Scars of Bourbon finishes their song, granting the young people their turn at dismay. "Thanks everyone, we'll be back later." Paul Vangar waves, "stay tuned for the play."

The more settled of the crowd put down their wine cups and re-engage in conversation. The youth pick theirs up and sulk amongst the settled.

"I think I know every line to this play by now," says Beren sitting back and crossing his feet.

"Oh I love Prometheus Bound," says Khloe.

Leo disjoins himself from thoughts of omega-killing at talk of the play. His mother has calmed, which helps him do the same. He takes a deep breath. "So I gotta sit through this again?"

"Zoe's playing Io this year," says Anastasia.

"Good," says Leo. He sets to gulping the last of his drink. "Then she'll be dressed as a cow; Matter of fact, it'll be worth watching just for that."

The stage crew moves with great efficiency to remove the music scene in favor of the theatrical. Stomachs not yet filled rush to the banquet tables for second servings. Drinkers who've had well more than their fill rush to do the same anyway. Within a few minutes, the great work of Aeschylus is ready to stage.

For a moment all artificial lights are extinguished. The fennel stalk torches cast a dim glow over the stage where the director makes his way to the front. A spotlight then beams down upon him, and he wastes no time in delivering the play's argument:

"When Kronos, son of Uranus, was king in heaven, revolt against his rule arose among the gods. The Olympians strove to dethrone him in favor of Zeus, his son; the Titans, children of Uranus and Earth, championing the ancient order of violence, warred against Zeus and his partisans. Prometheus, himself a Titan, forewarned by his oracular mother Earth or Themis (for she bore either name) that the victory should be won by craft, whereas his brethren placed their sole reliance on brute force, rallied with her to the side of Zeus and secured his success."

Leo rests his chin on his knuckles.

Blah, blah, blah.

The director, a small, half-bald man wearing the tragic of theatrical masks, frays his hands wide into fists on the word "secured." He then pauses.

Khloe smiles and leans forward in anticipation. Leo reaches for the carafe and pours obnoxiously loud to give his sister greater effect. The director seems to notice her venomous glare and continues:

"His triumph once assured, the new monarch of heaven proceeded forthwith to apportion to the gods their various functions and prerogatives; but the wretched race of man he proposed to annihilate and create another in its stead. This plan was frustrated by Prometheus, who, in compassion on their feebleness, showed them the use of fire, which he had stolen on their behalf, and taught them all arts and handicrafts. For this rebellion against the newly-founded sovereignty of Zeus, the friend of mankind was doomed to suffer chastisement – he must pass countless ages riveted to a crag on the shores of Ocean in the trackless waste of Scythia."

Thus he concludes: and with a low, one armed bow, the play begins.

Prometheus Bound tells the story of Prometheum's major deity from the inclination of Aeschylus. The work itself dates back several hundred years before the Reckoning. Though many accounts exist from other classical writers, the playwright's Prometheus is the character people commonly attest to.

On stage the noble omega wails his sorrows in chains:

"Ha! Behold! What murmur, what scent wings to me, its source invisible, heavenly or human, or both? Has someone come to this crag at the edge of the world to stare at my sufferings – or with what motive? Behold me, an ill-fated god, chained, the foe of Zeus, hated of all who enter the court of Zeus, because of my very great love of mankind. Ha! What's this? What may be this rustling stir of birds I hear again nearby? The air whirs with the light rush of wings. Whatever approaches causes me alarm."

Regardless of the testimony, all accounts speak of the eagle sent every night to eat his liver. As an immortal it would always regenerate by morning. Thus was the punishment of Zeus for the theft of fire.

Anastasia nudges Leo awake. "Hey, Zoe's coming on soon."

By the time Leo rouses, a beautiful brunette wearing a cow's nose circles the stage. Her fluid, animated movements draw the attention of the crowd: her nose Leo's. The free-spirited and lively Zoe Qwynshing commands the role of the inquisitive damsel in distress.

"Io: What! Shall Zeus one day be hurled from his dominion? By whom shall he be despoiled of the scepter of his sovereignty?

Prometheus: By himself and his own empty handed purposes.

Io: In what way? Oh tell me if there be no harm in telling.

Prometheus: He shall make a marriage that shall one day cause him distress.

Io: With a divinity or with a mortal? If it may be told, speak out.

Prometheus: Why ask with whom? I may not speak of this.

Io: Is it by his consort he shall be dethroned?

Prometheus: Yes, since she shall bear a son mightier than his father.

Io: And has he no means to avert this doom?

Prometheus: No one --- except me, if I were released from bondage.

Io: Who then is to release you against the will of Zeus?

Prometheus: It is to be one of your own grandchildren.

Io: What did you say? A child of mine will release you from your misery?

Prometheus: The third in descent after ten generations."

Prometheus prophesizes one of the twelve labors of Heracles; the slaying of the eagle as pictured on the vase art. People tend to regard his power of foresight as his greatest quality after stealing fire.

The play concludes a short while after. Again the stage crew busies themselves like a company of working ants. This time they prepare for the final event.

Most at the Maquari table watch their progress as well as any sign of Zoe with the other actors. When after a while she doesn't appear, that same majority put on long faces.

"Maybe she had interviews too," says Leo. He fills another cup with a smirk. Beren shakes his head and reaches over to be refilled too.

"Hey, everyone!" says a female voice from the rear of the table. She wears a red patch-like headpiece on her right temple to match the silk chiton cut above her knees. Her vibrant green eyes glow a shade brighter as she looks from person to person.

Leo knows she bursts at the seams for recognition of her performance, so he sits back and takes a deliberate sip of his wine. Beren makes Leo a knowing glance and sits back himself. Anastasia makes them both knowing glances and speaks up quickly, "Hi, Zoe, you were great up there."

"Oh thanks, Annie!" she erupts. She pulls Anastasia into her lean muscled arms. Anastasia looks more like a younger child in Zoe's embrace, reaching only her shoulders in height.

Zoe served with Environmental Aesthetics during her Social Service. She then continued to study drama at the Academy. An impressive physical specimen, she is as deadly in a dress as with her kladimans weapon.

Beren, intimately aware of her skill at the maolance, which is a kladimans form of a spear, lifts her in the air with his hug.

"Not a bad looking cow."

Zoe sets down and recovers her stance. She quizzically squints one eye as she pushes her hair behind her ears. "Uh, thanks, B."

"I think she looks better with the nose," says Leo. He takes a long sip of his drink and gets up slowly.

"Good to see you too, Leo," says Zoe feigning a scowl.

Their taunting expressions allay over an embrace and kiss on the cheek.

Pandora pays particular attention. Her aspect heightens to its peak at seeing the four friends reunited. After a brief pause where it seems she might jump out of her rotochair, she sits back in a state of contended ease.

"Wow, you look great Ms. Maquari," says Zoe. She moves away from the group and kneels next to Pandora. The young beauty doesn't hesitate to take hold of the maimed, discolored hand laying on the armrest.

"Hi, Zoe," Pandora squeezes as best she can. "I'm so glad I got to see you as Io. I know you made many people happy with that performance."

"Aww, me too!" says Zoe lightly clapping her hands over Pandora's. "And I promise I'll be even better next year."

"Oh don't worry, honey. That was everything I needed."

Leo turns at the comment. Pandora doesn't notice him right away, then looks up and gives him a tender smile. He'd like to feel assured enough to return it, but something tells him his mother only makes it for him to feel assured.

"So, Leo," says Zoe, "I don't see your guitar. Aren't you playing the Music Contest?".

Leo contemplates his mother a moment longer before answering. "Oh, nah, I don't think so."

"Vangar's judging, buddy. He'd probably be a shoe in," says Beren.

"Alright. Why don't you borrow Zoe's costume and go sing one of his songs. I'd play for that."

The Music Contest encompasses all genres, from electronic, to orchestral, to Scars of Bourbon. The winner is often nominated Festival Artist for the following year, and sits as head judge.

A shift in stage lighting indicates the first act is to come.

Myriads of artistry ensue beginning with a female acapella group dressed in classic robes. A DJ follows, lacing a melodic tune to techno in the midst of a light show.

A grey beam shines on the Maquari table. Leo follows its track to see it settled on his mother. Only then does he notice his mother settled on him. Her neck is once again hunched; her expression reaching, as though he is much further away than two seats.

Leo ducks over and kneels next to the rotochair.

"Everything alright, Mom?"

"Can you play me my song" she says quickly, "just one last time?"

Every time she's asked him to play "November Rain" it was always "for the last time," knowing well his aversion towards it.

This time, however, something in her tone prevents him from refusing her outright.

"In the contest you mean? How bout I just play it at home?"

Pandora makes no response but to appear absent. Almost as if she did not hear anything. Leo waits a bit longer, then swallows the saliva built up in his mouth.

"Alright," he says uneasily, "I'll just see how it goes." He turns towards his seat.

A sharp pinch stops him before he makes it two steps.

"Why can't you just play her the song," Khloe lashes, "is it that bad, really?"

"Shut up," he says, jerking his arm away. "I told her I'd play it at home."

"She asked you to play it now," says Khloe pointing her red colored nails down at the table, "so she can see you up there in front of everyone, to feel proud you played for this."

"It's just a stupid festival."

"Not to HER!" Khloe pauses to suppress her disgust. "It always has to be about you, doesn't it?"

Leo glowers and returns to his seat.

The next group sets up unceremoniously on stage. Leo takes no notice anyway. His eyes remain lowered under the weight of Khloe's words. Little by little they penetrate the recesses of his chest, until..

"Hi all," says a tenor, middle-aged voice ringing over the festival grounds. These words, though simple and said in a cheerful tone, quickly penetrate past Khloe's. "Got a familiar one here from our very own Festival Artist."

Leo's eyes stay down, but grow darker by the second. On stage, Aeschylus Serelin makes an indulging bow to the judges' panel, then nods to his band.

"Talk about a shoe in," Leo whispers to himself, "son of a bitch."

Aeschylus's band chooses the Scars of Bourbon breakout single "At War." The song, dating back to the times of the Reckoning, thrusted Paul Vangar into the spotlight as a lead man and songwriter. It also spoke greatly of the turmoil surrounding the early 21st century.

Though the band playing it now covers it with justice, a song counted as one of Leo's favorites sounds defiled to his ears.

Pandora, on the other hand, listens serenely to the vocals of her ex-husband: unaffected, unflinching. The others stop halfway between listening and trying to avoid glancing at Leo.

Anastasia chances to see how Leo reacts to his father playing so open and unexpectedly in his presence. She discovers he's not even looking.

Leo takes no notice of anyone around him, and soon his indignation turns him inward. Roots of compassion he once felt as a young boy become overshadowed by empty years of adolescence.

He raises his eyes to the man on stage performing with such freedom and vitality: freedom from life, vitality to live. He then turns to the woman in the rotochair.

Fists clench at the sight of his mother without two legs to walk on, two fingers to feed: trapped, in essence, of life.

Pandora's eyes flash open wide for a second, then slowly close altogether. Her finger continues tapping.

Leo abruptly stands facing his father's band.

You don't get to steal the show, Dad.

Before anyone can speak he marches at Khloe.

"I'll be back."

With that he stammers off. Pandora's eyes slowly open but remain lowered as Leo weaves in and out of tables. Anastasia watches him disappear into the darkness that has now fallen outside the Pi.

The contest goes on with several acts for the next 45 minutes or so. During this time many heads from the Maquari table turn many times toward the Maquari house. With nothing to show, the final act now takes the stage.

"I guess Leo bailed for the night," says Zoe checking once more.

Khloe scoffs and rolls her eyes. "He said he'd be back."

The final contestant, a harpist, plays a rendition of the popular folk song "The Ashes of War." Though played instrumentally, the tune still evokes much of the resonating feeling of the Aftermath of the Reckoning. Her performance brings the contest to a light, yet beautiful conclusion a short time later, and her bow signals the near end of the festival.

Paul Vangar rises from his judges' chair and begins to mount the stage. Halfway up the ramp he stops. A fast moving figure to the right approaches through the darkness.

A second later Leo appears shoving his way past the cauldron. He strides forth holding his guitar to the side as though it were his kladimans blade.

"I think we have time for one more," he says in Paul's direction. Before Paul can respond the crowd voices their approval through shouts and hollers.

Beren fuels it further by standing to clap. "Woooooooooo," he shouts through cupped hands. He then pinches two fingers between his lips and belts a piercing whistle. "Maurileho!"

More and more join until Vangar finds no way out of joining himself. He cedes the stage with a nod and walks off clapping.

Leo is already set. The flames of the torches reflect off the top of his maple colored Reynolds. Its steel wound strings send a glare eighty yards to the end of the Π.

All the cheers and encouragement pass over him like wind. Festival or basement, he's come for one person.

He spots his mother amongst the mess of crowd goers. For a long second they hold contact. Without breaking, he strikes the first note to the pre-Reckoning classic, "November Rain."

The bronze tone of the acoustic guitar's midrange sets the tonic point to the lightly plucked arpeggios to follow. Such a gentle touch from such a powerful and devastating arm. All for the perfect rendition of a song he dislikes to even hear, yet knows so very well.

Familiarity guides his fingers over the fret board to the point his hands do all the thinking. His consciousness detaches little by little. Soon he only hears himself as a listener.

This day the strings resonate deeper. They cycle in harmony, charged with energy Leo wouldn't know how to express through words.

He settles in further and further. The crowd begins to blur and eventually becomes a sea of faceless ornaments. All except one…

He meets his mother's eyes in the space halfway between the stage and seats. The music recalls earlier memories of playing her the song. Oddly enough, in some memories she looks much younger than he ever remembers seeing her in his lifetime.

Pandora again shuts her eyes slowly. She doesn't tap her fingers, just takes a deep breath.

Leo's singing voice lifts the first verse off the ground. The second he sends soaring toward the eagle. The Pi chills under its force:

"Been through this such as long long time
Just tryin' to kill the pain.
Cause lovers always come and lovers always go
And no one's really sure who's letting go today."

Pandora at hearing those lines turns discreetly toward Anastasia. She looks on the face of the girl she thinks of as a daughter in law and cannot quench the welling tears. She turns away before one reaches her cheek.

Leo continues on with the same intensity throughout the final sections. By the end of the song, both he and his mother are exhausted.

A grand applause erupts on the final chord. Paul Vangar stands with surprising speed for his age, this time prompting the rest to join him. The addition of vocalizations bring the noise to a level no Devers amp could reach.

Leo, without so much as a nod, descends the stage as though it were any other occasion. He pays no mind to Vangar doing his best to reach him, and slings his guitar over his shoulders just before he reaches the Maquari table.

"You ready to go?" he whispers in Pandora's ear.

She nods assent.

Leo glances at his friends who have stopped clapping. He glances a little longer at Khloe who never did to begin with. Then with no further ceremony, he switches the rotochair to manual and pushes his mother away.

All eyes follow their departure.

"Ooooooooo-k," says Zoe. "Why not just leave when you might have won one of the biggest music awards in the city-state."

"I don't think he was in it for the contest," says Beren.

Anastasia keeps quiet and continues looking on after them.

Khloe, until now with a hard look down at the table, appears to contemplate her next move. After a few short seconds she scoffs, makes her goodbyes, and hurries after.

The way home passes in silence. The light from the festival gives them clear passage to the edge of the field. The moon takes up the charge as they move through a small patch of woods separating the Maquari property from the festival grounds.

At the house, Leo hooks one of his powerful arms under his mother's thigh and the other on her back. He then shifts her entire weight to his left so as to pull along the rotochair and scan in at the door.

He wonders which arm she used to carry him when he was the baby.

Once inside he brings her to the master bedroom and lays her gently on the bed. He sets down the rotochair and guitar while she does her best to find comfort on the reputed cloud mattress.

Leo steps back to her side. As he looks down, he recalls the image of her younger self that came to him on stage. It returns to him so vividly it almost replaces the old, faded face below him. In what he sees she can't be much older than he is now: soft, healthy skin complimented by bright hazel eyes: her hair a more lush form of the strawberry blonde she's always had, only now embellished by a highlighted strand of blue.

He begins to lose himself in the illusion. He wonders if it even is an illusion at all. As he's about to open his mouth, the door chime indicates a visitor has been granted access.

The sound breaks Leo's concentration and he looks up quickly. No one appears at the door. When he looks back down again, he finds the illusion was in fact a delusion of the harsh reality of his mother's state.

Khloe enters a second later and they trade places with no words exchanged. Leo stands off as Khloe removes their mother's pants. The tinge of embarrassment once felt at tending her hygienic needs has all but evaporated. Leo maintains a straight face. Pandora turns hers away.

Khloe finishes shortly and dresses Pandora in her blue nightgown. The effort costs Pandora a few moments to recover. Afterwards she finds her daughter's skin and rubs the top of her knuckles against it.

Khloe catches her hand and leans down to kiss her withered forehead.

"Try to sleep. I love you."

Pandora fights to raise her arm high enough to touch Khloe's face. Once she reaches, however, a faint smile runs along her lips, though the part of her hand that touches is black and long since dead.

"I love you too."

Khloe hesitates, then turns to leave.

"I'll be back tomorrow," she manages to say to Leo on her way out.

"Mmm," says Leo, still facing his mother.

When Khloe leaves Leo regards Pandora under the soothing light of the solar lamp. Her body lies limper than usual: like it's already fallen asleep.

Her eyes though, a second before weak but tender on Khloe, start swelling in focus of some unidentified point. Soon she stares up with such intensity one would think a fury were trying to escape its cage. Her iris grows redder and redder as she doesn't blink.

"Mom."

His voice doesn't break her gaze which has now turned to fear. She begins lightly twitching in the face, cheeks becoming pale then flush.

"Mom," says Leo, laying a hand on hers.

The twitching stops. She makes a few blinks.

Leo wraps his hand fully around her wrist. "Did...did you like your song?"

Her eyelids close for a second longer and reopen slowly. The flame has abated to the cool of the present.

"Oh, it was beautiful, honey," she says faintly.

Her aspect again carries her away to a distant place. It reads the same intensity, but not of fear.

"Remember riding along," she says just as distant, "listening to it...in the car?" Her voice nearly cracks on the last word.

The car?

The question sends Leo for a loop. Not only has he never listened to it in any vehicle with his mother, but autos are the only type of vehicle a private citizen has. Cars are almost exclusively for dromo racing.

Leo considers before answering. "Yeah, Mom. I remember."

His response brightens her up to the point of a smile. She then seems to relax and settle into her pillow.

The mention of the song, however, reminds Leo of the reason he played tonight in the first place. He does his best to push it from his mind, much less burden his mother, but it gnaws like a fiery itch.

"Listen, I'm sorry Dad ended up in the contest like that. That flib, who knew he would show up and..."

"Don't be so angry," says Pandora in lucid tones. "He didn't know."

Once again, Leo reals at the words that come from his mother's mouth. They've gone to the festival every year as far as he can remember. Normally, his mother's defenses of the man who left her to her means and infirmity vex him to no end. There may have been lots his father didn't know, but their presence at the Prometheia was not one of them. Something tells him, though, that his mother didn't mean it like that anyway.

Pandora takes a labored breath, then another. She starts bouncing her right forearm off the blankets. Her eyes open, and immediately shoot to the ceiling where she looked so hard before.

"Mom," says Leo again. He wraps his hand a little harder around her wrist.

Her body does not remain limp. It starts twisting and convulsing as though someone were attacking her. The fear returns.

Leo's grip provides for more steadiness than comfort. He reaches across with his other hand to steady her more.

"You have to finish it, Leo," she says stabilizing a bit, "finish it for us."

"Finish what, Mom?" he says. He relaxes his hands a bit. A pang of uneasiness, however, piques his gut.

"I'm so sorry Leo," she says. She turns her head to his side, "I wish I could help you more."

Pandora clasps Leo's hand with unexpected force.

"Mom, you've done enough, it's not your fault. I...I'm helping you now."

She squeezes even harder fighting back tears. "Find a way... SEE the way, like Grandpa and Emrick. Believe. Find me."

Leo pushes the pit in his stomach with all his weight until he's mostly convinced himself her rambling is due to fatigue. Her words, however, he cannot prevent from taking root. She's always been one to mean what she says.

"Come on, Mom, it's been a long day," he says. He gently releases his hands and places her arm under the covers. She does not resist, but reverts directly to looking at the same spot on the ceiling. Her lips continue muttering her last words.

Leo waits a short time until she calms, then a bit more 'til she sleeps. He leans down and kisses the side of her cheek, listening to make sure she still breathes.

Standing up straight he pulls the covers a little higher over her body. For a time he watches her chest rise and fall. Then he just watches.

Once satisfied he turns to go.

"Lights off," he quietly commands.

He pulls the door softly behind him as he leaves the room.

Tomorrow would be just another day.

CHAPTER 3 – TOUCH OF THE KERES

"It's time," says General Alexander Maquari from a lone establishment off the autoroute. The location Leo vaguely recognizes as a spot towards the outskirts of Eulimnos heading into the mountain region. The man he recognizes quite well.

Nonetheless, Leo doesn't react. The shock of being addressed by his dead grandfather impedes all physical response; mainly given the last time he saw him, the General was an invalid at the point of expiring.

Now in place of the sick elderly stands a sturdy middle-aged man just beyond his prime. Though patches of gray appear around his head, he still retains the shaggy brown Leo knows of him having in his youth.

The General looks past Leo impatiently.

"Let's go, both of you," he commands.

A young man wearing chinos and a white collared polo brushes past Leo's shoulder.

"Is our Mother already in the auto?" he asks.

"Yes, and we need to hurry."

The young man turns, "come on, Leo."

Leo's mind fights for air at seeing the older brother he knows only from pictures. Suffocating quickly he covers his eyes with his palms. He rubs and rubs until his mind settles enough to give his eyes another chance.

Before he can even try though, a rumble in the atmosphere breaks his concentration. The sky grays, and a gust of wind slaps his face like a whip.

Something in the energy of the sudden weather change tickles a sense of warning. He decides even dead relatives might be of welcome company. As he means to join them, a pair of bright red taillights racing out of the lot indicates they didn't wait.

"Hey!"

He wonders why they'd be in such a hurry. He then recalls his older brother's use of "our mother." If that were the case, it could only mean one person they raced off with, and one reason why they did.

His eyes open wide in the direction they departed. He starts frantically searching the parking lot for any way he might catch up to them. To his great exaltation he sees one vehicle remains on the far side. It appears as if he had willed it into existence.

He runs off immediately, fists clenched. As he nears, however, he realizes he's not running toward any normal auto.

"Oh shit, a car."

Only a few times has he driven a dromo racer at Mountain Speedway.

Climbing in, he does a quick review of what he thinks to be the necessary controls. He then fires the ignition. Pressing cautiously on the accelerator, he begins pursuit.

Night's black chariot has already begun its sweep across the fading sky. He risks a little more speed. The mountainous contour of the landscape reminds him of riding through the Orgon Vale in Appalachia.

With visibility decreasing, he tries fiddling with the levers to find which activates the lighting system. He instead finds the wipers, and almost ends up off the road. The swerve reminds him to keep two hands in place on the wheel.

He soon catches sight of the taillights speeding around a sharp bend. Following such maneuvers feels like riding Beren's tail at the Speedway.

He takes the curve comfortably. On the other side, however, his grandfather's car scatters a heap of dead leaves. It swirls in the air and plasters to the windshield, again blinding him.

He slams the brake. Tires screech momentarily but this time he knows straightaway where to find the wipers. Once his vision clears, though, he no longer finds himself in anything resembling the Orgon Vale.

Thick forest lines the road to both sides. The passage narrows, and all trace of day now vanquishes.

An air of familiarity creeps into his mind.

The headlights pick up the dry and varied colors of the foliage. Their proximity to the car forms a natural tunnel of sorts. Despite the uncertainty of the path, Leo knows there's nothing for it, so he plunges headfirst.

His mind then takes him to the previous day training on the Shadow Fighter. The familiarity he started feeling now registers full on. He recognizes this wooded area as the place he traveled through in his daydream.

Once that connection is made, the world he once felt again comes alive. Only now he feels it in much greater vibrancy.

It urges him through the tunnel of foliage. He soon feels the essence of his mother. To his great chagrin, the essence is one of fear.

Cold air begins seeping through the vents. Night claims full dominion over the starless sky. Leo maintains speed, and between gripping the wheel and the drop in temperature, his knuckles go white.

Branches hang over the road like claws. A building wind sets them in a motion. The thrusts resemble the wings of a predatory bird. Leo feels himself the prey.

Through all his preoccupation the auto has moved out of sight. He's even lost touch with his mother's energy. Shaking his head and slapping his cheek, he runs deeper into the maze.

The moment he hits the pedal the sky erupts in a deep rolling thunder. It ripples across the sky and through the vents of the car. Leo wipes a dry forehead.

The road then leads to a small hill a few dozen yards ahead. Without sight or knowledge of what lies beyond, Leo imagines anything from demon to dragon.

Driving into the ascent at such speeds sends sparks from the front bumper. It also sends Leo's torso hard into the steering wheel. This reminds him of the use of the safety belt which he then quickly fastens.

It does not, however, remind him to decelerate over inclines. Hitting the summit at around 60 mph the car goes airborne several feet. Leo reels under the awkwardness of weightlessness and losing control. Fortunately for him, the car lands on a straight stretch of road going down.

At the bottom of the hill, however, a pair of red oval eyes glares in his direction. Its sheer size would suggest something as big as a Chimaera. Leo's knuckles again go white from the pressure of his grip.

Through his mind flash bared teeth, sharper than any he's ever seen. They appear in a series of three as though belonging to three separate jaws.

Before anything else appears, his foot reacts to a lingering command and slams the brakes less than 15 yards from the glaring red eyes. The tires scream to a halt nearly on top of the would-be predator.

He then realizes the red was nothing more than the taillight of his grandfather's auto.

It sits in a crooked position on an extended shoulder of the road.

The gravel pull-off.

He knows the matching sequences of his daydream cannot be mere coincidence: riding along a rural road, the woods, the foliage. He then remembers the last thing he saw. With that in mind, he makes a slow, impending turn of the head to the far right.

Looming high into the night, an elm tree stands at the edge of the gravel. Its pale glow defies the heavy darkness shrouding the others around it: its rich leaves do likewise with the dead foliage.

Leo turns away, then looks back. This is a tree that should only be at the bottom of the lake.

Impossible.

Notwithstanding, to see it in open air, in its full form, leaves little room to deny its true beauty.

As he pauses a split second to admire, light, invisible claps begin sounding from above. They first appear faint, then become stronger. They quickly form into a consistent pattern which reminds Leo of the branches moving over the road.

He hurries the rest of the way to the auto. Once there he glances over the external frame. No damage.

He grips the middle of the auto and pulls the doors apart. Inside very little remains. He finds no trace of his brother or grandfather anywhere. Only his mother...

Pandora, wide awake, stares ahead with a hard face but quivering lip.

"Where are they?" Leo says leaning in.

She doesn't respond. Nor does she seem to notice he's even there.

What Leo notices, however, is that her strawberry blond hair looks much fuller on her head: styled, moreover, very like to the way it was before she got sick.

He also sees her hand lying in her lap. Five fully formed digits extend from old but clear skin.

Leo smiles and grasps it.

Then, the world shifts.

The atmosphere slows and perceptions darken. Sound stifles to a numbing tone.

Leo feels a pit swirling in his stomach as if trying to decide which way is up. All the while he does his best to keep hold of his mother's hand.

Just then a faint clap peaks through. The next intensifies, and the ensuing twice as loud. The ones that follow keep to the rhythm he heard earlier but move to such close range they have gone from claps to heavy whooshes.

Leo musters his bearings enough to risk poking his head around the auto door.

His body instantly tenses.

Wading the air above, a horrific creature scrutinizes him. Soiled, venous wings flap the pattern of the wind. Sinewy arms hang at its side. They terminate in reaper-like claws blotched in dark colors.

Raiment follows suit. It clings to the body in fragments as though the only clothes it's ever worn. Leo raises his eyes cautiously to the face where he sees the first degree of anything human. Thin, lifeless hair run down both cheeks from a part in the middle of the head.

Judging from its overall composition, he imagines the creature is made to at least partly resemble a woman.

As the image sinks in deeper, Leo realizes what confronts him.

Keres: death spirits.

The glitch in his consciousness incites greater intensity in the Kere.

Its feminine lips part to reveal a row of fangs polished and filed to purpose.

Most of all though, its eyes begin swirling in deep-pitted sockets. They produce a neon yellow light that entrances Leo like a pair of magic jewels.

It is not, however, in his direction they look.

Mom.

The Kere shudders as though reading his thoughts. Just then two more arrive. They simultaneously move into pack formation and match the wing pattern of their leader. All as one, their weight shifts forward.

Fear melts into Leo's instinct and he jumps out from behind the door. Without even thinking he already finds himself in pugilist stance.

The Keres do not miss the mortal challenge. Their eyes swirl faster and wings pick up speed. All at once they launch forward in a fury.

Leo does likewise and unloads all his strength into an overhand right. In the blur of light and speed he aims between the bright yellow ovals of the leader. At the moment of impact, though, he hits nothing but air.

Recovering quickly, he looks back to the auto.

It's already empty.

"Mom!" he cries. The Keres, however, are already carrying Pandora away. The leader clamps an arm while the others each a leg. They head straight in the direction of the elm.

For all Pandora might resist, her only struggle is to keep eye contact with her son.

Leo begins chase with all the speed he can conjure.

The leader, several yards ahead, detaches and dives headlong into the base of the trunk. It disappears on impact. On the tree, however, it leaves a familiar imprint.

The "K."

The symbol looks just the same etched in the wood as when he first saw it. Only now he knows what it means. That ominous feeling pushes him even harder.

Just as he does the second Kere makes its own dive and vanishes like the first. Leo doesn't even have time to react before the last of them follows with Pandora.

As it descends, time seems to slow. Leo's eyes widen at seeing his mother being pulled down. The trauma on Pandora's face, however, washes away. It softens, and in her eyes Leo sees a desperate sadness dying to escape.

He lifts his arm to reach out.

Her lips part.

"Leo."
And she's gone.

△△△

Leo wakes disoriented, drawing deep breaths. He sits up with a jolt. He begins looking side to side but nothing immediately registers.

The poster screen on the wall reals images of Paul Vangar in his prime. Leo watches them slide as his breathing calms.

His right hand, for some reason, continues to grasp at something. It finds the familiar warmth and softness of his wool comforter. Comfort itself, however, does not acknowledge he's home, in his bed.

The fenestrator on the opposite wall is set to "glass: transparent." Outside, Dawn's chariot breaks the horizon. A red sun peeks through.

Just another day.

Leo swings his feet on the floor unable to block out all that replays in his head. It appears so vivid he wonders if that was the real and this is the dream. Regardless, the spot on his mind with his mother's image blisters real enough for either.

It was just a dream. Just a stupid dream.

The sensations, however, feel as raw as when they were inflicted. His chest wrenches to the tightening of the path; ears cringe to the clapping of the wind; body paralyzes to the glare of the death spirit.

Only confirming his mother sleeping soundly would put him at ease. So simple, so routine, yet he doesn't move.

Yellow swirls blare behind his eyes. Flapping wings flitter around them. The "K" burns in the tree.

Find me.

With great effort Leo brings himself to his feet. He steps off, and manages a few paces to the door. Looking back he again notes the sun in its red form. Though not a terribly uncommon occurrence, this day it spreads over the land in a darker hue, closer to a crimson.

He looks back to the door. Swallowing a mouthful of dry saliva, he steps through.

Slowly he gropes his way through the house he could navigate blindfolded. His audible range tunes into the most questionable of silences and deviations of sound. His hands grasp every object as though carrying an oppressive weight on his back.

As he approaches his mother's room, the weight turns into numbing flame. It spreads from his chest like wildfire, and scorches his nerves to sand.

He stops before the door inches from his nose. He listens for anything from a rustle in the sheets to an insect on the pillow.

Hot breath kisses his lips from being so close.

Hearing nothing, he reaches out with a different sense. It roams over the inside of the room like a probing device trying to perceive the slightest detection of energy. Even the anxiety he felt of her while riding with his grandfather would bring the greatest of ease.

Yielding nothing once more, he takes no immediate action. He just breathes and takes in breath. The warmth of carbon dioxide gives at least some proof of life.

He then looks down and places his fingertips on the latch. Drawing one last flow of air, he exhales, and pushes open the door.

He looks first to his mother's bed. What he sees makes him think he might not have woken up after all.

It is empty.

He rushes over and pulls back the covers. No signs of trauma in or around. The rotochair remains unmoved, as does seemingly everything else for what he can see.

He shuts his eyes and rubs his palm into his temple.

Just then the sky opens a little more. Intensifying rays pass through the fenestrator. They expand enough to outline a figure sitting in the old brown chair underneath.

"Mom?"

Leo's murmur cuts through the idle energy packed in the room. It seeps over every inch and trickles into every crack. Finding no recipient, it echoes back louder than it left.

"Mom!" he exclaims, though sounding even softer.

The unmistakable hand lays on the armrest. Its horrid condition serves as a chilling reminder of just how awake he really is. He notices it closes around something, what little flesh of the fingers remains to even close.

By now the burning panic has returned to his gut. Though he's found her, his apprehension grips stronger than ever over where she actually is.

He begins inching forth on stiff limbs. His brow furrows into a focused glare. While only a few feet, it may as well be his last mile.

Once at the back of the chair, he remembers to breathe.

His eyes stay forward, and back stays straight. He barely has the strength to place one of his meaty hands on the outside wing.

Wrenching his jaw, he leans forward and around.

There his mother rests with the same expression on her face as when she last looked on him from the tree.

The sun rises higher. Its warmth reaches her open eyes. For a moment, the light reflects deep like burning coals.

For a moment...

CHAPTER 4 – THE MANTIS

The tisk of an uncapped bottle pierces the white noise of the Pronoian River. Leo, sitting on its west bank, tilts back a Hoffman's Lager Top.

The flow pouring down his throat matches greatly the rate of current flowing before him. The cool liquid filling his belly does much the same with the crisp air of late Autumn. He ingests a mouthful of both once he sets down his drink.

With his free hand he begins fiddling with the bottle cap. He turns it over several times, but doesn't bother reading the text on the flip side. Indeed, it's the only one he plans to have.

After another long sip he turns to one of his oldest friends and wisest counselors: the river.

What's attachment worth if everything has an end?

The intention of his statement spreads far across the water. The question itself hangs in the air of his mind. He waits patiently until the condensation of the Lager Top starts dripping over his fingers.

The coolness rouses him, but the river remains silent.

Leo hunches forward and digs his elbows into his knees.

Why can't I feel what I know I should?

He shuts his eyes and allows the sound of the current to flow through his senses. Once at peace he submits to its grace. He tries to ask the reason why agony won't besiege him, why he sees the blood but doesn't feel the wound. Human emotion and the nature of impermanence: questions only a river could answer.

Nonetheless, the river doesn't cooperate. Nothing more than lovely patterns reach Leo's mind, as though viewing a hallucinogenic screensaver.

Leo looks down at the bottle in his hand, then tips it back again.

Reality will have to suffice.

He stuffs the bottle cap into his pants pocket and pulls out something else. He looks on it a moment, then begins fingering it in circles much like the cap.

It is a torn piece of parchment: with the last words of Pandora Maquari.

He thinks of the coroners arriving the previous day. While Khloe went to admit them, he knelt beside his mother's chair and lowered her eyelids for eternal sleep. Her hand still lay on the armrest in the closed position. He then saw what she was holding, and with some effort pried the note from her grasp and concealed it before anyone entered the room.

He now examines the vague and simple message:

"Use Your Illusion."

That his mother felt it was worth her life to drag herself to the chair and write this baffles him to no end.

He looks back to the river. Downstream to the left stands the archaic Portland Bridge where he and his friends have spent so much time. He'd often run out the door of his house without even a goodbye...to be with them.

He turns away. His fist closes around the note. He then lifts the bottle to his lips and downs the rest of his drink in one gulp.

For a second he squeezes the parchment even tighter. He ultimately releases it, though, before it crumples completely.

Shoving it back in his pocket he rises to leave.

The stations for the tram and electro rail lie a short distance from the river, respectively. Both, however, sound unappealing; that involving the midst of others. So he passes them by and decides to walk.

He opts for the solitude of the tracks over the exposure of the residential neighborhoods. They feel solid under his feet, unlike most else. And as the path he and his friends usually take, he enters into the protective cocoon of energy left by so many good times.

Soon after his departure, darkness threatens to fall, and the moon to rise. Houses nearby activate lighting systems. To the south the Pegeian Forest comes alive.

Two small boys play with synthetic Kladimans blades at the edge of their land share. They stop when they catch sight of a powerfully built individual in a fitted, long sleeve sweater moseying head down. This young man hops off the track and kicks a rock on the ground. When he catches up to it a few yards ahead, he kicks it again: and so on until passing out of sight.

"Hey, wasn't that the Maurileho?" says the older of the two.

The younger shrugs. "My point," he announces.

The brother, who's kept his eyes and mouth wide open on Leo, turns back to his sibling. Before he can manage a "huh?," a glow-in-the-dark blade tip taps him in the gut.

The little one raises his hands and races off toward the house.

"Mommy, I got him! Mommy, I'm the Maurileho!"

The older stomps the ground and begins chase.

The long miles home leave Leo to his thoughts. His mother many times spoke to him of the afterlife, mostly as a little boy and about his older brother. At the time he was too young to understand, and once older understood too much to believe.

"Living in Excellence should be the goal of all living," she would say, "no soul should carry burden to the afterlife." To this he would nod and go about his business.

He pictures her face far from unburdened when last he saw her. Yet as her entire life was devoted to Excellence, he assures himself if Elysium exists, she now certainly roams its fields.

Arriving home Leo enters the house by moonlight. To the right, the door to his mother's bedroom remains halfway open. He stands before it, and again he listens.

This time, a flutter catches his ear. His chest immediately tightens into a scalding fist. The last such flutter he heard signified a gang of diabolically scorned women with yellow eyes.

What ends up "fluttering" out of the room, however, is the tiniest of ladybugs. It pauses on Leo's shoulder in its ever continuing expedition for a cracked fenestrator. Normally Leo would take his finger and flick such a pest onto the floor. This time, though, he lets it rest until it's ready to leave.

Fed up for the day with attempts at understanding, Leo starts ambling toward the basement. The thought of laying on his silver couch seems the most welcoming option. He then remembers leaving his J.T Tasker on his mother's bed stand from earlier in the afternoon.

Again at her door he brings himself to cross the unfamiliar threshold of a room he's known all his life. Retrieving the thin, rectangular device he activates a small virtecran in colors of red. A bubble of "new message" calls his attention. He clicks the icon and sees a dossier whose title will not penetrate past his eyes:

"The Last Will and Testament of Pandora Maquari."

The words look more foreign than anything else. And yet, there's something more real about them than actually finding his mother the way he did earlier. He stares a minute longer, then drops into his mother's chair.

The document annotates the typical division of belongings amongst surviving offspring. The house, the land share, the auto, will now be owned in equal parts by Khloe and Leo.

Leo frowns at the thought of compromising anything with his sister. He then notices, however, that a few items have been bequeathed directly to him.

The first is a vintage copy of "Use Your Illusion" by the Pre-Reckoning group Guns N' Roses. Leo recognizes the antique disk in the side image of the file. More than anything he wonders over the correspondence to the note in his pocket.

He shakes his head.

All that over some stupid album.

He nearly takes out the piece of parchment again to finish crumpling. A part of him wishes he'd never found it. Knowing his mother, though, all of her actions and words held a degree of worth, so he cannot dismiss the potential significance over these.

He looks back on the virtecran to continue reading. Much to his dismay, the second item doesn't prove any clearer.

"Caras Maquarion: Grandpa's Estate."

Caras Maquarion?

Not even the name rings a bell. The only other residence he knows of his grandfather having owned was a modest apartment in Prometheum Proper dedicated mainly to affairs of state and the Guard; and the house in which his family has lived for three generations has certainly never been called anything but home.

A footnote underneath the strange inscription reads:

"The key is yours if you wish to take it."

Leo furrows his left brow and turns his palms up to the side. One palm raises to his temple. After a bit of rubbing, he sits back in the chair and scrolls down the page.

The final bequest is more a service than item. It charges him with constructing a funeral pyre capable of floating.

She wants to burn on the lake.

This message he understands on a personal level regarding his mother. Nonetheless, ignorance weighs less than understanding.

A pang of discomfort tickles in his chest. It threatens to spread, but just gets lost somewhere in the abyss.

Maybe this is all just another dream. Maybe to sleep is to wake up.

Leo taps the browser closed and brings his feet up on the chair. He locks onto the residual presence of the last person to sit there. His eyes quickly close.

Sleep carries him to a place of open fields where he wanders unfeeling.

Just another dream.

ΔΔΔ

Leo wakes in the morning with his arm draped over the armrest as his pillow. His hand faces down and closes around some small object. Turning it over, he sees through a half open eye it's his mother's note. He rests his head back down.

Nothing comes to mind as to how it escaped his pocket: nor why he decides to open it again now.

"Use Your Illusion."

He fails to draw any significance other than the old album containing his mother's favorite song.

He relaxes his hand.

Was there something about how I played it that night?

He then thinks about the estate his grandfather supposedly had. Not many now living would be able to confirm this or not. He considers asking Khloe, but doesn't feel like having to justify why it passed to him instead of both: indeed, if he could even justify it to himself.

A twinge of frustration passes through him. It nearly turns to resentment toward his mother for leaving him with such conundrums, if not leaving him altogether. Even the positive energy of his mother's chair doesn't help sway his negative reaction. Even considering her death in that very spot just one day before.

Leo sits up sharply and rubs his temple. He presses harder until he starts feeling a bit of relief. Little by little the nasty feeling dissolves into the cloud of others already amassed.

He leans forward digging his elbows into his knees. He sets to thinking on who might be able to help him with all these strange puzzles. After his mother, he quickly exhausts a small list of names who would fit the bill.

All but one...

△△△

Leo boards the tram later that day for the short ride to Anastasia's grandfather's estate. It lies on the high side of Lake Maquari, across the way and to the east of Leo's house.

Halfway there he questions the soundness of his reasoning for even going. A skeptic consulting an ancient mantis. That is to say, Leo consulting a 100-year-old man from the Pre-Reckoning world who claims to see life without time.

The cultural Renaissance in history inspired many to declare and even establish themselves as "seers," or mantis. Several proved fraud, and Leo's disposition has always prevented him from believing in the rest.

Leo isn't looking for fortunes, though. He only seeks answers from the man who was his grandfather's best friend and might know something about the estate and the note. For although Leo has always regarded him as peculiar, he wouldn't deny the confidence and wisdom of his words.

A part of him desires Anastasia to go along. For all her piety, however, she might be one of the few believers who doesn't consult the old man: though Leo knows the problem not to be faith in his guidance, but faith in him: faith she lost when he failed her father.

The estate sits a ways from any road or neighbor, deep into a hill bordering an open plateau. That Leo spots the path surprises him; so many years since he last used it, and so much smaller than the child remembers it in his mind's eye.

Crossing the small bridge over Hellebore Creek reaffirms he chose correctly. As children he and Anastasia would pick the yellowish-green bulbs lining the sides, or stare down at their reflections to see who would be turned into a flower. All this while their parents attended to "business:" all this until Anastasia's father was murdered.

Leo pauses at the rail and listens. The scents and feelings associated with this place resurface without the need to draw on any memory. The pale smell of dead foliage piling up for someone to play in: the innocence of a dry late autumn breeze rising up from the water. He wonders how many pieces of people's lives flow in that current.

He continues on until the sound of the creek fades behind him. The property itself, though beautiful, has long since been tended. Indeed, for not the height of the great house he might have missed it altogether. Heavy brush and vegetation form a natural hedge against the side of the path.

Makes sense for a hermit.

The walkway leading to the manor is walled with brick murals. Vines now obstruct what was once a dramatic tapestry of classical legend.

A break in the growth reveals a horse crest helmet. Leo sifts through and opens the scene of Hector falling to Achilles' spear shaft.

He removes a bit more and sees the musician Orpheus, enchanting the hellhound Cerberus with his lyre. He finds it strange a mortal would use nothing more than a stringed instrument against such a beast, all in an attempt to rescue his dead wife from the Underworld.

He then comes to a scene he didn't expect: a man standing alone in the midst of heavy rain holding a blade at his side. He is overlooking a lake from a summit nearby.

"Your grandfather," a soft raspy voice speaks from behind. Light footsteps accompanied by a gentle tap move a bit closer. "In the Sacred Rains, viewing the lake that now bears his name."

Leo continues looking but no longer sees.

"Mom's dead," he says, still facing the wall.

"I know."

Leo lets out a faint chuckle through his nose and begins to turn around. "I guess news even gets up here."

"Not all news travels by the *Times Current.*"

"Right."

The two regard each other with mutual interest: Leo amazed the man still breathes and the man as much that he breathes to see Leo again.

"And how is Anastasia?" asks the wrinkled man in a cardigan.

Leo would like to say fine, but somehow responding reassuringly feels like a betrayal. He sticks his hands in his pockets.

"She's your granddaughter, sir. You could always ring to find out."

"Yes, well, she's not exactly jumping to my calls."

"Then maybe you should learn to ping, Mr. Wildyn."

The old man curls his thin lips into a half smile, "Emrick will do."

Leo nods, then Emrick pivots slowly with his cane signaling Leo to follow. He moves fairly well for his age, with only a slight hump in his back and faint limp in his leg as a result of a chronic injury sustained during the Reckoning Wars.

They come to a door which, given the grandeur of the manor, is composed of nothing more than a non-finished wood base. In the center hangs a hefty metal ring looped through the mouth of a grisly old man.

Emrick grasps the ring with his bony fingers and knocks a combination set to a particular rhythm. On the last tap the door creaks open. Leo reaches around to push it the rest of the way but finds it especially light given its breadth.

"Thank you, Leonidas."

Leo scoffs at the mention of his full name.

They enter a lobby that seems more spacious than outdoors. The room hasn't aged nor modernized in its simple aesthetics, containing polished hardwood furniture complimented by a grand staircase leading to upper levels. The general lighting of the room reflects the chestnut shade of the house's interior.

Varied pieces of artwork adorn the walls. In one painting stands an extravagant row of tall buildings glittering in the night. Two in particular tower above the rest in twin formation, like a pair of giant pillars anchoring the city.

"Is that...?" says Leo, stepping closer.

"Yes, it is."

"The ruins of New York."

"Before they were ruins of course."

Citizens of Prometheum learn much of the Age of Decadence in Lyceum: "age" referring to the latter part of the 20th century up to the Reckoning in the early part of the 21st: "decadence" referring to the lifestyle that had become custom in many parts of the world. Amongst the years of such a deplorable time includes the fall of the great city that once symbolized a nation, the spirit of which has now been abandoned to the archives of history.

"Those two buildings, though," says Leo, flicking his head toward the higher ones, "I don't recognize them so much."

Emrick looks on Leo a second before answering. "They were destroyed at the turn of the century." He looks down and pauses again. "Not generally attributed to the Reckoning, but an early sign one could argue."

Footsteps descend the staircase. Leo doesn't turn.

"We have a guest, Master Wildyn?" says the voice of a bubbly young man.

"Ah, yes Dion," says Emrick. The old man places a hand on Leo's shoulder and leads him around. "This is Leonidas Maquari."

"Oh!" he exclaims looking Leo up and down. "The Maurileho, finally ready to join us?"

Leo holds blank silence.

"He's here on a different matter," says Emrick. "Would you do me a favor and ask Camilla to bring two cups of *vin chaud* to the den?"

The young man takes his leave to complete his errand and Emrick proceeds in the direction of his office.

"So who is he, your butler?" says Leo as they enter.

"My apprentice. One of them, at least."

Leo stops in the doorway and looks behind him. "He seemed to be expecting me." He watches the so-called apprentice climb the stairs as though he were happy to do so. He turns back and eyes the old man. "And so did you in a way."

Emrick makes a slight grin and settles into a high backed leather chair. "I had an inkling your curiosity would outweigh your reason."

Leo's eyes squint in surprise. Still in the doorway, he folds his powerful arms and leans against the frame. A moment later he drops them and stands up straight.

"I came here to find out about my grandfather's estate," he declares.

Emrick places his right elbow on the hard wood desk and regards Leo curiously.

"So," he begins, "after a short life believing in nothing, you'd concern yourself over a place of worship?"

He brings up his other elbow. "After all these years, you come to my doorstep, unannounced, looking for answers from an old loon who claims to have visions outside the present?"

Leo struggles to maintain a stern face. He knows no witty remark will avail him of Emrick's insight. He does note, however, the old man's reference to a place of worship instead of just a place.

"Or maybe," Emrick continues, sliding forward in his seat, "what you're really after is guidance, not answers."

Despite the wrinkles and slabs of gray hair surrounding a bald top, the blue of Emrick's gaze shines as though having beheld nothing but beauty in his days.

Anastasia's eyes.

Leo reverts to folding his arms and leaning into the doorway. "You haven't answered my question," he says.

"Indeed I haven't. Yet how can you expect me to give a clear answer to a hedged question?"

Leo stares deeper into the old man who just stares deeper back.

"My Mom," Leo says after a long silence, "...mentioned you the night before she died." He relaxes his arms again. "She told me to see the way like Grandpa and Emrick."

"See the way to what," Emrick states more than asks.

"I don't know, she wasn't making any sense that night."

A middle-aged servicewoman interrupts carrying a tin tray of *vin chaud*. She sets down two steaming cups that fill the room with a relaxing aroma. Emrick tests and squints his approval to excuse her. He then nods toward the chair in front of him. Leo obliges.

"What you tell me," he sips again, "is a start. But if you've already declared your mother's words incoherent, I'll assume you've come only to renew our acquaintance."

Leo sets down the cup he was about to drink.

This old bag never quits.

Yet, something about not having to keep your guard up due to the fact of it being useless tickles Leo's amusement. In fact, he finds it quite liberating.

"Alright," says Leo with a studied look. He then takes a hearty sip of his mulled wine and delves into everything he's seen in the last few days.

Emrick listens with the patience time has granted him. The "K" on the tree, the little girl running, the fearsome creatures chasing their car in the woods; all this he absorbs intently. When Leo concludes he rests back in his chair.

"And you see all this as dreams and daydreams?"

Leo starts rethinking that guard thing.

"I guess."

"That's a lie or you wouldn't be here," says Emrick with greater force.

Bastard.

Emrick sits forward again and puts his elbow on the desktop. "Never mind believing," he says, "if you had just paid attention growing up you would at least understand."

Leo folds his arms. "What do you mean?"

"The Kappa is a symbol of death. The letter on the tree, then the Keres."

"Alright, but..."

"Then the tree itself, corresponding to the character "Mu," is a link between worlds. Not to mention it was an elm."

Leo looks away a second. He omitted the experience of the underwater elm tree in his recounting, but now begins to make connections.

"So what are you saying," he says looking back, "I should have seen it coming?"

Emrick tilts his cup and dries his upper lip.

"You did see it coming, you should have trusted yourself."

A loud chime conveniently interjects the burden of responding. Its melody consists of a four note arpeggiated sequence that brings Leo back to the time of running through the halls of the manor with Anastasia. A time almost forgotten.

A time.

The source of the chimes, a tall old clock utilizing a form of classic numerals, looks almost more like a face than mechanical surface.

Leo watches as the hands turn round and round on the nose. The more they turn the more arbitrary the numbers feel. With no start and no stop, they indeed might be the only thing he can think of to escape the condemned cycle of beginning and end. Never having been born, to never have to die. Eternal. To know it would mean to see time beyond the face of a clock.

It dawns on Leo that Emrick has been making his own connections.

"So," Leo says, still watching the seconds turn, "I'm supposed to be like you then: to see life out of time. That's the point to all this."

Emrick grins. "Would that be such a bad thing? It runs in your family after all."

Leo breaks from the clock on the word "family." His grandfather supposedly had it, but no one else he knew of..."

Emrick's aspect hardens. "My old friend had it. And your mother 'supposedly' passed it on to you."

Leo sits up in his seat. "My mother was no mantis."

"You sound so sure."

Leo knows his mother's beliefs would have allowed for the idea. Her belief in Prometheus, the omega of foresight, was profound to say the least. Yet one unsettling fact remains:

"No one who could look into the future would have ended up like her."

Not removing his eyes from Emrick, he adjusts his seating and eagerly grabs for his now cool hot wine.

"Leonidas." Emrick takes a breath before continuing. "Our fates are drawn only by the choices we make."

"What?" says Leo, nearly spitting his wine. "So my mom chose to get sick? Chose to put up with that deadbeat they call my father? Chose to follow that omega who never helped her out of any of it?"

The old man lowers his bushy eyebrows. "Careful, Leonidas. Your passions and selfishness cost your mother more than you can imagine in life, and no one should carry burdens beyond."

His mother's words ring eerily from the mouth of another. He makes no retort.

"Your mother is deceased, but not at rest," says Emrick. "She will only find peace when you do. Only you can save her."

The chimes of the clock hail another quarter hour past. Arbitrary moments for an undying entity: time ticking for those already dying, or dead.

△△△

The hour is well advanced when Leo returns home. Once inside he fills a glass of tap water and makes straight for his room: the following day he's to host his mother's funeral games. He also must wake up early to complete the floating pyre that sits half-finished on the side of the house.

He stops at his door. The fenestrator is set to "night shades: opaque," so the only light comes from the poster screen. Stepping in he sees it still reels images of Paul Vangar and Scars of Bourbon. He watches it a moment, takes a large gulp of water, then exits for the basement.

He pauses similarly in front of his silver couch but ultimately plops himself in it. The water he sets to the side, half empty. Laying back, he rests his head on the cushion and uses his arms as blankets.

No sooner do his eyes close than Emrick's words start swirling in his mind. "Time," "trust," "choice," "selfishness." They move like an agitated wasp, weaving and stinging at random.

Eventually, however, they morph together as one and settle into a single phrase:

Only you can save her.

Leo lifts his arm over his closed eyes in an attempt to block out the soundness of everything the old man perceived. At any point of it seeping through, he presses harder on his face, and the words start stinging all over again.

Fear gives him strength. It fuels his resistance of owning to his actions in thinking their effect could actually reach the afterlife.

The fact he denies the existence of an afterlife doesn't help: for his mother it was a very real place. What's worse, if she put herself there by choice...

Leo rises abruptly and kicks over the rest of his water. He makes a striking motion towards it as though it were the glass' fault.

To the right next to the wall he leans down and lifts up a square slab of carpet. Underneath he opens a small console and taps the drying mechanism. He doesn't wait for it to function.

Leaving the basement he goes outside and turns left for the garage. There he gathers balsa based lumber, tools, and an old J.T Tasker he designates for small jobs. Once ready he kicks closed the tool box and proceeds out to the side of the house.

The motion light picks up his heavy steps a few yards from the project.

It reveals a heap of wood strewn about in something that wants to look finished. Under the mess, a long raft-like structure begins to show form. It holds together only at the vitals, much like Pandora did overall.

Leo lets his materials fall to the ground and kneels to set his Tasker. Touching a few commands, a small virtecran appears from which he draws a Squ, or sequencer program, for building pyres. A voice prompt begins at the step he left off.

The instructions read at intervals according to the progress of the task. They will also intervene and offer corrections to mishaps. Though the voice sounds often in this case, Leo proceeds as though it were on mute.

Twenty minutes later three figures approach the Maquari land share. Leo stops his work and peers through the glare of the light. The visitors walk nearly in sync, slow but determined in single file. Leo doesn't need any more than silhouettes to know who they are.

Anastasia, Beren, and Zoe appear a moment later dressed in buttoned blouses, suit vests, and silk scarves. They pause before Leo, exchanging glances at him, themselves, and the ground. A few pairs of lips begin to curl up but ultimately retreat like a shy animal.

Leo regards them, then their outfits.

"I miss something?"

Zoe slides two fingers down her scarf. "My parents had a little get-together," she says, "for everyone being back from...the Academy, and the Guard." She rolls her eyes away a second. "We've been trying to get ahold of you all day."

The pyre-building squ spits out an array of construction reproaches which Leo quickly silences.

"Yeah, well," he says, setting down his tools, "I had a few things to sort out." He deliberately catches Anastasia's eye on his last word. "How'd you guys know I was out here?" he asks before she can return any gesture.

"We saw the light from Zoe's," says Beren, "so we figured we'd see what you were up to."

Anastasia, though the first to arrive, has not shown any particular eagerness to join the conversation. Since Leo's glance she's maintained a sharp, studied look on his face.

"We also wanted to give you this," says Zoe. She reaches deep into a purple bag with black trim. When she withdraws her hand, she holds up a gold medallion attached to an embroidered strap.

"You won!" she says pointing a finger in the air. She quickly lowers it, though, and uses the same hand to push her hair behind her ear.

Nonetheless, she raises the prestigious award even higher for Leo to see. A medallion of the finest gold, the engravings of which depict Orpheus taming the mighty Cerberus in the Underworld. The strap holding it features a string of fennel stalk weaving in and out of flame lit notes. It is a great honor to win the Prometheia's musical contest.

Leo simply stares. Zoe begins lowering her arms when Anastasia steps in and takes it up. Pinching the strap gently with her thumbs, she lays it around Leo's neck.

"Mom would have been proud," she whispers, holding his shoulders.

Her face so close, he turns his to the side.

"If only."

She backs away a few steps out of arm's reach. After a quick regard, she backs a little more.

The friends revert to searching for places to stare. Leo raises the medallion for a brief look, then lets it fall back on his rounded chest with a thump.

"So," says Beren after another few moments, "pyres are made better by moonlight, eh?"

"Couldn't sleep."

Beren nods. "Well," he says, looking to the girls, "neither can we."

The girls respond with tender looks. Leo allows himself a half smile.

He then looks his dear friends over once more. "We better get you guys out of those pretty clothes first."

The eight-handed team finishes the project within an hour. The teamwork makes him think of the few times he competed with Beren and Zoe in the Phalanx Division of Kladimo, which consists of small group, strategic based combat. Though the glory of solo competition still rules his heart, he finds the idea of collaboration appealing for the sense of relief it provides of assuming everything alone. Indeed, in the short time of constructing the pyre, he nearly forgets the true purpose of constructing it at all. That is, until someone mentions the funeral games.

"Thought you'd sit this one out?" says Beren with a smirk at Zoe. He refers to the dueling event, for which the two of them are so vigorously known.

"Why would I," she says. She steps in front of him almost nose to nose, "when it'll be so much more fun sticking my maolance up your ass."

Beren inches a little closer. "That's the only way you'll get to touch it anyway."

"Hey, guys," says Anastasia, looking to one after the other. She takes the tools from their hands.

They break directly and assume casual positions.

Leo steps away and taps closed the squ, then manually shuts down the Tasker altogether. He glances at the beautifully constructed pyre next to the suit bags holding the outfits. He finds it a shame to need a time like this in order to recognize the truth of friendship.

Taking up the clothes, he hands them over one by one.

"Thanks...guys," he says when finished.

Beren claps him by the forearm. Instead of the typical slide up the arm into a fist bump, though, he pulls Leo in for a one-armed hug. "No problem, buddy."

Zoe moves in next. "See you tomorrow, k?" She hugs with a kiss on the cheek and joins Beren. "You coming, Annie?"

"I'll go in a bit," she says in Leo's direction.

"Whatever you say sister," says Beren. He throws a heavy arm around Zoe who elbows him in the ribs. They turn to go and are soon well into the night. Little by little their voices fade over the far side of the lake.

Anastasia, though facing Leo's direction, finally looks up at Leo who's been looking at her the whole time. She lowers her eyes, but brings them up again quickly.

"Um, so, how are you?" she says as if she didn't understand her own question.

Leo stares at her and almost grins.

"I'm top. And you?"

Anastasia makes no reply as he starts collecting his materials and heading toward the garage. He expects she will inquire over his earlier glance, and also that he will have to confess seeing Emrick. For the time being he applies himself to re-arranging the garage.

Anastasia waits, then starts following. Finally she stops and crosses her arms. "So what things needed sorting anyway?"

Leo sets the Tasker on his Muscle Caliber home gym and returns the last of his tools to the storage box.

"I went to see Emrick today." He keeps his back to her and punches the code to secure the tools.

Her arms drop. "What? Why?"

Leo debates mincing his answers, but decides one Wildyn seeing through him was enough for one day. He then turns, leans against the workout system, and starts relating the particulars of his day.

Anastasia listens as patient as her grandfather. She adjusts position a few times, but not in her facial expression which remains only attentive.

When Leo finishes she stares at him a moment, then nods and looks down. "And what did he say?"

Leo goes back to sorting through his things. "He said the tree was important, like some portal or something."

Anastasia starts at the mention. She adjusts positions again.

"Don't worry," says Leo, checking her over. "I didn't tell him about the lake."

Given the insight and perception of everything the old man discerned, Leo wouldn't be surprised if Emrick could talk of the shape of the leaves, and their significance. Much like he did in explaining the "K" on the tree.

The "K."

"A symbol of death, the Keres," Emrick said as though tutoring an unruly Lycean. Perhaps as unruly as he claimed Leo to have been in Pandora's life: her life leading to the "K," wrenching her down...

"Then," says Leo, pausing on a random action, "he started saying how Mom's not at peace."

He again hears the clapping of wings and the gripping of claws.

"and that only I cou..."

His mother's face.

"Could what?" says Anastasia leaning her head in.

Leo looks up and sees he was actually meant to finish his sentence. "Nothing," he says. He returns to his things, moving the Tasker from the Muscle Caliber to a better view atop the storage box.

"The worst," Leo goes on before Anastasia can respond, "is he thinks she actually chose to end up like that."

Anastasia starts moving toward his area. "How could someone choose that?"

The blankness on Leo's face melts the closer Anastasia gets. He turns slowly and catches the radiant blue of her eyes. For a moment he nearly sees Emrick standing before him.

"If you see like a mantis," he manages to answer.

Anastasia again looks for her pockets. This time she at least finds them.

"Well, I know you've never really thought of your mother that way, but..."

"I don't believe any of it. She always lived in excellence, or virtuously, or whatever the hell they cram down our throats. There's no way she thought she deserved that."

The notion remains, however, that not all choices are made based on what one deserves. Though Leo may choose that way himself, he knows his mother did not. For now, blaming the invisible demon of illness at least pacifies the doubt.

Anastasia regards him closely, opens her mouth, but relaxes her jaw before any syllables find their way out.

Leo flushes. "He asked about you, though," he says.

The flush transfers to Anastasia. She turns her body away. "That's nice. I'm glad he's ok."

Leo shakes his head and takes a stride to her front.

"Listen, Staj, I get your whole Dad being...you know...but that doesn't mean you cut the old man off. It's not like he had anything to do with it."

She doesn't look at him right away. When she does, she reaches out and lays the tips of her fingers on his skin.

"I'm sorry about your Mom. About...Mom. I'll see you tomorrow ok."

Her hand drops and she walks out into the night.

The hairs on Leo's forearm tickle on the places her fingers touched. They also leave a warm sensation, much like the visit of his friends in general.

The coolness of late Fall, however, will not be ignored. A breeze passes through the garage bringing goosebumps and a pair of recently fallen leaves. One sticks to the cuff of Leo's pants. Its three pointed tips mark it as White Poplar.

Leo reaches down and pinches the leaf between his fingers. The patches of bright red and yellow indicate at least a part of it still clings to life. Soon, however, it would turn brittle and brown and leave nothing for it but to pass on to Gaia from where it came.

The chill deepens on Leo's skin. A second breeze comes and the leaf falls from his hand, as if the wind were demanding it back.

He wraps his hands over his forearms. He knows he should go inside, but doubts it will be any warmer. Nonetheless, he follows Anastasia's path out, codes the door shut, and proceeds in.

He heads straight to the cabinet for a glass to replace the water he spilt earlier. Once filled, he drinks heartily for the night's efforts. The silence of the room presses on him at the intervals he doesn't drink, so he keeps the rest to his lips until finished. He then plops down at the table.

He'd like to feel tired if sleep were welcoming. Instead he leans back, crosses his arms, and stares at the front door. He stares until his pupils adjust to every line in the smooth texture. The inner knob especially, with its ergonomic contour and encircling warning light to indicate an entry.

Nothing lights this night.

Leo continues staring, nonetheless.

A soft beep from above the stove rattles the still air of the kitchen. Leo sits up and looks around. He glances once more at the knob then rises to check the time.

He runs his hand over the counter where his mother would take her nightly cup of chamomile tea. One of his fingers brushes an electric plaque on the stove top, but all is cold.

The clock, ever blinking, reads "00:00."

Leo stands at the kitchen fenestrator with the consciousness of it being tomorrow.

The moon's rays shed light on a few dust particles floating by his face. He wonders how anyone survives breathing such junk. It comes to no surprise so many died in the Pre-Reckoning world, as their dust clouds must have been a great deal thicker.

His eyes again adjust, and little by little start to distinguish the pyre sitting below the fenestrator. On to it he rests his mind.

Such tragic craftsmanship cannot stop the hint of pleasure he fights to suppress. To spend so much time and effort creating a product only to watch burn: his mother's life, a beautifully honed product destined to rise in smoke just as the most indolent of deadbeats.

Yet his mother's presence feels just as strong as when she lived. Her vitality, sharpness, comfort, surround Leo in such keenness Pandora could practically have her arms around him.

Leo turns quickly. Though no one stands there he looks back to the door and lingers for a time on the knob. Anticipation more than denial motivates his patience; the stronger he feels her the higher his expectancy. He begins to even question why they built the pyre in the first place.

A tap at the fenestrator startles him. He might have toppled another water if he hadn't left it on the table. Moving his head close to the glass, he peers from left to right. Nothing apparent but another breeze and moving branches. He continues looking in the instance of a hidden finger, or claw of a Kere. The only thing of substance, however, remains the pyre.

Leo digs his nails into the counter. That someone could have lived so pious and altruistic in life, to be punished in such a way does not weigh in the balance of things. To have chosen this fate seems a greater paradox. To "not be at rest" in either Elysium, Paradise, or even Oblivion is downright cruel. Even the agnostic mind senses an eternal injustice. Regardless, the pyre rests pristine despite its destiny to be destroyed later in the day. To think he actually enjoyed a project meant for condemnation. More so that something signifying the loss of his mother even became a *project*.

Leo grinds his teeth.

We should never have had to build that damn thing in the first place.

The twisting in his chest is a welcome sensation. He draws on it for power, resistance, and subsequently a heightened connection to his mother.

The silence, however, makes him realize it's really her absence that fuels her increasing presence.

He shakes it off and hardens his grip on the counter. Closing his eyes he locks on to the energy, and soon feels Pandora's essence flow through him. It contrasts greatly to the soothing, enduring dependability he knew of her in life. Anything but at peace as Emrick said. And the more he concentrates, the more it amplifies into something closer to slow steady torment.

"Can't you just leave her alone?" he pleads aloud. "Didn't you already get enough out of her?"

The "you" takes him aloof of solid ground, and the abstract takes root. The second person starts materializing in the reality of his mind. Armed with a definitive point, hate comes much easier to place. On it he channels the storm of his confusion until one notion solidifies in the midst of the chaos:

This is your fault.

The words form and are just as quickly consumed by fire and smoke.

He hears a moan. The air rapidly dries and he passes his tongue over lips he finds to be already chapped. Another moan, but on Leo presses.

Out of the smoke the elm tree appears in a cavernous domain. In place of the "K," however, the sorrowed face of his mother is carved in the wood. Leo charges and skids his knees over the stone floor to stop before the base. He begins scratching at the point his mother was taken. The more it proves ineffective, the harder he scratches, until no skin remains on the tips of his fingers.

Leo ignores any pain or repulsion a person might feel, and is soon tearing like a wild animal. His fingernails crack and break but doesn't slow him down. They then rip off altogether to reveal the mutilated beds of flesh underneath.

The sight of blood running down his hand feeds his frenzy even further. Yet seeing it has gone for naught, he clenches his fist and drops a huge overhand right to the lower trunk.

The impact pounds through the atmosphere like a bolt of thunder:...jolting him awake at the kitchen table. The pounding continues when he realizes someone is knocking at the door.

He stays a moment at the table examining his fist. The skin remains unscathed. Yet the pulsating trauma renders it difficult to readjust to the world people tell him is real. Another knock provokes him to just accept in order to shut the person up.

Who the hell knocks anymore.

Leo places his left hand on the knob, pauses, and opens.

The man, whose lips were initially pursed, hesitates at seeing a poorly rested Kladimans champion who's just spent the night staring at doors and punching at trees.

"Uh, good morning, I'm from..."

"I know who you are," says Leo venomously. He rubs his knuckles before continuing, "I'll open the garage."

Once the item is conveyed, the man quickly takes Leo's thumbprint and departs, leaving Leo alone with the delivery.

A weary Maurileho sticks his hands in his pockets and looks on it a moment. He then approaches in slow steps.

The long, black leather encasement lies flat at about five and a half feet. Leo rests his right hand on the zipper at the top. After a long hesitation, he slowly pulls down the smooth cover.

Each ripple of the zipper resonates throughout the room. It produces a sound as ugly as the task he performs. For the several seconds he pulls though, he only actually makes it a few inches. Then, he stops.

With disheveled curls lying about his head, his bloodshot eyes staring at the bag, he takes two fingers and carefully spreads the opening apart. He then peaks underneath.

As soon as he registers what he sees, his hands contract as though to claw again. Slowly but surely they curl into hard, compact balls. His body then tightens, face constricts, and fists raise.

After a heavy exhale, however, all releases.

He leans the weight of his upper body on the encasement.

Crying would feel a relief if anger and indignity had not already dried his well.

His jaw clenches stiff.

Only you can save her.

A ray of hope reaches the hollow tunnel of his eyes. It hits so strong it seems as if a spirit took possession of his mind. In a few seconds that hope transforms into something more of a fevered frenzy.

I'll save you, Mom.

With that he reaches for his Tasker.

Purpose has pointed him in search of something. He doesn't know what, only that "you" will be what he finds.

CHAPTER 5 – THE FUNERAL GAMES

A roar of engines calls attention to the road on the southern border of the festival grounds. Small cars of sleek design inch forward in rows a half dozen vehicles long. The circuit race is about to begin.

Second only to Kladimo, the sport of dromo racing enjoys immense popularity in the city-state of Prometheum. The compact assembly of the racers, coupled with their low center of gravity and aerodynamic wings, often gives the optical and audio impression of bees when raging in competition. Hence, the models are often assigned names associated with the insect.

Today the standard Drone models will race due to it falling outside the sanction of the CC Circuit.

Clear magnetic barriers protect both sides of the road outlining Lake Maquari. A layer of synthetic asphalt covers the solar plaques over which the A and M-Coaches usually operate around Prometheum. The race is a single lap, and denotes the traditional first event of the funeral games: the horse chariot race.

The festival grounds buzz with several dozen people ranging from friends, to family, to unknown citizens of the public come to pay respect. White, the color of mourning, blankets the area in a human quilt woven of their attire. Each square connects the man in the blazer to the teen in the graphic tee, the old woman in robes to the little girl in autumn leggings: all present to celebrate the transition of death with the vitality of sport, all occupying a block of time in the life of Pandora Maquari.

"Where the hell is Leo!" Khloe shouts at no one in particular.

The aforementioned's friends and sister convene at the southwest corner of the festival grounds, near the starting line of the race. Immediately following Khloe's tactful aim at civility, another chorus of engines thunders toward the sky.

Beren rises on his tiptoes in the direction of the Maquari house. For all he looks though, he doesn't lock on to anything specific. Setting himself down he runs a hand through his golden hair, squeezing a bit at the top.

"I'm sure he's on his way," he says, also at no one in particular.

"Awe," says Zoe using Beren's shoulder as an involuntary hoist, "this has got to be hard for him."

Anastasia glances at them both but remains silent.

After another failed attempt at ringing, Khloe flashes them all a look and stomps off. By that time her ear lobe is bright red from the overuse of her J.T device.

The crowd of mourners begins pressing harder for a better view of the race.

On the road, the drivers continue bearing their teeth with the gas pedal. A few helmets occasionally turn in the direction of the Maquari crew.

"Listen," says Beren looking toward the dromo cars, "we're going to have to get this thing started. Leo's MIA and his sister's losing it."

"I can flag the drivers," says Zoe. She snatches the green pennant from Beren's grasp.

"And I'll announce the event," says Beren holding up his empty hand. "Staj, could you catch up with Khloe and tell her we'll kick things off. She didn't want to do this anyway so that'll at least give her an excuse."

"Ok," says Anastasia, glancing in the distance.

The friends set off to perform their tasks. Beren maneuvers through the crowd in making his way to the podium where Leo is slated to deliver the eulogy following the games. Once there he stands off to the side and watches for Anastasia's progress in hunting down Khloe.

A patch of bleach blond hair amongst a sea of white signals her movements. Beren sees her utter a few phrases to Khloe who has her finger on her J.T the whole time she listens. When Anastasia's lips stop moving, Khloe looks to the ground, back to Anastasia, pinches her J.T, then throws her hands up marching off in a different direction. Anastasia stands speechless for a second. Beren waits until she turns and makes eye contact before he ascends.

"Hi, everyone," he says. He slides a finger over volume control. "Can I get your attention please."

He raises an arm.

The cars and guests calm to a purr. Many point at the podium and start making chatter.

"I'm Bereniko Braun on behalf of the Maquari family. I'm sorry Leo hasn't made it yet. He's a little indisposed and his sister went to check on him. I'm sure you understand."

Soft murmurs pass over the crowd.

"As Leo's like a brother though, I'm honored to open the funeral games in memory of the woman who was like a second mother to me: Pandora Maquari."

Talking turns to clapping at the mention of the deceased. Beren nods solemnly. Off to the right of the podium, Statesman Braun smiles with a keen look on his son.

Beren spots Zoe by the dromo cars and she gives him the green flag.

"So without further ado, let the games begin."

The opening event of the games stands as one of the most anticipated, despite the circumstances. Not since the times of Reconstruction have people been able to drive cars themselves. That practice now exists only on the track.

The roar returns with drivers anxiously gripping their wheels. Zoe takes long strides out between the cars, gently waving one of the flags at her side. Her fitted peplum dress draws more attention than the racers.

Taking a green flag in each hand, she raises them straight above her head. For a few seconds she holds in a final pose. Then, with a smile at each racer, she drops both arms like a whip.

Tires screech, burnt rubber fills the air, and so the funeral games for Pandora Maquari begin.

Mourners cheer as the cars run adjacent on the initial straightaway. Notwithstanding the shortness of the track, the drones will reach speeds nearing 100 mph, and closer to 200 on a standard size track. Blue 77 profits from his inside position by pulling ahead on Turn 1.

"So how did I do?" says Zoe. She flips the flags into Beren's hand.

"I'll let you know when you're finished," says Beren, replacing them with a checkered one before Zoe has the chance to draw her hand away. She snatches it and sticks out her tongue.

Before turning to the race, however, she looks at Beren sidelong.

"You know, B," she says, then pauses. "You sounded a little like your father up there."

Beren raises his eyebrows, but makes no comment besides "hmm."

Moving out of Turn 1, Blue 77 protects his new position by looping in and out at the beginning of the following stretch. The provocation sends the trailing drivers into aggressive tactics to counter.

One car, Yellow 25, manages to tap the rear bumper. As soon as contact is made, however, the lead car releases a hail of loose spikes that splatter over the road like shattered glass. The brunt fall under the tires of the 25 which immediately burst and send it swerving into the barriers of the track.

The grind of the impact is only overshadowed by the melodic siren that sounds overhead. Along with it, a bright yellow flare that covers the sky over Lake Maquari. This is the signal that a racer's been knocked out of competition.

As the spikes continue scattering, the subsequent three drivers react in time to activate their tire shells. The now second Red 38 even manages to fire a light projectile at the leader. Blue 77, however, has already initiated his rear shields, and the shot leaves nothing more than a graze mark on the silver coating.

Once fully on the next straightaway, the 77 launches forth at a speed putting more and more time between him, the runner up, and rest of the pack. The tailing driver, Green 17, makes some gentle maneuvers to avoid the remaining spikes, but does not have to resort to his tire shells. Each special feature used on a dromo car costs a certain percentage of the vehicle's energy.

Now on the far side of the lake, the drones become a haze of speed and a blur of sound. They pass by the weeping willows the friends would swing on when they were young. They move by the houses on the hills they've called home all their lives.

Within a matter of seconds, a sizable interval forms between the leader and the followers.

"77 all the way," says Beren.

Zoe eyes their progress on the opposite bank. "I'm not so sure, B."

Beren pushes his hair back and holds out his other hand toward the drivers.

"77's like two seconds ahead," he states as though Zoe were watching a different race.

"I'll take Green 17," says Zoe. She grips the checkered flag and starts making toward the finish line.

"You're on," Beren calls after her. "A week of laundry at the gym."

Zoe twists around in motion, winks, and proceeds to the side of the road.

By this time, Blue 77 has advanced to the three-quarter point of the long straightaway. The following three cluster around halfway, and Green 17 at a quarter.

Just then the track veers hard right over the northeastern corner of the lake. It quickly disappears giving way to the water underneath. Blue 77 is caught only half prepared with his tire floats and hits the surface hard. The impact causes him a sharp spin and nearly two full seconds momentum. Quick to react, however, he realigns, activates his rear booster, and launches forward.

Red 38 does not miss the opportunity. Having had a split second longer to set up, he initiates his floats and standard motor propellers. This function enables the driver to maintain a strong speed at only half the energy of a booster. Within a blink of an eye he is already within a car's length of the leader going around turn 3.

The third and fourth place cars, Orange 55 and Black 11, follow forthwith to hit the water. Both do so with relative ease. Upon activating their mechanisms, however, 55 makes an aggressive cut in front of 11. As he does his back-rear propeller becomes entangled with the driver's side propeller of his opponent.

All at once the propellers explode, sending both pieces and their cars flying in different directions. Orange 55 ends up flipping on its side in front of Black 11. Lacking control, 11 plows into 55 sending it into further rolls over the water.

Not a moment passes before two sirens sound, and 2 flares blast off.

With all eyes on 77 and 38 rounding Turn 4, Green 17 increases speed moving into Turn 3. He moves over the water with ease, making smooth agile maneuvers around the rubble of his former forerunners. Little by little he drifts toward the outside moving into the final turn.

Blue 77 and Red 38 now enter the final straightaway. Both favor the inside having come out of that position in Turn 4. Their engines scream almost in harmony.

They quickly approach speeds of nearly 100 miles per hour. Though 77 maintains about a car length's lead, 38 consistently closes the gap. The final legs of a race is when car energy comes into play the most.

Within a few seconds time the leaders run side by side. They begin by applying sheer speed. When 38 starts to inch ahead a few exchanges are made of swerves and light bumps. When he shows that his car will inevitably outrun his opponent, the 77 activates his tire blades.

Red 38 opts for an offensive defense and activates the tire blades of his own car. Together they clash in an array of clings and sparks that would make one think they were battling in a Kladimo match rather than just trying to pop each other's tires.

The dueling becomes even fiercer as they move over the final stretch. With the finish line in sight, all mourners stand on their toes to catch sight of the would-be victor.

The leaders then disengage for one split second. When all think they will simply floor the remaining few yards, they lean into each other with a loud smash. This vicious sound is only surpassed by the sharp pop of both driver's tires.

The remaining rubber screeches over the track in their attempt to keep from crashing into the barrier. It's all they can do to even keep moving straight ahead. With less than 15 yards to the finish, they muster all their cars can bear until...

The 17 flashes by them in a streak of green.

Mourners clap before the victor even makes it past Zoe's checkered flag. The 77 and 38 barely cross their battered cars over the finish line: this more from shock than mechanical failure. Beren's jaw dropping expression mirrors that of the drivers: but more over the loss to Zoe.

The Green 17 skids to a halt a few dozen yards beyond the checkered flag. He forgoes the typical tire burn of the CC Circuit's winner's circle. Once the others clear, he steadily makes his way back to the finish line, then emerges helmet raised.

"Don't feel bad, Berry," says Zoe resting an elbow on his shoulder, "you still have a duel to lose."

Beren's shoulders tense, and he brushes her off. "Yeah," he says, "I think I liked you better as a cow."

The two move off to the white draped prize table where, amongst a handful of dromo enthusiasts, the victor anxiously awaits. Once the Green 17 spots the tall figures approaching, the tan skinned, red headed dromans steps forth and offers his forearm. Beren reaches to receive it but Zoe cuts him off. The dromans' soft, freckled skin blushes as their arms clasp and they proceed to the customary kiss on the cheek. Beren shakes his head grinning, then greets the winner himself, minus the kiss.

"Great job out there," says Beren sincerely. "And you didn't even throw a punch. What's your name?"

"Ioannes," says the young man, making quick glances at Zoe. "Or John as most call me."

"Well, John," says Zoe. She steps in front of Beren. "It looks like this helmet's seen a lot of action."

Ioannes nods but doesn't look over the helmet. Zoe removes it from his hands with no resistance and starts running her fingers over dents and chipped motion decals of dromans, kladimans, and...Leonidas Maquari: the Maurileho.

Zoe's face straightens into something plain, and subsequently so does Ioannes'.

She hands him back his helmet and takes the victor's prize from the table. "What do you think about this one?" she asks modestly.

Ioannes' eyes detach from Zoe once he sees the white shiny dromans helmet.

"It's so light," he says, lifting it up and down. "And a Corb!"

"It'll keep your head on your shoulders," says Beren with a pat on the back. "Enjoy."

As soon as he leaves Zoe turns to Beren. She's about to speak when she sees Anastasia walking up from the crowd.

"Any luck?" Zoe quickly asks.

"No." says Anastasia. "Khloe went to the house and he's not there." She starts glancing about the grounds. "I'm not really sure where to look now."

A group of rambunctious children brush past Beren in the direction of the second event.

"We'll just have to keep running the games then," he says, watching his back for any more, "and hope he shows up."

"Oh gosh," says Zoe. She covers her mouth, "isn't he supposed to do the eulogy?"

"Yeah, he is," says Anastasia.

"He'll make it," says Beren. "Let's get this thing rolling though." He moves close to Zoe's side. "I think I'm ready for a warm up." He takes leave with a smirk.

Zoe returns the smirk and runs off in the direction of the bathhouses.

The following event moves to the lakefront beach where the wrestling is to take place. The crowd forms a circle about 40 feet wide to serve as the barrier to three sides, the lake itself being the fourth. For a mat, the soft sands of Lake Maquari.

Many PK's, or practitioners of pankration, occupy the front row of spectators. Ranging in size and age, they all share a look of determination, and exchange just as many looks between them.

Zoe arrives in her white sprinting gear to find Beren in conversation with the PK coach at the local gym, legendary Phil Palaistros.

Palaistros, now nearing middle age, was fundamental in transforming the combat art of pankration into a competitive organization. Sport pankration rose quickly into the leagues of kladimo and dromo racing as a favorite amongst Prometheans. Palaistros was its first champion.

"I spoke with Coach P," says Beren, jogging over to Zoe. "He's going to take over some of the PK related events."

Zoe snaps one of the straps on his white singlet. "Ooooooooookay," she says. She then glances over his shoulder and forms her lips into an "o." "Just make sure you make it back for the rest."

Beren follows her look and nearly forms his lips the same.

Standing in the center of the ring is a young man well-nigh 300 pounds. His arms and legs carry the girth of tree trunks, despite the slight belly protruding in his midsection. Nose crooked, dark skin calloused, his head reaches nearly six and a half feet into the air.

"Pux," says Beren, eying his would-be opponent. "That big oaf. I thought he moved to Pronoia."

"He did," says Zoe, "to train with *Silvio Belmont*." She pats him on the back of the shoulder with a smile. "Have fun, Berry."

Beren looks back to the ring.

"So much for my warm-up."

Pux Ramique, a few years Beren and Leo's senior, used to work with them both at the Eulimnos Gymnasium. Not the book type, he dedicated himself to the sport and was successful in many local matches, prompting his move to Pronoia to take residence at the gym of renowned champion Silvio Belmont.

Known for a heart as big as his suplex, he slaps his belly with both meaty hands and smiles his chubby cheeks into balloons.

"Heyyyyyyy yo, Braun," he bellows as Beren walks onto the sand. "Back for another lesson?"

Beren returns the smile before donning his earguards. "I'll try to catch you up on whatever Belmont forgot."

To this Pux throws his head back in a hearty laugh, then settles into position for business.

Coach Palaistros takes a minute at each corner to make sure both are aware of the rules on pin/submission grappling, as well as the regulations against striking and small joint manipulation. Once the competitors agree, he moves off, checks if everyone's ready, and makes a sharp blow on his old plastic whistle.

The gargantuan PK wastes no time rushing Beren in a display of speed uncommon for such his size. Beren inches forward toward the onslaught then pivots at the last second. Pux, however, does so as well and drives a shoulder into Beren's midsection, hoisting him off his feet. The impact on the sand sends particles flying everywhere, but also loosens the brute's grip around Beren's waist. From the ground Beren is able to use his wiry frame to wiggle out of the attempted mount.

Back on their feet, they circle the center of the ring amidst a round of clapping from mourners. Pux grins to the applause: Beren maintains calculated focus.

In the split second between Pux's heavy steps, Beren shoots for his legs and manages a tight wrap around his knees. In the split second that follows, however, Beren's body hangs upside down feet first in the air, then hard into the sand on his back.

Pux wastes no time moving into the mount and jamming his elbow across Beren's collarbone. Only then does Beren seem to react by hooking under Pux's arm.

The brute adjusts his leg position and applies greater force on Beren's shoulders. This frees Beren's right leg which swings up and around Pux's wide back.

Pux releases his grip on Beren's collarbone and shifts his weight into Beren's right side. Beren then slides his left leg up and over the giant's shoulder, curling his knee around the side of his neck. With that Beren's contracts his body and concentrates all his force on the jugular vein.

The massive PK thrashes his body around the sand, slamming Beren multiple times in all different points. Yet the grip holds.

Little by little Pux's chubby cheeks take on a crimson color under his dark skin. His power fails, and his will gives way. Finally, he taps Beren's knee with his right hand.

Cheering drowns out the whistle from Coach Palaistros as both competitors lie belly up in the sand. Pux revives first, rolling to his feet and slapping both sides of his head in rapid succession. He looks about, then down to find Beren still back to the sand.

Without warning he grabs Beren by the arm and lifts him to his feet one handed.

"Alright, Braun, alright," says Pux, nodding his head.

Beren takes a second to orient, removes his ear guard and runs his hands through his hair.

"Good match, Pux," he says. He reaches out to clasp his opponent's forearm.

The great PK returns the clasp fondly.

"Say," says Pux, "where's the lion at? I come to pay my respects."

Beren glances in the direction of Zoe. "We're not sure, big guy. Hopefully he shows soon."

"Alright, alright," says Pux, "I'll be seein' yah."

Beren makes his way through a series of shoulder punches from PK's and PK enthusiasts alike. He spots Zoe walking over from the prize table. As he moves to meet her, she is intercepted by Statesman Braun.

Beren pauses at seeing his father politely request the victor's prize from Zoe. She hands over a large medallion held by a white neck strap and follows the distinguished man to the edge of the sand.

"Fine job, son," says Statesman Braun holding the medallion in his hand. He looks his son over. "You know," he continues, "a career in state wouldn't hurt as much as being flattened by Pux Ramique."

Beren turns his head before pursing his lips.

"I won, didn't I?" He pushes back the sweaty hair on his brow.

The wrinkles on his father's forehead rise and crease. A certain intensity reads in his pupils. Only a flash, though, then both forehead and eyes settle slowly into a nod.

"You did," says Statesman Braun. He unravels the medallion. "And this belongs to you."

With that he drapes the white silk over Beren's neck and takes a step back to view.

Beren turns over the gold piece to see the front. The engravings depict two stout men in bitter strife: one, a colossal specimen, attempts to lift the other but is off-balance in one of his legs.

"Ajax lifting the cunning Odysseus," says Statesman Braun. "But failing when Odysseus strikes the back of his knee."

Zoe peeks her head in. "Kinda like you, B," she says, "with that triangle choke on poor Pux."

"Poor Pux?" says Beren, rubbing his collar bone.

Just then Anastasia emerges from the crowd. Straight faced, she rises on her toes to hug Beren.

"Congrats," she says.

Beren cringes a little bit under the embrace but smiles it off in good humor. "Thanks, Staj."

"Oh," says Anastasia, stepping back, "sorry." She then turns to his father. "Statesman Braun."

"Hi, Anastasia." He greets bowing his bald forehead. He then puts a finger to his mouth, "might I ask," he says, "has Leonidas made contact...or *pinged* as you all would say?"

Anastasia first looks to her friends before answering.

"No, sir."

The great man nods. "I see." He then looks off toward the Maquari property. "While I can understand his not wanting to participate, I do hope he brings her body. Not just for respects, but remember..." He leans in closer, particularly toward

Anastasia. "No soul may cross the river Styx without passing to Prometheus through the gift of fire."

The blue of Anastasia's eyes takes on the white of Statesman Braun's collar. The reflection holds as she stares unblinking.

"Yes, sir."

Beren gives Zoe a look then steps around and very gently pats his father's back.

"We got it, Pop," he says, sliding his hand off. "Now, if you'll excuse us..."

Statesman Braun stays in position a moment longer then abruptly reassumes his normal stance.

"Ah," he says, "of course. In any case, I imagine it's Miss Qwynshing's turn to shine isn't it."

Zoe smiles and twists her body like a bashful little girl.

"Good luck," says Statesman Braun, taking his leave.

The three remain to watch him go. Once out of sight, Anastasia turns to Beren.

"Your father's right, you know. This is all getting worse." She looks away.

Zoe walks up behind Anastasia and wraps her in her lean muscled arms. "It's alright, Annie. Leo knows about that stuff he mentioned too."

"Leo doesn't believe in that *stuff*," she says, breaking from Zoe.

No one immediately responds. Finally, Beren lays a hand on her shoulder.

"You know how Leo is. He wouldn't show up to his own funeral."

Zoe opens her mouth and squints her eyes. "Hell-oooooooo, like anyone *could* show up to their own funeral."

"Shut it Zebra, all I meant was..."

"Zebra!" she says, stepping forward.

A reference to her pubescent days when she and Beren got along like water for chocolate.

"Listen, Berenikkle, you wait til our duel, Pux will feel like a massage when I..."

"Guys!" says Anastasia, moving between them. "Not the time."

Both drop their heads.

"Let's get set up."

Anastasia walks off toward the far end of the sand where the sprinters are already lining up. The other two remain still until Zoe turns up her chin and struts off. Beren shakes his head and combs his fingers through his hair.

Once the start and finish lines have been temporarily tattooed to the ground, the footrace is set to begin.

The lanes, also marked, cover the distance from one end of the beach to the other: roughly 50 yards. As an open gender event competitors consist of mostly young men from the local gymnasium.

One other female, however, presents herself as the last runner in lane 8. Zoe sticks her head out from lane 6 and looks down the way. The young and very tall adolescent catches her eye but quickly lowers her head.

Zoe waits, and little by little the girl raises it up again. When she finally reconnects, Zoe smiles and gives her a wink. The girl's lips part into a smile twice as big as her counterpart, revealing a row of partially crooked upper teeth.

Just then Beren raises his hand from the opposite side. Mourners and competitors stand at attention as he signals to Anastasia next to the lake. She acknowledges holding a flairbow, a device that shoots an explosive into the sky to mark the beginning of a footrace.

The flairbow rose in popularity as more and more hearing-impaired individuals started competing in field-oriented sports like athletics. Complaining they were unable to hear the auditory starting signals, a solution was invented that would allow a visual to go with the sound. After a time, it became a standard overall.

Anastasia lifts the crossbow-shaped apparatus and aims it at a 60-degree angle downfield. Runners set, the flairbow releases, and all watch as the projectile flies into the distance. After a few short seconds a sharp blast fans over the grounds. A shower of red sparks follows that transform into doves as they fall.

The runners take off. Clumps of sand spray into the air at the initial charge. Within a blink of an eye a jagged pattern forms across the line to indicate the runners' position.

Before long that line moves into a clear shape. It expands to a wide breadth and comes to a point at lane 6. Here Zoe already leads by a length of a full body.

Her long legs carry her further and further ahead, pumping like a dryad dashing through the woods. Some in the other lanes glance over and begin slowing down. Others put on labored faces in contrast to the breezy look on Zoe's.

Beren and Anastasia stand at opposite ends of the finish line. The crowd is already applauding around them. In a flash, the tall frame of Zoe whizzes by in a blur of white, sand still spraying from her feet.

She comes to a stop just after the painted grass. Paying no mind to the other competitors finishing, she makes her way over to Beren, hands on hips and barely breathing above average rate.

Though her body approaches him head on, her head looks in every direction other than straight. Smirks appear on both their lips but do not move into smiles.

She stops before him and continues in her same behavior. Bit by bit their smirks grow. They peek at each other at slow, then rapid intervals until a burst of laughter erupts from their lips.

They embrace each other fondly.

"Good job, Zo," says Beren.

"*Thank* you," she replies, tilting her chin in the air. She pushes her shiny brown hair behind her ears.

"Maybe next time though," he says, "you can warm-up with Pux and I'll run the race."

Zoe slaps him in the gut.

"No excuses, buddy boy. We're up next."

Anastasia comes over a moment later. In her hands she holds a fancy pair of white Giulian sprinting shoes.

"Great job, Zoe," she says handing them over, "you won by more than 2 seconds."

They hug and kiss. "Thanks, Annie."

Zoe rubs her thumb over the winged decal at the ankle of the shoe. This is the signature icon of Giulian's sporting line. The label makes reference to the old god Hermes, who was a messenger known for his speed and cunning.

At the finish line, many of the male competitors roam about with their hands above their heads, still breathing heavily.

"Who got second place?" says Zoe.

Anastasia giggles before answering. "Lane 8 did, the girl."

Alone amongst the winded young men, the other female competitor stands with her hands clasped before her. Her long shorts hang a size too big around her skinny legs, her shirt a size too tight over a budding chest.

Zoe looks over to find the girl already looking back. This prompts the runner-up to quickly turn her head away. Once again, though, Zoe waits, and when the girl looks up, she waves her over.

A smile not quite big enough to expose the crooked teeth forms at her mouth. She then starts making her way but continues to hold one hand in the other.

Her true height becomes apparent the closer she gets. By the time she reaches Zoe, they nearly stand at eye level.

"Hi there," says Zoe.

The girl's honey-brown eyes flash between Zoe's face and neck.

"Hi," she says. She releases one hand to push her dirty blonde bangs to the side.

When she doesn't move to greet, Zoe steps forward and takes her forearm. The girl's body tenses at the contact. Once they kiss on the cheek, however, she begins to relax into her former anxious pose.

"What's your name?" says Zoe.

She starts keeping her eyes up a little more. "Ephebeia. But... my friends call me Effy."

Zoe grins at Beren and Anastasia.

"Weeeeeeeell, Effy, I'm Zoe..."

"Qwynshing," says Effy, unclasping her hands, "I know."

"Oh," says Zoe. She flops her head toward Beren. "I didn't realize my name was so well known."

Beren shakes his head.

"You're a great kladimiss," Effy goes on. "I...I train with maolance too."

"Could have fooled me," Beren whispers to Anastasia.

Another slap to the gut.

"I'm glad you like kladimo, Effy, and the maolance: because now I'm going to give you the opportunity of watching how we use it on an overgrown lunk with a golden mop."

Effy chuckles as Beren runs his hand through his hair, then tucks his braid behind his ear.

"Two zebras," he whispers, only to himself this time.

His hands move over his abdomen when Zoe looks back, but no strike follows.

"Good luck, Zoe," says Effy.

Zoe continues on Beren. "Oh don't worry, sweetie," she says, "this won't be about luck."

Beren smirks and moves off toward the bathhouses.

Both friends adequately "warmed-up," it is time for the dueling. The closest event to resemble a kladimans match of the solo bracket, the funeral games duels function much like the contests of the Scout Division. Competitors wear a fitted body suit over protective plates. Each plate contains sensors that illuminate a different color when hit. Each hit counts as one point.

Competitors may win in a variety of ways suited to a kladiman's style: knock-out, submission, judge's interference (J.I), or being the first to reach seven points. There are no time limits.

Beren and Zoe present themselves at the arms table in their protective gear. Zoe, normally in purple, wears a white one-piece outfit with Giulian cleats. Beren opts for a tight fit top over a cingulum and sandals. They do not communicate but for an occasional sidelong smirk.

Next they choose from a series of kladimans weapons. Light and very blunted, they also are infused with illuminating sensors that react to each blow. This light only appears on the outline of the armament.

Without hesitation Beren grabs for what has become known as his family legacy: the twin blades of Braun. Each double-sided and of medium length, Beren whirls them round simultaneously then holsters them in his open back sheath.

Zoe, too, selects her bread and butter: the half-moon maolance with white ponytail at the end of the shaft. Gripping it eagerly she tosses it in the air, twirling the tail like a helicopter seed. She then drives it into the ground leaving the tip to vibrate by her cheek.

She blows Beren a kiss.

"For when you yield."

He smiles and shakes his head.

Finally, they don their helmets. Most skilled at kladimo design a personalized headpiece once they start actual competitions. On the face of Beren's, two blades cross at the nose and terminate just above the chin. The gold finish matches the color of his hair. Lining the crown are mini twin blades, each with a bright red stone in the middle that fluctuate in intensity given the heat of the brow. The helmet once belonged to his father.

Zoe's also fluctuates in color, but over the entire face in black and white only. In the light, the classical mask of comedic theatre: in the dark, that of its tragic counterpart. The visage alternates at random times in the face of an adversary, and does not react to anything prompted by Zoe.

Hundreds of spectators pack on and around the sand. Their three-sided circle forms a boundary roughly the size of the wrestling margins. Growing increasingly dense, however, that margin grows smaller by the inch.

Coach Palaistros leads Beren and Zoe through a narrow passage he makes between the people, and each part for opposite directions. He holds up a hand and waits for the crowd to stop pushing forward. He then nods to both duelers and steps away from the center of the ring.

Beren and Zoe set. The crowd again becomes restless and presses the boundary of the ring. All look eagerly to Coach P who searches his shirt cuff and pockets for his whistle.

Little by little the chatter dies down as Coach continues frisking himself down to his toes.

When the grounds slow to a murmur, a large crow passes overhead followed by the silhouette of its flight. At the point it reaches the sand, it releases a piercing caw, and neither competitor waits for any further signal.

Beren charges in high position, dropping quickly to meet Zoe's thrust to the mid-section. As their weapons clash, flashes of red and blue mix to make purple.

He uses her momentum to twist to the left and make a follow-up cut at shoulder height. Zoe recoils and the crowd gasps at the force of the blow parting air.

Zoe moves to the offensive, keeping Beren beyond striking range with light taps of her maohead. She then proceeds to rapid twists, giving her maolance a larger appearance from the spinning ponytail.

Beren feints a few times then finally commits to a break in her rhythm. He uses both blades to pin one of her thrusts deep in the sand. Sliding to the right, he sacrifices one to shift his weight for a strike. Before he can execute, however, Zoe shoots up her maolance and scores a point to his chest, lighting the protective plaque yellow.

Beren reacts before the crowd has a chance to cheer by reaching his blade up and under Zoe's weapon. Bobbing low he guides it over his head then unleashes a savage blow to Zoe's shin guards sending her four feet into the air. Before she hits the ground he is already following downward with his other blade.

The crowd skips a breath as Beren's blade stops less than an inch from Zoe's forehead. Beren starts raising his other arm in victory when he notices a strange pressure on his chest. He looks down to find Zoe's maohead resting comfortably against his heart. Just then her helmet face changes to the white of the comedian.

"After you," she says.

Beren shakes his head and presses his blade against her mask. She responds with force to his chest.

One mourner declares "draw" followed by several others. Coach Palaistros acknowledges and again reaches for his absent classic style whistle. Not taking time to search in more than one pocket, he quickly steps in and separates the competitors.

Beren and Zoe withdraw but keep their arms in position. Amidst rising applause, however, they begin to relax.

Beren is the first to lower completely. Sheathing the blades on his back, he walks over to Zoe and offers a hand. This she ignores, and springs to her feet with the help of her maolance.

They stare at one another through the peep holes of their helmets, Beren crossing his arms, and Zoe placing her hand on her hip.

"How's the leg?" Beren finally says.

"Hmmmmmmmmm, not as bad as your pride I imagine."

They remove their helmets and maintain firm expressions. When Beren's starts to break, Zoe sticks her chin in the air, but soon breaks too.

Coach Palaistros returns forthwith and has them both hold out their wrists. On them he scans a short, red colored barcode. Beren and Zoe watch as the lines and numbers dissolve into their skin. They look up at one another more pensive than excited.

"Well fought, kids," says Coach P. He speaks in his typical stern manner. His hard brow and crooked nose match the inflection of his voice.

Just then Anastasia comes up from behind.

"Hi, Coach Palaistros," she greets, "you dropped this in the sand."

With that she holds out his old whistle of no identifiable color.

"Ah," says Coach P, eagerly accepting. "Thank you, Miss Wildyn."

Anastasia nods and the coach moves off tucking his whistle under his shirt.

Beren and Zoe remain silent.

"Hey guys," says Anastasia. She looks down at the spot on their arms where Coach P scanned the red code. "So what is it you got?"

Neither immediately responds. Beren then takes another glance at his wrist.

"They're tickets," he says, "...to the Pronoia Invitational."

Silence ensues amongst all of them now. The bustle of mourners passes and fades into the background. The dual victors keep their arms extended as though somehow contaminated.

Zoe pinches her skin in the area of the code.

"Ayyyyy," she says, yielding nothing, "is that really so soon?"

Anastasia takes on the pensive look of her friends.

"I didn't think it had been that long."

The Pronoia Invitational stands as the pinnacle of kladimans competition in the Twin Cities of Prometheum and Pronoia. It is also the most widely viewed of all broadcasted athletic events in the region. The upcoming tournament will mark one year since Leo's devastating loss to the great Feidor Yazinov: a loss which left him in rehabilitation for many months along with a second scar to his face.

"Well Annie can have mine," says Zoe to Beren, "cause I don't plan on just watching this year."

Beren shakes his head.

Anastasia turns away at the comment and looks in the direction of the Maquari house.

"My gosh," she says softly, "where are you, Leo?"

Another shake of the head in Zoe's direction and Beren places a hand on Anastasia's shoulder.

"Come on, Staj. Nothing to do but keep on," he says.

Before he can follow with his other hand he raises both in the air to catch a laced, oval-shaped ball.

"Enough rest, Bereniko," says Coach Palaistros a few yards away. "Time for the next event."

Beren looks first to Anastasia. She nods, and they all move off.

The pigskin toss derives from one of the few competition sports kept intact from prior the Reckoning. Football enjoys the majority of its popularity in flag form at Lyceum, and full contact in recreational adult leagues.

It comes to no surprise when the tall quarterback from the local league heaves a Hail Mary 80 yards down field to claim the victor's prize.

Archery follows, finally catching the attention of Anastasia who has stood aloof of most events. She steals quick glances at her friends arranging a series of bows on the arms table. When they move to the far end of the sand and activate the target Squs from a pair of J.T Taskers, she can't look away. The virtecrans expand upward, six in a row and take the form of five white circles swirling around a red bull's eye.

Beren and Zoe catch her eye simultaneously. She hovers at the edge of the festival grounds towards Leo's house. They smirk at one another as she looks away, then Zoe jogs over.

Anastasia continues avoiding interaction even when Zoe's towering stature stands right before her.

"Staj, honey, don't kid yourself," says Zoe.

Anastasia doesn't respond but to glance at the spot on the lake behind the podium. This is where Leo should have brought his mother's body on the funeral pyre.

Beren runs up behind Zoe. "Come on, Staj, you got this." He adds a love tap towards the row of competitors already lining up at the targets.

The fingers on Anastasia's right hand curl the slightest bit. She watches as the archers select bows and move back into place on the shooting line. Many pull on the string to test the draw weight, and hold it out toward the target to feel its balance.

A slight grin passes over her thin lips, a grin that soon becomes a sorrowful smile.

"I'll do it."

She pauses.

"Mom would want me to compete."

The small group of archers gathers at a distance of forty yards from the Squ targets set at the western end of the beach. Each circle displays a number to determine the shooter's final score after three shots. A bull's eye is worth 10 points.

The shooting proceeds in collected exhibitions of marksmanship across the board. Competitors range from adolescent girls to elderly gentlemen, all utilizing a bow system custom to their needs and limitations. After five archers have completed their rounds, the high score remains a solid 29.

Anastasia steps forward as the final competitor. She holds a basic-style compound bow using only fixed sights as opposed to the more common zeroing technology. In the shooter's circle she takes up a specially designed carbon arrow that employs a flu feather set to fly at a predetermined distance. Looking downfield, she nocks and attaches her mechanical release.

Before drawing she looks behind as though someone were standing at her rear.

"I remember, Mom. Arm bent, stay loose."

With that she pulls and fires.

Her round begins well with the first two arrows scoring tens to the center. On the third, she takes an extra moment and regards the placements of her shots. She inhales deeply as she concentrates, then moves an inch to the left. One more breath and she draws. Exhaling slowly, the arrow fires from the bow.

It flies through the air somehow producing a crisper sound than the previous two. Arriving on point, though, it doesn't penetrate the target, but rather plunges in the back of the first splitting it in half.

"A Robin Hood shot!" a fellow competitor exclaims, unbothered by losing.

The other archers scowl but applaud the poignant skill.

Anastasia just stares.

As the cheers and clapping rise, Zoe runs up to her friend and envelops her in a suffocating embrace.

"That was great!" she says holding out the victor's prize: a state of the art Cameron homing sight with rectal magnification.

Anastasia doesn't move but to wipe the side of her cheek.

"Oh, honey," says Zoe. She pulls Anastasia in once again.

Seeing his friend's sobs drawing a sympathetic spectacle, Beren lightly encourages the crowd to follow him to the site of the next event. Before turning, however, he looks off toward the Maquari house, and shakes his head.

Zoe, after taking her time consoling Anastasia, takes the penultimate game by default. Her repute and commanding presence at the ready deters any potential challengers from throwing spears against her, especially in a feminine jumpsuit.

By the time the final event arrives, the mourners are looking more and more frequently in the direction of the Maquari house.

"I can't believe this!" says Khloe stomping up out of nowhere. "Never mind Leo, my mother's body isn't even here."

"Maybe we can check the house again," says Anastasia.

"You guys can do what you want. I'm done looking and making excuses for him. I need to figure out what to do with everybody here."

The three friends watch Khloe walk away with her hands in the air and still grumbling.

"He really is cutting it close," says Beren.

"I just hope he hasn't done anything stupid," says Zoe.

The final event is pugilism. Rules permit all forms of standup striking, yet competitors primarily use their hands. Wraps must secure and protect wrist to knuckles at all times. Headgear is optional.

Justly, the revered Pankration legend from the Eulimnos gymnasium steps into the designated area. Coach Palaistros, though several years beyond his prime, has maintained fantastic shape to compliment a head of only partially graying hair. He's approached his retirement years with just as much vigor, working extensively with Eulimnan youth as well as upcoming PK prospects. The warm welcome he receives reflects such dedication.

"Khloe better think fast cause they'll probably defer to him," says Beren.

Zoe and Anastasia keep a sharp eye for any would-be challengers. No one, however, shows signs of stepping forward. The ovation for Coach P continues, and after another minute Zoe hands Beren the victor's gloves.

Beren is about to declare when he's cut off by a young man wearing a headpiece made of rope and tassel. Long dark hair runs down his back in a braid held fast by a sharp metal ring. On each major joint, a white fringe hangs loose a few inches. Many tattoos cover his mocha skin, but most notable is the vivid tiger extending the length of his left arm.

"And what do we got here?" says Beren.

The young man moves opposite the honored coach, brings his right fist into his left palm, and bows his head.

Coach P lowers his head in return, but not his eyes.

The tattooed fighter then begins performing a dance around the span of the ring. His movements, though ritualistic in style, closely resemble the forms of hand to hand combat when he pauses in motion.

"THIS guy knew Ms. Maquari?" asks Zoe.

"It's a public funeral, and the name is known," says Anastasia.

When the young man finishes with his knee high in the air, he and Anastasia make brief eye contact. She quickly breaks but looks back right away. Her eyes widen.

"Beren, this boy reminds me a lot of your grandmother's funeral games, the one Leo..."

"It's not," says Beren curtly, moving off onto the sand.

Anastasia looks to Zoe who keeps her head forward.

Ceremony observed, Beren checks the competitors' awareness of regulations. Once both have confirmed he moves to the center of the ring. He then makes a final signal to each side, lifts his hand in the air, and drops.

Coach Palaistros keeps to his aggressive, yet calculated tactics in moving immediately on his opponent with a series of jabs and combinations. Such tactics would often yield early victories in the matches of his prime. The tattooed fighter, however, bears the onslaught gracefully with use of fluid legwork becoming of his age, and no damage is sustained.

They move to circling the center ring. On an upstep Coach P lunges forward with a straight right that the younger fighter has already dodged. In return, a clash of bone pierces the crowd as the coach absorbs a crippling shot to the left knee, sending him reeling around the ring.

"Did you see that?" says Beren leaning his head in. "He kicks with his shin -- like the boran kickboxers do. I hope Coach is up on his standup game."

As if having heard Beren, Coach P sends a well-formed roundhouse to the midsection of his opponent. This the young man catches in his arms and delivers a brutal counter to the knee once again. Both Coach's legs go sidelong into the air and his torso hits the sand with a deep thump.

Many in the crowd cringe at the fall.

Away from the crowd, and the clamor of the bout, a lone figure staggers up the lakefront leading a floating item in tow.

On the sand Coach P pushes himself to his feet and closes his guard. He moves forward determined but unstable, keeping his legs tight and head low. Between absorbing punches and blocking kicks he manages to penetrate close range.

For a time he keeps the boran boxer at bay, throwing short hooks and uppercuts to the ribs and abdomen. The young man regains some distance with lazy jabs from his tattooed arm. The coach ducks, but on one strike the arm doesn't retract. Like the tiger paw clawing on his skin, the young man grabs the coach by the back of the head and violently drives his face into a rising knee strike, shattering his nose.

Mourners wince at the sound of breaking bone and blood splattering on the sand.

In the same motion the kickboxer goes airborne. The older man makes a vain attempt to raise his hands, but the younger fighter's elbow drives through, dropping like a hammer over the eye socket.

At the instant of contact the coach's knees buckle and he falls to all fours. The mourners gasp at impact -- then again when he attempts to stand.

"Beren!" says Zoe.

As shocked as everyone else he waves an end to the bout. The small medical team, along with many of Pandora's former nursing co-workers, move in to attend to the battered coach. When they do though, the disoriented man almost begins grappling with one of the paramedics.

Beren starts moving toward the confusion. He then stops and looks down at the victor's gloves in his hand. When he turns back, he finds the boran fighter standing alone, watching in collected ease.

Beren approaches in careful steps.

"Well done," he says, offering the prize at arm's length.

"Thank you," says the young man.

Despite the modest reply, a certain intensity burns in the pits of his light-green eyes.

"We were wondering though, how you knew Pandora Maqu..."

"Hello," a weary voice echoes over the grounds.

Mourners turn toward the figure holding himself up by the eulogy podium. Eyes widen, and many hands move to mouths.

"Leo," Anastasia whispers.

Leo sways side to side, looking rancorous and disheveled. His clothes are spotted and ruffled; eyes half shut in a cross between glare and fatigue.

"Why are you here?" he says through clenched teeth.

The world rotates at half speed behind his bloodshot eyes. He surveys through darkened perception the sea of white gathered for his mother. A handful he doesn't recognize. Over the rest he's convinced no one bothered to show up when the party consisted of an ailing woman not even able to change her own clothes.

"And now you decide to come."

He stares down the crowd more intensely, looking left to right trying to catch as many eyes as possible. In the blur he catches his father's standing a bit removed from the crowd. Leo jerks his head away just to notice the kickboxer standing next to Beren. His hand immediately moves to the scar above his eye.

He starts rapidly shaking his head back and forth, seeing the fist of the boran fighter at Victoria Braun's funeral games dropping into him once again.

"You shouldn't be here," he cries out through clenched teeth.

He shakes harder. A long moan reaches his ears followed by the sight of a "K." His mother's eyes reflect the rays of the morning sun but take none of its warmth: a note in her hand, the silence of her room.

"WE shouldn't be here." His lips quiver.

The sight of such a powerful person so thoroughly beaten down inspires solemn shock in more than one mourner. The Maurileho, the kladimans who challenged the great Feidor Yazinov in the finals of the Pronoia Invitational, breaking in the face of an invisible foe.

Anastasia brushes off Zoe's hand from her shoulder and begins making her way to the front.

A bird caws overhead. In spite of its keen ring only Leo and Anastasia seem to lend ears. Another caw, and the eagle over the elm flies directly above the podium and on to Lake Maquari.

Pandora's note unfolds in the recesses of Leo's mind. Emrick's words echo. All manifests.

Leo raises his head and turns in the wake of the eagle passing over the boulder where he and Anastasia would swim as children. A glimmer of hope reaches his laden eyes. Looking back, he makes visual contact with Anastasia, stopping her in her tracks.

Bye, Staj.

"Leo!" she cries.

But too late.

The young kladimans leaps off the platform and in one fluid motion lands and pivots off.

Anastasia doesn't wait for the crowd's reaction to take off after him. Face in dire effort, she bypasses all modesty shoving people left and right onto the sand. The only thing she catches, however, is the sight of Leo diving into the lake.

No ripples appear after the initial splash, nor do any air bubbles rise in the vicinity of the plunge.

Anastasia stands at the edge of the sand, one leg pumping the anxiety of her nerves. Now it is Beren and Zoe moving people aside to get to her.

After seconds to seem an eternity, Anastasia's feet spur into a sprint as her friends tumble into the spot she abandoned.

Mourners of Pandora Maquari watch in horror as a second life is thrown away to the fate of the first.

EPITASIS: THE UNDERWORLD

CHAPTER 6 – THE LETHE

A muffled splash sounds through the deep waters of Lake Maquari. Bubbles scatter as though running for their lives, and Anastasia propels through them with little regard to the risk of her own.

The clarity of the Lake affords a distant view yet no figures or disruptions signal the path Leo may have taken. Anastasia cuts through the water confidently, however. Rainbow scaled fish swim along beside her: all in a straight path due east.

In a few long seconds she comes within sight of a sparkle. A short second more and the sparkle flashes to reveal the bough of a tree. More limbs illuminate as she nears and soon the leaves begin opening in succession. The edges shine like sharp blades; the veins engorge like flowing streams: the underwater elm comes to life.

Once within arm's length of the tree Anastasia plummets fast toward the base. Her choppy strokes carry her further and further into the depths of Lake Maquari. Branches thicken as she descends, and clarity suffers but for the glow of the elm.

At 30 yards Anastasia releases a large air bubble and starts slowing down.

A widening of the tree gets her tangled in branches. She fights herself free then uses them as leverage to continue deeper.

In another few feet small bubbles begin trickling up from below. An occasional larger one passes by as she continues downward. Finally, thin patches of water float past contaminated with the tint of blood.

Anastasia pauses and wrenches her hand over the area of her lungs. As she does the red water starts rising thicker and more frequently. She reaches out her other hand to comb through it.

Though it breaks up on contact, blotches cling to her fingers as though drawn by magnetic force. It even begins to stain them as she rubs two together. Shaking it frantically off, she kicks down hard toward the bottom of the tree.

A disturbance at the base sends up even more bubbles and crimson water. Vibrations start resonating through the immediate area, and she is soon close enough to see the source.

Leo, face in demonic glare, tears at the trunk in a passion despite the blood pouring from his fingers. He attacks fully believing his nails are ripping over the "K" his mother was dragged into by the death spirits. If he could only get through...

A muted sound finds its way to his ears. Not the moan he expected, but an actual word...a name.

Leo.

Stopping suddenly, he looks left and right before up.

Seeing Anastasia treading above him stifles the intensity in his eyes.

His friend moves closer, grasping branches with one hand and clenching her chest with the other. She starts pointing rapidly toward the surface. The thought of moving away from the spot his mother was taken, however, feels like fleeing. His brow furrows and he shakes his head.

Looking back at the trunk he remembers the punch that seemed to break through the moment he awoke at the kitchen table. So cocking his powerful fist, he again unloads an overhand right straight into the perceived "K." This time, however, the only sound is a soft thump in the wood, followed by a loud yell from Leo himself.

A series of thick bubbles escapes at the cry. Leo clutches his mangled hand, simultaneously inviting the pain from the flesh wounds incurred at clawing the tree.

By this time Anastasia's face is red and contorted. She moves down to eye level with Leo and cups her throat directly before him.

Though Leo's face shows much of the same signs, he looks back to the trunk and begins pulling at bark with his left hand.

Anastasia reaches out to grab him but stops before her fingers even touch. She retracts her hand and rubs it on her clothes as though it were poisonous or contaminated. Stilling herself as much as her last bit of air will allow, she reaches out once more.

Her eyelids drop slowly as she touches the back of Leo's neck. Upon contact, the water simmers. The churning energy expands outwards and soon becomes an unscathing boil.

Leo stops his pulling and tries to swat at the bubbles. His hand, however, will not detach from the tree. He then moves to violent tugs which creates even more disturbance to the area. When the effort proves useless, he adds his legs for extra leverage.

Just then a white glow appears under his fingertips. It takes shape in the form of a small circle the size of a ring. Little by little, it grows larger and brighter over the surface of the underwater elm.

Leo turns his head from the light. He considers trying to pull away again, but instead lets out a large air bubble and presses his broken hand against his chest.

The illuminating circle expands into a blinding sphere.

Leo feels his fingers being sucked into it, as if the elm had developed its own gravitational pull. His feeble resistance serves only enough to slow things down. Bit by bit he starts to fade.

His consciousness slips faster than his body to the immense tow of gaping light. Heavier it weighs and heavier he falls. Finally, Leo spits the last of his oxygen, his eyes roll back, and on he descends into the depths of the unknown.

△△△

"Leo," says a soft voice.

It echoes louder as it fades.

Leo.

The name reaches him somewhere in the valley of where Hypnos carries his slumbering souls, and the place he leaves them awake.

A name.

It carries him through lush grasses and over fertile hills: high above, as though on the wings of the eagle.

My name.

Diving hard it plunges into a liquid mirror that shatters on impact. The despair of submergence returns. Leo's chest takes on the burn of suffocation once again.

His body thrashes. He kicks and flails. Trying to reach the surface seems like the world had flooded over.

Finally, the auditory sound of a voice breaks through to his ears.

"Leo."

The name registers, and he breathes his first.

Air comes as water to a desert tongue. Indeed, the heavy dampness passing through Leo's lungs implies an infusion of the two.

The ground, however, does not correspond to the padded wetness of the air. Solid floor outlines Leo's body lying flat on its back. It penetrates past his massive build, and digs into the vertebrae running up his spinal cord.

The discomfort activates his fingers. They scratch over stone, chilly and granular. That they even work at all surprises him after being so damaged by punching the tree.

Though he hears no more names, a near silent splash lands above his head. Every few seconds it repeats. When he comes to expect the next one, it skips a beat, and a droplet of water rolls down his cheek.

The texture of the dribble irks him more than the hardness of the ground. As such he manages to raise a limb. Before his hand reaches his face, however, another arrives first.

The soft touch opens his eyes forthright and sends him sprawling away on his hands and knees. In the same motion he moves into a backward roll. Landing his feet he springs straight up and lunges forward.

He stops mid punch.

"Staj."

Anastasia lowers her arms slowly from in front of her face.

"Damn, Staj, I didn't..."

His eyes move away from his would-have-been victim. They scan left, right, growing more intense by the second.

A cavernous setting opens up before him. Ridged boulders span a dim interior so far as light permits. On the ceiling where he would expect a row of sharp stalactites, there is only darkness.

"Leo," says Anastasia, reaching out to him.

He starts recoiling, faster and faster.

"Leo!"

A stray stone sends him crashing to the ground. Once down he finds he has to hold up his head by himself in order to keep it flat. He then realizes there *is* no more ground.

Turning over, he pushes himself onto his knees and looks out over the bare expanse. His eyes adjust slowly. As they do he is able to discern sparse, glossy reflections on a wavy surface.

Water.

A few dozen yards out a current becomes apparent. The light takes on a bleached shade in the ripples, and seems to shine stronger in that particular spot.

Leo looks to the right but a jagged bend in the boulder line blocks his view.

With Anastasia carefully observing he huffs a labored breath and stands. He starts along the stony bank minding each step of his feet. The glare on the current shifts the further he gets. He follows it until reaching the curve in the path.

He halts.

At a distance downstream, a lone island glows in a ball of majestic brilliance. No sun nourishes it from afar because its own light emanates from within. It bathes the natural landscape in white from sand to field, tree to hill. At the far reaches of the isle, a tower reaches the top of the domed radiance.

Anastasia makes her way to his position and stops to his rear.

Leo keeps his eyes on the island.

"What the hell is this place?"

Anastasia lifts a hand to his shoulder, but drops it before touching.

The question hangs heavier than the air.

"Erebos," she finally says. "It's the Underworld, Leo."

Swirling emotions and a blur of his latest experiences race through his mind. The "K" in his dream, Emrick, looking into the eyes of the mourners, the eagle calling him home. Everything jumbles once he hits the water of the lake: even what he thought was a clear intention. Now sober, his reason returns.

"No way," he says, crossing his arms. The muscles on his arms tense. "There's no way..."

"Why?" Anastasia interrupts. "Isn't this what you imagined?"

She walks in front of him. Leo looks away from the island but not at her.

"I dunno, I...hey, who says I imagined anything?"

"You jumped in the lake: and after Emrick told you about the elm being a portal."

Emrick, she calls him.

"He doesn't know anything about that tree."

"But WE know it's no ordinary tree."

The image of his mother's face flashes through his mind. Her head being sucked into the "K," Leo tearing after her. All followed by the hard right hand he dropped on the trunk that at first sounded like thunder, and second shattered his knuckles like a twig.

Leo holds up his right hand, flexes, then drives his fist into his other palm.

Nothing. No break, and merely a trace of former pain.

This has to be another dream.

He lets his hands drop and rubs them against his denim pants. Indeed, even they remain unaffected after being underwater for so long.

Anastasia again tries to get his attention.

"I thought this was what you wanted."

This time Leo looks back.

"I did -- I do, I guess -- this is freakin' crazy."

Anastasia folds her arms and puts her weight on her right heel. "Only *you* would deny what you want when it's right in front of you." She lowers her head when Leo turns his.

He glares wondering at the full meaning of the statement, but quickly dismisses it as some kind of girl code.

He returns to glaring, however, when he takes into account Anastasia's quick and ready answers to all his doubts. He likewise observes her to appear in complete comfort despite being sucked into a Matapan cave through a tree in Lake Maquari.

"I gotta say, Staj," he says, now trying to catch her attention, "you seem pretty...ok with all this. Almost like you knew we'd end up here."

She reaches for her pockets, but finds there are none to reach for.

"Well, I...I just thought," she says, refolding her arms. "Emrick said only you can save Mom, and if that's true this is where we'll find her."

The words splash on Leo's face like freezing water.

Save Mom from death. Damn.

Leo looks over at the island, down at the water, back to the rocks. He tries recalling the moment he entered the so-called Underworld.

Suppressing lake water weighs on his mind. His hands tingle at the thought of thrashing. The impenetrable tree, the burn in his chest: blackness.

Leo clenches his fists and locks his elbows around his head.

"I don't even know what's goin' on."

After a few seconds he lowers his arms. He takes a long look around the shadowy interior. Finally, he puffs a resigning exhale through his teeth while shaking his head.

"Either way, I didn't mean to bring you into this."

Anastasia steps to his front again.

"You didn't, Leo. You just believed."

The comment brings amusement to his face.

"Believed, huh? And that's all it takes? Ha! You know, we're probably just dead and we're right where we belong."

Leo laughs again, and this time the cave responds in echoes where light does not touch. It fades in the slightest increments until reaching depths he can only imagine.

The amusement disappears.

He waits for his voice to pass into a whisper before relaxing his limbs. When it seems the last bit has died away, he turns to Anastasia.

The last bit, however, does not die. It builds speed even and takes on a harsher sound than the mouth it left. It then starts gaining volume and moves swiftly back in the direction it came.

Leo steps in front of Anastasia. The unlit hollow swells with a noise that now sounds more like his name than his laugh.

A pair of swirling yellow eyes flashes through his mind. If he knew Keres could speak, he would half expect the demonic wenches to burst into the light at any moment and drag him and Anastasia to wherever it is demonic wenches go.

The cackling gets louder. Anastasia ducks behind Leo's broad shoulders and places her hand on his back. Leo puts up his guard.

At the moment it emerges, both cover their ears as Leo's own hoot washes over them twice as loud as when it left.

The silence that follows relieves, then unnerves. Leo waits a short minute before moving.

He keeps his left arm raised and approaches the visible part of the high rock. Once in reach he runs his hand along the gritty surface. Where the light stops, however, the rock stops as well, and his hand falls into nothingness.

"Great," says Leo. He inches back a bit. "Probably just woke up half the dead, or Cerberus."

"I didn't think you believed in three-headed beasts."

Leo turns quickly. "I don't, I...whatever."

"Leo," says Anastasia, moving closer, "this could be real or not, but you *are* here, and I know you have your reasons for coming."

Leo throws up his arms at the assumption. He opens his mouth to speak but Anastasia puts her fingers over his lips before any words can form.

"I don't need to know what they are," she says. She drops her hand slowly. "But try to forget the rest and think about them: think about her."

The look on his mother's face before being torn down by the keres appears almost as clearly as when he saw it again on the chair where she died. He wonders to the cause of such sorrow: departing that world, leaving him, feeling betrayed by Prometheus whom she had always so faithfully served.

Stupid omega.

To think of all the revered deity took from his mother in life, only to find out he hadn't granted her peace even in death.

Leo's right hand squeezes much as it would around a blade grip. In thinking more about Prometheus, he wishes he had both the omega and the weapon in front of him.

The chance of encountering his mother's killer, however, has him consider what else he may encounter on the way.

He looks back to the hollow darkness in the rock. The eerie sensation running down his spine makes him realize there's much more to this place than he might imagine, and not all as pretty as the island downstream.

His ears, still ringing from the deafening cackles of his rebounded laugh, go on perceiving the echoes from the tunnel. In the louder portions he remembers discerning his name. If no keres have yet come for him, however, only three people come to mind who would actually call it in a place of the deceased: his grandfather Alexander Maquari, his older brother Alexi, and his mother.

He continues staring into the darkness.

"You're not going to say the Maurileho's afraid of his own voice, are you?" says Anastasia.

Leo glares over his shoulder, then turns and brushes by her.

He walks over to the riverbank and regards the white island. He considers the ugliness of his mother's final days set against the immaculate purity of the land mass on the water. It seems fitting her afterlife would merit such a place, if only "not being at peace" merited the same.

He glances back at the tunnel then forward again to the isle. Even if he believed he could reach his mother somewhere in the course of that passageway, without a light source they would have no way to navigate. With the isle at least, there stands a chance of meeting Prometheus, assuming white shiny islands in dark caves are the kinds of places an omega would be.

Or, at best, he would discover it all to be just a bad dream. Emrick's words would result a bunch of crap, and he would find his mother young and healthy in the paradise she belongs.

"Alright, Staj," says Leo. He nods to himself. "You win. Let's do this."

Anastasia tilts her head at him and moves to his side. "You want to go there?"

"You got a better idea?" he says, peering back at the high wall of rock and shade.

Anastasia makes no contradiction, but she can't help looking on the current of murky water.

"I'm working on that," says Leo. "Let's at least head up-stream and see if we can get any closer."

As she accepts, Leo takes one final look at the dark tunnel, then moves off.

The path along the rocky ridge winds according to the river's contour. Footing becomes easier the closer they near the island. The great light source reveals high elevations to their right complimented by the occasional passageway to cackling tunnels. On the water, reflections shine with the poignancy of deflecting mirrors.

Leo and Anastasia make no comments but to observe their surroundings and keep one hand running along the cool surface of the rock. At one point Anastasia slips on a stone hidden by the shadow of the ridge. Before she can even begin to fall, however, Leo's arm shoots out and clamps onto hers. Only after does he even turn his head around.

"Watch it," he says.

Anastasia relaxes but keeps hold of his arm. He looks down where they join. After a quick glance back up, he dismisses it and continues on, Anastasia in tow.

The riverbank starts progressively widening the closer they get to the area of the isle. It also becomes much easier to see with the added light. Within a dozen or more yards, Leo starts discerning a large object at the edge of the water.

"Hey, you see that?" says Leo.

Anastasia squints as they quicken their pace.

"It looks like a big...raft," she says.

Leo squeezes his eyes shut then opens them wide, afraid he might be looking at a mirage.

Once they arrive close enough to confirm Anastasia's suspicion, Leo slows and keeps close watch on the surrounding area.

"Almost too good to be true," he says.

They both stop before their means of crossing a river not likely swimmer friendly.

"I'd say it is, actually," says Anastasia, stepping closer.

"What do you mean? It's right here, touch it."

"No, I mean it just seems too easy."

She kneels down anyway and runs her finger along a log. She then touches one of the thick vines weaving through the main frame.

"Oh come on, who's the skeptic now?" says Leo.

Despite his remark, he takes another long look around while Anastasia examines the raft. He focuses especially on the deep tunnels that now appear clearer in the rock.

"Maybe someone's expecting us," says Anastasia, rising from her knees.

"Or setting us a trap," he replies.

Now Leo kneels down. At closer look he sees the logs to be of a mid-size diameter. The thin, gray bark easily betrays the type of wood they came from.

Balsa.

The wood used to build his mother's pyre.

Leo stands up abruptly, then bends right back down and starts sliding the heavy construct along the ground.

"What are you doing?" says Anastasia.

"Let's go."

With one final heave, the raft drops into the water. Leo steadies it by keeping one foot on the platform and one on "land."

Anastasia remains in her position.

"Wasn't this supposed to be a trap?" she says.

"If it is, it's time to spring it."

The pupils of Anastasia's eyes tighten slightly, but she eventually steps forward.

The raft wobbles nearly as much as her body while she boards. Leo then remembers to offer a hand. Once settled, he kicks up a long oar from the floor and pushes off hard. Only one time does he look back, and the high jagged rock already appears like toy clay.

Leo paddles longways across the current with surprisingly little resistance. The oar seems weightless as it cuts through the water. Underneath his feet, his body itself somehow feels lighter. Maintaining a straight route presents no difficulty.

Seated in front, Anastasia observes the strange reflections in the water. They sparkle at a variance consistent with the summits of the ripples. As the island enlarges and light thickens, the variance becomes much wider spread.

Her hand moves to her wrist and rubs a bracelet glittering much the same way. After fiddling with the stones, she twists it into a new position. This leaves a ring of skin much lighter than the rest of her hand.

Despite the tightness of the band, she would never think to take it off. It was a gift from her father when she was a little girl. It has not left her wrist since the day he was killed.

The reflections grow brighter the more they absorb the increasing light. Instead of sparkles, however, they start taking on a slower, more composed quality. Anastasia sticks her head carefully over the side of the raft.

She flinches immediately. The recoil rocks the raft so hard it nearly sends Leo overboard.

"Damn, Staj, what are you..."

"Look!" she says pointing at the water.

Leo follows her finger. Standing affords him a clearer view of the spot she found so frightening. He hones in on the reflections.

"Those flashes," he says. He stops rowing. "They look like..."

"Faces!" says Anastasia.

Leo focuses a little keener and quickly confirms her suspicions: floating prisms of still human faces.

His eyes widen, and he returns to rowing in greater vigor.

Anastasia stays aloof of the raft's edges for a time. Little by little though, she inches closer. Eventually she risks a second peek.

This time she finds a prism directly under her nose. Again she pulls back, but not as violently. A second look even relaxes and makes her smile.

The image is of a boy, far too young for the Underworld. His scruffy brown hair falls over a face as pure as the twinkle in his eye.

Although a still, the image appears as vivid as if the boy were actually looking up from the water itself. His sweetness brings out Anastasia's squinting smile. She even pretends he's real and makes eye contact. Once made, the reflection expands into a wider view of the boy's surroundings, and the boy moves.

He cups his hands on a river bank very like to the one they just departed. Bending down he scoops a large drought of water and drinks deeply. He allows a lengthy few seconds for it to pour through his body. His eyes show great sorrow as he waits. Then, after a long blink, they reopen and know only peace.

"Ahhhh," says Anastasia.

"What is it?" Leo immediately asks.

"Um, nothing, it's just..." Anastasia returns her attention to the prism.

Leo tries looking over her shoulder still with the idea that demons will rise from the prisms at any moment to ambush them.

Anastasia, fascinated, then extends a gentle finger to touch the boy's two dimensional forehead. Her finger only ends up wet, however, and the image dissipates altogether under the contact.

She sulks momentarily, but the disturbance her finger created morphs into a new image: someone running in the midst of a chaotic battle zone. From the vantage point it shows the back of the little boy. Firearms of Pre-Reckoning times blaze around him into crowds of camouflaged soldiers and fleeing civilians.

The boy's pattern is erratic. His eyes, however, search intently. Maneuvering through strewn bodies and falling rubble he spots a woman huddled in a doorway with a small girl.

The woman yells for him and he hurries in her direction. Relief crosses her anguished face. It nearly becomes a smile until the boy is stopped in his tracks.

The woman releases a muffled scream as he falls to his knees. Turning on his back, he fingers a gaping hole in his chest. The wound pours blood from his lungs then to his mouth. His final thought appears of the woman in times of peace.

Anastasia jerks back, rubbing her fingertips into her temples.

"What is it?" says Leo.

She does not react but to cover her mouth. Her other hand moves to the center of her chest; she presses, then breathes deeply. Looking back at the prism she finds the boy returned to still form.

Exhale.

"We're almost there," says Leo. He looks down on her and around the raft.

The boy slowly sinks away and another flashes in its stead. This time Anastasia turns away.

All thoughts of water demons soon disappear from Leo's mind as the White Island rises before them. Set against the opposite bank, the glowing sphere appears like the sun on the horizon. A defined aura becomes visible at its brightest and enshrouds the haven in an atmospheric dome.

As they approach the threshold of this semi-sphere, Leo and Anastasia exchange a look, but not of distress. The white rays then enfold them in their protective embrace and quickly penetrate through the pores. A numbing ecstasy moves over them. Between the intense light and sensation they close their eyes. When they open, their raft skids to a halt so sudden they both go flying off its platform.

Both land face first on a warm beach.

Leo lifts his head. He dabs the part of his chin that collided with the ground, expecting lesions or burns of sorts. All he touches is fresh skin.

"Staj," he says looking down. "Look at this sand."

He takes a handful and lets it sift through his fingers.

Anastasia cups some in her hands. "It's so soft," she says. It slides off her palms. "Really light, too: like it's been bleached."

The fine quality reminds Leo of the sands in Pronoia: walking on its shores...with Thais. Thinking of her makes one of his scars itch.

"Leo," says Anastasia.

He runs his palm down the side of his eye until the itching of his scar stops.

"The sky," she says, "it's only blue. There's no clouds either."

Her excitement heightens. Leo watches her a long moment as she admires the natural phenomenon, then looks up above.

The deep blue indeed contrasts greatly to the painted sky of Prometheum. He recalls the very conversation he had with Anastasia on his mother's bench, on what would be the day before she died.

I once read it was the ocean," Anastasia said to his wondering what gave the sky color.

Leo looks down from the sky and onto the water. His eyes shoot left to right.

"Staj," says Leo rising to his feet, "what happened to the cave?"

Anastasia's attention remains on the vast blue.

"Huh?"

"The cave, Staj, where did it go?"

For what seemed a domed island with finite boundaries now extends as far as the eye can see. The waters, blue as the sky, maintain a constant flow like a river but open in a body more like a lake.

"I...I don't know," says Anastasia.

Leo looks at her sidelong waiting for her to remember some hidden piece of magic or alternate way out. When she simply continues staring, he moves to her front and squares his shoulders.

"What do you mean you don't know?"

Anastasia makes to respond, but shrinks back in the face of Leo's presence. She lowers her head.

Leo turns away in disgust and steps to the edge of the water. He searches intently for any signs of flashes or still images. When none appear, he blinks and searches again.

He switches to the horizon. Rubbing his eyes he focuses harder and harder thinking the aura might have somehow caused an optical illusion. To think, even if he did find his mother, there would be no retreat but an endless flow of blue.

Suddenly the soggy air and gritty stone of the cave are a great deal more appealing than the soft, rejuvenating sensations of the island. Looking out over the boundless open space before him never felt so constricting.

Leo leans over and sets his hands on his knees. The weight of the situation presses upon him. A primordial prison, as beautiful as anything Gaia could create, without a sun, yet as bright as can be.

For a moment he forgets his real purpose for being there. He starts thinking how crazy it was to have even come and what he could do to save himself now.

A pang of guilt stops any further thought. He closes his eyes tightly and digs his nails hard into the flesh around his knees. At the point the skin would break, a loud roar cuts the silence of the sandy shores.

Leo jumps immediately into guard position. Both he and Anastasia look around for any sign of its source.

"Didn't realize there were beasts in paradise, Staj."

"I don't see anything."

Anastasia stops surveying the coast and focuses on where the brush line begins a few yards ahead. A small break appears a foot or so wide. She moves off.

Leo makes to follow but first runs back to the raft where he takes up an oar.

They arrive at the opening in the verge at the same time. Anastasia peeks through. Though no exit is apparent, the diameter seems to continue on like a man-made path. Before she enters, however, she takes notes of the peculiar greenery.

"These leaves are so big," says Anastasia, rubbing a soft, segmented leaf three times the mass of her hand.

Small to midsize trees rise deeper into the brush. Light, scaly bark covers trunks much thinner than that of the elm.

"It's like an old heritage photo," says Anastasia.

Leo looks over his shoulder and tightens his grip on the oar.

"Pre-Reckoning," she goes on, "something of the southern regions."

"Yeah yeah, like Pronoia, right?" says Leo.

"Further than that I think."

"What? Uncharted Lands?"

"Well, they weren't uncharted then, they were stat..."

A second roar rings out, shaking Anastasia's hand off the leaf.

Leo lowers his base and quickly starts scanning the area: for not only did the sound come from much closer, it contained a far more savage tone than the first.

"Let's go," he says, plunging into the brush.

The greens of the slender path slap off their shoulders as they run as quick as visibility will allow. Leo uses the oar to chop at the thicker parts. Anastasia does her best to keep up.

Moving deeper along, the color begins to vary on the fingers of the leaves. The high pace makes it feel like running through a kaleidoscope. Leo, however, is reminded of the narrow road he travelled in the dromo car while pursuing his mother in his "dream." The colored foliage tossing about to all sides: the flap of the Keres whipping hard overhead. He can nearly hear it now.

The second roar closely resembled the harshness of his cackling laughs from the cave. He can only hope that if any such creature would manifest in this place, they would be susceptible to his attack. Perhaps to touch them, however, would mean he's already dead.

The two continue, and in a short time the path widens to where they can hurry through side by side. The oar becomes unnecessary but doesn't leave Leo's hands.

Soon the colors start morphing back into solid green. The path widens even more, and another opening appears several yards ahead.

Leo speeds up. Out of the brush he sees not water nor sand but grass and sky. The similarity to the terrain of Eulimnos drives him even faster. He thinks it could even *be* Eulimnos, and that he's actually running out of another dream.

He emerges like a dromo racer across the finish line. Before him the ground drops hard into a low valley. A small pond sits to the right, bordered by a lone white willow moving to a breeze he doesn't feel.

Beyond unfolds into a series of rolling hills. The undulating contour nearly brings him to the waterfront of Lake Maquari where he would view the Orgon Vale of the Appalachia section of Prometheum: and if he lifted his eyes even higher, he would see the Gifted Flame burning as strong as ever atop the Tower of Winds.

When he looks up now, a white tower stands in its place. The color reflects closely the radiance that gleamed from the dome when they were approaching the island. And as he saw then, its top knows no end but the sky.

Leo loosens his grip on the oar and almost smiles.

In the next moment, however, he is blindsided by a ferocious blow which sends him flying through the air. Only his hard collision with the soft ground reminds him he's not meant to fly.

As he fights to suck air back into his chest, he considers having just once felt such force in a blow: from the blade of Feidor. He half expects his great foe to be standing over him when he attempts getting to his feet.

"Leo," says Anastasia, scrambling to his side. "Stay down -- just stay down." She looks over her shoulder and clings to Leo's arm.

"What?" says Leo.

He jerks his arm from Anastasia's hold and reaches for the oar.

Though merely a long piece of wood, the feel of something hard under his fingers sends force to his limbs. He grips tighter. The threat of imminent danger tickles adrenaline untapped since the time before his rehabilitation.

As he rises, his face nearly matches the intensity of his competition days: the face of the Maurileho.

Anastasia closes up, takes a step back, then stills herself just to his rear.

Leo turns. Just as gradually as his spirit built, however, it now falters.

Pacing before them in eager steps, a gigantic white lion whips its tail back and forth, up and down. Thick muscles ripple under a tight coat the color of the tower. They cover more than twelve feet from rear to flowing mane.

Leo remains still and follows the beast with his eyes. Only in Lyceum lessons surveying pre-Reckoning predators has he seen such an animal. Even in those times it was from a distant world. It now exists only in lore, and by word of the occasional fanatic who claims to have seen one in the Uncharted Lands. Indeed, his own Kladimans epithet, the Maurileho, derives from the creature meaning "Black Lion."

As the shock wears off, however, he quickly realizes he's not confronted by any Kladimans opponent.

His hand starts sweating around the oar, his heart pumps faster. The lion's pacing quickens as though detecting the surge of blood.

It's at this point Leo takes closer note of the lion's features. Tucked behind its massive shoulders he sees a wing joint resting close to the body. The wings themselves blend so well into the torso they're barely distinguishable. What he does discern, however, is more skin and veins as opposed to feathers or fur: much like the wings of a bat: much like the wings of the Keres.

Leo slowly slides his right foot to the rear and jostles a better grip on the oar. Still avoiding direct eye contact, he lowers his gaze to the pattern of its steps.

His own eyes widen slightly.

In place of a padded set of paws, thick scales cover four digits passing for feet. Talons the size of blades extend from each.

Leo thinks of the eagle over the elm resting on the boulder back home. He remembers when last he saw it there: the piercing glare it threw him and Anastasia with those narrow, penetrating eyes.

Even the mental image causes Leo to look away. The flinch, however, stops the lion in its tracks, and Leo quickly finds eyes much of the same bearing into him from a few yards off.

These eyes, though, appear more as black, hollow pits. The glossy reflection lends much to the quality of the prisms in the river. Indeed, looking into them feels like looking into a window as dark as the soul he imagines it having.

Leo lowers his center of gravity. By now blood and adrenaline have overwhelmed his poise to remain still.

The lion responds by arching its back and leaning head first over its front talons. Its gaze intensifies into slits. The thick whiskers under its nose curl revealing the white of sharp fangs underneath.

The thought of dying again enters Leo's mind. He wonders where the soul would go if it's already in the Underworld: if his body would remain mangled after being shredded by a monster: if somehow his death would release his mother from whatever held her back.

As the great lion takes a few careful steps forward, Anastasia makes a supplicating glance at his side. He sees through the corner of his eye not only a look of fear, of will to live, but also dependency and despair.

At that moment something trickles past his own fear. It touches a point beyond the ego yet remains within an extension of the self. Preservation becomes not only an instinct, but a duty.

Leo returns the gaze to the strange beast with the same intensity it's given. At this the lion spreads its wings, opens its jaws, and lets out a mammoth roar with two rows of pointed fangs.

Though painful to bear, the booming sound brings Leo back to the sands of Pronoia when he stepped out to meet Feidor in the finals. The crowd cheered just as loud. His guard hung perfectly from his left hand: his blade from his right. Never did he physically feel more at his best.

He now brings the oar to the front across his body.

The memory serves as a keen reminder that although he's not trained in earnest for quite some time, he is a Kladimans of the Warrior Division, a Maquari, and above all: the Maurileho.

With that, both lions launch forward.

Leo takes aim at the ridge of the nose and drops a hard downward cut with a two handed grip. At the second of contact, however, the lion lifts its massive frame into the air and glides over Leo's head, grazing a few hairs in passing. The force of Leo's miss sends him into a forward roll and back to his feet.

Circling back the lion squints its dark eyes and begins pressing forward. Leo backpedals, twirling the oar end over end in rapid turns. He keeps careful watch through the blur.

The lion does likewise, and as it advances faster it concentrates on the cycles of the oar. Leo recognizes the tactic as one he employs himself: that of timing his opponent's movements in preparation of a strike. Before he can alter his rhythm, however, the first strike comes high and quick.

Only Leo's lightning-fast reflexes enable him to parry the heavy talon to the side. Just as fast, though, is the follow up from the opposite limb.

A prompt succession of blows ensues, each with increasing speed and force. Within less than a second Leo's footwork has him backtracking with his spine arched at 180 degrees.

Under normal circumstances he would continue drawing his opponent in then use his momentum against him with a hard pivot and counter. His feet now, however, will not obey his wishes and soon succumb to the overwhelming press.

Head over heels he tumbles. Yet before the lion can pounce, Leo springs to his knees and delivers a fierce two-handed swing of the oar. The edge finds its mark. It lands square on the jawline of the beast's giant head with enough weight and force to shatter any type of bone.

The only thing that shatters this time, however, is the oar.

Leo lifts his hand stinging with vibes and stares at the splintered end now half the size of the original. The lion remains in the same position: unfazed, unscathed.

Leo takes a few steps back then steadies himself on the defensive. The intensity in his eyes no longer matches the lion's. His stance lacks form, and the oar hangs off-balance in his hand.

Though what's left of it has formed a sharper point, he knows it will be of no effect against the impenetrable fortress standing before him. Hitting it indeed felt like hitting a wall of diamond.

He looks to Anastasia who's taken refuge in the tree line. He then quickly turns away before the expression on her face causes him to lose heart.

The lion bears its teeth, snaps its wings. Not bothering with any more swatting it thrusts hard with its hind legs and propels headlong into the air. The 10 feet or so gives Leo just enough time to react and tuck his head into a tight forward roll. His timing puts him just under the lion's belly at the summit of its leap.

Moving out of his tumble he thinks to attempt some kind of feeble counter to the beast's eyes or throat. Yet before he can even stand, three razor sharp talons tear into the top part of his right shoulder down to the left half of his lower back.

His voice bellows a cry he didn't even know it could produce. Only Anastasia's is louder.

The lion then tops them all with a deafening roar that carries all three voices clear across the vale.

Despite the crippling pain, something of the deep sting coupled with the lion's energy builds up a surge in Leo's chest. A glance at a frightened Anastasia adds to this. He knows he's her only defense, and that if he gives up she would stand no chance against the lion.

He grabs for the oar. Fighting through the extreme volume permeating through the atmosphere, he fires at the beast mid roar.

The oar shoots through the air like an arrow from a high-powered bow. To Leo, though, he sees every rotation, end over end until the pointed side disappears into the depths of the lion's jaws.

The sound cuts. The echoes trail off into the distance.

The great beast shakes its head and grinds its teeth. It begins stumbling around.

Leo falls to one knee and reaches a hand behind his back. Through the tears in his shirt he feels the warm stickiness coat the backs of his fingers. He does not look. He only hopes the smell is not too strong.

At the moment he brings his hand around, the lion stops and turns its head his way. Leo does not rise, nor stare back much, but does curl his right hand into a fist in what he believes will be his final recourse.

He wonders if now is perhaps the time he would wake up: back in his room, like after the Keres.

His giant foe, however, shows no sign of disappearing, nor does the soft ground beneath his knees.

The lion begins flicking its tail in a circular motion and pumping its wings outward. Leo rises slowly. He cocks his arm as the beast steps off straight towards him. When he thinks to throw what he knows will be nothing more than a bump to a brick, the fearsome creature takes to flight and passes directly over his head. Leo turns in surprise as it sails high in the air toward the mountains and the tower. Only when it moves out of sight does he relax his fist and return to his knee.

CHAPTER 7 – THE ISLES OF THE BLESSED

Anastasia runs out from the brush and drops down at his side.

"Oh my gosh," she says, hesitating, unsure where to place her hand on his back. "These cuts...are you alright?"

The gashes across his back form deep incisions well past the skin into the muscle. Blood pours generously from the wound well down to the other parts of his back, as is evident from the deep stains to his once white shirt.

"Don't worry about it," says Leo. He keeps his head to the ground. "Just a scratch."

Anastasia tucks an unsteady hand under his shirt and lifts, accidentally brushing one of his cuts. Leo immediately winces.

"These aren't just scratches, Leo."

She holds up her blood-stained fingers, searches her pockets with her other hand, then realizes again she has none. Still in her mourning outfit from the funeral games, she wipes on the white of her ruffled trousers.

"Yeah, well," says Leo trying to stand, "it was a lucky shot."

Anastasia attempts to help him up but he shrugs her off. With all his adrenaline run dry, he feels each shred of torn skin and ripped muscle fiber as he uneasily makes it to his feet.

He exhales through gritted teeth. "I should've never stopped seriously training."

"You were hurt," says Anastasia, "and...Mom needed you."

Leo remembers the long road of rehabilitation following his loss to Feidor. For months his mother nursed him back to health, possibly at the cost of her own. Once healed, he became nurse to her, and was unable to return to the level of training required to compete in Kladimo. There was always a part of him that resented her for it.

Leo grinds his jaw and suddenly the pain to his back seems not only right but just. He tenses his muscles to augment its acuteness until trickles of blood start seeping out the already congealed areas.

"Leo," says Anastasia. She places a soft hand on his forearm. She then looks down a ways into the vale.

"Let's just get to that pond," she says. "The water might help."

"Yeah, or suck us into our own reflections."

Anastasia hurriedly moves off. Before she can take more than two steps, however, Leo snatches her by the arm and pulls her back.

"Wait," he says. His eyes fix on the willow down by the pond. "Someone's down there."

Anastasia follows his gaze to the tree where indeed stands the figure of a man in the shadow of the chorded branches. He leans against the trunk with folded arms and one foot across the other, toe in the ground.

Anastasia watches. Leo calculates.

The man simply stares.

Though Leo wouldn't be surprised if the guy suddenly transformed into a minotaur, something in his aspect tells him he won't.

Either way, if they walk away now, they would be heading toward nowhere with an unaccounted-for creep on the lurk. This not to mention a giant, flying lion that just tried to eat him.

Nonetheless, a man would at least have the ability to talk, and would hopefully be willing. If not, the potential of facing a creature of plain flesh and fingernails feels nothing of intimidating after a lion. Even the searing pain running down his back does not dissuade him from this.

"Let's go," he says.

"What?" says Anastasia.

"Come on."

Leo winces on the first step but quickly establishes a pattern of not swinging his arms too much as he moves. Anastasia trails close behind with her hand extended as if any second she might have to reach out and catch him.

They slowly descend the sharp decline into the heart of the vale. Leo keeps his eye trained on the man amongst fits of throbbing when he'd lose his footing or shift his torso too hard.

He never thought so much could be connected to a body part he can't even see.

In short time they stumble onto flatter ground. The man remains still, and Leo considers that if this guy were going to turn into a minotaur, he would have already done so.

Now at close range, they see this man they found so random appears to be much of the younger sort. He wears a white form-fitted polo and boot-cut jeans around a pair of sneakers marked "Converse." Over his clean face and shaggy brown hair is a dark blue cap bearing the symbols "NY."

Leo slows down and looks left and right. The minotaur seemed more fitting.

The young man picks up their pace and moves out to greet them, all smiles and ease.

"Leo," he says warmly.

The guy extends a hand, which Leo scrutinizes. He then looks left and right once more.

"Yeah, maybe," he says, "Do I know you?"

The offered hand retracts and runs up under the "NY" cap. It brushes through a head of curly locks. Leo cannot deny a slight resemblance to himself.

"Not like this I guess," the young man laughs. "I'm Alex, your grandfather."

Leo stares a moment, then makes his own laugh. The laugh returns much like the cave, though, when the tension to his torso sends a shock of pain from the top of his shoulder across to the bottom of his back.

"You're really Alexander Maquari?" says Anastasia paying no mind to Leo cringe.

"Para servirle," says Alex, imitating a bow.

"What was that?" says Anastasia.

"Oh, nothing."

Leo swallows down the last ripple of pain and sets to looking over Alex's physical features. The broad shoulders, dark brown eyes, light brown oily skin: traits he remembers up to his grandfather's death a few years ago which leaves him unable to completely dismiss the claim of parentage. Yet as he remembers him, is as a wise respected old man, not the clothing model wearing an unheard of brand of sneaker and hat with random letters on it.

"Listen man, my grandfather is like a legend where I come from. And I might not know what this place is all about yet, but when he died he was really old and really sick."

Alex chuckles again and folds his arms.

"Sorry...dude, you don't think I'd still be on my deathbed after I actually died, do you?"

"Dude?"

"Never mind."

Anastasia regards carefully the young man who says to be her old mentor. She runs her eyes down his athletic frame and back up to his high cheekbones. She pauses for a long moment on the dark brown hiding his pupils.

"It is him," she says as if speaking from a dream. She walks up to Alex and cups one of his hands into hers. "It's your grandfather, Leo, when he was our age."

Alex smiles down at her and Leo takes a long, labored step forward. He glances at their joined hands.

"And if I had to guess," she goes on, "we're on the Isles of the Blessed."

"Right you are!" Alex says, breaking away to clap. "Same Annie as I remember." Alex wraps her in a hug and kisses her cheek. "Only now a pretty young lady."

Anastasia blushes. Leo raises his eyebrows.

"Yes, sir," she says.

Alex places his hands on her shoulders and looks on her with pride. "Leo wouldn't be here without you. And call me Alex by the way."

"I think I will too if you don't mind," Leo cuts in. "Can't exactly call a 20-year-old Grandpa."

"I'm 94."

Anastasia covers her mouth as Leo puts on a goaded face. The lines of Alex's smile bring Leo back to the time when his old grandfather would approve of his winning a duel, singing a nice song, or just making one of his cynical comments. The more he settles on the feeling, the less he has to doubt the essence of the man he sees as exemplifying a better side of himself.

"A spirit's not a body, Leo," Alex continues. "You can have people who are really bad off physically, but with sound mind, and vice-versa. No matter what age or sickness I had in life, I always saw myself as the restless young gamer from Queens ready for another adventure like Bilbo." Alex spreads his arms in display. "That's how we pass on, especially the Blessed."

Leo makes no reaction whatsoever. Only "Bilbo" rings the slightest of bells.

He does, however, begin to imagine how his mother might have seen herself at the height of her own age and sickness: what she'd look like with all her limbs, all her fingers, the color of healthy flesh on her skin. He doubts he would even recognize her, much less in the body of a twenty-year-old.

Such an aesthetic, however, would likely be reserved for the sound of mind as Alex described. Given the state of his mother's, he worries she would look any different at all.

Anastasia steps off a few paces and takes a long look over the vale.

"Where is everyone else?" she asks. "Why is it we only see you?"

Alex grins. "You see who you're meant to see. Don't forget, you're not one of us."

"Us?" says Leo. "You mean you and that giant cat flying around here? By the way, thanks for the help back there, *Grand-pa*."

The strong expression sends another shot of pain up Leo's cuts. This time he suppresses the grimace with Alex facing him directly.

"Help?" says Alex, stepping closer. He curls his lip and nods in consideration. "What is it they call you in Prometheum? The Maurileho?"

Leo glares into him.

"I didn't think *help* was something the "Black Lion" ever wanted."

Alex folds his arms and remains planted in front of him. The challenge and proximity of an able bodied individual incites Leo's combative spirit. His body, however, promptly forfeits.

Alex glances over him with a studied look.

"--which is probably why you'd rather stand there and suffer than ask for something."

Worry returns to Anastasia's face at the mention of Leo's wounds. She hurries to his rear and sees the drying blood grown dark and hard.

"I was saying maybe the pond water would help," she tells Alex.

"It might," says Alex, still looking at Leo. "If Leo believes it will."

Anastasia steps around to his side and tries catching his eye.

"It's worth a shot," Alex continues. "You made it this far; I wasn't even sure you'd be allowed that much."

The hard look on Leo's face drops. "You knew we were coming?"

Alex unfolds his arms and shrugs.

"Of course," says Leo, "the whole "life without time" thing, right?"

"Not quite. I showed you the way, and you made a choice. Luckily, so did she."

Leo manages a step forward.

"What do you mean YOU showed me?"

"The Blessed can go where they please anywhere in the Underworld. We can also visit the living, in their dreams."

Leo recalls the roadside pull-off where he encountered Alex and his older brother. No one gave him time for questions, and he was soon struggling to trail them in a dromo car whilst being pursued by Keres. The end of that chase led to the "K" in the tree and the loss of his mother.

Alex keeps a keen eye on Leo's thoughts.

"You left that raft, didn't you?" says Leo.

"I did."

Both Leo's jaw and hands clench at once as he looks away. Around them all a light but sharp breeze picks up, rustling the small green leaves of the willow vines together. Ignoring equally the wind and sting to his back, he begins turning about.

"You had this all planned out: where the hell is my mother then?"

The intensity of Leo's gaze coupled with his facial scars would be menacing in any world.

Alex, however, calmly interrupts his seething by placing a hand on his shoulder. "She's not here, Leo. She's dead, but not passed on."

"I've heard all this," says Leo, striking his arm away with a hard parry to the wrist. "Where is she?"

When Alex simply looks back at him Leo takes a step forward. Anastasia quickly steps in between and sets both hands on his shoulders.

"Leo."

He looks aggressively on where she touches but makes no move to get her away.

"I asked wh.."

"She's at the boatman's ferry," Anastasia blurts out. "On the other side of the Styx." She lowers her head. "Charon won't take unburied souls across."

Leo looks down on her sandy hair, then to Alex who nods in confirmation.

"You knew this?" he says to Anastasia.

She looks up and he takes a large step backward letting her arms fall limp from his shoulder.

"I...,"

"I didn't need a family reunion, Staj," Leo interjects, pointing his finger at the ground. "Or did you really just need to see Alexander Maquari cause you wanted to check him out as a 20 year old."

Anastasia stares into him for a moment. "This isn't somewhere you just walk through," she says. "We needed a guide."

"Fine. We got one. Let's go."

Leo stumbles off but a firm grip latches his arm out of nowhere. His conditioned reflex jerks away. One particular finger, however, digs into a sensitive spot under his skin and detains him with little effort.

"No," says Alex. "Take some rest, you're not even healed: you don't know what you're getting into."

"And you do?"

"Enough to say you should take my advice. We'll go together, soon."

Leo glares into his grandfather but the look he's met with belongs to no 20-year-old. Though clear and radiant, its depths reach places born only of the wisest and labored of eyes. Its aspect matches the force of Leo's yet motivated by strength rather than passion. Even his hand grasps with the command of a patient steady hold free of fear or despair. At that moment Leo realizes it is not grandfather Alex who confronts him, but rather

General Maquari, hero of the Reckoning Wars. In simply a touch and look he senses the power that brought him to his station in life. Without further protest, therefore, he complies and makes his way slowly around the willow toward the pond.

Anastasia takes a step in following but Alex holds up a hand. He watches until Leo plops down by the water, then turns toward Anastasia. When he does so he's resumed his initial smile.

"Don't worry about him," says Alex. "I'm happy to see you at whatever age you see me in. So, how is my old friend?"

Anastasia breaks eye contact. "Oh, my grandfather Emrick? He's fine."

"I didn't think you'd have an answer."

She looks away completely this time. "I haven't seen him in a while."

Alex pauses but stays facing her. "I remember when Leo was born: it was right after his brother, Alexi, was diagnosed. He brought life back to the family, always laughing and smiling." Anastasia turns her head to the scarred, solitary figure sitting by the pond.

"He was fairly young when I got sick: my lot for living through the old Reckoning Wars I guess."

Alex leans his neck around to regain her attention. "I know losing your Dad wasn't easy."

She turns away once more.

"But he died for what HE believed in, not what Emrick or anyone else put into his head."

She looks off in the direction of Leo and wipes under her eye. He places a hand on her shoulder.

"It's not too late you know."

Alex also glances Leo's way.

"Alright, alright," he says patting Anastasia on the back, "enough of that. Come on, there's some things I need to give Leo."

ΔΔΔ

Leo kneels before the pond with his hands on his knees. He imagines he should be drinking it, but instead just stares. The vibrant clarity runs much akin to the waters of Lake Maquari.

The richness, however, takes from the deep blue of the Blessed sky.

He thinks to himself that with a single gulp he could probably live 1000 years. He thinks of his mother: if only she could have just a sip. Instead, she's trapped in limbo by fault of his: for not only did he fail to complete her funeral rites, he left it so no one else could either.

He contemplates what it would take to reach a place belonging to neither his world nor this one. Monsters, demons, omegas, the trials for his audacity: all the same.

All the same.

"Leo," Alex calls from behind.

Leo continues looking on the water for a short time longer. Then, making it to his feet, he walks back to the tree without having had any at all.

Under the willow lie a few items he doesn't remember seeing when walking by earlier. Alex draws the first. With his back still turned he holds it up and takes a moment to admire.

"I have some things for you: gifts you might say."

The great general steps back slowly and presents the item just as slow: a creamy white electric guitar with a solid body the shape of an 8. Three golden pickups underline a set of bronze strings, complimented by a row of four equalizing knobs at the base of an overall design Leo doesn't recognize.

Leo accepts and considers it curiously.

"Never seen one like this: and man is it heavy," he says.

"It's a vintage Les Paul. None were ever made again after the Reckoning."

Leo begins to strap it on, winces, then decides to go to one knee. He sets the smooth inlay over his thigh and takes a pick from his pocket.

"It was mine," says Alex. "I always wanted it to stay in the family."

Nothing but guitars and kladimo blades could distract Leo from a fixed purpose in mind. This being one of them, he delves into a rapid mixolydian scale in D. Up and down the fretboard his fingers fly. So poised is his concentration he completely forgets he's entered a subterranean realm to save his mother from death: or that he plays on a guitar gifted by his dead grandfather with cuts running down his back from a giant lion with eagle's talons.

Once his fingers slow, his mind comes back to speed.

"Uh, thanks...Grandpa," he says looking around. "Listen, Alex, not to be ungrateful but what good is this thing going to do me here?"

"Like I said Leo, no one knows what's in store for you, not even me completely. But if it makes you feel better, I have something else more for your...frame of mind."

Alex shows him the next item.

His eyes light up. "Now we're talkin'."

He hands the guitar off to Anastasia and wraps his hands around a large, vanilla colored aspis guard.

"It'll shield you from head to hip," says Alex.

Leo turns it around, remarking the engraving of "M" in script-like calligraphy. He runs his hand over its elegant lines and etchings. He then pauses, looks closer, and furrows his brow.

"Is this *wood*?" he says.

"It's willow, from Eulimnos."

"A willow aspis? I'd be dead in two strokes."

Leo barely has time to raise his arm before Alex drops a crushing blow with a blade seemingly conjured out of air.

"How did that feel?" Alex asks a wide-eyed Leo.

"I barely felt a thing." Though the pain to his back would strongly suggest otherwise, the guard did indeed absorb the full power of the strike. There was also something peculiar in the sound of the blade he didn't know Alex even had: and indeed no longer sees in his hand.

Leo looks back and forth between Alex and the guard.

"It's no trick, Leo. It's Aether."

"Aether?"

"The fifth element," says Anastasia, "it's used in Alchemy." She steps up eagerly.

"You got to be kidding me. That stuff's not even real."

Alex chuckles and adjusts the brim of his cap. "That's quite a statement coming from a guy who just fell into a tree and is talking to his dead grandfather."

Leo scoffs.

"It can be a devastating weapon once you learn how to use it," says Alex, no longer laughing. He points to the thumb gadgets on the rim of the grip, "I had some mechanical modifications done, too, but the rest will have to come from you...like with this."

He pulls out the final gift.

Leo takes what appears to be a slab of white stone. At the touch of his hand, however, it becomes more animated than a beating heart. Light streams of pulsation run up through his wrist and out to his arm. For what he thought would be a rough surface feels more like a smooth, adhesive marble underneath. Indeed, his fingers wrap around as though gripping a blade.

He looks up at Alex. "So what is this, a vibrating blade grip?"

Alex shakes his head. "Focus your energy and give it a squeeze."

Leo regards his grandfather for a moment longer then tightens his grip. He thinks of his mother stranded on the opposite side of the Styx. He thinks of all the injustice that brought her there. He thinks, if he could only confront Prometheus, blade in hand.

All at once something zings forth from the stone. Its pallor is dark and gleamy like the eyes of the white lion: its texture sharp and thin. A moving, cloudlike pattern circulates over its surface: about 2 and a half feet end to end.

A blade.

Leo looks over the item in his hand, hardly believing he would ever hold such a thing. He waves some basic strokes to make sure he isn't imagining. Again something in the sound catches his attention.

With a swifter stroke he lends a careful ear and perceives the faint whisper of a voice. No words manifest, which gives to the quality of being more vocal than spoken. As soon as he might discern more, though, it dispels into the recesses of his mind, like an echo of a dream.

"Don't tell me," says Leo, "more alchemy?"

"Among other things."

"*Among other things,*" says Leo under his breath.

"The blade will learn to listen to you, if you learn to speak to it."

When Leo ignores the "among other things" guideline, Anastasia quickly steps aside Alex.

"It responds to emotions?" she asks.

"It responds to state of mind," he says only to her. "Emotions can play a part, but alone they're too fickle and can limit you."

At the sign of a tête-à-tête, Leo steps to the side and continues his modest strokes. The blade cuts through the air so easily it causes little to no pain to his injury. When waved in succession, it sounds more like a chorus than one random voice.

"What are its limits?" Anastasia asks, watching Leo fondly.

"Depends on its master. But it's not a magic wand, it's an extension of the person."

Anastasia turns her neck toward Alex but pries no further.

Leo, meanwhile relaxes his grip on the blade and it dissipates. He holds it up to his face, nodding approvingly. The contour of a blade grip under his fingers makes him feel right at home. Despite the oddity he's much more eager to go forth armed and injured than healthy with an oar in his hand.

"Thanks, Alex," he says walking back over.

"Take care of them," says the General. "Now, you guys get some rest."

Leo takes a wide look around at the bright and sunny vale, warmed by no particular sun. Though certainly fatigued, a mid-afternoon nap in the open is not quite what he had in mind.

"It's still light out," he says.

"It's always light out; we don't sleep."

Alex brushes by the two of them and starts heading toward the hills.

"Where are you off to?"

The young General stops slowly and swings his arms as he turns around. "Oh, out for a little promenade."

"Promenade?" *Where does he get these freakin' words?*

Alex grins. "Something like that...; anyway, try the grass, it's softer than down; it'll take you right home." With that Alex departs. He "promenades" through the fields, admiring the tall grass, winds, and white tower. Never does he alter his pace. Then, in what seems like a few seconds, he passes out of sight completely.

Leo turns to find Anastasia already having taken Alex's advice. He takes a long look around before doing so himself. The last place he stops is in the direction Alex walked, and up in the sky where the lion flew.

"We'll be ok here," says Anastasia. "We can't go anywhere without him anyway."

Leo doesn't respond, but slowly gathers his items and drops them on a spot near her.

Trying to settle down he first falls to his hands and knees. When the initial sting passes, he attempts a shoulder. Little by little he manages to work himself into a side position on the grass he finds to be exactly as Alex described.

The softness and comfort gives him confidence to perhaps try more of his body. Indeed, the soothing contact seems to penetrate well past the skin. As such he begins a slow, tense roll over.

Inch by inch his back meets with the grass. The only discomfort is the part not yet touching. When he's almost completely lain, he releases the tension holding him up and plops down the rest of the way.

The grass immediately welcomes his weight. It adjusts like a cloud mattress for the contour of his torso to the point he thinks it's his bed.

Once stable, soft blades start gripping his clothes and skin. He does not resist. They then seep up through the tears in his shirt and move over his wounds. The tickles they provoke almost make him laugh. The relief they provide almost makes him forget.

Such overall security he's not felt in a long time. For as much as he'd like to give himself over fully, however, the fact he lies exposed in a place where beasts lurk in land and air prevents him. He can only imagine what they may look like in a place not as beautiful. He also finds himself noting Alex's absence more keenly than anticipated. Before he allows his eyes to close, therefore, he takes his new blade in hand.

Sleep comes the moment he submits. In his dreams, though, he has not moved. He sits where he now lies looking into the distant hills. The sky dims and assumes the colors he associates with Eulimnos. Something draws him to a particular point on the horizon; a feeling, tender and broken.

He reaches out with his energy and feels for the source. The closer he gets, the more it amplifies. As it does though, the burden becomes heavier to bear, and he now senses beyond the outlying feeling to a core of something much more forceful.

The surge presses hard against his skin and quickly breaks through toward his own core. What he felt as tender and broken becomes sharp and desolate. It spreads like wildfire. He jerks his neck hard right, left, but the hold has already sunk in too much to shake.

As it magnifies his left hand closes into a fist and locks across his chest. His right hand does likewise, but around the grip of the aether blade.

At this point the source reaches out to him. It jars his spirit back and forth reflecting the pattern of a dromo car. The motion gets increasingly fast and erratic, which compounded with the moving despondency, overloads Leo's senses to the point of bursting.

He jumps up thrashing at the air. He tears at his own body until he feels the burn of his fingernails on his chest. His efforts combine with the faint notion he thinks he's only dreaming.

Despite that little reassurance, however, the source only beseeches him harder.

Therefore, as a measure of last resort, he clenches his teeth, animates the blade, and slices down the side of his leg.

Leo jolts awake to the brightness of endless day. Anastasia remains sleeping, and the sky has returned to its solid blue.

He runs his hand across his chest. No tears to his shirt. When he makes to adjust his position, however, a sharp sting shoots up the side of his leg. He reaches down to a long tear in his pants becoming more stained each second.

Quickly he grabs for his shoulder and rips off a short sleeve. The thin wrap does little around his bulky thigh so he ends up tearing off the other one as well.

Once at least slowed, Leo rests forward on his hands and marks the spot in the distance where he connected with the source. Unsure whether it still exists or only seems so from just waking up, he trusts his heart as to why it ever came.

"Mom."

Grabbing his things he gets to his feet. He uses his good leg, and is careful not to tighten too much in his back. Much to his surprise no pain arises from the area of his cuts.

He reaches a hand over his shoulder and fingers through the tears in his shirt. His fingertips find skin: hard, numb, but skin.

He looks down at the grass and considers dropping on his side to give his leg a chance to heal. A pang from his dream, however, sends his arm clutching across his chest. It quickly passes but he finds himself once again facing the direction of the Styx.

So attaching the blade to the inside of his guard, he tightens his bandages and makes to leave. He looks once more on the beautiful guitar Alex left him, but decides it would only be a burden to carry. His only other hesitation occurs before Anastasia.

He regards her a moment: his best friend, willing to go into hell for him. That she slumbers so peacefully comforts him.

"Sorry, Staj. I gotta do this one alone."

He kneels slowly beside her and runs the back of his knuckles over her soft skin. He takes a wide look around the strange place he is about to leave her all by herself. He rises nonetheless, trusting Alex will soon return, and hopefully send her home. With that he breaks into a fast jog toward the source: toward Pandora.

Trudging through the hills proves more relaxing than fatiguing in fact. The gash on his leg holds steady. Compared to deep incisions delivered by talons, it seems like nothing more than a nagging scratch.

To his left, the brush remains wildly colored. To the right: the tower appears to grow taller with each step. Even in a slow run he discerns different levels, seemingly cut from stone and glazed with some magical brush. The scenery abates his drive to purpose in spite of his desire to keep it.

He soon reaches a wooded area. Nothing of giant leaves over scaly bark, though; instead the familiar oak, maple, hemlock, and birch of Prometheum.

Running in reminds him of chasing Beren and Zoe through the woods of Eulimnos.

Once under the high cover of the canopy, he follows the only open path in sight. It weaves around thick trunks in a sharp series of bends. The winding makes him recollect the narrow road in flight from the Keres.

Just then a wide shadow appears on the already darkened floor. Leo, keeping pace, lifts his eyes to the treetops and spots a winged silhouette keeping pace right along with him. Its sheer size doesn't leave room for uncertainty as to what it is.

Leo quickens his strides. Though armed with mystical weapons he gets the sense the lion won't be opening its mouth so wide again anytime soon. And against its hide, he doubts even an aether blade could penetrate.

The path begins tapering the further he advances. Overhead he hears the cracking of branches in rapid succession as if the beast were trying to descend. He then realizes that while the thickening woods hinder his progress they also hinder his enemy's, protecting him for the time being. He thus refocuses ahead and concentrates on his maneuvers.

A second or two later the sound of a river reaches his ears. A straightaway following a sharp turn reveals the great body of water about fifty yards away. Unfortunately, the path leading to it widens into an open funnel.

Leo breaks into a sprint. He already hears the cracking branches above when he turns to look back over his shoulder. He finds the beast looking on him in full span of its sinister wings. In quick calculation, he estimates 40 yards to the top of the canopy: and the same to the river.

He moves into the deepest run he can conjure. Not since serious kladimans training has he pushed so hard.

25 yards to go.

A loud break above signals the woods have relinquished their protection. Leo presses his weight, doing all he can to keep footing on his now aching leg.

15 yards.

Wing flaps draw heavier and nearer. The path now extends to the size of a road. No beach appears beyond, but, as though a mirage, another raft awaits identical to the one he came on.

The surge of relief he feels disappears just as quick, however, when he realizes it's attached to the bank by a long thick rope.

In the split second that covers the last five yards, under pressure from the ferocious energy just at his neck, he makes the decision to attempt the only move that will both release the raft and not slow his flight.

Planting hard with his injured leg, he thrusts himself airborne, tucking his chin to his chest. In one fluid motion he detaches the blade, conjures it, and manages to cut the rope before his body is completely upside down.

At the same time, though, he also realizes he did not have enough force to execute the twist. At best he hopes to land on his back.

Just as his torso comes about, however, a fierce blow sends him upright and hurling. The world turns into a chaotic blur. Right-side up and upside down become one. He is quickly reminded of which is which, though, when his chin and breast plate collide hard with the grooves of the raft.

Despite the pain, the force drives the raft outward over the water. As quickly as possible Leo gathers his remaining wits and scrambles to his knees. He turns to find the lion circling back for another attack. Remaining in low position, he sets his guard hard before him and keeps the tip of his blade hidden just behind.

As the lion rounds the last of the trees it launches headlong at the raft. Its widened eyes depict a more purple shade than black, though just as hollow. It is there Leo fixes the point of his weapon.

He cocks his arm, shifts his weight, but at the moment the beast reaches the water it pulls up and away as though there were an impenetrable barrier separating them. Leo keeps position as it settles on the bank.

For a short time they hold each other's regard. When the lion shows no further interest but to watch him float away, he relaxes his arms.

As he gets to his feet he takes up the long oar lying across the floor. He then glances momentarily along the coast for any signs of Alex. Seeing none, he turns and sets to rowing.

The deep blue waters extend as far as he can see. He wonders how long the illusion will hold before the dark of the cave unfolds around him. The vastness of the matching blue above makes him consider looking back one last time at the bright, lonely Isle with no sun. As soon as he turns his head, though, his eyes fall on the white aura forming the protective dome around the island. He oddly doesn't remember it ever changing.

What he does remember, however, are the somber depths of the cave.

When he looks forward again he's surprised to so quickly spot another land mass: a dark coast, the edge of which is visible only by the grace of the Isle. It stretches as far left and right as he can tell, thereby leaving no recourse but to continue straight.

Within a few dozen strokes tall weeds brush along the side of the raft. The river underneath becomes progressively shallower. When it eventually becomes too much to row he dismounts and drags it the rest of the way through about a foot of water.

The raft slides to a stop on a grassy, saturated bank. Leo throws down the oar but takes no step forward as his pupils struggle to dilate in the obscure environment.

Behind, the White Isle glows at near distance. Its rays fall on the uncharted land in the color of moonlight. Little by little Leo's eyes adjust. When they do, he sees nothing more than an endless terrain of the tall grass and weeds he's already encountered.

A deep exhale breaks the silence. He takes another breath leaning over, hands on his knees. Running toward nothing seems to be exactly what he found.

He thinks of Anastasia lying near the willow tree. He hopes she doesn't wake alone. He even thinks of Alex who likely knows more about what he's doing than he does himself.

He stands up straight. Though dim, he takes a long reaching look over the desolate field. His eyes furrow into slits trying to pierce the haze. When they close altogether, he moves a hand over his stomach.

Despite the futility of his impulsive flight from the Isle, the pull in his gut creeps back little by little. Somehow it makes the dismal abyss before him seem a bit clearer. Somehow he knows straight is the way to go. Firming his resolve, he takes a step forward.

No sooner does his foot hit the ground that a comet falls from the sky. The trail of light illuminates the area like a cluster of lightning bolts thrown all at once. The only thing that overshadows its awesome power is the booming impact that knocks Leo right off his feet.

From the ground Leo immediately reaches for his aspis guard. He gets up quickly and assumes a defensive position with the guard hanging low.

Before him rises a man-like creature, twice his size holding a two-handed war hammer. Hairless and slits for pupils, his body is a magnificent physical specimen but for a gruesome scar shaped like a lightning bolt running shoulder to hip.

Leo recoils and almost lifts his fingers to his own scar.

A near spitting image of the dreaded Feidor Yazinov. If he didn't know any better, he would think his great rival died just to face him again in the afterlife.

"Why are you here, Leonidas Maquari?" As it speaks, an embedded flame passes deep behind its eyes.

Though the stature resembles Feidor, the voice barrels slow and deep as if a bother to even use. It chills Leo to hear his name spoken in such a tone by such a creature who shouldn't know it.

"Who the hell are you?" says Leo, reaching for his grandfather's blade.

CHAPTER 8 – MENOITIOS

Anastasia wakes to a cool breeze tickling her nose. It smells of fresh mist and fruit infused with a touch of rose petal: a lot like the sweet air blowing off the Pronoian River.

In the back of her mind she can almost hear Zoe and Beren bickering over who got the better kladimans finish. She imagines them all dangling their feet over the edge of the Portland bridge, high above the water. These were always her favorite times, when time itself seemed to not exist.

Home, friends, and the strange blue sky above parts her lips into a smile she barely notices having made.

She gets to her feet. Standing feels nimbler than usual. Not just physically, but also everything else starting with the death of Pandora up to the Underworld somehow seems alleviated following a sleep that could have lasted a full day.

The grass from where she rose still bears the imprint of her body. She sets to wiping her already sullied white clothes from the certain dirtying of sleeping on the ground, but finds there is in fact nothing to wipe.

She instead runs her hands down the side of her cheeks. The extreme smoothness and sensitivity gives her the impression she wouldn't need even a dab of makeup, not that she really wore any to begin with.

She slides her fingers up through her hair and feels a lot of the same. Just as she begins to enjoy it a little too much, she hears someone approaching from behind.

"Le – oh, hi, Alex."

"You slept well I'd say."

She drops her hands quickly and wraps her arms around her waist. "Um, yeah, thanks." She makes him a quick smile then glances over his shoulder.

"He left," says Alex.

Anastasia looks back into the "young" General. "What do you mean? Where?"

Alex steps a little closer and places a hand on her shoulder, which she allows to remain. "You know why he's here."

"He thinks he can save Mom -- that he's supposed to." She bows her head slightly. The notion sinks in deeper now that Leo's vehemence is not there to insist. She shakes her head. "Either way he's going to need my help, our help. He's almost got himself killed trying to get this far."

A spark of tenderness crosses Alex's eye. He curls the side of his lip and places his other hand on her free shoulder. "I hope he realizes what he has before it's too late."

Anastasia looks up then quickly away. Alex finishes his smile, stepping off to the side.

"It's time to decide," he says. "Know now, that even though your presence may comfort him, there's not much else you can do. Your gift can't save him this time."

Her shoulders slouch as she exhales. She nods nonetheless.

"This was his choice," says Alex, "even I can only guide him. The rest is his fight."

"Fight?"

Alex steps back to face her but offers no response.

"I understand," she resigns.

"Alright."

Alex returns to where he was, but this time stays in position a time looking far afield. Ever so gradually his expression sharpens. "Come on then. He's not far."

The two set off on the same path as Leo. Passing up through the vale and over the hills, Alex sticks to the course while Anastasia views her surroundings. Once in a while that view takes to the skies. Accompanied by one of the Blessed, however, she feels secure nothing would seek to harm her. That is, if anything even exists to harm someone who really belongs there like Alex.

In a few more paces she's looking off to the right. Like Leo, the great tower catches her eye.

"Does anyone live there?"

Alex drops back and glances in the direction she stares. "Omegas mostly. But the realm is primarily ruled by Menoitios."

"Prometheus's brother," says Anastasia. "How did he end up as ruler?"

Alex claps his hands behind his back: a habit he took to later in life when walking in discussion with a student or protégé. "Well, as you know, he was killed by Zeus in the war of the Titans: a thunderbolt to the chest that sent him into Tartaros."

She nods. The War of the Titans, or the Titanomachy, was a conflict between the old Olympian gods and the Titans, sons and daughters of primordial gods Ouranos and Gaia. It arose from an old prophecy stating that one day a son of Kronos would eventually overthrow the father, which led the ruling titan to devour every child he had.

When at last Zeus was born, his mother Rhea tricked father Kronos into eating a rock instead of the baby. Zeus was then given refuge in the safety of the mountains. Once fully grown, he rescued his siblings and declared war on his father. Menoitios took part in this war. Prometheus did as well, going so far as to side with Zeus and aid him in victory. Anastasia never understood how Zeus could strike down Menoitios being the brother of the one who helped him win.

"Wasn't he just killed for being so proud and insolent?"

Anastasia considers all she knows about the Lord of the Underworld: his birth to parents Iapetos and Klymene, his being the most glorious of his brothers. Such glory, however, went along with a violent and rash disposition. Combined with a hubristic personality, it was never going to end well when thrust in the presence of Zeus' own glory and hubris.

With these thoughts of Menoitios in mind, Anastasia looks again to the white tower: the pristine beauty, the elegant construction, the calming tranquility of all it oversees: all *he* oversees.

"He was," Alex replies, "so you can imagine what he was like when he had his chance for revenge."

"The Raising of Olympus."

"Right. Remember, omegas can be imprisoned but they can't die. So it was just a matter of Prometheus freeing him."

They ascend to the summit of one of the larger hills. Down the bottom of the other side, a long row of trees comes into view.

"He went after Zeus, then?" says Anastasia.

"Cracked his skull with that hammer of his. Zeus might have known, Menoitios means "doomed might"."

Anastasia takes another long look at the tower and over the terrain.

"So was this his reward for beating Zeus?"

"In a way; but Menoitios had been down here so long he couldn't be bothered with the living anymore. Aside from that, he can keep watch over Zeus, and the power of the Island can keep watch over him."

Though she struggles to make a stark distinction now, she remembers the feelings passing from the cave to the Isle. Air soothing her lungs like pure aloe; sunless rays flowing through her pores, warming away all the aches of life.

She runs a few fingertips down the side of her cheek again.

"It's true I've never slept the way I did earlier: never in such peace. So maybe it's really the perfect place for him."

"There yah go."

Just then Alex halts. He reassumes the sharpened gaze he put on before they left. It focuses on the woods. This time though, it sharpens to the point of trying to pierce through the density and hone in on something in particular.

Anastasia sees nothing but trees. She waits patiently, then finally opens her mouth to inquire when a booming clap of thunder strikes it shut. The force sends shock waves from a distant sky that penetrate to the internal organs. The echoes reverberate nearly just as strong.

Anastasia claps her hands over her ears and drops down cringing. Alex waits poised until the final echo dies away. Despite the silence, Anastasia still hesitates a moment before uncovering her ears and rising.

She looks off in the direction of the final sound.

"I thought Zeus was in Tartaros?"

"That wasn't thunder. We have to go, take my arm."

Anastasia says no more and obeys. The moment she makes contact the Island disappears.

ΔΔΔ

The giant figure grips tighter on his hammer in response to Leo's impudence.

"I'm Menoitios. Now you will answer my question."

Leo moves into side position but is careful to keep the blade un-conjured in the grip.

"I'm here for my Mom."

Menoitios snorts. "Self-righteous child. There's nothing less she'd rather see."

The notion catches him off-guard. Though hindsight has begun to show him his many faults growing up, it has also shown that his mother never faltered despite the fact. That she had would've been easier to bear.

"I-I'm her son, and I'm getting her out of here."

The great omega leans closer. Though still at a distance of five yards, his towering presence over Leo forces the young mortal to lean his neck back in order to keep eye contact.

"And you thought it would be so easy to take from my realm," says Menoitios. "You're a little boy, Leonidas, come to cry because she made choices you don't understand."

"Choices I don't buy," says Leo regaining his fire. His hand tightens around the grip and he begins to circle. Menoitios stays facing forward.

"She was a good person who trusted in scum like my Dad," says Leo, "who spent her life believing in things like you, and look what that got her."

This prompts a grin from Menoitios. "Your vindictiveness blinds you, little boy."

The mighty omega waits patiently until Leo's completed a full circle and is again to his front. Once clear view is re-established, he goes on with a condescending tilt of his neck.

"What if I told you her sufferings were of your doing: that *you* were responsible for her death."

The comment slows Leo's pace, but only for a second. "Bullshit. Who's being vindictive now."

Menoitios laughs hard and deep. He begins taking small steps to mirror Leo's.

"You're right, Leonidas. Rest assured: it was *I* who planned her demise: I ruined the love of her life, I killed her firstborn, *I* drove your father away."

Leo squeezes his weapons harder.

"I left her with two unruly kids, a disgrace to her name."

"Shut up," Leo grunts.

"Best of all: I gave her the disease that chopped her limb from limb, torturing her mind and body even to the afterlife. *I* killed her,...little boy."

The taunting works. Rage burns away any fear Leo might have had of his powerful opponent. He points his blade in defiance, and conjures it to purple flame.

"You son of a bitch. You son of a bitch! You took her from me!"

With that Leo charges; eyes damp and bloodshot and face of single purpose.

Menoitios raises his weapon likewise, grinning as he sidesteps a savage overhand cut that sends a hard, discorded tone from the aether blade.

Leo off-balance, the omega plants a heavy foot into his side sending him sprawling.

He recovers only to see the devastating hammer raised high above in the shadows. All his energy immediately pours into his guard as the only recourse.

The Lord of the Underworld then brings round Zeus' Bane and unloads a monstrous blow, striking the guard like thunder.

ΔΔΔ

The world dims around Anastasia as though nodding off into a sweet dream. Indeed, she even finds the apple tree by Lake Maquari flush in the prime of summer.

She reaches out. A taste of home would be nothing short of ambrosia during the holidays. Just before she can grasp the apple, however, a shudder jolts through her body, and she wakes standing amongst tall weeds with her fingers around Alex's arm.

"You alright?" says Alex.

The swirl of purple flame in front of her brings her to bearing quick enough. "Leo."

The guard astonishingly prevents any damage to Leo's person, but the force knocks him several feet across the ground.

Two times down humbles his passion. The flame of his weapon abates, and he slowly gets to his feet with a studied look on the omega.

He steadies his breathing through gritted teeth. For a second his blade even goes green. Running his eyes from head to foot, the gruesome scar spanning the breath of Menoitios' torso reassures him that even an omega can bleed: and never has he met one more deserving...

Ducking low he gains the inside with an upward cut toward the groin. Menoitios grins again as he effortlessly blocks that then a series of quick shorthand strikes that follow.

When Leo attempts a lunge, Menoitios uses the hammer head to redirect Leo's momentum. He then in the same motion lands a cross cut to Leo's head with the butt of the hammer.

Anastasia gasps as a light spray of red splashes on the ground. Leo lands just next to it and feels the warmth flowing down his ears. He uses his remaining shirt to wipe what he can before quickly returning to position.

Before he can fully regain footing, however, Menoitios throws a lunge of his own which Leo manages to send high with an upward block. Seeing an opening he slashes for legs the size of tree trunks, but the giant omega jumps as though they were the lightest of springs.

A counter swing of the hammer sends Leo backpedaling. Unable to form a clear strategy with his right hand, he remembers his left and the mechanics of the aspis guard. He presses the button most salient under his thumb. Doing so he hears a click and the guard fall loose in his grip.

"Dodge this, asshole."

With a long stride Leo throws all his weight forward and launches the guard. A green and purple line manifests between the airborne saucer and the handle he retains. The same colors spit off the edges of the projectile as they rotate with the speed and crispness of a well thrown frisbee.

For all its precision, however, Menoitios catches it as though it were indeed nothing more than a spinning piece of plastic. A violent tug follows, sending Leo flying one way and the guard another.

Anastasia rushes to go to him but Alex catches her by the shoulders. He says nothing as she feebly struggles, remaining intently focused on his grandson's next move.

Leo staggers to his feet. A long wipe of his forehead and cheek smear a mixture of mud, sweat, and blood. He stills himself with a heavy exhale. Without guard he switches to a two-handed grip on the blade.

Menoitios' cat and mouse face has now all but disappeared.

The Lord of the Underworld moves to the attack. Overhead shots rain from left and right in strokes as quick as a light blade.

Leo backpedals keeping his blocks defensive and compact. The force knocks him side to side as he only applies enough resistance to avoid being overwhelmed.

Both force and pace quicken, however. In an instant Leo finds himself in an onslaught even Feidor never brought forth. Instinct and guesswork become intertwined.

In one of the two Leo cuts to the left in anticipation of the next stroke. His blade, however, is never met.

Before he can react a hard hammerhead drives into his gut. Menoitios wastes no time following through by sending the butt of the hammer rising into his chin. The impact does not throw him far, but when he falls he drops flat on his back.

The mighty omega walks slowly over toward his beaten challenger. Stopping over him he holds the head of his war hammer inches from Leo's battered face.

"Yield," he commands.

Leo spits a mouthful of blood. His mind and body war over their next move. On one hand, a quick parry and roll to the right might free him of the colossal weapon's reach. On the other hand, seeing that very weapon up close in its full colossal size makes him realize that a few cuts and bruises were a grace compared to the devastation it could cause if its owner actually decided to fight.

Despite any part the omega might've played in his mother's death, he would be no good to her by adding himself to that list.

With nothing else for it, Leo detracts his blade.

"Yield," he says.

Anastasia breaks from Alex and runs straight past the mighty Lord. Kneeling down she immediately tears off another piece of Leo's shirt and starts dabbing the blood from his head and chin.

Menoitios casts her a condescending glance. He then steps aside, and sets his massive arms atop his weapon.

"Alexander," he says.

"Menoitios."

Leo perks up at hearing any type of greeting uttered by a creature who seems to do most of his talking with a war hammer.

"What all does he know?" asks the omega.

Alex shakes his head.

Menoitios probes the fallen mortal and his companion at his side.

"Underneath," he says, "you may be worthy after all:...favored of my brother."

Leo slides onto his elbows but makes no reply. Menoitios, in any case, doesn't wait for one, and turns his back to them in facing the direction of the Isle.

"How fortunate you really are," he says, "to have death as your end; living each moment as its last." He turns his thick neck back down on Leo. "Even that you seek to ruin."

Leo furrows his brow on the immortal Titan.

Ruin?

Though a word he's always associated with death, to consider it in the opposite sense strikes him harder than the butt of the hammer. He thinks of the devastation wrought on Staj's family after the passing of her father: he imagines the misery his mother must have known when his brother Alexi died: he recalls all he's known since she's been gone herself. "Fortunate" is the last term he would apply to that lot.

Still staring up at the Ruler of the Dead, he almost betrays a look of insolence.

Menoitios now turns fully around and folds his arms across his scar.

"I will grant you one chance to reach your mother," he says. "One, chance. The rest will depend on you,...little boy."

Leo lowers his eyes. From his place on the ground, soiled of blood and dirt, beaten in body and spirit, he wonders how dependable he would really be to anybody.

He thinks of leaving to save his mother: all his resolution, all his promise of avenging her of Prometheus and the omegas. His fall seems that much harder now given how high he started from.

Combined with his own behavior toward his mother in life, he begins to consider what truth there may be in Menoitios' comment about her not wanting to see him. And if the rash omega was right about that, Leo fears what else he might have been right about.

What if I told you that you were responsible for her death...

Though inconceivable, the very notion weighs on him so much he's not even sure if he can get up. He then wonders if he should even bother.

Anastasia answers at least part of this question by pulling him to his feet. Leo obliges mainly from lack of will to resist. Still in a daze, Anastasia nudges him toward Menoitios and the pending opportunity he's just been granted.

"Oh..yeah..alright, Menoi...sir," mumbles Leo.

Menoitios glares unamused then turns to Alex who bows in turn. The omega nods, then without further ado assumes his slow walk into the shadows of the field. Little by little his large frame becomes one with the darkness.

Leo watches with eyes half closed. If the great Lord's coming seemed like bringing him to his fate, his going seems like leaving him to his doom. His words undermined everything Leo set out for. One fell swing of the tongue inflicted more damage than several from his war hammer.

With that he dabs his chin with the back of his hand. His skin meets with drying blood and a sharp sting.

"Oh man," he says with flailing energy. "So now what?"

"Now what!?" says Anastasia. She turns on Leo, suddenly not as concerned about the fact he was just nearly squashed like a bug.

She opens her mouth to finish her remonstrance when a rustle in the weeds breaks the silence of the atmosphere. A gentle breeze, and a sun breaks far in the distance on an expanding horizon.

The rays shoot across like an arrow from Apollo. They hit the river bank and the tall weeds crumble into grains of golden sand. Spreading further they push toward the outer expanse uncovering a field of red roses bedded in fragrant grass.

Tree groves spring up in various patches to add intervals to the lovely landscape. Day awakens at all corners.

"Welcome to Elysium," says a strong baritone from behind.

Anastasia's eyes go wide, her hand raises, and she stifles a cry.

CHAPTER 9 – ELYSIUM

All turn but Anastasia. Before them stands a tall man of sturdy build with hands clasped behind his back. Mostly bald, a crown of ruffled blond hair lines the bottom half of his head.

Despite being under the regard of so many eyes, his stern face regards only one amongst them. Little by little it softens on the long sandy blonde that might have resembled his own hair in younger days.

Leo looks hard on what he feels an insolent stare at Anastasia by an unknown. He doesn't imagine Alex would allow anything to harm her, yet his young grandfather *did* just stand by as he got pummeled by an omega, only to say hi to it afterward. In either case, he still holds his blade from that duel, and he now lets it settle back into combat grip.

Oddly enough, though, the more he looks on the man, the more a vague familiarity creeps in. For some reason Hellebore Creek flashes through his mind: running around Emrick's estate as a child with Anastasia, pressing their ears to the door under the staircase, trying to hear what their parents were doing in secret; all this until one parent was no longer there.

Realization passes before Leo's eyes and he nearly fumbles his blade. At the same time Anastasia turns.

"Daddy."

The man smiles as his long-awaited daughter looks into him, eyes welled with tears. Anastasia needs no more than a second before she rushes into his massive arms.

"Hi, Annie," he speaks into her ear.

The sight of Anastasia burying herself into someone's chest takes Leo aback. Always so reserved, he never imagined her showing such open affection, much less toward her long-deceased father.

When he considers her alternatives, though, embracing the dead doesn't seem so strange. With no boyfriend he knows of, a mother more than emotionally absent, and a lack of siblings to commiserate with, her only outlet is a small group of friends who have always treated her more as a stable constant than a feeling person.

"I knew you'd find me," says Anastasia, her voice muffled. "I'm sorry I never came this far before."

Anastasia's father draws her gently away. "It wasn't time."

The comment furrows a few lines on Leo's forehead. He glances at Alex for some visual clarification, but all he gets is a casual look of "search your feelings for answers you should already know," or something like that.

The burly Elysian gazes deeply into his daughter, as though trying to recover all the years he lost in seconds.

"Here you are, all grown and pretty," he says, running a hand through her hair.

Anastasia tries to hold, but a growing smile turns into red on her cheeks. She ends up looking away.

"You're a lucky man, Leonidas," he says. He eyes Leo, a warning Leo heeds more than the attached remark. Anastasia casts her father the same warning glance he casts Leo.

"Uh, yes, sir," says Leo. He approaches with a careful eye of his own.

"Might not say the same for you though, honey." The middle aged man scrutinizes Leo head to toe: starting with the stained sleeve wrapped around his leg wound, continuing to the long tears down the back of his shirt; upward his eyes raise to the other missing sleeve, ending on a face and chin of dried blood under the scars that were already there.

"You look like you fought an omega, son."

"I did."

"Ah, backbone, but no brain."

Both Leo's hands clench, and he begins estimating what it would take to drop a man of his size and training.

"Alright, Silas, don't scare them off too quickly," says Alex, walking up from the side.

Silas Wildyn bows his head, "General, sir."

"Captain."

Alex assumes a slightly greater air of Guard Official than before. Despite his youth and easygoing appearance, Silas doesn't seem to take him any less seriously.

"Leo," says Anastasia. She takes her father's arm. "This is my Dad."

Leo takes a moment to swallow down his indignation before answering.

"Yeah, I kinda got that...even without a brain."

The side of Silas' mouth curls up and he steps forward, extending one hand and keeping the other behind his back. Leo sees Anastasia watching anxiously from the corner of his eye, so he doesn't hesitate too long before extending his own.

When their hands meet, Silas takes him in an iron grip Leo's only half convinced was fully unintended. The power he feels travels well up the arm, well over the torso, and well into something non-material altogether. Leo imagines he must have been hard to kill.

The last of this force he sees in the bright blue radiating from each eye: so much like Anastasia's, and like hers nearly the same hue of the Blessed waters.

Holding eye contact Leo responds with a good dose of his own strength. When it registers on Silas' face, the captain raises his head slightly and looks carefully on the battered youth.

"Well then," he says. "The Maurileho himself."

Leo's grip loosens at hearing his kladimans alias spoken by someone long dead before it was even coined.

Silas's mouth curls again and he releases likewise, stepping back to his daughter.

"Alright then," he says to Anastasia, "let's get you rested." He looks Leo up and down once more. "And a surgeon for these... scratches."

Leo takes a quick glance side to side. "Wouldn't think people need hospitals in Elysium," he says.

"Don't worry, little lion. The water from my grove's a panacea."

A what?

"Let's go."

Silas wraps an arm around a star-struck Anastasia and Alex steps in behind. After a few paces, the General looks back over his shoulder and nods for Leo to follow.

It takes a minute for Leo to relax the face he's put on over Silas. He steps off though, knowing they are at least moving in the right direction of the Styx, and his mother.

Moving into the field, a low draft blows the long blades of grass on a waving tilt, like a loose head of hair by Lake Maquari. Each time it blows a tussle of rose petals springs into the air, taking several seconds to glide to the ground even after the breeze has already stopped. It also sends out a fresh scent with every pass.

At first Leo senses the distinct smell of the roses. Then it starts shifting: first to the velvet of Kalpoor perfume, much like Zoe and his mother wore at times: then to the sweet staleness of autumn, and the myriad of colors flowing over the Appalachia region on the far side of the Vale.

Leo thinks of evenings at the lake with Beren and Zoe, chatting over kladimans feats and admiring the foliage in the distance. He remembers Anastasia joining them, but mostly just admiring the foliage.

He wonders what his friends are doing this day, night, or evening, or whatever it is up above. With all that separates them, he has a hard time deciding if he's stuck in Elysium or they're stuck in Eulimnos.

Leo runs his fingertips over the rose blossoms as he walks.

He imagines what might have been of his conflicts with the White Lion and Menoitios had Beren and Zoe been at his side. Zoe keeping them at bay with the long point of her maolance: Beren disarming with a slight of his twin blades: and Leo delivering the yielding blow: just like in the team division, yet all armed with aether.

"What do you think?" says Alex appearing out of nowhere.

Leo snatches up his hand and wipes it on his hip. For the first time he misses home.

"Nothing," he says.

"I meant about this place?"

Before answering Leo sniffs the tips of his fingers: a robust aroma of baked goods.

"It's alright I guess...a bit like the Isle." He sniffs once more. "There's something different though," he says. "Like, more home. More human."

"People retain their memories here."

Leo looks far into the distance and sees nothing but roses, tall grass, and random groves.

Right. Who I'm meant to see: no one.

He looks to his grandfather. "Looks like you kept yours."

"The Blessed do, but there are many more Elysians. Perhaps you feel what they've brought with them."

Leo thinks more on what he's brought *to* them.

"You see the sun," says Alex. "They have stars too."

Though the sky keeps the strange solid blue of the Isle, a sun at its center does make it seem more like home.

"It gets dark here?" says Leo.

Alex affirms. "And people sleep."

"That's pretty human."

The small ensemble continues toward the groves when Leo begins to notice flickering images over the fields. A closer look reveals silhouettes of what he soon identifies as people. Nothing more can he tell though, because they never fully materialize and dissipate like phantoms after a few split seconds. He does, however, see enough to know these blissful dead do not remain idle in their elysian afterlife:

A pair of burly men grapple through the roses. While they vie to win, neither seem to mind should they lose. Both are nude.

A group of young women wearing long elaborate dresses chase a flower posy through the air. Nothing more do they accomplish than tipping it in a different direction, yet on they chase, on they laugh.

In another area, three men of similar complexion, one old, one young, and another in between, play catch using large leather gloves and a red-laced ball.

Finally, an eternal couple makes love as though they were to die all over again.

Leo shakes his head. "I definitely see *some* people here at least."

"They don't control their materialization like the Blessed, but you still only see glimpses. Don't forget..."

"I'm not one of them I know."

Up ahead Silas veers into one of the wooded areas abundant in a single type of tree. Whitish-gray in leaf and bark, they stand over 30 yards in height and mesh together to form a dense canopy overhead. The upper portions remind Leo of the ruffled hair an acquaintance of his once had in Lyceum.

He stops a moment and takes hold of one of its three pointed leaves. He rubs his thumb over its veins that spread over the surface like veins from a hand.

"It's Leuke," says Alex, again out of nowhere, "White Poplar in common speech."

"Where'd they get 'Leuke,' then?"

Alex takes one of the leaves in his fingers as well. "From the nymph whose name it was. She was taken by Hades, then transformed into this," he says. He waves his hand around the grove, "Metamorphoses."

Hades. One of the old gods, once ruler of the Underworld domain.

"Guess she had a pretty bad day," says Leo. "Hades too when he got his head cracked by Menoitios."

Leo releases the leaf. "Whatever happened to him anyway?"

"Hades?" says Alex. "Oh he's here: down in Tartaros, that is."

A smirk crosses Leo's lips. "Jailing the architect; I hope they changed the locks."

The density of the poplars begins thinning to reveal a wider path as part of an expanded tree bed. Ferns of light red and green array the floor around and about the trunks. The ground itself, while mostly bare, takes on a tint of maroon and accommodates each step as though stepping over clay.

In short time they arrive to the sweet hiss of running water. Just around a bend, a small waterfall feeds a natural pool bluer than the waters of Lake Maquari. The mist it creates floats over the pool in slow motion and sparkles all colors of the rainbow whenever touched by a penetrating ray.

"Home sweet home," says Silas.

Leo looks around for any signs of shelter or human commodities but all he finds are colorful arrangements of flower bouquets and fruit-budding plants set near the water. He supposes the tree canopy would be enough to call a roof.

"Esta en su casa," Silas proudly states.

Neither Leo nor Anastasia react to his welcoming statement.

Silas frowns, "just make yourself at home. Actually, no, come with me."

Silas walks over to the edge of the pool and kneels down. Dipping his hands into the deep blue, he cups and scoops a handful of water.

"Drink this," he says, drinking first himself. "Then go rest." He holds out a hand which Anastasia takes and he guides her gently down.

As she makes to follow suit, however, a splash of water shoots up from the pool soaking her face from hair to chin. Silas laughs before she knows what hit her then splashes again. A match ensues, with the two eventually moving to their feet. Leo watches as Anastasia chases the powerful man like a toddler running after a young parent.

Once they've disappeared into another part of the grove, Leo bends down and takes their place by the pool. He doesn't reach for any water. He simply waits for it to settle, then leans over.

The reflection, clear as a mirror, feels ice cold under the warm sun. The battered face looking up contrasts sharply to the mental projection contained within.

A sullen hand rises in the water and stops over the lines of his scars. Down it traces until moving to the fresh wounds on his head and chin.

The touch of his finger produces a relieving sting. So lightly he presses, then harder until the pain provokes tears.

He focuses his mind past the overly assuaging effects of Elysium and draws forth the dark wounds of motivation, still bleeding from his mother's loss and now affected by Menoitios' taunting words.

These thoughts renew his vitality, his purpose. He seeks not healing but justice, a clarity for which only pain will afford.

The water remains still.

Leo rises and follows the pool line deeper into the grove. The sound of the waterfall amplifies with each step, as well as the spray of the colored mist. Both envelop him in a cocoon apart from the world.

He chooses a spot under one of the larger, more eroded Leuke. Resting his head in the arms of its roots, he watches the bubbles foam into the pool from the falling stream of cascade.

Little by little he closes his eyes. He closes his eyes and opens his ears, listening for the counsel of the white noise.

ΔΔΔ

"Three bodies go missing in the Eulimnos section of Prometheum," says an attractive young reporter wearing a flower in her hair. Behind her stand dozens of mourners and almost as many rescue crews bustling about.

"This is Amara Cruz reporting from Lake Maquari on a day meant only to grieve for one death. Earlier today mourners gathered for the funeral games of Pandora Maquari, former infrimiary and daughter of renowned General, the late Alexander Maquari. After impressive displays of skill and athleticism, Leonidas Maquari, son of the deceased, was set to deliver the eulogy speech when all took a turn for the worse.

"He'd been MIA all day," a tearful friend Zoe Qwynshing explains. "Then he comes all a wreck, saying these random things."

"We figured it was because of his Mom, you know?" says another close friend, Bereniko Braun, son of Statesman Boukoletes Braun. "Then all of a sudden he takes off and dives into the lake. So I'm not really sure."

The scene grew even more puzzling when childhood friend Anastasia Wildyn followed suit.

"Leo was always...special to her," says Miss Qwynshing, "and she was a great swimmer, so it didn't surprise me when she tried to save him, just that she never came back up."

And as if the situation couldn't get more mysterious...,

"Leo was in charge of the funeral pyre," says Master Braun, "which he left down a ways. After we called for help we reeled it in...but it was empty."

Search teams continue to scour the lake and its surrounding areas for any signs of the young man and woman. An investigation is also underway to recover the body of Pandora Maquari in order to complete with the necessary funeral rites. This is Amara Cruz for the *Time's Current.*"

Emergency lights color the white of mourners unsure who to mourn. Idly they stand waiting for any piece of news regarding a disappearance. They attempt not to stare at any unfortunate family members, lest one stares back.

"Look, it's Annie's Mom," says Zoe. The two of them stand aloof of the mourners and the commotion of the crews.

Beren shakes his head. "At least her daughter missing got her outside."

Silas' widow, Zellas Wildyn, sought refuge in drink following her husband's death. A blend of sorrow and resentment toward his companions made for a bitter cocktail for anyone involved with her to swallow.

"Oh, she looks horrible," says Zoe. The aging woman's once gleaming blonde hair now lays disheveled and a few shades faded down her back. Her clothes prove not much better: clinging to more than covering her body in a worn material meant to resemble an evening robe.

"She looks normal," says Beren.

Zoe casts a reprimanding glance. "Maybe we should go to her."

"You can go. She doesn't like me."

"Give her a break, she just..." Zoe's voice cracks. She folds her arms and looks away. "B, it's been a half an hour."

Her face contorts as she keeps a steady look on the spot where their friends submerged. Turning back to Beren she keeps the same look, as though she herself were now the one under water.

Beren lowers his head. "Leo's strong. And Staj...you know. She'd go to hell and back for him. There's no way a lake could best them."

Zoe looks as though she wants to believe him, but instead turns again to wipe her face. Beren nearly does the same. He then pulls his remaining friend into his shoulder.

Lake Maquari buzzes with marine boats and divers ranging an area of probable circuits. Land crews scour the surrounding area, utilizing scent-tracking horses far up the water's edge.

A frazzled Khloe appears followed by a group of civic inspectors. "Beren, uh, guys, these shieldsmen need to check the house, so..."

"Don't worry, we'll be here."

Khloe acknowledges the courtesy with a nod and absent look: an erratic cat declawed.

When she doesn't make to move, Zoe reaches out and offers a consoling squeeze of the hand to remind her the shieldsmen patiently await. Though Khloe doesn't squeeze back, partial awareness returns to her eyes and she goes off with the inspectors. Zoe then returns her head to Beren's shoulder.

She sinks in deeply: clinging to her remaining quarter and obstructing a bothersome earlobe to the sound of their missing friends. Although her eyes remain open and barely blink, they serve only as inanimate mirrors to the commotion passing before her.

"You know," she says softly, "I feel like I'm looking through their lives like they've happened already."

Beren looks away from the drone of lights and motors and peeps down at his friend. For a moment his expression also goes blank. As it then grows darker, he shakes his head sharply to the side and reverts quickly back to the lake.

As he does so he spots his father consulting with search leaders amid the confusion. He tries reading the Statesman's expressions, then tries not to. He eventually has no choice as his father turns to approach.

Statesman Braun keeps a steady, yet careful regard on the two as he makes his way through the field of inquiring mourners. Stopping before them he maintains the same look but doesn't immediately move to speak.

Zoe precedes him by releasing herself from Beren's arm and stepping forward.

"So that's it? They're just giving up?" she says.

"They've done all they can unfortunately."

"What!?"

"They couldn't have just disappeared," Beren says more to himself than anyone else.

Statesman Braun nods in understanding. "More divers will be sent out to the deeper parts of the lake...in case..."

"In case what?" says Zoe.

He places a hand on each of their shoulders and applies a bit of pressure. "I need to find Khloe and Ms. Wildyn," he says.

Zoe shakes him off and steps to the side.

"Khloe's at the house. We'll tell her," says Beren.

The father acknowledges, takes one last glance at Zoe, then moves off.

Beren goes directly to his friend, taking her in his long arms. She resists slightly and keeps her head turned, but once she runs out of places to look she sinks into his shoulder once again.

Across the way Statesman Braun continues in the direction of Zellas Wildyn. The ailing friends follow his own direction for lack of anything appealing to watch and even less of anything appealing to say.

Zellas Wildyn stares hard and indignant at Statesman Braun in his final steps to reach her. As he delivers his message, her withered face turns to scorn as if he'd drowned Anastasia himself.

At that point Beren and Zoe turn their heads to the ground. Little by little the world around them cools to a simmer: mourners leave to mourn elsewhere, motors cease, splashes calm, and the few remaining divers probe out beyond the realm of rescue and into that of recovery. Soon, the simmer goes cold.

Zoe's body goes limp and she nearly slips out of Beren's arms. "This can't be happening," she says, hand over nose and mouth. "Why...why would Prometheus let them die like that?"

Beren bites hard before answering for the supposed champion of men. "Omegas don't control our lives, they only influence our choices."

A hard shove nearly knocks Beren to the ground. Zoe's beautiful brown hair falls over bloodshot eyes.

"So where did THAT choice come from," she says, shaking a finger at the lake.

No reply.

The choke in Zoe's throat conjures a lump in Beren's. A welling of emotion to fill the void once occupied by their comrades. Together they come and release the valve. Together, their friends endure.

They huddle close on the way to the Maquari house still in the white of their sporting outfits. Over the fields they walked so eagerly to come, they now tread with heavy foot to leave.

Passing through the tree line the house comes into view. They see the last of the gray coated inspectors filing out with no great novelty to their step. A frazzled Khloe follows, not so close behind.

Standing in the door port she catches Beren and Zoe approaching from the corner of the property just past Pandora's bench. She examines their faces like Beren did his father's. Once it registers she stomps her foot and lifts her head sharply away.

Zoe scampers ahead and hugs her tightly from behind. Beren follows quickly and wraps an arm around both. Khloe doesn't move.

After a minute she pulls away, fanning her face rapidly with her hands as though struggling to retain any denial that might escape.

"I can't stay here," says Khloe. "Guys, do me a favor, write Leo's legacy. I wouldn't know what to say anyway." With that she leaves.

The two look after her with no words to utter and no motions to react.

"Let's just go in," Beren finally says with little energy, "maybe we'll find something the Shields missed."

Zoe accepts with even less energy, and in they pass through the open door.

The house remains exactly the same as the day before, and the day before that: table to the left, master chamber to the right, kitchen fenestrator above the sink. Once inside, however, Beren and Zoe pause and take long looks around. Little by little they inch their way in, cautious not to disturb the stillness.

"That smell," says Zoe, leading with her nose, "it feels so old."

Beren takes a sniff. "I don't smell anything."

"I didn't mean the odor."

Beren just looks on her a moment and lowers his eyes.

He then steps to the right where he comes face to face with the door of Pandora's chamber. After a long hesitation he leans in and lines up his eye to the thin crack between the door and panel.

Inside, amidst a heap of strewn items, sits Pandora's chair. The solitary item remains positioned as though ready to receive someone. All it receives for now, however, is the dust falling like mist through twilight's rays.

Zoe takes a seat at the kitchen table. She slides her finger into the red flashing comp port and it processes her molecular makeup. A virtual screen then appears demanding her username and password. Completing the required fields grants her access to her satellite drive.

"Quill," she commands.

The screen shifts into an outline of a keyboard and word processor. Her fingers move forward, but don't quite make it to the keys. After staring another minute the following words type out on the screen:

"Leonidas Maquari, born 11/11/2059. Died...kdaekn"

Her fingers tremble over the typos. They then rake through her hair on both sides until settling over the temples. After rubbing a few seconds she makes another attempt at typing, but only ends up leaving the chair altogether.

Beren comes up behind the empty seat and looks at the screen. Once the words register he leans his weight on the table and turns his head to the side.

"You're sure you want to do this now?" he says, partially looking back at Zoe. When she doesn't respond he turns his head all the way.

Zoe catches his eye. Before answering she wipes her face.

"They'll need it soon anyway," she says. Abruptly she moves and brushes by Beren.

Stilling herself she completes her phrase: "13/16/2080."

The month of Meton, named for the classical Pre-Reckoning figure who coined the metonic cycle now used in Prometheum, is an intercalary month that only appears 7 times every 19 years. As such, no candles would be lit for Leo or Anastasia's Moros, the term for the day of their passing, until the next blue moon in 2083.

Beren slowly pulls up a chair.

Both fixate on the screen for quite some time, waiting for either a way to go forward or a way to go back. As neither contribute, the inanimate cursor doesn't either. It counts to a long sixty before anyone speaks.

"I don't even know what to say," says Zoe. She crosses her legs and sets her chin in her palm.

Beren also adjusts in his seat. "What did he have going for him?"

After considering a while she sits back and folds her arms. "He was into music, great guitar player and all that."

"Yeah, and he won at this year's festival," Beren proudly states.

"He probably would have been next year's Festival Artist too," Zoe follows just as proudly.

The rising excitement strikes a harmonious chord to an otherwise discorded character. Both Beren and Zoe get caught up in the moment. As the energy dies, however, so do their faces go down. As it fades completely, they see the harmony was the only real discord of it all.

Zoe slouches and goes back to typing. As the part of Leo's festival win appears on the screen she stops and lifts her fingers.

"Remember when his Dad won?" she says.

"Yeah. It was right before he and Ms. Maquari split up."

The forecast for that year's Festival was only set for cloudy skies. As Aeschylus Serelin took the stage, however, a surprise storm hit, sending many running for cover. Yet Leo's father stayed, and went on to play an original song entitled "Run" which speaks of a broken man afraid to face his demons. Though soaked and chilled, his voice and guitar rang over the fields so beautifully that many suffered the same fate to listen until the end.

"People always thought that song was about Ms. Maquari," says Beren, "but it kind of made me think of Leo's older brother, Alexi."

"How? We never even knew him."

"Most of the song was about the past, and he hadn't separated from Ms. Maquari yet."

Zoe shrugs her shoulder then types a few more letters. Again she stops.

"What's with Leo's Dad though; you think we should mention him too?"

Before Beren can answer Zoe cuts in.

"You think *Leo* would want him in this?"

It takes him no more than a second to have his answer.

"Yeah, not really," he says. "People'll recognize him through his grandfather, and mother anyway."

Though Zoe has her answer, she does not write any words. In fact, she sits back altogether and closes up. Only a touch from Beren's hand seems to rouse any response.

"Grandfather, mother," she says, "brother, Annie..."

She moves off the chair and walks over to the fenestrator.

"My gosh," she says looking out. "That family...*our* family."

Beren stays at her back and buries his chin deep in her shoulder. Both take hold of one another by arms and hands. On this occasion, however, they squeeze much tighter than usual.

Outside a few deep divers resurface at the edge of the Maquari property. None have anything to show, none have anything to hide. As they move off, another apple falls from the tree by the bench.

"Come on, let's go," says Beren in her ear. "We can do this another time."

"No," says Zoe, breaking free. She takes hard steps back to the table and braces herself in the chair.

"What else then?" she says.

Beren hesitates a moment at the fenestrator. With one more glance outside he moseys back to his chair.

Once seated he stays at Zoe's back and keeps his eyes to the ground.

"The obvious one, I guess: The Maurileho. We can't forget about that."

Zoe smiles her first in a while. "I'm sure you wouldn't mind."

"Ha, he had you too."

Best friends and greatest rivals, Beren, Leo, and Zoe competed since childhood, pressing each other's limits to the point that outside competition seemed easy. They bested each other fairly equally when it came to recreational sports, but Leo claimed the edge in hand to hand combat.

"I had to let him win at some stuff," says Beren, making a smirk that quickly disappears.

Zoe stops typing and hangs her head toward Beren. She doesn't make eye contact.

"He got into it heavy after his Dad left."

"Into pankration?"

"And kladimo. I figured it was a way to unload whatever he was going through. And boy did he unload."

The devastation Leo wrought on his opponents at Lyceum was quite brutal at times: hidden anger unlocking hidden skills, unleashing dormant savagery. The sport marked an overall first step into a new world for him.

"Yeah I remember that," says Beren. "He wasn't allowed to spar in school after a while, but then he got into local competitions at the gymnasium."

"And won some too," says Zoe shifting in her seat, "against a lot older guys."

"But then," says Beren. His eyes revert to the floor. "At my grandmother's funeral games..."

Victoria Braun, a contemporary and associate of Alex and Emrick, died a ripe old age of natural causes. In life she was so astute and austere some believed she would humble death into passing her by. Such qualities, however, proved quite productive in the construction of Prometheum.

"It was supposed to be me in the games," says Beren, speaking low. "I was expected to participate a lot as the grandson. But when it came time for the pugilism, my father called me away for something. Leo took my place."

Zoe frowns at the side of her mouth. "It wasn't your fault. Leo was, being Leo, out to prove himself."

Beren keeps his head down.

"*He* got himself that scar, not you," says Zoe placing her hand on his knee.

"I know, I know," says Beren. "Which one was it even?"

"The one *over* his eye."

Beren winces. "Yeah, that guy really got him."

Leo never returned to serious competition in the PK ranks again. He would thereafter typically only don gloves for the occasional sparring session at the gym, or a workout with the Shadow Fighter in the basement.

"You know when I first saw that guy today, I thought it was him," says Zoe. She leans forward and rests her chin between her thumb and finger.

"The guy who beat Coach P?" says Beren. "I thought that too. The style and..., they even looked a lot alike."

Both consider in the ensuing silence.

"Do they even teach that style around here?' says Zoe.

"Not that I can think of. That guy doesn't seem like he's from Eulimnos, or Prometheum even."

"I wonder why he came then."

"Yeah. I wonder."

Neither comment further on the subject. Beren rises and moves about the kitchen while Zoe finds more to type. In the end she's able to summarize Leo's feats at PK as best she can to favorable effect. Anyone reading would think he continued to a prosperous career mixing with the likes of Pux Ramique and Silvio Belmont.

Zoe taps a full stop and sits back in the chair. Crossing her legs, she reflects a time on the screen.

"What about his other scar?" she says.

Beren walks up behind and folds his elbows on her seat back.

"That one cut a lot deeper," he says, "in a lot of ways."

Following his turn at pankration, Leo shifted all his focus into the sport of kladimo. Opting for the mid-size xiphos blade and guard, he trained under the guidance of promethean champion Aero Warner and quickly became a local phenomenon. His victories soon earned him the epithet of "The Maurileho."

"He was on top of the world: winning. Then it all went down...hard."

Zoe looks over her shoulder. "The Pronoia Invitational."

Beren nods. "*Feidor.*"

Considered the greatest all around fighter of the Gemellan Cities, Feidor Yazinov revolutionized kladimo. The emphasis on skill and precision in hand-to-hand combat brought forth an overwhelming challenge to the traditional paradigm of power and speed. His fame led to new training strategies in Pronoian gyms. His undisputed status spread it to Prometheum.

Zoe lays her head in her palm. "You know, though" she says, "Leo beat himself more than Feidor: and a lot over his ex-girlfriend, Thais."

"What do you mean? She wasn't even there."

"She was there," says Zoe. "She wasn't in the crowd, but she was there."

"Well, *I* was there, and all I saw was Leo gassing out and getting caught with a hard cut to the head."

Leo's injuries proved much more extensive than a cut down the side of his eye. With six broken ribs, soft tissue damage, and a destroyed knee joint, he required several months of rehab and home care, which his mother administered despite her own declining condition.

Zoe rolls her eyes back on the screen. She goes on typing. "He *was* one of the youngest to ever compete in that tournament," she says.

After a few more taps on the keyboard she pauses and returns her chin to her palm. "You know," she says, "writing this makes me think how sad it was he wasn't happy."

The comment doesn't earn an immediate response. Beren, in fact, looks away for a time, staring off at the blinking colon of the kitchen clock.

"Leo had it out for the world," he finally says.

"Leo had it out for himself," says Zoe after an equal pause.

The clock continues to count seconds moving into late afternoon. Zoe glances out the fenestrator. The shifting sun beams redder than usual, casting a fiery hue over the rest of the color filled sky.

Turning in her seat, she faces Beren directly.

"With all Leo had going for him, it was just never enough. Losing, or even getting setback would make him bitter, feeling sorry for himself, you know?"

When Beren doesn't respond she places a hand on his knee.

"He was never *going* to be happy, B."

Beren turns his head sharply away. He then rises altogether leaving Zoe's hand to fall on the chair. After a long pause in the middle of the kitchen floor, he turns to his last remaining friend and exhales deeply through his nose.

"He was like my brother," he says. "I don't want to remember him that way. I choose not to."

Zoe rises likewise and stands before him. As their sad eyes meet, her mouth opens ever so slightly, but closes around the hot breath that might have formed any words. She instead just nods.

With only each other left to hold they proceed to do so in wake of the void Leo and Anastasia once filled.

Outside, the red sun sets over a wounded Eulimnos, drawing to a close the 16th day in the month of Meton.

When finally the friends release Zoe makes no further action but to return to her seat. For the next hour she types, cries, smiles, then types some more. By the time she finishes any reader would question the merit of Prometheus to take a life so young, full of promise, and happy.

ΔΔΔ

Leo wakes to the white sounds of falling water. Millions of particles a million different ways dropping to create just as many frequencies that mix into one. Nothing more homogenous, nothing more monotonous, yet nothing more soothing than the beautiful blend it creates.

Behind Leo's eyelids flash red images of virtual screens. They bounce around his mind in the form of symbols, letters, and phrases. He keeps his eyes closed, though, and remains on his side until all fades completely.

Rolling onto his back he returns to the rich dome of blue under which he's either fallen out of or into a dream.

All the same.

The synthetic sun afforded to Elysians burns high above the land so far under his own. He hopes a ray would somehow reach his mother in whatever darkness she finds herself. Something to tell her he's coming.

In the meantime he reverts his mind to precisely that land he calls his own. There he finds the lot of Beren and Zoe's words still lingering. They begin circulating the more he focuses, and soon grow into a whirlwind he only provokes by trying to calm.

When he finally manages to bring them together, they settle like a torch in the pit of his stomach.

They think I'm dead.

He takes a deep breath, inhaling the sweet scent of green. It savors of freshly cut grass on a dewy morning in Eulimnos. It's the most he can ask for against the notion of his companions thinking him deceased.

I guess they would.

The water-muffled voices of his other companions remind him that he indeed isn't, not here at least, yet. That he still feels life it never occurred to confront death. Running into a lake was not a question of drowning. In the third person, however, it was suicide.

Taking into account the scene he occasioned to mourners doesn't bother him. Considering he did not take into account his friends, does. He can still feel his own absence in the vicarious tones of Beren and Zoe's consciousness.

Leo rolls back onto his side. The noise serves to drown out the Underworld around him. When he closes his eyes, he almost feels like he could reconnect to the minds of his friends just by quieting his own to the point of silence.

Until now he's not really thought about the significance of tapping into the thoughts and experiences of others across dimensions. Perhaps starting from a surreal dimension itself sets the bar on what to consider natural and otherwise. This compared to fleeting visions on mundane Eulimnos.

It amazes him to note how all-encompassing his perspective was of Beren and Zoe: one mind, really.

He'd almost believe it a positive thing until he remembers there's a reason why people are conditioned to not speak their mind so openly about others.

So I'm a proud and bitter "could have been" who pities himself.

While he reeled at the fact of seeing his own legacy written, it was the unwritten that carries a much more permanent stamp.

A heavy drop of indignation seeps into the long running well of affection he holds for his friends. He wonders if Anastasia would think as they do. He then remembers it was only one who risked "suicide".

Only one.

Leo rises and makes toward the direction of the voices he heard earlier. Walking along the sweet flowing pool he runs a hand along the jagged surface of his scars: scars wrought by fist, blade, and perhaps other things, as his friends would think.

The violence of all three churn about into a ball of confusion: victory, defeat, bitterness and pride. They sear in his chest, and would pierce his heart but for nearly tripping over a slumbering Anastasia.

Curled up on a bed of yellow, white, and blue, her light blonde hair completes the tapestry of flowers. They make room for her as if they knew she were coming, and welcome her home as though she were born of the same roots.

Her father was right, he thinks regarding her.

Her purity of complexion and heart diverges sharply to the battered form standing before her.

She is the unlucky one.

Leo tries to see under her eyelids to know what she dreams, willing it a beautiful dream that would carry her home. He wonders if his not existing would free her of a burden, then considers his existence free of hers.

The thought empties a part of him he didn't realize had any substance to void. Experiences torn in half in the absence of what made them whole. A panic ensues, followed quickly by the process of replacing her in the memories that comprise most he's lived of his short life.

Once rebalanced, he again considers the burden of her existence.

Harmony, peace...

Staj.

He begins leaning down. He's just placed a knee at her side when a booming voice nearly throws him down altogether.

"Leonidas!"

Leo scrambles to his feet, attempting to avoid the opening eyes of Anastasia waking with him so close.

"Uh, yes, sir..." he says to her father standing with his arms akimbo.

"Get your blade. It's time for training."

"Training?"

"Training. Something you young punks think you don't need after you win a match or two."

Leo stares hard after Silas as the brawny captain makes his way out the grove. He then glances down at Anastasia, who gives him only a shrug and sleepy smile in return. With an aggravated flick of his hand he trots off toward the tree where he dropped his weapons.

Silas abruptly turns up ahead.

"No guards. Let's go."

Anastasia sticks her head up as they make their way through the trees. When they've almost passed out of sight she jumps to her feet and scampers after a few steps. She watches until they reach the fields. Once gone, a squinty smile comes to her face which she takes her time to enjoy. It still remains when she turns to go back to her bed of flowers.

"You picked a nice place to crash," says Alex walking over from the pool.

"Crash?"

"Never mind." He grins. He then surveys the ground around which he and Anastasia stand. The grin returns, this time complemented by a nod.

"The Bouquet of Persephone."

Anastasia moves quickly to the side at knowing she stepped on something with a name. She then takes a closer look at the bed she spent the "night" on: yellow stigmas of Crocus, blue bulbs of Iris, white petals of Lily.

"These were the flowers Persephone was collecting when the old god Hades took her," says Anastasia.

"That's right."

She bends down and takes a sniff: another, then again even deeper. With every breath the flowers lean in closer her way.

One of the lilies next to her comes so far as to touch her skin. Though she giggles and recoils from the tickle, she stays where she is.

With more and more flowers abounding, a shift in the sun splits rays through a different break in the canopy. One of them finds the spot of the Bouquet. As the fresh light drapes the petals, they spread and start pumping as though sucking on their mother's breast.

Anastasia's eyes glow as she looks around her spot. She then follows suit by claiming some of the sun for herself.

Holding out a hand she turns it over and over slowly under the growing warmth. A smile comes to her face. Then, in the rays bathing her palm, light particles of crystal pollen rise into the air. She waves at them with the back of her hand causing them to scatter and swirl.

Looking down she sees the source: the entire bouquet drawing breath at once: stigmas and stamen opening to release their ecstasy of seed in perfect concert.

The fragrance intensifies with each release, bombarding the senses. Cream, spice, clove-like sweetness enter Anastasia's nostrils like the smoothest of vapors.

Her eyes close at will. She reverts to sniffing, then inhaling altogether. As the clouded aroma grows larger Anastasia brings her hand in and grasps her virgin colored shirt. A few more breaths and she's clutching outright.

A few more: and all is released.

She opens her eyes to a still bed of flowers. The sun has shifted, and no sparkles pepper the air.

She turns her head slowly to find Alex a few feet off. He stands with his back against a tree, arms crossed, failing at fighting off the grin that wants so much to form on his lips.

Anastasia quickly looks away. Eyes darting in all directions down she runs a finger across her own lips while risking a few glances back at Alex.

The young general does his best to catch one and hold a reassuring eye complimented by an unassuming laugh.

"Persephone had good taste, no?" he says.

Anastasia finally commits to facing him and is able to return a timid smile.

"Yeah," she says, "good taste."

She looks back down on the flowerbed and remains in observation for some time. Her face slowly changes into something of deep thought. Extending a hand, she gently brushes the vibrant blue of the Iris.

"I've always believed in Prometheus and the omegas," she says, still rubbing the petal. "But sometimes I wonder what stories like that really mean."

Alex walks over and sits cross-legged beside her. He doesn't respond, but tilts his head slightly in her direction.

"I mean, are they real?" she says. "Or just allegory?"

Off in the distance, through the pillars of trees, a clash of aether blades sings over Elysium. Harsh, staccato tones mix with the bronze harmony of baritone. Though distinct, the precision of their orchestration indicates only the most trained of hands.

"Well," says Alex. He keeps an ear to the chorus and an eye to Anastasia. "What *is* real?"

The question draws her from the sound but doesn't elicit a response. She raises a brooding eyebrow in Alex's direction. Still considering, she reaches down to the blue Iris and touches it one more time.

"Is it what you see with your own eyes?" Alex goes on. "If so, who'd believe you're here."

"I believe I'm here," she says.

"Well, there yah go. I think it's all much more subjective than people realize: reality is what you believe to be true."

The statement brings some relief to Anastasia's struggling expression. "So," she says looking back at Alex, "it's really about choice?"

"And faith. For some it comes easier than others."

The comment earns him a warm, trusting smile from his former protégée. "It must have been easy for you then," says Anastasia.

Alex chuckles and sits back on his hands. "I was a non-believer half my life."

The trusting smile becomes a pair of wide eyes. "Really?"

"There were all kinds of religions in my time," says Alex, "I never took to any of them."

Anastasia stares at Alex's mouth as though rainbow colored bubbles were pouring out. She then looks down and shakes her head. "At least I know where Leo gets it now."

Alex smirks.

Off in the distance the blades continue to ring. Not having noticed before, Anastasia now sees that the flowers tend toward the sounds of Leo and her father. A quick survey of the area shows other plant life doing the same.

Most astonishing, however, is the position of the sun: where a second ago rays were piercing the canopy of the grove, there now remain none in sight. In fact the sun has shifted its position altogether. Far over the fields it presently shines in a location that would have taken hours to reach back in Eulimnos.

Anastasia just stares off.

"So what changed that for you?" she says, turning back to Alex.

"As I'm sure you know," he says, "Christianity was the most widespread religion before the Reckoning. In this part of the world at least."

She nods.

"It started to decline heavily at the turn of the century. I wasn't the only one, you see."

"Was it because of the wars?"

"Later, yes. But at first it was mostly skepticism."

The pre-Reckoning man, likely speaking in the form he was in those times, sits up, then forward. He places both elbows on his knees and two fingers around his chin. His aspect takes on an air of distance and regret.

"Then *some* Christians got desperate," he goes on. "Sects started forming, radicals who thought the reason people were losing god was because people no longer *feared* god."

Anastasia shifts her body his way. After facing, and considering him for a time, she says, "So they brought back the fear."

Alex nods. "And essentially that's what they called themselves, The Fear."

Eulimnan history notes the Pre-Reckoning groups once known as terrorists. As with anything dealing with perspectives, however, historical facts often become biased and distorted, focusing more on overt acts than the ideologies behind them. Alex, though, did not need history books, nor was he looking to write any.

"It wasn't just Christians of course. Islamic terrorists existed for years before, but their reach was limited. The Fear was at home, and a lot bigger."

"Did they cause the Reckoning?"

"No. They were a snowball of an avalanche. What they did do was put a sour taste in people's mouths over Christianity. It wasn't fair of course, because they were just a few bad apples of a group whose true believers stood for something totally different."

Anastasia, though affected by the tale, takes on a brighter face and proud smile. "Is that when you revived the omegas?" she says.

Alex shakes his head. "It wasn't me who brought back the gods of antiquity."

General Maquari is often credited as the conduit of mythological renaissance. His leadership under the guidance of Prometheus instilled a following of the old Titan in the stronghold of the Atlantic region and what was to become Prometheum. The Sacred Rains falling over the Final Battle solidified this image and marked the end of the Reckoning.

Anastasia, at Alex's revelation, looks on him as though speaking to a phantom from another world.

"Relax sweetheart, I'm not a fraud. It just so happened that during the time of the Fear there was a young presidential candidate named Sage Watkins who had a background in the Classics. Now I doubt he believed in anything he was saying, but he was able to take advantage of all the distaste brought on by the terrorists to offer an alternative: ancient Greek culture."

Modern Protheans typically shirk at that expression, as though parts of their own culture were recycled rather than first-hand. Anastasia is no different.

"It had already started really," Alex continues. "In movies, TV, literature, art; people were getting into it through the media. The iron got hot and he hit it: hard; it was brilliant."

Anastasia's face grows longer. "How could media make people believers?"

Alex lets out a hearty laugh at that comment. "Back then, the media was more powerful than any god or omega. It could put you under a spell with its language, and blind you with its images: to anything other than their agenda of course. It was like Big Brother all over again."

"Big Brother?"

"Oh," says Alex, "never mind. In any case you wouldn't understand growing up in Prometheum. These days the word 'media' isn't even used the same way."

Alex returns his chin to his finger and looks off toward the fields.

"It's funny though, right? Our faith. Of all the holy reasons you'd like to tell your kids, in the end it was all a game of politics."

Anastasia stays silent for some time, mostly staring blankly at the ground. When a break in the aether chorus cuts over the sky, it rouses her a bit and she looks back at Alex. "So...this President Watkins: was he the one who converted you?"

"No," Alex snorts. "I liked it out of general interest, but I wasn't buying into it any more than that."

A ray of hope crosses Anastasia's face.

"My 'conversion,' as you would say, was genuine. When I was a teenager I started having these dreams--random stuff at first, or so I thought. Eventually though, they started forming patterns, patterns that once I learned to recognize, I was able to use to predict events in my life."

"Like Leo?"

"Like Leo. Only he rejects what he has. Abilities, you see, aren't gifts: they're tendencies. Seeds that are planted but won't grow unless you cultivate them. And that starts by accepting them."

Her face brightens at the notion. The insight resonates. The seed was what led her to the underwater elm as a child, acceptance what got her through to the Underworld as a young adult.

"Leo's time will come," says Alex confidently, again glancing at the fields. "I dismissed mine too in my own way."

"What do you mean?"

The aether blades recommence from beyond the grove. Now a longer legato collides with a firm base: like a heavy wave crashing into rocks.

"Well, prophetic dreams were nothing new. People had been claiming to have them for centuries, whether legit or not. So one day I got curious and googled it."

"Googled?"

"Oh, right. I mean I performed a web search to acquire the necessary information," says Alex, spelling out the words with his hands. He smiles.

Anastasia stares a moment longer before his words register. "Oh, yeah, you beamed it," she says.

"Beamed?"

"Never mind."

The two fake straight faces for a minute, then break into the laughter they used to share when they chatted as old man and adolescent. Around them a few of Persephone's bouquet abandon the music and redirect toward the laughter. Some even open into cup shapes like radio dishes.

Alex's face relaxes first, "and that's how I found him: that's how I found Prometheus."

Anastasia carries her laugh despite herself. "The founder of Eulimnos found himself on the net."

"Would you rather I said I found myself listening to a river like the Siddartha?"

"The Sidd...I won't ask."

"'The Titan of foresight,' the website read." Alex curls two fingers in each hand for quotation marks. "Just a myth: but the more I read the more I got interested. And the more I got interested the more I started opening myself up to the possibility. Then, it was like he was with me all the time."

Alex again leans forward and looks off a ways. He allows the natural sounds to reclaim the ambiance.

"My dreams became visions under his guidance," he finally says. He then turns his head sharply back at Anastasia and slaps his knees with both hands. "Then something else funny happened."

Anastasia makes an overly pronounced nod and nearly rolls her eyes. "You became General by betting on a dromo race?"

"No. Well, not quite. Back then there wasn't mandatory public service, or a 'draft' as we'd call it. You either went in out of high school or joined ROTC in college."

Terms as foreign as another language, the younger generations of Prometheum struggle to recall their lessons on the historical equivalents of Lyceum, Admiral's School, and the Academy.

"So I joined the Marines and did my ROTC at Penn State." Blank stare.

"But instead of majoring in STEM, I studied philosophy, learning more about Antiquity."

"That was the funny part?"

"Oh, right, no. The point is, I was only a second lieutenant when things got crazy: eventually so crazy that I often found myself giving more orders than taking. Squad fighting, guerilla fighting." His head and hands stress every word he says. The words seem to animate reliving the times.

"I'd win more often than not thanks to my particular 'gift,'" again with finger quotations. "Even though there was no time for official promotion, the results brought more and more people under my command."

"So how did you become General?"

"Right, the funny part," he says. He points his index finger in the air. "You see by that time I was firm in my beliefs, so I didn't keep quiet about how I kept winning and who was to credit. So oddly enough, after all that time not buying into President Watkins' scheming, I became the very poster boy for his campaign."

Old broadcasting often depicts General Maquari alongside President Watkins. The vibrant, wild salt-and- pepper haired politician shaking the arm off the handsome soldier waiting for his hand back.

"It always seemed like you two were the best of friends!" says the girl who just discovered some singers lip-sync.

"I was his own Jesus Christ. Once I came along there was no need for speculation. I was living proof of his claim on the old gods. As you can imagine, he won the election, and when he did, he made me General." Alex concludes with a slight frown.

Anastasia mirrors the frown, but with an added pinch of empathy. She then leans her head around, making sure she catches his eye.

"History would have been a lot different without you," she says, holding his regard. "You earned that title, Alex, through choice, not politics." She touches his knee.

The General of modern legend takes a moment, but ultimately places a hand over hers. "Thanks, sweetheart. I'd like to think so anyway."

Leo and Silas return a moment later from their training: no signs of trauma or even sweat: just keen eyes from heavy concentration. Overall neither appears the worse for wear, though any worse for Leo might have meant not returning.

"Your boy here isn't half bad," says Silas addressing Alex, but looking at Leo. "He might make it out of here yet."

Leo huffs through his nose. "I'll send you a facepost at Yuletide."

"Thank you, Captain," says Alex.

Leo brushes by Silas and makes to set down his aether blade.

"No, Leo. It's time to go," says Alex.

Anastasia jumps to her feet. She begins looking frantically back and forth between Alex and her father. "Do we have to? We just got here. Leo should rest a bit and..."

A strong hand on her shoulder halts her discourse. Her father leans his bald forehead down at her and smiles reassuringly. "It's alright, Annie, I'll be going along too."

Relief crosses her brow. Silas pulls her deep into his side and whispers in her ear, "You didn't think I wouldn't be spending every minute with my little girl while she's here, did you?"

Through tightly shut eyes and seeping tears, Anastasia manages a smile.

"Besides, I couldn't let Orpheus here have you all to himself," he adds, leering at Leo. He gets a scoff in return.

Leo steps off a short distance away. He places his hands on his hips and looks out through the trees of the grove.

More and more as the adrenalin wears off from his training does the pain from his wounds come back. More so, the pull to the west he felt on the Isle of the Blessed from both in and out of his dream. The pull in his chest: the call to his mother.

He doesn't waste time trying to reconnect to what he already knows is there. Rather, he marches straight over to Alex.

"Is it time to get Mom?" he says in low tones. He follows by taking hold of Alex's arm. "Are we headed to the ferry?"

Alex looks on his grandson then down at his arm. "Not yet," he says. He pats Leo's hand. "We have other realms to pass through first."

When Leo's grip tightens, Alex simply brings around his other hand and applies a small amount of pressure to the area on the inside of Leo's thumb. The grip quickly releases and Alex walks away.

Leo puts on a sour look as he massages his pressure point. Indeed, the mention of "realms" in the plural did not escape him. Odd, he finds, he can only think of one other navigationally necessary. Nonetheless, he decides not to pursue it further, knowing they would at least be moving westward.

"Alright, off we go," Alex announces. "Off to find the Ring."

"What?" blurt Leo and Anastasia in unison.

"Oh, right, never mind."

CHAPTER 10 – THE PLAINS OF ASPHODEL

The Maquaris and Wildyns make their way from Silas' grove back to the rose fields. Leo takes up the rear. When the others have passed far enough out of sight, Leo stops and takes one last look at the waterfall. He then turns West, and no other direction thereafter.

Once out they hug the tree line, heading further and further away from the world they know as real. On the way they pass by an assortment of fruits ripe to Elysian freshness. Green, red, orange, yellow: they seem to appear as fast as Leo can imagine them. The Maquaris, at least, pick eagerly to their liking.

Leo wonders if Elysians even need to eat -- or himself for that matter being in Elysium. Hunger doesn't nag at him like it did in the world above. Nonetheless, the sweet spectrum of colors lining fruit bushes as tall as Beren and thick as Silas makes him realize he doesn't care.

"So how was your training?" says Alex, biting the last of a strawberry.

The question delays in reaching Leo's ears as he gazes off toward the western horizon. When it does, he wipes the watermelon juice from his face, spits a few seeds, and says, "Alright, I guess."

Alex picks another and eats, glancing back at Leo between bites. "And that's it? You must've learned something; Silas knows what he's doing with a blade."

"I don't need blade training."

"Not with most blades, perhaps, but a blade like that you do."

Leo looks sidelong at his grandfather and takes a final bite of his watermelon. Chucking the rind in the bush, he recalls his session with Captain Silas Wildyn.

"An aether blade's an extension of you. If you're not at peace in here," says Silas tapping a thick finger on his chest, *"you can't be at peace with it."* He awaits Leo's move in full concentration.

Leo attacks, barely heeding his council. He delivers savage blows with a darkened blade until Silas parries him off balance with the last.

"Hear how it sounds? Rough, and deep."

Another series of hard cuts confirms the auditory observation, the blade reverberating like an old organ.

"Think orchestra, not Scars of Bourbon. Flow..."

The latter term brings him not to Chopin but to his mother's favorite song. For although he abhors it in general, he cannot deny the sonorous quality of the guitar solo which he now plays through his mind.

Swinging his blade in his next offensive, the organ becomes a light synthesizer.

"Not bad, but power only goes so far. Know when to take instead of give."

Another exchange, and Leo allows Silas to take more initiative. He does his best to wait patiently until finally the burly Captain commits too much weight to one side and Leo gently redirects him off balance.

"Better," Silas grumbles, recovering his posture. *"Now, your hand. It can crack a man's skull, or rub your baby girl to sleep; just by thinking. The hand is the limb to the blade. Think, and the blade will obey. React with a clear mind, and you won't have to think."*

Leo takes a deep breath, tuning his mind to his opponent's. Silas moves first, but Leo has already countered. He feels the weight of the blade adjust to the type of maneuver he dictates. Everything moves in slow motion to the point that when Silas offers his midsection, Leo spots the hair on his flesh before striking with the flat of his weapon.

Silas nods. *"Now look at your color."*

Leo lifts his blade to reveal an opulent blue, rich as the Elysian sky.

"Your anchor's blue."

"Why's yours bright red?"

Silas' face hardens and takes on the shade of his blade. "The blade tunes to the person, and peace of mind is different for everyone. Enough talk, boy. Let's go."

Leo grabs a strawberry in passing before he responds to Alex's statement. He takes it down in one bite.

"I got what I needed out of it," he says after a long pause. Finishing, he disposes of the sepal.

A soothing breeze dances across the fields, churning the fragrances of the rose buds. The sun lowers ahead. Its setting seems like the falling sands of an hourglass extinguishing the time granted him by Menoitios. Approaching the end of the tree line, he picks one last fruit from the brush and quickens his step.

No sooner do his teeth sink into a juicy pear than a great heap of palatial ruins appears to the right beyond the trees. Broken pillars around a solid foundation of a design made for royalty. A blemish in an otherwise flawless realm.

Leo nearly ignores it but asks anyway, "What's all that?"

Alex now matches his step to his grandson's apparent haste. He gives him another minute to note the remains, especially the marble texture of the collapsed roof.

"No guess?" he says.

Anastasia falls back with her arm around her father's waist. After a quick glance she says, "I think it was the palace of the old god Hades."

A smile comes to her father's face. "That's right, Annie." He squeezes her shoulder, "I'm glad to see *someone* payed attention in Lyceum."

The slight earns him another scoff from Leo.

"This is where the Olympians made their final stand," says Alex. "Their last stronghold, guarded by spells and other creatures."

"Like the Hekatonkheires?" says Anastasia.

"The Hekatta what?"

"The Hundred-Handed, right," says Alex.

Leo turns his eyes toward to the ruins to avoid the looks of smugness burning into the side of his head from Silas.

Examining the breadth of the foundational slabs he can only imagine their composition in Promethean terms. To see them as they are now, snapped like twigs, brings even further awe as to the sheer force it would have taken to drop such a structure in rubble.

Leo muses, "that must've been a hell of a fight."

"Not as much as you might think," says Alex. "Especially with Prometheus calling the shots. You see, this fortress was well protected, so he knew cunning would be the only way to make any kind of end.

"How did he do it then?" says Anastasia.

Alex points upward. "He used the sky to draw out Zeus."

"I thought this was considered a different cosmic realm to the one back home?"

"Exactly."

"Well, Zeus must've known that, no?" she says.

"He did. But he assumed his brother Hades had control over everything. So when he stepped out to face Menoitios in single combat, he thought he would have the full power of his thunderbolt, but he was wrong. The powers of gods and omegas don't extend to the primordial."

"Prometheus knew that, Zeus didn't, and it cost him a hammer to the skull!" bellows Silas.

"Cut off the head and the body will fall," says Leo, mostly to himself.

After a few more hurried steps he finds he no longer hears any patters behind him. He turns to see the others have veered off toward the fallen palace. Throwing up his arms he doubles back and considers going on alone. The image of the White Lion, however, checks his rashness, considering what happened the last time he broke from Alex.

He thus pauses, looks hard on the setting sun, and slowly pivots his weight in the direction of the scrap pile of scenic attraction.

Coming up from behind he still remains aloof of the party. The shadows cast on the ruined palace do not extend as far as he might have imagined given the sharp angle of the sun. Indeed, though the sky starts to show some color, it is still nothing like the Promethean sky back home. Observing such phenomena, he nearly trips over one of the many slabs strewn about the grass and roses.

Nobody notices. He then maneuvers through a few pieces until coming to one of the pillars. Leaning down to touch it he's surprised at how smooth the surface is for concrete. He's even more surprised at how cold it feels given the fertile climate of Elysium, almost as if the pillar itself once had life.

Seeing the damage and how brutally that life was taken makes him think of the wrecking aptitude of Menoitios' war hammer.

He touches his head and chin.

He then recalls Zeus came *out* to face him.

"How did the palace get wrecked?" he asks without looking up.

Alex takes a few steps his way. "Well," he says, "there was the initial onslaught, but the rest was the duel. Don't forget, even without his thunderbolt, Zeus was still Zeus."

The destruction inflicted to the great fortress makes Leo realize just how much Menoitios was toying with him. Studying the patterns of impact, he imagines Zeus taking his brother's trident as defense against the hammer. Monstrous blows pass between them, leveling pillars and heaving bodies until Menoitios cuts sharply to the right and...

"Leo," says Alex. He and the others stand together waiting in the fields. "Time to go."

Leo looks to where they all were a second ago, then back at where they are now. Abruptly rising he glances down at the pillar once more. Just an old slab of rock.

The four continue until the light of Elysian fire begins to fade. Darkness falls on the distant horizon and begins its slow steady crawl from one side of the dome to the other. Flowers close the closer it approaches.

Leo pays it little mind walking with his head down. The diminishing roses underneath pass in a red blur: his steps the beat of a lonely bass.

When he finally does look up, he realizes the sun shouldn't be setting in the direction they're moving at all. A panic sets in thinking they might be going east: the wrong way. He twists in his tracks and remarks the sun not actually setting in any direction. Its rays beam as high and bright as ever in what would be a few hours behind in Prometheum. Bright as they may be, though, they only fan out to a certain extent.

He at first dismisses it to another oddity of his surroundings: why would rays extend all the way over people who don't even want to be seen. He then notes that in the few seconds he's thought about it, he's been looking directly at the sun without being blinded himself.

The mental realization makes him turn his head more than any actual hurt to his eyes. Without risk of harm though, he takes a chance looking back at the natural phenomenon he would not likely be able to look straight at again.

Though typically depicted as yellow or red, Leo senses more a neutral color as if all the colors of the sphere had been blended into one. Though typically of flame he finds the topography to closer resemble a flowing sea of lava. Finally, though normally neglected in a direct sense, he wonders if its rays do not reach all corners on purpose: he wonders if here *it* wants to be seen too.

Taking in the benevolent ball of fire, he thinks on how dependent people really are of its warmth, light, and energy to even live. In that sense it doesn't surprise him civilizations in history would worship it as a god. In fact, it makes much more sense than worshiping a character on a page that only survives through the sensational stories people believe. Who gives who life really denotes the nature of power and what is worthy of reverence.

In such vein of thought Leo lowers his eyes. He reclaims his step but does not bother to catch up with the others.

Moving into the growing darkness of whatever direction Elysium feels like calling it, a new light begins to shine. Little by little specks of sparkling glitter freckle the sky. The more that appear the more they take form, and the more that take form the more they become identifiable as the patterns of stars.

Constellations foreign to Eulimnan eyes drape the sky in an array of clusters. When taken as a whole they seem to take on the form of a geographical place with fixed boundaries, resembling a map. Brightness varies across the board, and every few seconds a star shoots out.

"There's another one," says Anastasia pointing across the sky.

"Do you know what they're for?" says Alex.

She hesitates. "I know they're particular to this realm, but... no."

"They're people," answers Leo, appearing from behind. He stops and throws his guard over his shoulder.

"Good, Leo," says Alex.

Leo makes sure to appear extra proud for Silas, who grits his teeth while trying not to notice.

"Each star represents a living being and his/her vitality," says Alex.

"So, the brighter the star, the greater the spirit," says Anastasia.

Alex nods, "And when they become shooting stars,..."

"They die," says Leo.

"Yes, they join us."

Leo imagines how his mother's must have been. Despite her horrid condition, there is no doubt her vitality would have rivaled the brightness of the reverent, temperamental sun of Elysium.

Thinking of where she died he stares up and widens his perceptions. He runs his eyes from side to side, then allows his mind to assume control of the picture. Little by little a framework takes shape.

"If I had to guess," he says, "I'd say those two big ones over there are the Gemellan Cities."

Alex nods. "And Eulimnos?"

Leo concentrates. He relaxes his acuities to sift through the mess of sparkle. Finally, a profile of something he would see on a Sat-Scan map catches his attention. "Right there: the oval one on its side."

He does not wait for Alex's confirmation. Maintaining his focus the oval soon expands into a large map unto itself. Bodies of water emerge, including the all familiar northeastern lip of Lake Maquari.

Following his senses brings him to the boulder over the elm, then to his very own home. Inside he finds two individuals rummaging through files and belongings.

His files and belongings.

Beren.

Zoe.

He quickly breaks the connection.

"What is it?" says Anastasia.

Seeing his friends as they were in his dream reaffirms his assumption it wasn't actually a dream at all.

It also reaffirms his fears.

The chilling threat of his mother's body being burned before he reaches her now becomes a cold reality. He always assumed there would be search parties of Shields and Inspectors. He never thought it would be his own friends to undermine him. He doubts his friends ever thought they'd be the ones to condemn his mother. Without a clear conscience, Pandora cannot pass to anywhere a clear conscience would go .

Time was running out.

Anastasia looks back and forth between the star filled sky of Elysium and the star dazed head of Leo. "How do you know it's Eulimnos?"

"What?" says Leo. "Oh, I dunno, just look."

After lingering on him a second longer, Anastasia turns and peers up at the sparkling tapestry. Her eyes strain, then squint. Her face assumes a level of energy like to how Leo's looked. Hers, however, struggles and falters.

She sighs.

"Annie," says Silas, "they're not going to change for you. You got to look past the surface. Pick your spot and ease your mind."

Anastasia looks up at her father then back on the stars. She does all she can to abate her forced will in favor of a gentle reciprocal exchange.

At one point her eyes brighten and shoulders start to rise. After another few seconds though, that strained look returns to her face and her body begins to tense.

"Easy sweetie," says Silas, rubbing her shoulders. "Don't force it."

Relaxing, however, she loses the connection, and her shoulders slouch.

Yet before she can accept defeat another pair of hands assumes position. Comforting, though not rubbing.

Under the touch her shoulders regain posture. She hears directions from a familiar voice but doesn't care to turn and see who. Her eyes blink long and slow, and her neck tilts gently back.

"Stay loose," the voice indicates, "give yourself over. Take in what they have to show."

At these words the haze lifts to reveal an eagle eye view of the Maquari home. Zooming in, Beren and Zoe sit solemnly preoccupied at the kitchen table. They do not speak, just remain close. Nothing moves but the cursor to the clock over the stove.

She adjusts her view to her own home, where her mother sits in similar circumstances weeping over a bottle. The woman's dirty blonde hair mats to her face: some from tears, some from snot. She curls up in the nightgown she never really takes off and pours over old family pictures showing her as a young, healthy, beautiful woman standing aside a strapping soldier in uniform and holding a baby girl with hair of the father.

Anastasia pulls away, closing her eyes. "I don't want to see anymore."

The hands don't move and neither does she. Something about them wraps the painful images in a cocoon of protection that, if wrapped long enough, would grow wings and fly away as something beautiful.

Finally, she turns ready to thank Alex for his guidance. She instead finds Leo, and her tongue fails.

Their eyes gravitate and lock. Even Leo fumbles his typical remark. It's a look that surprises them equally, though for different reasons.

"Hmm, hmm," Silas coughs. Leo's hands fall and they both look down.

"What's wrong, Annie?" says Silas, eying Leo as he moves between them.

Anastasia glances quickly at Leo herself before answering. "It's Beren, and Zoe, they think we're dead. And Mom, she…"

Silas's face drops. "I know."

Anastasia looks up surprised. "How?"

"It's how we keep track of people. How I've watched you all these years."

The loving daughter opens her mouth to speak, but instead falls into her father's burly chest.

Leo steps off and reasons through Silas' explanation of the stars and what he sees as the relative geography of Prometheum. He then broadens his range to consider the stars that appear outside the territory of the Gemellan Cities. As he does, they begin to form clusters of their own in concentrations denser than just the random set of lifeforms.

"This is a cosmic view of Gaia, isn't it?" he says.

Pre-Reckoning maps clearly marked boundaries of the former continents. Most today, however, include only the Gemellan Cities.

"So there *are* people out there," he says without confirmation of his first statement.

"You should have seen it *before* the Reckoning. Twenty times as bright," says Alex.

Leo traces his knowledge of old geography to pick out the regions of North America and the United States, once a prosperous land brought low by decadence. To see its profile on a template of immaculate stars one would think nothing ever happened. Yet the wars of the Reckoning extinguished more than just human life.

The desolation wrought on the civilized world first severed communication on an international level. The American nation followed, unable to keep a centralized government.

Survivors turned their attention locally to areas less affected, claiming and defending it as though it were conquered territory, like Prometheum. Following the Sacred Rains, a peaceful alliance formed with Pronoia, a nearby city-state founded by a settler of Prometheum.

Aside from a few minor colonies in between, however, no other civilization has reached out from elsewhere.

"I thought it would look different," says Anastasia, discerning the boundaries Leo spoke of.

"The unknown triggers the imagination," says Alex.

"But pre-Reckoning seemed like a completely different world."

"It was. In more ways than you know," says Alex reflectively. "The Rains, though, didn't affect the land masses, just the topography."

Man battered nature in the Age of Decadence to the point of giving it cancer. The Rains fell as a panacea, issuing life into a broken spirit. By its grace the primal world became lusher than ever: though tales circulate of it having awakened creatures unknown to the fifth generation of man.

Leo notes how wide-spread the stars extend beyond the geographies of the Gemellan Cities. "Why don't we know anything about these others?" he says.

"You tell me," says Alex shrugging one of his shoulders. "Even now that you know, would you go back and look for them?"

Leo makes no response.

"They're obviously not in a hurry to see you, so..."

Still nothing.

"The appetite for expansion died years ago," Alex explains. "It started with Manifest Destiny, continued abroad, then blew up in our faces: literally. Wanting more just leads to wanting more."

Leo sees the wisdom in Alex's words--in learning from the mistakes of history. Prometheum itself was founded as a counter-reflection of pre-Reckoning folly. Nonetheless, he often wonders what lies in the Uncharted Lands bordering his city-state, or across the ocean where people used to fly.

"Alright, enough history," says Silas pulling his daughter in, "let's get moving." Alex falls in behind the Wildyns starting back west, east, or north. Leo hesitates a moment, thinks of looking in on Beren and Zoe again, but ultimately just files in behind the rest.

The stars glare sufficiently to light their way for a time. They soon, however, grow sparser, as do the roses of the field. Within a few blinks of an eye, both sky and ground have changed altogether.

In place of the lovely red of Elysium, a greyish flower with pale tubers starts popping up between their feet. It dominates an expansion vast and wide. This expansion, however, appears more plain than field. The sweet smell of scented life all but evaporates.

Up above the stars have vanished to all sides of the spectrum: as if wiped clean by a dusty cloth leaving a residue of overcast cloud.

Behind the overcast, a pale glow filters through to provide enough light for visibility.

Leo suddenly finds it harder to breathe. He looks to the others but sees only Anastasia in the same predicament. "Why's the air so thin here?" he says, clutching his chest.

"Because there's no one to breathe it," says Alex.

Leo coughs, "Some hospitality."

Anastasia, after a labored breath, bends down and picks one of the dull flowers. She fingers and sniffs. Holding it outward she regards its texture, then brings it in again.

"Asphodel," she whispers. She scans the vast plains, blanketed with thousands of flowers identical to the one in her hand. "We're in the Plains of Asphodel."

The area on the near side of the river Styx serves as the place of disembarkment for Charon's passengers. Once judged by the Three, they then proceed to their final destination by the will of the Fates.

Although part of the itinerary, even Alex and Silas show temperamental signs of the realm's draining effects.

Leo surveys their surroundings. "Plains of Asphodel, huh?"

Cough. Spit.

"Yeah, well, I'll buy the shirt the next time through. Let's get to the ferry. Besides, I heard they got gh..."

The words catch in his throat.

A flash of something the color of the clouds whisks by to the right. Before he can make out anything of what he saw, another passes to the left.

His hand moves to his blade.

Now looking back and forth he falls into a defensive stance. He removes the blade from his guard expecting anything from Keres to the White Lion. In focusing on the sides, however, he misses what has now appeared directly to his front.

Immaterial apparitions of creatures that were at least once human. Their vaporous quality mutilates their facial features to the effect of burning skin. The smoky fumes rising from their heads would confirm as much if not for the lack of any recognizable smell.

Anastasia clutches her father. Leo remembers he can no longer do the same with any parent of his own: not that he ever would.

"It's all right, sweetie," says Silas.

More come. Their numbers now count several rows back to all sides. The ones to the rear pass to and fro as though their wits have been stolen. The ones to the front remain still and fixated on the group as if summoned by the scent of blood.

Leo holds off no longer. Conjuring the aether blade he lunges forward and throws a heavy overhand cut to the lot in front. As his blade comes down, however, it meets with something firm and ungiving.

Leo looks to see the tip hovering just inches over the nearest apparition. He then realizes what stopped him was Alex's hand still clamped to his arm.

"That won't be necessary," says Alex. "They can't hurt you."

Leo regards more the hand on his arm than the man it belongs to. Ultimately, though, he relaxes and lowers his weapon: yet the blade remains conjured.

Leo stares a moment at the "ghosts," then waves the blade in front of one's face. A swish of violet. A flat tone. No reaction.

Leo continues staring as if not fully convinced.

"Why do they look like that: so dumb," he asks.

"The Plains of Asphodel is for those who lived relatively average lives: that in the ethics sense, and how much you've contributed to society."

The one closest is a male spirit wearing old, rugged clothes. He babbles something unintelligible with his tongue hanging out. Through his cloud filled eyes not even former signs of vitality exist.

"This is what average gets, huh? Cloudy with no chance for a bath," says Leo.

"They may look brain dead but they don't suffer. In fact, they don't feel anything."

"I guess they wouldn't mind."

The Wildyns move off first, Silas at the lead. They have no trouble passing as their movement incites the apparitions to do likewise. Alex follows the path they've set.

Leo waits another second for his pale friends to disperse before joining the group. Once they've cleared to his satisfaction he starts in slow steps toward the others. Only then does he de-animate his blade. He does not, however, reattach it to the guard.

Within a few yards most of the apparitions have disappeared into the gray terrain, or just disappeared. One, however, still lingers. It maintains a short distance behind Leo with eyes into his back.

At each step Leo takes, however, it takes the equivalent of two, had it legs to actually take them. In short time it comes within a few body lengths. Such proximity does not go unnoticed.

Leo peers over his shoulder now for the third time. More than any visual though, he somehow senses its presence. He finds it odd to feel energy off an inanimate being. Nonetheless, he's not one to take risks.

Placing his hand back on his blade he allows the creature to continue approaching. A keen look forward is all he needs to monitor its progress. Once at arm's length, Leo makes a rapid spin and cuts sidelong to the neck.

This time, however, he's the one to still his own hand.

Holding his blade against the creature's jugular "vein," Leo regards what appears to be a spirit of the younger sort. So young in fact, he can hardly imagine it being in the same realm as the babbling dim-wit they encountered before. It almost makes him regret that it is. An eerie sensation pinches his core.

The spirit remains perfectly still, blade yet at its throat. The stillness clarifies its features by settling the vapors rising from its face. As it does an uncanny feeling passes through Leo.

Leo's own face relaxes and he begins focusing more on the spirit's complexion than that of his weapon raised. Something in the light jawline and moderate cheek bones recalls a vague familiarity: almost as if looking into an old picture.

Leo slightly squints.

"Alex," he says..."Alexi?"

Heavy footsteps come up from behind. "Give me your hand," says Silas, grabbing it before he offers. He draws the blade away from the spirit's throat and removes it from Leo's hand. Before Leo can even react, Silas slices him at the palm.

"Daddy!" yells Anastasia from behind,

The gesture shocks Leo too much to pull away. Though a small cut, the bleeding inflicted by the aether blade has already spread over his entire hand. Before it can spill Silas quickly tugs his arm forward and allows it to pour on the spirit.

Anastasia, looking back and forth between her father and Leo's latest wound, steps between and places her hands on their arms. While making a vain attempt to pry them apart she glances at the spirit...and stops.

What was once barely more than a frame of rising smoke now starts materializing into a profile of body and limb. Color forms around its feet and creeps upward like giving life to a cartoon. It turns brown over tan chino pants then white over a collared polo. Flesh follows, revealing a face of fair skin under straight, light brown hair.

As self-awareness settles a light blue ignites in its eyes. They first find Alex.

"Hello, Grampa," says the adolescent boyishly.

"Hi, Alexi."

The great General hugs his grandson like old times: times never known to Leo, as with the brother standing before him.

When Silas moves to greet him Anastasia takes Leo's wounded hand.

"You're going to run out of shirt pretty soon," she says, ripping around Leo's midsection.

He continues with his fossilized stare as she applies the torn fabric to his palm.

"Hey," she says. She reaches for his chin but doesn't touch it. "Relax. You look like you've seen a three-headed dog. Remember where you are."

"Right."

Leo exhales and takes a step over toward his deceased sibling. Only one step though. From a short distance he regards just how much of his mother's resemblance he took. He might even think him the lucky one were he not dead and flitting around aimlessly in overcast heaven.

Leo eyes him curiously. Though his brother appears as he does in old photos, for some reason Leo imagined him much older in person as opposed to a few years younger.

Alexi smiles brightly. He, for one, does not seem curious about their encounter.

"Uh, hi," says Leo, mainly to break the silence.

"Hello, Leonidas. Or, 'Hey Leo,' as you might prefer."

One of Leo's eyebrows raises.

Are you sure we're related?

"Yeah, Leo's good," he says. "How did you know, you see me in the stars or something?"

"The stars?" says Alexi, peering at the gray sky. "No, but your blood sustains me."

The cut on Leo's hand still stings. He glances at Silas. Although he acknowledges the Captain's purpose in his actions, he doesn't doubt a grain of pleasure might have passed in performing his task. When Silas grins back, he knows.

"Asphodel spirits can only animate with blood," says Alex. "Otherwise, all feelings and memories of their human life stay dormant."

"Wouldn't want that."

"Blood is code, so, he already knows you a bit."

A twinge of distress crosses Leo's eye. He quickly suppresses it to make himself believe no one noticed.

"May I ask why you are here," says Alexi.

Leo pauses. "You mean you don't already know?"

"I can only sense your inclinations, personality, and such. Don't worry, little brother," Alexi smiles gaily.

"I wasn't worried," says Leo quickly. *Who you callin' little?*

Alexi's pending expression indicates he hasn't forgotten his question.

Leo sighs. "My mother...oh, Mom, I mean, is dead."

"Ok. But why are <u>you</u> here?" he asks with no change of tone.

His brother's lack of emotion astonishes and irritates him. He lets it slide to the notion that he's probably forgotten how to feel after being inanimate for so long.

Nonetheless, he does not immediately respond. He in fact looks hard into his brother for having the audacity to pose a question Leo really hasn't dared pose to himself since he jumped into Lake Maquari. Even now, with the words spelled out in front of him, he dare not still.

What he does do, however, is recall Emrick's words. Emrick's words and his mother's message.

"I'm gonna find her," he finally states, "and save her—-" He points a stiff finger toward the dull gray of the Plains. "From this."

Alexi contemplates. He then looks to his grandfather who makes no sign one way or the other over Leo's statement.

"Come on, Annie. Let's take a walk," says Silas to his daughter.

Anastasia glances at Leo then joins her father. Alex gathers his old guitar from Leo's things. "Get some rest," he says, "we leave in a little bit." He then walks off, settles on a patch of ground, and starts strumming.

Leo curses them in silence for leaving him alone with the captain of the Archimedes club.

"So, let me guess: you expected a strong, arrogant, lunk as an older brother?" says Alexi.

This freakin' guy.

"I dunno. I've only ever seen you in pictures."

"Well, sorry to disappoint that I'm not more like you."

Did he just take a shot at me?

"Uh, yeah, no problem."

Alexi strays a few paces and sits. His cheerful expression and fixed gaze never seem to alter; and now he faces Leo.

Leo glances at those who've abandoned him. Only now does he return his blade to the guard. He ultimately obliges his brother by joining him, but is careful to sit a few feet outside normal conversation range.

Alexi continues staring.

Freak.

"So, uh, what did you do when you were...yah know...alive?" says Leo trying to jolt his brother from his aggravating trance.

"You mean did I win tournaments and bring glory to the Maquari name?"

"Sure."

"Well, first of all I'm not a Maquari, I'm a Serelin. And second -- no competitions; I played French horn in the school orchestra."

For the first time Leo's expression changes from outward to somewhat down to earth. That is, were they not in the Underworld.

"I didn't know you liked music," he says.

Alexi twists his head and adds a little more smile to his already existing one.

"It was my plan to play for my public service," he says. "But," he snaps his finger across his body, "didn't quite make it that far."

Again the apathy over death strikes Leo as odd. Though in looking around, perhaps death was just the beginning of another life. Alexi indeed seems more alive as his dead brother than the one he never knew in Prometheum.

Leo then remembers the state of the quirky French Horn player when he nearly cut off his head with the aether blade. And yet, despite being nothing like The Isles of the Blessed or Elysium, the Plains of Asphodel was still a place of no suffering in or out. Suffering was for the living. So in that sense, maybe Alexi's reaction makes the most sense of all.

Nonetheless, as someone still attached to that difficult world in spite of reason, Leo feels bad for the pain his mother must have felt at his brother's passing.

Alexander Serelin died of a sudden heart condition at the young age of adolescence. Some found the circumstances suspicious, given no prior record of health issues. For better or worse, though, it was only ever regarded as an unfortunate tragedy.

"So Mom's here now," says Alexi, matter-of-factly. "Will she come to us?"

Leo looks down hoping Alexi does not already know the answer to that question.

"No. She...she hasn't crossed yet...long story," says Leo. He looks up in tentative glances waiting for the follow up.

"Was it her diabetes?" says Alexi.

This time he looks up sharply. "How did you know about that?"

"She was diagnosed when I was little. Though, it wasn't much then, as long as she kept up with her pills."

Pandora did not disclose her illness to Leo until well into his teens. Even then, her condition remained stable for many years.

Leo turns abruptly and enters into a pace. "She did keep up. She did. That's why I don't get how she ended up so bad."

"She would've needed different ones over time, and more of them."

The drastic period of Pandora's decline happened over the past year. As if overnight, the infectious disease spread mercilessly to her hands and feet. It soon saturated the skin into a mess of purple flesh.

Her first amputation followed what felt like no respite from Leo's costly and tedious road of rehab. This, of course, brought on by his extensive injuries at the hands of Feidor.

The tournament.

Before Leo can replay any gruesome scenes in his mind, a childlike giggle draws their attention to the plain. Anastasia clings to her father's neck as she pretends to fly like a bird. She looks nothing more than a little girl with her hair waving and face scrunched in pleasant fear.

Seeing her would bring warmth to the most dormant of hearts.

To think of the emptiness she must know, the piggyback rides she's missed; and yet never to have wallowed or sought sympathy brings a lump of shame to Leo's throat.

What a beautiful creature.

Light footsteps approach to his rear. "So what are you waiting for?" says Alexi.

Leo peers over his shoulder to the annoying gaiety in his periphery.

Little bastard.

"Wh-what do you mean?"

"I may be a yoyo, but no clarinet was safe from me back in the day."

Leo turns. "Clarinet?"

"And take it from me, you haven't kissed til you've kissed trumpet lips."

"I'll take it from you, man."

Leo turns back to the Wildyns.

"Then stop wasting time," says Alexi. "Stop taking for granted."

"Taking what for granted?"

"Her. Your life. Take it from me."

A door long since closed opens a crack. Leo peeks through at the possibility of giving himself over again, of dropping his guard and embracing the intimacy of connecting with somebody. Another glance at Anastasia, and the door shuts tight.

The tournament.

"She's better off this way. Away from me."

"I wonder what she'd say about that."

No comment.

"Well, if you don't want her, maybe I'll..."

Leo shoots his brother a glare without fully comprehending his words.

Although he never thought of himself with her, he also never imagined her with someone else. The thought perplexes him. As far as he knows she's never had a boyfriend. It would seem unnatural.

Alexi doesn't laugh: only continues in his queer delight for which Leo recognizes no source.

Leo shakes his head. "Whatever. Come on let's go. We need to get Mom before..."

He stops.

"Before what?" says Alexi.

Leo continues facing away. The fact of his mother being at risk as a result of his own actions brings his feelings on the matter to the forefront of his conscience. As such, he has an inkling his brother already knows what.

"Nothing," he says, stepping off.

They find Alex a ways away, sitting cross-legged in the asphodel. He strums gently on his amp-less guitar. With his head down he sings an unknown, yet not totally unfamiliar tune to Leo's ears.

"Mama put my guns in the ground.

I can't shoot them anymore.

That cold black cloud is coming down,

Feels like I'm knockin on heaven's door."

Alexi doesn't wait for any subsequent verses. "Time to go Grampa," he says.

The guitar stops.

"What was that song?" says Leo, grasping Alex's forearm to help him up. He notes the similarity in hand complexion to his own: smaller for a male with thick veins to pump blood to thick muscles on the forearm.

"Just one I used to play when I was younger. This place reminded me of it."

"It's gotta be ancient if it talks about guns."

Firearms and weapons of mass destruction, as they were called, played an integral role in the Age of Decadence. The ease of pulling a trigger and the sorrow it invoked put such a sour taste in the mouths of those who survived the Reckoning, that no more were manufactured. To even speak of them became taboo.

The Maquaris set off with the Wildyns filing in. Anastasia, locked to her father's arm, smiles over her shoulder in a way only rarely seen: eyes squinted, but of more than a passing fancy. They glisten over a mouth full of teeth feeling secure in a world where everything's right: where everything's whole: where nothing is abandoned.

Leo doesn't know how to respond after his brother's words, but seeing his friend so full of the love she deserves brings at least a closed mouth smile to half of his face in acknowledgement.

The plains roll before them in uniform dreariness. Spirits will occasionally float by but Leo no longer reaches for his weapon. Shock has already given way to intrigue, with him most of all.

The non-discriminatory nature of Death astounds him.

A man of prime physical condition halts a short distance away looking off into nowhere. He wears only athletic shorts, and poses a musculature to make even Leo jealous.

An older man in ceremonial robe stands hunched with years on a bad leg. The cross hanging from his neck Leo recognizes as some old religious symbol.

As he flits away, a little girl in a spring dress takes his place. It reminds Leo of the girl he saw running through the festival grounds. Though void of emotion as all in the realm, Leo interprets the youth and innocence of her face as a crime of nature for having let her go.

Again the question of justice perturbs him. What, he wonders, really determines fate. The Moirai, Prometheus; or do people really choose their paths as his mother *supposedly* did. He shakes his head as the little girl moves off, feeling as though saving his mother would somehow bring justice to the girl as well.

Alexi brushing by breaks the thought that grips his mind. Leo furrows his brows for a second then takes note of just how little weight he felt in his brother's shoulder. Though smaller in stature, Leo's association of relative force with a person that size runs amiss, sending a signal of disquiet to his senses: a break in the rules, a glitch in the balance. He considers if somehow his own matter differs from the dead.

Alexi scurries ahead and veers off to the right. Visibility is difficult in the gloom, but it looks as if he stops and takes a seat in the middle of the plain.

Leo dismisses the detour as another of his brother's peculiarities. The Wildyns, however, veer off as well.

He throws up his hands. "Did I miss a sign for attractions or something?"

Alex makes a light smile, "Go see."

"You know, I'd rather not," Leo flashes.

Another step to the right would feel like losing an hour of his real purpose. The impatience swells, a fear even begins to grip. He wonders if time passes the same in the world above as down there, if a concept of time even exists for the dead.

The dead.

Imagining his mother floating around with her tongue hanging out seems like little recompense for living so virtuously and enduring such suffering. The thought angers him. Though he's unsure whether that anger arises from the injustice of her fate, his part in it, or her choices that would have made it all her own.

He exhales to a slow blink. In that split second to open his eyes the sky has grown darker. Nothing of night, but heavy in the murky saturation of rain clouds.

The greatest remaining visibility lies on the distant horizon. With his eyes naturally gravitating there, he perceives the silhouette of a lone figure pacing back and forth. That it does not immediately appear human keeps him on his guard.

As his eyes adjust, he indeed notices it being carried by four legs rather than two. A head the size of a lion's mane makes him almost wish they would adjust no more.

For a moment it stops. Facing Leo it extends its bat-like wings to their full extension. Before Leo can even react to grab his blade it lets out a searing roar across the plain.

The roar, however, carries no sound.

The part that sears is the excruciating pain from the claw marks running down Leo's back. The closed skin seems to tear open in slow progression. As the air hits, the sting returns in fresh form. His hard cringe does nothing but to amplify the sensation.

Given the momentary nature of a roar Leo expects relief that never seems to arrive. The agony instead travels upward into his head. By the time it gets there he can now hear the sound of the lion full well.

He drops to his knees and smacks his temples from both sides. The harder he massages, though, the louder the pressure builds.

At last resort he attempts to block from within. Focusing all his energy on the intrusive force, the sound, if not the pain, begins to subside.

It is quickly replaced, however, by a series of images. Striking flashes of scenes darting through his head: soft fingers running through brown hair: those same fingers mutilated and discolored; a "K" in a tree, a glimmer in an eye; a perturbed figure on a dark, lonely river bank.

"Mom!"

Leo nearly jumps to his feet. Though he expects a murky horizon, giant lion, and his grandfather to be standing next to him, he finds Alex has already moved off with the others, and nothing looms in the distance but the same somber Asphodel sky.

He takes a breath. His eyelids return to their normal aperture.

"Look, Leo, there's a seat for you too," says Alexi.

Leo ignores the fact there might be a chair conveniently set in the middle of nowhere. Though he'd like to ignore the lot of them, looking into the distance once more gives him the feeling that doing so would bring him to nothing good. Such thoughts lead him to see what exciting park bench his brother has found now.

Leo stops to the blind side of the Wildyns. He observes, indeed, two chairs conveniently set in the middle of nowhere.

The empty one sits about a foot and a half off the ground with golden limbs and no back. The other, occupied by Alexi, sits higher in both height and design. The regal bends in the legs extend to arm rests and a back higher than anyone could need.

Leo crosses his arms. "Well gee Alexi, that's just swell." "Can we get moving now?"

"Don't you know what this is?" says Anastasia, walking over and leaning down between the chairs. She rises holding two golden sepultures: one crowned by bull and one by eagle.

Leo remains arms crossed. "What?" he says after a few seconds, "is this Menoitios' royal café or something?"

"Not Menoitios, Leo," says Alexi. He reaches behind the master chair. "Minos!" Alexi raises a thicker, more elaborate sepulture topped by the once devastating weapon of the god of gods.

Leo keeps a straight face regarding the lightning bolt, but casually turns to the side once he realizes what all that means.

Minos.

The Judges.

Under the reign of Zeus, when it came to the lives of deceased souls, Minos, Rhadamanthys, and Aiakos served as arbiters of truth. All three sons of the Thunder God led mortal lives and were appointed judges in the Underworld for their governing of justice as leaders of men. Rhadamanthys dealt primarily with souls from Europe, Aiakos from Asia, and Minos oversaw all with the final vote.

Leo imagines their absence to mainly be due to the change in power and the imprisonment of the Olympians in Tartaros. Nonetheless, it is not their association with the dead that unsettles him.

He takes a few steps away from the group and looks hard to the left. He recalls a passage from Plato's Gorgias once discussed at the gymnasium: "These...shall give judgment in the meadow in the dividing of the road."

Must have been a metaphor.

In any case, the dividing refers to one direction leading to Tartaros, and the other to the Isles of the Blessed and Elysium. As Leo continues staring in the direction they came, he realizes solar panels are not a requisite for marking location.

The Plains of Judgment.

Looking no different from the Plains of Asphodel and really only an extension thereof, Leo did not notice any deviation in their course. Nonetheless, he rests reassured that once Alexi finishes in the play area, they would be making due south to the River Styx.

Anastasia approaches the kingly sepulture and rubs her hand over the golden thunderbolt.

"I never understood why Zeus made Minos head judge," she says, letting her fingers slide off. "How could someone who fed tributes to a Minotaur be considered just?"

Alex walks up and also regards the sepulture. "It's a common misconception," he says. "You see, there were, in fact, two Minos's from the same family. The first was a son of Zeus and Europa, along with Rhadamanthys, and a benevolent king of Crete. The second was his grandson, son of Lycastus, and the one we associate with the labyrinth. Obviously, it was the first Minos who sat in that chair."

Alexi adjusts his position, tapping the arm-rests with each hand. "Can I see those," he asks Anastasia. "I'll trade yah?"

She hands over the two smaller sepultures and takes hold of Minos'. "That's a relief, I guess."

"Ironically," says Alex chuckling, "it was the "good" Minos who prompted our destruction."

The statement even catches Leo's ear who impatiently waits to the side.

"HE brought about the Reckoning?"

"In a way, yes. You see, Zeus himself supposedly educated Minos in the ways of lawgiving, which set him apart from the others. It also gave his word more credibility."

Anastasia paces a moment, then hands the sepulture to her father. "But what would make him want to destroy us?"

Alex wraps his knuckles with his left hand then fixes his baseball cap to the side. "Well, imagine reading novels with nothing but sad endings: it would start to affect you after a while: and that's exactly what the Age of Decadence did. So many foul souls passed through that Minos eventually gave up on humanity and counseled Zeus to purge the population."

"Like the Deluge?" says Anastasia.

"That's right: and if you remember, only Deucalion, Prometheus' son, was spared in the flood along with his family. This time, no one was meant to survive."

"Until Prometheus interfered."

"Voila."

"Huh?"

"Oh, nothing."

Leo, while finding the history lesson somewhat interesting, hopes it has ended and opens his mouth to speak when his brother beats him to the punch.

"Why do these other sepultures have bulls and eagles on the top?" says Alexi the same way he might ask why the planet is round.

"The bull topped one belonged to Rhadamanthys, as it was in that form Zeus seduced his mother Europa."

"But why the eagle?" says Anastasia. "I thought that was the symbol of Prometheus?"

Alex takes the sepulture from his grandson. "Symbols change according to what gives them their meaning, and from whose perspective." He twists it in his hand.

"In the time of Zeus, the eagle represented the all-seeing nature of a high god, and was also the means by which he tortured Prometheus. Therein lies the connection: at that moment a supporter of Zeus would see him enacting justice on a traitor, whereas others would see a martyr of sorts who sacrificed for the good of their people."

"And the eagle symbolizes that sacrifice, of all he suffered for us," says Anastasia, deducing Alex's point.

"Voil...oh."

"I got it this time," says Anastasia smiling.

Silas glances over his shoulder at Leo but finds him pacing head to the ground.

"There are many examples of that kind of thing from history, especially pre-Reckoning," says Alex.

Anastasia moves closer while Alexi goes about admiring his chair.

"Like what?" she asks.

"Well, the Christian cross for one. It was much like the eagle for the Romans: a torture mechanism for administering justice. But when the son of their god, Jesus, died, it became a symbol to inspire his followers: really to the point that most forgot its original purpose."

Although most follow the widespread faith in Prometheus, the city-state of Prometheum does not discriminate against other religions. Indeed, many minor sects of Christians can be found in various parts of the Gemellan Cities, making their cross recognizable to the common eye.

"There were some symbols, however, that went the opposite way," says Alex with a change of tone. "You might've heard of World War II from your Pre-Reckoning classes?" Alex pauses reflectively. "If they only knew what a real "world" war was back then."

Anastasia tilts her head at him patiently.

"Anyway, the enemy of the time was the Nazis, and their symbol was a swastika. It looked something like this:"

Alex points his finger in the air and draws six strokes at forty five degree angles for Anastasia to visualize.

"What that really was, you see, was a modification of this:"

He does the same only at ninety degree angles complimented by four intersecting dots.

"Its original meaning comes from Sanskrit, a language of Hinduism, and represented good luck. The Nazis adopted it as the symbol of the Aryan race, or the race they saw as superior to all others. Because of Nazi barbarism, you see, it developed an extremely negative connotation thereafter, and ended up standing for all the atrocities the Nazis committed. Weird, huh?"

Anastasia raises her eyebrows but remains speechless. She considers the area of the three judges then begins to show doubt.

"There was one other thing I..."

"Hey, hey," interrupts Leo, stalking up to the group, "do you mind if we continue class on the "road," he says curling his fingers in parenthesis, "we're wasting time here."

Anastasia casts him her reproving face which he knows to mean one thing.

"Jerk."

The word does not come from Anastasia, however.

Leo looks to Minos's chair somewhat in shock of how he was addressed.

"Don't be such a jerk, Leo," repeats Alexi as though he were telling off a bully in the Junior Lyceum cafeteria.

Leo stands dumbfounded which brings Anastasia's hand up to cover a laugh.

"You tell him, Alexi," she says.

Even Silas' glare changes to a good natured smirk in watching Leo falter.

The scrutiny tweaks Leo's pride, but all he manages is a "hmph" as he stammers off.

"You were saying, Annie?" says Alex.

"Oh, uh, right: I remember there being more here, according to the art," she says waving a hand over the area. "Where are the Keys of Hades, and the Gnosian Urn?"

Alex and Silas exchange a look at the mention of the latter.

The Keys were entrusted to Aiakos, a son of Zeus and Aegina, who held them as long as he served as judge. The Urn belonged to Minos, who would enclose and shake souls reluctant to own the truth of their lives.

"Turns out," says Silas with a careful look at Alex, "both are missing."

"Missing?"

"They went unaccounted for during the Fall of Olympus," says Alex. "But I wouldn't worry."

"Right," says Silas. "Besides, I'm sure Menoitios has changed the locks since then."

Anastasia disregards the attempt at humor and gives both men wary looks.

"You're probably right," she says. "Menoitios would know who enters, and what good would a judge's urn be to anyone."

Her father clears his throat. "Alright, let's be off before Leonidas has another temper tantrum."

Alex, Silas, and Alexi assume rank: yet instead of proceeding south, they turn right. None seemed troubled by leaving Leo behind nor putting quick distance between them.

Anastasia scurries over to where Leo stands, back turned, staring away toward the south.

"Come on, it's time to go."

Leo turns with a hard face that drops at seeing the others heading West.

"Where the hell are they going?" He hurries off. "Hey!"

No one seems to hear, nor pay any mind.

Anastasia catches up in a few steps.

"Why did they just take off?" says Leo. "We need to go THAT way," he points behind.

As they proceed further, the quality of the air again changes. Dry, slightly warmer: a raspy fume tickles Leo's nose.

"You smell that?" he says.

He sniffs deeper.

"Seriously, it smells like something's burning."

"I smell it too," says Anastasia. She takes an anxious look around.

They search the horizon for signs of fire but notice nothing abnormal. "Can these plains even burn?"

"No, *they* don't burn," says Anastasia with an apprehensive brow.

The three deceased move ahead at greater pace. That no one seems nervous over the potential of wildfire causes Leo much suspicion.

He feels the touch of gentle skin take his arm as Anastasia falls in at his side. With all the supernatural oddities, she looks comfortingly human in her misgivings.

The odor grows stronger. Heat kisses their faces but isn't the reason they sweat.

Leo struggles to identify its origin. "Something's not right here. Alex is off. It's *south* from the Plains of Judgment to the

Ferry and Stygian Marshes. And we're still going west."

The heat intensifies and visibility darkens.

"There's only one place I know that burns here," says Anastasia pulling closer into Leo.

The three family members stop ahead at a fair distance. They stand shoulder to shoulder looking down.

Leo and Anastasia approach with heavy feet. Darkness thickens, yet a new light flickers ahead. Halfway to Alex they see its source.

Flame.

"I thought it couldn't burn here," says Leo.

"It's not the plains," says Anastasia in somber, conclusive tones. "It's a river."

Leo's brow raises. "A river? But the only river that burns is the Phlegethon, and that leads to..."

Both their bodies tense. Leo halts altogether and turns his head back toward the direction of the ferry, then slowly returns it to the flame.

"Why would Alex even bring us here? Mom's nowhere near us!"

Anastasia glances at her father then tries to pull Leo on.

Leo resists, focusing his senses southward. He struggles to find the lure he felt to his mother.

Nothing.

"Son of a bitch," he says, breaking from Anastasia moving into a jog.

"Alex..., Alex!" he barks.

Alex turns once Leo reaches him.

"This isn't where Mom is, we have to go back."

"The only way back is forward," says Alex calmly.

Leo steps aside his grandfather and is immediately blasted by the full force of the heat. Through his shielded eyes he sees the current before him flowing like lava more than water. Fire coats the surface from end to end.

In the distance beyond, the bronze walls of Tartaros loom as a shadow in the night.

"Into this? You're crazy."

"Look to the flames," says Alex. "You know who will answer."

Leo shakes his head and looks hard on the young man in the baseball cap. His doubt meets with eyes full of years and confidence.

"Look to the flames, Leo," he says slower.

Leo first looks to Anastasia. She clings to her father and appears as if saying farewell to a loved one she knows must go. The flames flicker up her face and dance in her eyes. She makes no move to contradict Alex.

Some believe Prometheus can be accessed through the fire he gifted man. Some: such as Alex. Regardless of what Leo believes, the quasi human wall of family and friends standing behind him suggests he would be looking into the flames whether he wants to or not.

Resigning himself to the task, he exhales through closed teeth and turns for the river.

The hot fumes again make him recoil. This time, though, he holds. Little by little the skin on his face assimilates to the extreme it's not meant to endure.

He steps.

Sifting through the confusion of the flames he channels his concentration on one point. The brightness is agonizing. He fights hard the disposition to bring up his hand to shade.

His squint, however, gradually opens wider. As it does an energy pours through him that makes him forget about heat or brightness of any kind. Soon the flames become a variance of orange and red colors prancing about in the sweetness of dance.

He steps again.

Though nothing manifests resembling Prometheus or notions of foretold events, a break in the flame opens in a small circle. As it grows the fire begins to take form around it: an upper and lower, long teeth, yellow eyes. Flames flare wildly to the side from the head and neck.

Once large enough to encompass Leo's torso, he sees only the dark abyss swirling into an entrancing cyclone. He soon loses sense of place, followed by sense of self. Somehow his body reacts to some unknown stimulant that forces him into a final step.

As he does, the jaws drop.

Falling feels like drifting to sleep.

"Leo!"

CHAPTER 11 – THE PHLEGETHON

"You were amazing today," says a perky, pale skinned brunette with her cheek pressed against Leo's.

Before Leo can respond or gather any indication as to who it is, she shuts his mouth with a hard kiss.

The lips, lined and firm, recall something from a shallow grave. Leo's hands think the same touching the bare skin of her lean body.

This has got to be a dream.

Then, he sniffs.

As the air flows through his nostrils all thoughts of dreams flee from the vividness of a familiar scent: euphoric jasmine blended with a teasing pinch of fruit. A scent, *the* scent.

"Thais!" he says, pulling away.

His old love smiles with eager eyes. "Calling out my name a little soon, aren't yah?" she says, looking down.

Leo follows her look to find them both in bare skin amongst other things. He shudders. The fight between recognition of place and lack thereof in time sends his eyes darting all around.

The first thing he spots is his maple colored Reynolds guitar. It rests amongst a heap of practice blades and other training equipment.

Second, under a fenestrator of red trim, a series of SnapShot frames lines a bureau against the wall. The first is a motion shot of him and Beren after a victory in Kladimo. The next is a still shot of Khloe and her family. And last: the last is a paintbrushed shot of his mother when she wore a purple saffron in her hair during younger years.

Leo's eyes now move down where he finally spots his camo patterned Guard uniform he was apparently wearing not long before.

This at least gives him enough to make out the room as his quarters during Public Service.

There's no way I can be here.

"You ok, babe?" says Thais. She guides his chin toward her with her index finger back. "Don't tell me you're too tired to see the moon," says Thais.

The expression cuts him deep. A few weeks after they started seeing each other, they checked out an ORV (off-road vehicle) to explore some mountains in the Appalachia section of Prometheum. On their way back to quarters, they pulled off into a secluded field.

Leo followed her into the back seat where they had a few Lager Tops waiting. Accepting hers, Thais lowered the windows and rested her head back on the door.

"It's a full moon," she observed.

Leo leaned across her to peek out the window.

"They say people do crazy things on the full moon," she added softly, hooking a finger through his belt loop.

Leo looked down on the face that always showed the purest love for him in the twinkle of her eye: the face, that despite Leo's disbelief, managed to look past the thick layers of fault and smile upon something only she seemed to see.

There they had their first time: and "to see the moon" became code for any time after.

"No I was...I was never too tired for that," he says.

Though his use of the past tense escapes him, he fights to understand whether his statement serves as a response to her question, or consolation for all the pain he would bring her. The notion of even dreaming of such a time brings a heavy weight to his heart. The possibility of consciously reliving it: dread and confusion.

Nonetheless, as she sits before him none of what she will live has yet entered her mind in the slightest. Her aura is pure, clean, and safe from him. Her smile shines the way it did at the height of their relationship.

He remembers this moment: right after winning Qualifying to represent Eulimnos in the Pronoian Games. He and Thais then stole away while others celebrated the day's events in Prometheum Proper.

She loved to watch him compete, and always took such gentle pride in victories.

He was hers, and at the time Leo was convinced he felt the same.

Beholding her on the bed makes it so easy to relapse. The playful brown eyes; the strong, feminine form, all meant for him. Simple love, too hard to appreciate.

Seeing her so happy breaks his heart. Hindsight swarms like a nest of bees stinging their guilt as a lingering poison.

Leo turns away before his eyes go bloodshot from a welling tear.

"Hey, you must have got hit harder than I thought today," says Thais. "Come."

She pulls in and wraps tight around his neck. "I'm so proud of you, Leo. I hope I'll always get to see how special you are. I love you."

The kind words run blades over his skin. If she only knew, she could have run then and there.

"I love you too," he says in truth.

He hides his face over her shoulder, but the warmth of her embrace recalls the affection of her presence. The surge shoots through his gut and out to his limbs. He pulls in deeper attempting to squeeze it out, and perhaps offer some comfort that will settle just as deep in her.

Thais' lips touch his neck, gently sucking each of the sensitive areas she knew so well. Leo clenches his teeth but offers more of his skin anyway. He tries even harder to resist in his mind. His body, however, responds to the arousal despite him. Submitting feels all too natural.

Yet so does Anastasia.

ΔΔΔ

"I'm going to miss this," says Thais a while later. She flicks Leo's curls.

"I will too," says Leo.

She buries her head in his thick shaven chest. "You're so sweet."

Thais Kava, a year older than Leo, was at the point of completing her two-year public service. During that time she had served as an infrimiary in the Guard. It was she who was on duty when Leo came in with a minor training injury to his arm.

A native of Pronoia, she opted for the less-common path of completing her public service away from home. Her trust in her free spirit proved quite fruitful. By the end she had chosen a career, had several unique experiences, and found love. Nonetheless, she would soon return to Pronoia to start her License in medicine at the Academy.

"I remember wanting to get your attention," she says giggling, "and putting that pipe cleaner octopus in your store space." She looks at him straight on. "You never told me how you found out it was me."

"Ha," Leo remembers. "You never told me how you got into the guys' storeroom in the first place."

"You first."

"You started it."

"Fine," she says, propping herself on her elbows. "It was a night you finished training, no one was really around. Since you guys don't pay much attention who walks into your storeroom, I just threw on a robe, popped up the hood, and snuck in as someone was leaving. Didn't even need a thumbprint."

Her smugness is endearing. A smile even cracks on the side of Leo's lips.

"Then I just hid in a bathroom stall til you went to shower."

Leo's smile grows a little bigger. "You were watching me the whole time?"

Thais covers her mouth. "I might have peeked a little."

She shows the same bashfulness as when he confronted her with the toy octopus: the same that made him forget someone had broken into his personal store space.

"K. Your turn."

Leo knows he can't match a female peeping Tom but a promise is a promise.

"Your scent," he begins. "I could smell you on the pipe cleaners."

Thais raises her eyebrows as though he had quite matched her.

"Oh! I didn't know I had one."

"You do. And it's strongest like this," says Leo, breathing in the erotic odor of jasmine and sweat still clinging to her body.

The playfulness makes Leo nearly forget his doubt on the present. Coupled with her smell, he might have believed Alex somehow sent him back in time.

Thais giggles and taps his shoulder away. She then pulls a sheet over her naked body. "So sweet."

Her smile fades into reflection, and she takes hold of his arm in a firm grip. "Don't forget about me," she says. "And make sure you get down to Pronoia. You promised, remember?"

"I remember."

Thais nuzzles her head into his chest and says no more. Her breathing slows, and at the point Leo thinks she's asleep she wraps her arms around him as if he were slipping away. Leo almost wishes she had never let go.

She soon dozes off but Leo fights the desire to follow her into sleep.

Thais saying goodbye did not prompt the sense of loss Leo anticipated in himself. Over the following months, the flame that fueled their relationship began dying in Leo, with no other reason aside from the absence of something to feed it.

Communication dwindled to the point of a ring every few weeks. Though fully aware of the pain it caused Thais, Leo could not find the motivation to do more. Eventually, she cracked.

A long message of lonely meditation ended their relationship officially. This was a month before the set visit to Pronoia. Having already purchased a ticket, however, they agreed that Leo would still go as a friend.

He wishes Alex would send him to relive that decision.

Leo watches Thais' bare chest rise and fall. Short, savory breaths, weightless of the future, weightless of him.

Oh Thais, I'm so sorry.

He tucks his head into the side of her breast and listens. Her strong heart pumps a tender flow out to all it touches. In the beat he sees her face, ebbing between one world and another. In the rhythm he hears himself, dancing a song of blades in the Grand Coliseum.

∆∆∆

Regaining awareness, Leo finds himself walking along the musty docks in Pronoia. The moon lights the way, and the lanterns of the Thetian Islands decorate the bay like fireflies. Couples claim their territories to all sides.

Thais walks to Leo's side, head down. They do not hold hands.

It is Leo's final night on an awkward trip cut short.

They take seats in the corner of a murky bar and begin by saying nothing.

Drinks arrive. Sips thicken the air. On a full night's rest, Thais looks like she hasn't slept in two days.

"So you fight next week?" she says.

Leo takes a long swig. "Yeah."

She nods then turns her head away.

Over the previous two weeks, Leo acted as normal as possible to avoid discomfort, even renewing physical intimacy which to him was mostly physical.

"I hope you can beat Feidor," she says, still looking away. "I hope you can find whatever you're looking for."

At the first sob, Leo remembers the desire to leave then and there. Imagining a second chance, Leo had all the right words rehearsed. Now given that chance, real or not, his heart will not obey his tongue.

Thais turns back with a look not so much reproach as incomprehension: like a severely beaten puppy.

A look of the deepest hate would have been easier to bear.

By this time the tears flow freely. Six months ago Leo took a cavalier attitude to the fact, hiding behind the idea of a spectacle to avoid confronting it. Now, he just lets her cry.

"I'm sorry. I – I just can't control it," she says, trying to fight it off.

It's ok, Thais.

Leo lowers his head feeling two inches tall.

This must be Tartaros, hell, or whatever. Why would Alex send me here if it's got nothing to do with Mom.

An urge tells him his hold on the present is slipping. He starts feeling lighter and more disconnected to the emotion pouring out in front of him. He knows afterwards there would be no other memories to revisit if he had something to say.

Keeping his head lowered he scrambles to find the words he rehearsed a thousand times in his mind in the years following their separation.

They were so perfect. They would have made everything alright. And yet...they don't come.

In a final desperate attempt he lifts up his head and manages to blurt

"Thais!"

An elegant, middle aged woman cocks her head in surprise.

"Passage," says a rail worker.

Leo's pupils fluctuate as if adjusting to light, but his hand lifts anyway to have his thumb scanned. The woman does likewise.

"Sorry," says Leo, turning away to stare out the glass.

The woman smiles and waves her hand. As she does, the solar light of the cabin flashes over a dark, marble ring bearing the symbol of "v." She eyes Leo curiously before resuming her reading of a large book with a pentagram imprinted on its cover.

Leo pays her no mind. His head continues churning over the lost words he intended for Thais. Along with the passing flatlands outside, however, they soon become a blur: as do the images of Thais herself.

Leo rests his head against the transparency and watches the fleetingness of what he cannot control. Bored of this, he adjusts his perception to inner glass. In the reflection he sees his face with only one scar. He thinks to run a finger over the smooth skin he doesn't even remember having, but refrains. He might have deserved that second scar just as well at the hands of Feidor.

The sobbing face of Thais returns to his mind but quickly morphs into Anastasia. To hurt her the same would wound him deeper than any scar: to love her would be raising a blade above both their heads. For her sake, he'd be better as he's always been.

He carefully places Anastasia back in her rightful place.

As the sunset closes upon him, he succumbs longing for dreary plains and hellish rivers.

△△△

Leo packs his gear with haste of the departing rail: guard, suit, plates, footwear. He does one final check on the integrity of his xiphos blade and sheathes it to go as well.

For the final item he slows down a bit: the headdress of his namesake, a jaw of black steel surrounded by a mane of the same color; over the side of the face, razor sharp silver incisors.

The headdress that perpetuated his alias "The Black Lion": the symbol of the Maurileho. He places it carefully in his competition bag and runs upstairs.

Turning the corner into the kitchen, Pandora Maquari appears in the flesh.

"Mom," says Leo, stopping short.

"Your tea's almost ready," she says dryly.

Leo regards her as though witnessing a mental snapshot come to life. His mother wearing her leisure grey and orange sweat suit, advanced in middle age but still with a hint of her younger beauty under wrinkles and faded hair: the appearance he remembers her by.

Though Leo bursts inside, it also recalls the time of his teenage years, much of which was spent bickering over petty conflicts with his mother. He imagines a lot was due to his own attitude, though he certainly didn't attribute much to himself at the time: and this for the time he was even around.

His father leaving provoked a retreat of sorts from family life. In fact, any memory at all of her surprises him given his mental and physical absence over those years.

Watching her feet bustle around the kitchen and fingers tapping on the buttons of digital appliances reassures him that she wasn't always the pain-ridden cripple who suffered so greatly toward the end of her life. Watching her in her routine, he sees, despite his own wavering, she never really moved.

"You know," she begins. Leo remembers this lecture. "You're not in the right mind to be doing this."

The tournament.

"You won't be going against the boys from your own gymnasium. This is the Pronoia Invitational. And Feidor."

Feidor. "Yeah, ye..." Leo begins to challenge in his teenage "spare me the sermon" tone. His words come out as a natural reaction to pressure. They stop over the surreal happiness and confusion he feels at seeing his mother alive. Suddenly a scolding becomes just a way to hear her voice. He gently recants. "I know."

Pandora eyes him suspiciously before continuing. "No, you don't, honey. If your spirit isn't balanced, at best you won't get seriously hurt."

A tingle passes down the side of his eye where his second scar has not yet been inflicted. To think that cut would be the least of his rehabilitation: to think what his mother would have to endure. If only he could tell her.

"I'll be fine."

"Leonidas." Pandora places her hands on her son's muscled shoulders and softens her expression. "Leo, you can't go on blaming yourself. Thais; she's not your fault."

Leo turns his head and resists slightly but she clamps tight.

This time, Leo notices one set of fingers clearly stronger than the other: the stronger in the hand she kept.

"Hearts change, honey, and they don't take orders. Don't try to reason through something that's unreasonable by nature."

Leo's mind sees his mother's advice as perfectly reasonable, yet he can't accept it. Not then, not now. He lowers his head with no retort.

Through the corner of his eye he notices some discoloration in the weaker hand. He even sees a slight variation in posture. They are the fingers that would eventually be amputated.

"What's this?" he says, taking her hand.

This time it is Pandora who turns away. "Oh, it's nothing, honey," she says, withdrawing it.

His brother's words ring loudly from the Plains of Asphodel. *Her pills.*

The time of the tournament coincides.

The urge to scream and warn her overwhelms him, yet somehow he knows it would be futile. Moreover an eerie caution seeps through him about letting anyone know their future. So instead, he takes her into his powerful arms and hugs her close. This also serves to buy time in blinking away a tear.

The uncharacteristic fervor of affection shocks Pandora's eyes wide open, but she accepts it with as much of her own.

Into the embrace Leo pours all his love. Love coded in life, unveiled in death. Somehow, he knows she receives it, despite being no more than a conjured image likely of Alex's doing.

A chime at the door interrupts the moment. Before separating, Pandora whispers, "just remember what I said." She then pulls away, still surprised but quite happy.

She continues eying her son carefully which causes Leo to hurry toward the door. "I'll get it," he spits out.

He opens and reacts just as quick to the person on the other side.

"Staj!"

Anastasia recoils from the unaccustomed enthusiasm over her presence.

"Leo? Hi."

Arranged much simpler in denim, a low cut top, and ponytailed hair, she has never appeared more beautiful to Leo.

He rushes forward without thinking. The astonishment in her eyes is all that reacts. As he means to embrace her, however, the only thing he hits is the opposing blade...

of Feidor.

△△△

It takes three moves before Leo realizes where he is.

The Dueling finals of the Warrior Division comprises victors from two separate branches of semi-finals. Each kladimans may choose two weapons to use. In this case, Leonidas Maquari versus defending champion Feidor Yazinov consists equally of xiphos blades and aegis guards.

Indeed, Leo has never met a worthier opponent. Equal and exceeding in power and speed, the threat of failure has never lurked so close. Its presence both drives and frightens him to the limits of his abilities. In the end though, it would take more than sheer skill to beat Feidor.

The two exchange a flurry of hard cuts which rings throughout the arena like a clashing of thick icicles. Feidor presses forward with a strike from his signature guard: a mid-sized pearl colored weapon in the shape of a pentagram. The champion follows with a low cut from his equally signature curved long blade of the same color.

This Leo oversteps and turns into a swift counter kick. Feidor, though, absorbs this, and with a twist of his arm flips Leo head over heels to the ground. He then continues with a huge downward swing that sends the air screaming on its descent. From his knees Leo manages to parry and quickly rise to deliver a guard strike to the back.

The two regroup by circling in a small radius. Ravenous beasts smelling the blood in their prey.

Feidor's imposing figure casts a shadow in the sand. Facing him feels like facing a monster come alive: his headdress made of the jaws and teeth of a Great White: scar ridden skin over a stocky frame using very few protective plates. This he sacrifices for the sake of being able to move his 6 foot 5 body like a man 50 pounds lighter.

The loudness of the vast expanse around them rises anticipating the end. Competitors usually rely most on the crowd's energy late in a match when fatigue looms against their will.

For Leo, he would listen to Thais' cheers. This he would attest to hearing above thousands.

Now though: silence amongst screams.

He had never competed in a tournament without her. Lacking her support feels like fighting with only one hand: her sheer absence like fighting naked with no body plates.

In the earlier minutes his mother's advice kept Thais' presence at bay.

It's not your fault.

Now battered and breathless, however, one reaches deeper within.

What he finds instead of motivation is a broken girl who cries her innocence. Tears of blood stream down her face. Leo sees it is he who holds the twisting blade.

His shoulders droop.

Not a moment later does Feidor charge for the kill, driving Leo back with a fury of precise combinations. A rising cut well placed on the chin sends both Leo and his headdress flying.

The violence of his fall sends the crowd into a roar. Both they and the great champion lift their arms expecting Leo to submit. The Maurileho, though slow to react, keeps hold of his blade and makes it as far as his knees.

Feidor approaches Leo still dazed. He moves swift yet not rushed. Once before his wounded foe, he lifts his blade high into the arena air.

Leo lifts his eyes in a starry haze. The figure in front looks even larger than Menoitios. The sun gleaming off his blade and guard make him actually seem more terrible and majestic than the mighty ruler of the Underworld.

Though Leo's muscular instinct begins lifting his blade in defense, the tormenting thought of Thais prevents him from committing to the effort. To even block Feidor's cut seemed unfair to her. That she bleed whilst he not. That she suffer whilst he win glory at a sport she invested so much in.

Only suffering pays for suffering, and only suffering will heal Leo's pain.

In the original match, Leo lazily raised his blade against Feidor's savage strike, resulting in a deep gash running down the left of his eye. The blood felt cathartic for Leo. He then sought more.

Although Feidor cut him no further, he delivered devastating body shots to the ribs and knees preventing Leo from rising again.

The loss of blood and difficulty breathing nearly sent Leo into shock.

The last thing he remembers was Anastasia in the arena dabbing his face with her shirt. The next thing he remembers was waking in the infirmary several weeks later. This was followed by his mother's exhaustive efforts at rehab for many months thereafter.

Mom.

Now again with the blade hanging over him he thinks of all his self-indulgence cost his mother. More importantly, the hand she placed on his shoulder: the hand doctors would chop leaving her a cripple.

The suffering he wished for himself would end up his mother's burden: a burden leading to her...

No.

"NO!" he shouts with a surge of fire.

Feidor's strike hits nothing but sand. Leo, rolling to the side, counters with a hard cut to the elbow sending his opponent's long blade flying to the ground.

He then wastes no time following up, attacking like an uncaged animal. The rage on his face and fear in his eyes look far more menacing than any lion's headdress.

Feidor bears the onslaught with crafty maneuvering of his guard until Leo locks it in and spins around. Then with a savage backhand he strikes the great champion flush to the back of the temple. This sends blood and shark's teeth splattering in all directions.

Feidor's fall shakes the ground.

An unaccustomed terror penetrates the scarred, leathery skin of the bald man as the young Maurileho raises his weapon to finish.

The crowd's screaming deafens. Its energy intoxicates. Yet Leo pays it no mind. He eyes the wound he's inflicted on his foe and drops thunder with the edge of his guard.

ΔΔΔ

Leo's eyes open to relative silence if not tranquility. They first perceive the coarse darkness. As more and more light enters, an extremely robust structure begins to take form just off to the right. He soon sees it is made of brass and circles higher and higher until passing out of sight. From his position on the rigid ground, he makes it out to be a set of enormous walls.

A new light enters. It touches life where he imagines his scar would no longer be. When he touches back his fingers find Anastasia's.

"Staj," says Leo, pulling her close.

Her body tenses, then relaxes into his.

"Hi, Leo."

Leo holds her for an extra second to make sure she's real.

"I think I won. I think I beat him," says Leo. He gets to his feet quick and a bit uneasy.

"Beat who?"

"Feidor! And if I did, maybe Mom's ok."

Anastasia looks over the groggy eyed mess standing in front of her and makes no comment.

"Don't you remember?"

"Leo," she says, "you didn't beat Feidor."

Leo's hand moves to the side of his face where a long patch of skin has less feeling than the rest.

"That's impossible," says Leo. He scrapes his scar harder and tries his best to ignore that he ever accepted those experiences as orchestrations of Alex. "You were there, you saw it!" He grazes the part of the chin where Feidor struck him and it swells with pain.

"I can feel where he got me. How can you not remember?"

"I do remember, but not that way."

Leo shakes his head and paces a few steps. "I don't get it then, why would Alex send me there?"

"It wasn't me," says Alex, walking up with Silas and Alexi.

Leo quizzically glares at his grandfather. "Well look who's back," he says. "You got any other fire rivers to jump in? Why don't we stop to see Typhoeus, I hear there's a petting zoo in the Pit."

"Leo, you remember what Menoitios said: what happens down here depends on you."

"Yet where I go isn't real," says Leo. He presses on his chin, "somehow."

"What is real?"

Leo flicks his hand in disgust and looks away.

"Did you find answers?" Alex follows.

Thais' tears return to his mind: Feidor's blade to his chin. Both culminate in the sensation of a weakened hand resting on his shoulder.

He grinds his jaw for a good many seconds, but ultimately sighs.

"I guess, yeah," he says brusquely.

"Then real or not, should it really matter?"

Leo looks ahead to the massive structure some believe to be Hell. It weighs largely on Leo's skeptical mind. And yet...there it is: the high walls looming directly in front of him and the rest.

Even its fiction inspires believers toward a certain path in life, a benefit even a skeptic cannot deny.

"Relax, Leo," says Alex when his grandson doesn't respond. He looks him over, "and take a break. You look like you just went a few rounds with Feidor Yazinov."

"I did."

"Really?"

"Real enough."

"That works for me."

Leo paces a few more steps toward the wall. Looking down he examines the uninviting ground for a place to "relax." He then spots his substance of choice when coping: the guitar.

Taking it up he plops down and begins strumming. The white Les Paul his grandfather gifted him plays beautifully, though without an amp sounds hollow. Anastasia sits down beside and listens to him finger through a Scars of Bourbon lick.

"You should play that next year," she says.

"Next year?"

"At the Prometheia. You'll be Festival Artist."

Aeschylus, his father, played a Scars of Bourbon song for the Music Competition this year.

"No thanks," says Leo, ceasing to play.

"Then do November Rain, with that," she says, pointing to Alex's heirloom.

His mother's favorite song, despite being pre-Reckoning. The electric version requires a full band and orchestra. Leo fingers through a part of its famous solo to see what he remembers.

"Nah, that song's ancient," he says.

Nonetheless, in the damp air outside the Walls of Hell, even clanky strings sound divine producing the sounds of that melody. He continues playing.

Anastasia regards his face with a soft yet somewhat frightened look. As his fingers keep moving, his mind seems to move further and further away from the present.

"What?" he says without lifting his eyes.

Anastasia reacts a bit startled at his somehow feeling her stare. She quickly collects herself. "I thought you were dead."

Leo stops. "Huh?"

"Or whatever that means here. You walked into the river."

Entrancing flames float through his mind like a dream: the jaws of the lion, the submission of falling, landing in his Service quarters with Thais.

"Well yeah, but...actually, I don't even know how I got here." Leo glances at the river of fire several dozen yards behind them, then at the towering walls of bronze right of where they sit.

"You were on the ground when we got here."

Leo starts to consider, then just grins and shakes his head.

"How did you guys cross?"

"Alex. He can..."

"I know I know. The Blessed can blah blah blah." He continues strumming.

"You saw me then? If you relived Feidor, that is" says Anastasia.

"Yeah. When you had your short hair and dressed like a guy."

A hard slap to Leo's meaty shoulder rings through the dark expanse. This is followed by an equally dark glare Leo expects to precede her typical "jerk" designation. She instead poses a question. "Who else did you see?"

Damn.

"Jerk" would have been better.

"Uh, Mom...Feidor...you, and...Thais, a bit."

"Oh," she says looking down. "I guess it was a nice memory then."

"No, not really," he says, a little indignant.

Anastasia's eyebrows raise at his tone, then relax. Leo returns to playing.

Alexi joins them a second later in his gay, yet neutral tone.

"Glad to see you kids playing nice. Mind if I pop a squat?" says Alexi. He sits and crosses his legs before anyone can answer.

Anastasia smiles over at him fondly. Leo pays him no mind.

Though Alexi doesn't necessarily return the smile, something in the depths of his blue eyes shows a twinge of how he once might have reacted. He then looks on Leo. His expression remains the same despite having been ignored. He stays that way for a good few minutes.

"You're a lot like Dad when you play," he finally says.

Leo fumbles a lick, then picks up his strumming a little rougher. "I'm sorry to hear that."

"Why sorry? He was quite the guitarist."

Leo stops altogether and looks into his brother.

"But not the father."

Anastasia rises to leave when Leo snatches her arm. "You don't need to go anywhere. Stay."

"What makes you say something like that?" says Alexi.

"Listen, I don't know what he was like in your time, but when my turn came he'd already checked out."

His grip remains on Anastasia's arm, only tighter.

The deceased adolescent horn player from the Plains of Asphodel kneels down to be at eye level with great Maurileho of the Warrior Division.

"You're right, little brother, you don't know."

His hand loosens a bit on hearing this. Anastasia's attention also peaks and she resumes her position next to Leo.

"He was such a great Dad. I miss him just as much as Mom."

Sentimental words seem alien when associated with Leo's father. Holding him on equal terms with a person such as Pandora Maquari: incomprehensible.

"Are you sure we're talking about the same guy?"

"I'm sure. He was always with me, he always had time. We'd play every day when he came back from the studio. When I started studying French Horn, he'd do accompaniment on his guitar. And then..."

Alexi's expression changes for the first time since being re-animated. His cheer flattens, his expression dampens, and he stares distantly toward the iron gates of the wall.

"Then...when I got sick...he'd lay with me until I fell asleep: like when I was little and had a nightmare. Only now he was the one having it."

The ice around the image Leo keeps of his father begins to drip despite the cold of his will. His brother paints such a different picture from the neglectful, self-absorbed wanna-be rock star he'd always known. Yet somehow he's unable to completely dismiss what Alexi says.

"It was so hard for him to see me that way. He made me feel better acting like it didn't. Eventually, though, it was like he was the one dying, so I acted for him."

These notions grind against Leo's perception like being told the world is flat. He fights through memories he's stowed away to find a shred of the man his brother describes. When he puts all those noble characteristics together, though, all he sees is a stranger.

"At the end I couldn't talk or open my eyes, but I could still hear. He didn't know that. Then, he lost it; crying over me and hating Prometheus. It was worse than being sick."

Though still out of character with his father, the straight simple nature of Alexi coupled with the vividness of his recounting presses heavy on Leo's will.

"I knew he'd suffer as long as I lived. So I let go, for him."

Alexi turns to his brother looking more human than ever, while Leo never felt less.

"He was my best friend. Be happy you play like him."

With that he walks away. Leo keeps his head down while Anastasia dabs the wetness from under her eyes.

"Why did he have to tell me that?" says Leo.

"So you'd understand."

His brother's story combined with the tournament he never fought have drained him the energy to try.

Instead, he lays back and rests his head on his arm, eyes open.

Anastasia places her hand atop his. Then, steeling her nerves, she slips her fingers through.

A butterfly flitters in Leo's stomach, but settles faster than he expects. Its beauty breeds peace in his chest, and his eyes close.

ΔΔΔ

"Attach document," says Zoe folding a lock of her luscious brown hair behind her ears.

The TeleComp's voice prompt asks for a recipient.

"*Time's Current* Editor."

Beren sits back one leg over the other.

Neither say "send."

They sit in silence staring at the file summarizing their comrade's life. This, when only days before they were watching him play for hundreds at the Festival, along with Pandora and Anastasia.

Zoe glances back at Beren, frowns to one side, then gives the command.

A receipt confirmation beeps. It cuts through the air of the lonely room. Leo's obituary is gone.

"Now what?" says Beren after a time.

"Yeah…, right."

TeleComp shuts down.

Zoe rises and her hair falls over her face to one side. She does not bother pushing it away. The bags under her eyes look like she's been awake for days. Her white garb from the funeral games looks as though they've been worn just as long.

She turns from Beren and starts for the door. No footsteps follow, however. Turning back she sees her forlorn friend still staring in the direction of the TeleComp.

"Aren't you coming?"

Beren rubs his palms over his eyes and around his disheveled hair. "We're not done yet."

"There's nothing more to do, and I really just want to go home." Zoe crosses her arms around her waist.

"Ms. Maquari is still missing," he says getting up. He's sure to set the chair carefully back in its place. "We might as well check for any leads."

"The Shields are doing that."

"They don't know the family like we do...or did," he reluctantly corrects. "Leo might have left something we would get but not them."

Zoe massages the back of her neck but doesn't outright refuse.

"Besides," says Beren, "this might be the last thing we can do for them."

The solemn statement prompts a lazy smile on the part of Zoe. The look in her eye prompts more the solemn part. Finally, she drops her arms to the side as if to say "where do we start."

Beren nods and makes straight for the basement.

"You think she's down there?"

"Not exactly, but Leo was before she went missing, so, might find something."

That "something" hangs in the air between them. The notion of not only looking for a rotting corpse, but that of a loved one for whose son they've just written an obituary. Zoe returns her arms to her waist.

"Um, you go ahead, B. I'll just...take a quick look in the rooms."

She enters Pandora's lending no eye to any search. Sinking into the great woman's chair, she hugs her knees and leans her head back into the cushions. The closeness invites her to sink in deeper, and she doesn't resist.

Outside, the sun sets as ever.

Nearly dozed off, a peculiar reflection catches her eye from the closet. Amid a line of old clothes, it flashes again. She slowly unwraps her body and peels herself from the chair to go see.

Pushing aside racks, her hand bumps into a large glass-colored object. She pulls it out to reveal a classic style fixed bow: angled limbs connected by a neon red drawstring. She lifts and tests the pull.

"Whooa, this draw weight has got to be seventy pounds."

Bows with limbs of seventy pounds or more are typically designated for hunting big game. Hunters themselves generally reside in the small mountain communities outside Prometheum. Otherwise, they are used for combat.

Zoe spots a bow quiver; also a hunter's tool for its silence in motion. A half dozen arrows fill it, each ending in two yellow fletchings and a white cock feather.

Zoe pops one out and it slices clean through a heavy coat hanging nearby.

"Oh gosh," she says, holding the tip in front of her face: three prongs of razors meeting at one point.

A broadhead.

"Why would she need a weapon like this?"

Zoe sets it back down where she found it. She then notices a rather large box a little deeper in the closet. From its breadth and durable outer cover, it seems to be some type of Preservo product. On top it is labeled "2049" in graphic letters.

"This is older than Khloe," she says, reaching down. She places her hand on the box and hesitates. A quick glance at the bow, though, and she sets to opening.

A puff of air spits as she unlatches the protective lid. Inside contains a number of old trinkets from handheld music devices to surprisingly fashionable makeup. Zoe pulls out an old J.T Tasker and notes its significant weight.

She next finds a paper copy of the famous novel *The Ashes of Rebirth*. Written during the Reckoning years, it recounts author Charles Alvarez' experience of great sacrifice and loss, most notably of the woman he intended to marry.

Underneath a heap of other novels is an old-fashioned computer device. There is no virtual screen outlet. As it seems to unfold like a book, Zoe lifts up the top very gently.

This produces a creak that sounds as slow as she lifts. The unsettling noise ringing through the silence of a house recently vacated by death nearly causes Zoe to drop the computer altogether. Though she manages to retain hold, she ends up looking over her shoulder before returning her hands anywhere they were.

Once assured no death spirits have come to reprimand her curiosity, she makes a sharp exhale and turns back around.

"Get with it, there's no one there," she says.

Now with the blank screen fully visible, she places her fingers next to what she thinks is the power button. She makes no move to press. She just contemplates the dark reflection looking torn between amusement and hesitation.

"Pandora shooting bears at 100 yards?" she ventures.

She thinks it over a second more.

"Just a peek."

The laptop starts at the push of a button, which Zoe finds insecure. A beautiful portrait appears on the desktop of a young Pandora with Aeschylus and a light haired little boy. All smile and appear very united.

Zoe purses her lips to the side. "If they'd just stayed that way."

She looks closer at the boy and notes the slight build in addition to the light hair. She tilts her head to one side. "If that's not Leo, it must be Alexi, the brother who died." She clicks on the photos icon to see more. Many follow along the same vein.

One tab, however, is of solid color. It is marked "Generation 6." The contents therein contain one solitary image.

Zoe opens and enlarges. Eight people pose together with conviction on their faces: each armed and very familiar.

To the far right holding a spear stands Zoe's mother, Gaya Qwynshing. She wears the standard combat gear of the time that used heavier body plates.

Next to her is Bouko Braun resting his hand on the shoulder of a woman Zoe does not recognize. While his customary twin blades cling to his back, she carries no apparent weapon. Neither do her clothes conform to the rest: long, satin robes hanging like a fancy dress.

A lean, darker skinned man occupies the center of the photo. Zoe gasps at the resemblance between him and the boxer from the funeral games: long braided hair and a tiger tattoo. He holds a pair of tonfas.

Aside him, an older man in a blazer leans on a crutch. Small, oval spectacles rest out on his nose. He also displays no weapon.

The final two position themselves the closest. A sturdy man wraps his hand around a young woman's shoulder. The woman, with long strawberry blonde hair, reaches across her body to lock her fingers into his. He holds a long blade while she a bow: the same bow as from the closet.

Zoe covers her mouth. Anyone seeing the photo would believe them a couple if they didn't already know them as Pandora Maquari and Silas Wildyn.

"Oh-my-god. Talk about skeletons in the closet."

Zoe picks up the laptop and exits the room.

"Thank gosh *Leo* never saw this."

CHAPTER 12 – TARTAROS

"Annie," a strong voice commands.

Leo rouses to see Anastasia lying on her side. With no dreariness in her eyes he's not sure if she slept. They are still holding hands as Silas' expression standing over them indicates.

"Come on, get ready," says Silas.

She moves to obey her father when Leo pulls her back sharply. "No," he says.

The two glare at each other. In place of the bald fatherly Captain Leo sees a young bladesman with a mind toward his mother. His protective and even possessive sense rouses at the threat of an outsider moving in on something of his own. Silas very well may see Leo in a similar light.

Nonetheless, something in Leo's knowing look registers on Silas' face. Though he tries to match Leo's intensity, a wariness begins to grow over what Leo may say.

The image of the old picture remains burned in the forefront of Leo's mind. It even fights to escape his lips. For the time being, though, Leo pushes it aside and opts for the second mystery nagging at his brain.

"What's Generation 6?"

A faint relief flashes over Silas, quickly turning back to doubt. "Well, uh," he grumbles.

"It's ok Captain, it's time they know," says Alex appearing with Alexi.

Anastasia looks on Leo less curious about what he said and more content that he was able to derive such a term. For several years Leo has only made allusions to things he's seen in dreams or "daydreams" as he calls them. Never before has he committed so openly to a vision.

Alex sits beside him, "you saw something?"

Leo hesitates a moment and throws a final reproach toward Silas.

"Zoe, she...found an old photo."

Alex smiles: not for the photo.

"Mom was in it," he continues, "she was holding a bow. The others I knew were Zoe's Mom, Statesman Braun, and…Silas."

The big Captain sits and beckons for his daughter. This time Leo releases her hand.

"What do you know about the Raze of Olympus?" says Alex.

Before Leo can answer a faint draft passes under his nose. It's warm and damp like a humid day, yet putrid as though blowing from the lungs of something unsavory. The White Lion immediately comes to mind, strong enough to tickle the hair on Leo's forearm. He doesn't believe it would approach, however, with Alex so near: nor can he imagine a source of a breeze in such a dismal place.

He then addresses his grandfather's question, looking at no one in particular. "They say Zeus wanted to kill us, and Prometheus stopped him."

"They say, and it's true. The race of men, pre-Reckoning, were actually the fifth generation created."

Leo braces himself for another tale he's supposed to believe.

"Prometheus' son, Deukalion, founded one after the Deluge. Others you know from Homer."

To imagine even "fictional" men as a different form of man from what he'd always imagined seemed strange.

"When man was first conceived, Epimetheus had the job of apportioning traits."

"Prometheus' brother," states Anastasia.

"Right. But being a fool he gave out all the useful qualities to animals and left man with nothing."

"Oh that must be why animals have fur, claws, and heightened senses," says Alexi.

Basic biology at schools also monitored regeneration in insects, a remarkable trait followers also attest to the foolishness of Epimetheus.

"Zeus thought to balance the equation with the 6th generation, so he had a formula drawn from the earth. At that time you see, human ingenuity was running rampant in the mechanical arts Prometheus stole. It was thought that if humans had more primitive abilities, they wouldn't go to such extremes for self-preservation."

Leo makes a reluctant nod. "Makes sense," he says.

"It does, until Zeus determined that Generation 5 was far too gone to be rebalanced, and would never lose the lust for power."

Lycean lessons on ethics often refer to the Age of Decadence as an exemplar on living without temperance.

"So better to do us in, huh?" asks Leo, finally sticking his head up.

"Pretty much, and there came the Reckoning."

Only a time in history for most living. For those who lived it, such as Alex, the word signifies much more.

"We lost so much," says Alex in a distant, quieter tone. He takes a moment before continuing.

"Anyway, once it was finished, the formula was sealed in an urn and guarded away...until Prometheus found out where it was. He never gave up on us, though if he did I wouldn't have blamed him."

To hear such a statement from a positive and reputable man like Alexander Maquari would surprise any Promethean. Coming from a stable society where the culture demands a natural equilibrium with their environment prevents them from understanding Alex's world. Furthermore, to hear such a champion of Prometheus showing the slightest bit of understanding on the part of Zeus, whose name carries a negative connotation, is like seeing a lamb side with a wolf.

"So what did he do?" says Anastasia.

"He managed to procure the formula and began mixing it in the clouds. Before he could finish, though, Zeus caught him. That began the War of Clay."

The final series of statements peaks Leo's interest for the first time in the narrative. He hangs on one particular word.

The clouds.

He looks to the darkness of the sky, or ceiling, or whatever they would call the upper regions of the bank beyond the Phlegethon. He thinks of the white clouds of Eulimnos scattered across the colored sky: how his mother would enjoy them sitting on her bench next to the apple tree. He thinks of himself at her side, then realizes he will have to invent that memory, for he never took the time to do so in life.

Picturing Lake Maquari, however, recalls another image he recently acquired: that of his grandfather overlooking the lake region he would settle. The mural he saw in the entryway of

Emrick's estate. Alex stood on the summit of Emrick's property drenched from head to toe from the heavy rain falling around him.

He begins to piece things together.

"The Sacred Rains," he says mostly to himself.

Alex waits. "Keep going," he says.

"That was the formula." says Leo.

"Very g..." Alex begins.

"If it was," Leo interrupts, "that means..."

The photo from 2049 runs through his mind as it did over Zoe's eyes. Gaya Qwynshing, Bouko Braun, Silas Wildyn, and Pandora Maquari: from left to right the parents of his friends. An entire folder dedicated to a single photo with the peculiar name of...

"It's us," says Leo. "We are Generation 6."

Anastasia's smile reaches the point of her customary squint. Alexi seems content just to be able to call himself something new. And Leo: Leo keeps his head hung like he's just been told he was adopted.

"I've never met anyone with fur or claws," says Alexi.

"The qualities aren't necessarily animal," says Alex, "and it isn't everyone. Many have gifts people wouldn't understand." He glances at Anastasia, then settles on Leo. "And others they'd rather hide." Leo leers at his grandfather but keeps his head down.

"Remember, the Rains were only part of the formula, the rest is still out there."

"Out where?" asks Anastasia.

Alex makes a long face and looks off, catching Silas' eye on the way. "Hidden and protected," he reveals.

"Sucks for everybody else," says Leo.

Alex rises abruptly, "that's exactly the kind of thinking Zeus would want from the people he meant to destroy."

When he stands the rest follow: Leo the slowest. Alex keeps his shoulders squared toward his grandson and a hard finger pointed at his chest. Once again his persona takes more the General than the boy from Queens.

"We made peace but nature was left unbalanced," Alex continues. "It won't be long before the wrong person figures it out and takes advantage. That's not what your parents fought and sacrificed for."

The last word draws in Anastasia. She regards her father standing attentive with his hands clasped behind his back. A sadness pours over her eyes, and she takes a few labored breaths before speaking. "Is that what happened, Daddy?" she says. "Did you die looking for the urn?"

Silas moves to face his daughter and places his hands on her shoulders. "Yes, Annie. One of our team, Vince Yeerum, turned on me. I was alone, after training, and he shows up out of his wits. Attacked me without saying a word."

Anastasia breaks eye contact and looks up and down her stout father. "But...couldn't you defend yourself?"

"I held my own," says Silas, rubbing her shoulders with his thumb. "We were both unarmed, but there was no beating ole Vince hand to hand. His style was lethal, and he could use every part of his body as a weapon."

Anastasia cringes under his fingers.

The man from the Generation 6 photo crosses Leo's mind: the one with the tiger tattoo. Though he may not be fond of Silas, he feels for Anastasia likely projecting a scenario of her father being beaten to death.

Anastasia turns her eyes to the barren floor. Her breathing becomes heavier, and an uncustomary darkness flushes over her face. "At least Statesman Braun killed him," she says.

Silas raises his brow. "Too bad too. Vince was a good guy."

Her head pops up. "A good guy?"

"He was. I'll never forget that deranged look he had that day. Something was off, but I never figured out what."

"Can't you just ask him?" says Leo.

"No I can't just ask him," Silas says at Leo. "Souls that come here can't be reanimated."

"You mean...he's HERE?" says Anastasia pointing to the dark walls.

The flash of sinister satisfaction betrayed a moment earlier begins to fade. Before the intimidating bronze guarding the Pit once believed to cage the Titans, a note of pity touches upon her grief. It collides hard with the anguish of her father's demise.

Not knowing which face to choose, she buries the one she has into her father's chest.

"Mom would never tell me what happened exactly," she says, "or who did it. She just had me think it was some cold-blooded murderer."

Silas makes a knowing look to Alex. The General considers, and nods in return. Silas then whispers in his daughter's ear, "I know you've had a hard time with that, Annie, but it's time you get closure."

Silas takes her hand and moves off with Alex. Alexi follows up behind and the four of them head toward the tall gates embedded in the high walls of bronze.

You gotta be kidding me.

The notion of entering Tartaros does not unsettle Leo half as much as another step in the wrong direction to reaching his mother. The pressure mounts knowing the necessity of finding her before Beren. Again the idea arises of leaving the others behind.

Seeing such anticipation in Anastasia, however, stays the protest he has dying to release. The years of uncertainty written on her face mix hard with the fear of having it relieved. The closure her father promised she would likely never have a chance to attain again.

Although unsure of what this detour may cost, Leo does his best to suppress the tension swelling inside. After a few more breaths he realizes: *he* must follow *her* this time.

Alex continues leading the way to gates that seem to grow taller as they approach. Once within a short distance he waves the others off and goes on alone. He then places his hand on the crevice of the opening, applies a small amount of force, and waits.

The doors extend several yards wide and several more high. They share the contour of the bronze and appear so fixed to the structure one might think they've never been open. Several feet above Alex' head, two ring handles the size of tree trunks hang heavily still.

"There's no way he's pushing those things open," Leo thinks aloud. "Even a Blessed."

Just then a frame appears in the shape of a door. It glows as if under fluorescent light and is lined by a random pattern of classical letters. Anastasia immediately looks down at her bracelet, then back up at the door.

A second more and it opens: slowly and in complete silence. Behind reveals a narrow passage.

"Pretty neat, huh?" says Alexi.

Silas turns reprovingly on Leo before moving on.

"Yeah, pretty neat," says Leo.

Entering they do not find themselves at a lack for light. The glow seems to follow where they go: or at least where Alex goes, but no further.

As Leo draws his first real breath a thick mouthful of musty air fills his lungs. He then looks to the coarse stone lining the walls. Touching it with the back of his knuckle, it feels cold and damp.

They soon emerge on a ridge of large expanse. Wind greets them, flapping about as though a storm were occurring nearby. With light barely to see, the great Pit knows no end high or low.

"How did we get down this far?" says Leo searching up and down. "Actually, I can't even tell what far *is* here."

No one heeds his question. All keep attention, rather, on the corner of the ridge.

There, barely visible in the dimness, a battered soul jerks about. Similar in constitution to those in the Plains of Asphodel, its limbs create the appearance of white smoke when they flit. Each twitch moves his body several feet, yet his lips move continually.

"It's like he's trying to say something," says Alexi.

Each convulsion follows an inaudible utterance. He thrashes as though searching for a tongue that will never grow back.

Anastasia leans closer. She squints her eyes on his erratic lips and concentrates for several seconds between movements. "I think he's saying... "I didn't mean to." She ventures a step closer for a better look. Her own lips start imitating the formations of the spirit's. Eventually, she adds air and a voice.

"It wasn't me," she interprets. She then pauses a moment. "Why would he say that, Daddy?"

"Ah, Vince, I don't get you old buddy," says Silas.

"Vince!?" says Anastasia, recoiling from her father's killer.

Silas catches her from behind. Anastasia doesn't turn but keeps staring at the man who so drastically changed her life.

Her jaw wrenches a few times but is unable to remain clenched. In the end her head just falls forward.

By now the spirit has ventured closer to the rest. As his twitches become clearer, it turns out they are not twitches at all.

Leo moves cautiously next to Anastasia, looking behind her before he speaks. "Don't those moves remind you of something?" he says.

She doesn't notice him immediately, then slowly tilts her head, "huh?"

"Look closer," he says, "those aren't random jerks, those are kata positions. Kick, punch, elbow, knee."

She turns with limited enthusiasm but considers nonetheless. After a series of further movements, the kata or "forms" he executes begin to register on her face. "The funeral games," she says softly.

The kickboxer at Pandora's games performed a ritual dance of similar style before engaging Coach Palaistros in the pugilism event.

Vince's spirit passes just before them, allowing a slightly clearer view of his features.

"The braid," says Leo, "he's got it too."

Anastasia zeros in on his complexion. Vince's torment reads loudly on his face, louder than making any connections of familiarity. She focuses on his eyes, which, despite his anguish, show genuine repentance and a lack of understanding. She then follows his lips, and begins to show the same look on her own face.

She sniffles. "But why would he say that?"

Leo turns to find emotion already pouring uncontrollably from Anastasia: only that way would she allow him to see it so openly.

Embarrassed, she hides her head in her hands.

Silas again rubs her shoulders but she will not drop her hands to embrace him.

As a friend, Leo might have done the same or tried to lighten the tension with one of his remarks.

Now, in the depths of Tartaros, he takes her hands from her face and pulls her in close. Even Silas does not scoff as she lets out years of pent up feelings and doubts on Leo's shoulder.

The proximity does not feel as foreign to Leo as he would've thought. Her body joins together with his like a puzzle piece. After a few moments he forgets who's comforting who, and soon all seems lighter.

"I know some of this doesn't make sense," says Silas from behind. "But I need you to move on, Annie."

Anastasia shoots an incredulous look at her father. She then turns back to Vince.

After a while her head drops again.

"I'll try." She releases Leo and takes deep hold of her father. "I'll try, Daddy."

A relief passes through Leo he's not felt in some time. Given the overall circumstances, he's not sure he has the right to such a feeling. For Anastasia though he lets it pass.

Turning back to Vince he ponders the lonely spirit for quite some time.

"You know," he begins, "there's something I don't get."

Silas grinds his jaw. "And what's that, Leonidas?" he says.

"If this guy's saying he didn't mean it, and you said he wasn't in his right mind, then what he did wasn't really his fault."

"Could be."

"Like he was possessed or something."

"What's your point?"

"Why would he be here if he's not really bad?"

The question catches everyone off-guard. Most look to the other. When no one answers, everyone looks to Alex.

"As you know," Alex begins, "the three judges no longer exist. Rhadamanthus, Minos, and Aeacus were removed after Zeus' reign ended."

"So how is anyone here then?"

Alex raises his hands in gathering. "We choose our own fates."

Leo scoffs. "Who the hell would choose to come here?"

"Someone with a guilty conscience."

The old notion of rewards and punishments still exists for some. Their intuition of the afterlife permits it. Faith in Prometheus, however, does not subscribe to this belief.

"A person always knows who they really are in their hearts: whether their actions hurt or bettered their society in life: and that's where the problem is."

"Life is the problem?"

"Essentially, yeah. It's the secular effect on human emotions."

Any mortal in the Underworld could not deny the emotional effect of the atmosphere, especially the calming sensation of The Isles of the Blessed and Elysium. In addition, the lack of interaction with people on an everyday level invites less to rouse.

"In life it takes a person with incredible poise to trust his gut, and even more to make well-reasoned choices."

"Don't most people think before they decide something?"

"No. They decide what they want then find ways to justify it. The choice's already been made whether you realize it or not."

Running into the lake, Anastasia following, the reasons thereof...

"Society tempts and conditions you, puts like a veil over your conscience. When you die the veil is lifted, and that's all you're left with."

"Pride, vanity..."

"And love," says Anastasia.

"The choice is already made when they come here, their time here lets them figure out why."

The wind intensifies, throwing mist into the air. Vince goes on as usual.

"So there's really nothing here to punish him then," says Leo.

"If you're referring to burning or other eternal tortures, then no. It all depends on you."

"Right, like Menoitios said."

Leo turns back to Vince. Although without any physical suffering, Vince's mental agony deters any complaisance toward Tartaros.

"How long will he be here?" says Anastasia.

"Not forever. Just until he's purified."

"How will he know that?" says Leo.

"He'll know. And when he does, Menoitios will release him."

"To the Plains of Asphodel?"

"To the river Lethe where the two of you entered."

Both recall the vast river they crossed to get to the Isles of the Blessed, on what Leo thought was a raft his mother left. The faces they witnessed in the water come to mind: Anastasia in particular of seeing the young boy killed in the gunfire.

"The river takes their memories, doesn't it?" says Anastasia.

"They have to drink before they can pass on to a new life. They'll only know of their old ones instinctively and through dreams."

The wind develops a more consistent pattern and carries more condensation. A particularly hard flap rising from the ridge reminds Leo just how long they've lingered in Tartaros. He makes a knowing look at Alex: hard and impatient. Alex makes one back at Leo: just the opposite.

Leo can only imagine how much further Beren has come to finding his mother's body. He knows if he pushes Alex though, the General will put him in his place. For the time being he decides to hold his tongue.

In the meantime, Alexi wanders around like a curious puppy; Silas and Anastasia observe Vince more; and Alex remains in the same position, watching Leo with a patient look of anticipation.

Leo begins to pace to distract his anxiety. The conditions in the atmosphere, however, recall to him the myth of the monster Typhoeus: the storm giant born of Tartaros itself and sent back permanently only after challenging Zeus. He was said to have fifty hissing serpent heads in place of hands and vipers in place of feet. While his head was human, disheveled hair and pointed ears combined to lend a frightening compliment to eyes that flashed fire.

Leo takes a careful peek over the ridge. Down in the Pit he discerns nothing but darkness.

A small, ridged stone lies at the edge. He nudges it over with the tip of his shoe. Though he waits and waits, no sound of it landing ever returns.

What does come, however, is an increase in the wind's intensity. One gust throws a splash of mist in Leo's face. Another nearly knocks him off balance toward the edge.

All of a sudden the White Lion seems like a kitten compared to what a storm giant may be.

"Well," says Leo, wiping his brow dry. "Vince: super guy. Sorry he killed you, Silas, but I think we need to get moving."

The comment earns him the typical glare.

Alex approaches casually. "We're waiting on you."

Leo scoffs. "On me? I never wanted to come here in the first place," he says. He lowers his eyes to Anastasia right after the statement leaves his mouth.

"Then lead the way."

The uncharacteristic acquiescence stalls Leo for a split second, but he has no mind to refuse.

"Right, let's go."

Leo rushes off headlong into the dark passageway they came by. Fluorescent lights flash in rapid succession to the pace of his steps. When he realizes just how fast he stops to make sure the others have kept up. All that's followed, however, is darkness and silence.

A lone glow emanates from the walls where he stands. Little by little it falters, then goes out.

ΔΔΔ

"Leo. Hey, come on man, it's time for the archery."

Awareness returns on the festival grounds in Eulimnos. Multitudes of people in white line the field. For a moment, Leo thinks he's returned to his mother's funeral games.

"Don't you want to watch Staj? I'm sure she'd...appreciate you being there."

"Beren?" says Leo gaining his bearings.

"Man, you're losing it. Try to get a grip on your... daydreaming."

The doubt arises, however, from appearance more than unfamiliarity. Beren, much leaner than in present day, sports longer hair styled up by product. The last he looked like that was around the time of his grandmother's death.

Leo follows his friend nonetheless. The crowd parts easily for the two to pass. Given their sympathetic looks toward Beren, Leo figures it must have something to do with the Braun family.

The two manage to get a front row view of the archery range. At the head standing before all the competitors, Statesman Braun patiently observes.

"There's Staj, to the left," says Beren.

Her younger, plainer form does not surprise Leo half as much as seeing his mother whispering councils into her ear. Pandora, at a time before the diabetes took serious hold, carries herself nimbly even in middle age. She wears denim the color of the games with a form fitted top showing her body to retain much of the toned form from yesteryear. With her hair in full possession of its natural strawberry blonde, Leo grasps how beautiful she really was.

She continues giving council to Anastasia, often pointing to features of the bow and indicating range toward the target: all the while offering encouragement and affection with side hugs and gentle caresses. To an outsider, they might appear as mother and daughter. They appear so to Leo.

He never really took note of the depth of their bond. In fact, he doesn't even remember watching Anastasia shoot at that event. It makes him wonder if she shot at his mother's games, and how she might have felt if she did.

With a final word, Pandora kisses Anastasia on the cheek and steps off.

"They start yet?" a sporty teenage voice says at their back.

"Zoe," says Leo.

"Leo," says Zoe.

"Guys," says Beren. "It's time."

Statesman Braun lifts his hands and gives the command to nock arrows. He keeps one raised as he steps to the side.

"Commence fire," he says.

The first round flies like a swarm of killer bees. Anastasia's arrow hits the ring numbered eight of the Squ target, two outside the bull's-eye. A fair shot, though victors usually score tens. Between each subsequent round she peeks behind for tips and approval, like a child learning to write their letters.

Pandora's attentiveness never falters. Though in the end an archer from Pronoia takes the prize, she bristles with pride as she hugs Anastasia whose face of disappointment quickly evaporates.

Leo did not see his mother shoot much as a young adult. It seemed like a pastime she left in his childhood, and even then it was not too often. Nor was it with the bow Zoe found in the closet.

"Awe, too bad for Staj," says Zoe.

"Spear throwing's next," says Beren in Zoe's face.

"Then pugilism," says Zoe practically eye to eye.

The familiarity makes Leo miss more than just his mother since he entered the Underworld. The fact they think him dead in "real life" exacerbates the point. Nonetheless, they are the ones who remain if and when he should ever return.

"I'll catch up with you guys," says Leo brushing their arms as he walks off in the direction of the archers.

He leaves them practically touching noses. When they actually do touch, both recoil to the fact of having Eskimo kissed. Beren rubs his nose with both hands as though trying to rid himself of some deadly germ. Zoe rubs hers with one hand, and with the other sends a hard crack to Beren's shoulder.

As Leo makes his way through the sea of white, Beren's intended event rings ever louder in his mind.

Pugilism...

He rubs his left eyebrow; his first scar is not yet inflicted. He shakes his head unable to make sense of it.

What does Alex think this will do, showing me my failures?

"Oh right," he says to himself, "somehow it's me, not Alex."

"What was that, Leonidas?"

Leo follows the direction of the voice to find it leads to an old man in a chair. He is frail, gray haired, and a cane rests against his knee. Before the man can say another word a fit of heavy coughing seizes him.

"Alex? I mean..., Grandpa?"

"Who else?"

Interacting with his grandfather so much in the likes of a peer nearly replaced the image of the elderly man he knew as a boy: as well as the cancer patient he knew as a teen.

Leo looks on him as though he were a stranger.

"Ah, don't worry kid, all this is pre-Reckoning effects. Your world's a lot cleaner than mine was," says Alex.

"Right, yeah," says Leo.

"Everything alright?"

Alex's eyes ask more than his words, penetrating so deep he could be looking through Leo back to Tartaros.

"Uh, yeah," says Leo scratching the back of his neck and looking everywhere but forward. It feels like trying to lie to an omega, though he'd likely have better luck with Menoitios.

Alex curls his wrinkled cheek. "So will you be in any games today?"

"Might do the pugilism."

Alex nods deliberately. "Yes...I hear you're into pankration lately, and so is Bereniko."

"Yeah, he...got me started."

"Maybe the two of you can face off then."

If only.

Leo swears he catches Alex break eye contact and glance at the area above his left eye.

"Right, well, I got to get going," says Leo. "I'll see you soon, I'm sure."

The old General coughs, then makes a slight smirk before answering.

"I'm sure," he says. "And be careful, Leo."

Leo chooses the direction with the fewest people and goes.

Knowing Alex will soon die somehow does not unsettle Leo as it typically might; that is, being in the position of foretelling someone's death. To think of Alex young and healthy, roaming white sandy beaches and fruit filled fields, frequenting his loved ones at will: such a fate after a life of hardship and accomplishment seems only just, and offers Leo much more relief than grief he ever felt. Indeed, to think of Alex wanting to pass on to a simple life in the next world, Leo begins to understand him as simply "the restless young gamer from Queens" he described himself as on the Isles of the Blessed.

He looks back at his grandfather once more.

His mother comes to mind as he continues weaving through the crowd of people he has no desire to recognize. He runs parallels between her and Alex, and nearly takes comfort in thinking a similar fate awaits her: then he remembers that by his doing she remains alone on the abandoned shores of the Styx.

The surge of guilt would've stopped him in his tracks if it weren't for the surge of anger rekindling his resentment of the omegas and his father for all the pain they caused her: killing her child, leaving her a single mother, slowly dismembering her body.

His emotion, however, does not serve him like it used to. When he revisits his original intention of saving his mother from the dead, the weight feels impossible to shoulder. What's more, half his energy is already spent convincing himself it's even possible. Nonetheless, Menoitios granted him a chance, so on he walks.

Many have gravitated toward the spear throwing. Leo tries to spot his mother and Anastasia but it seems they've gotten lost in the mix. The eagerness of the crowd sends a flurry of butterflies through his stomach for the event following.

He scans the field for the fighter with the tiger tattoo, remembering the viciousness of his blows dropping on him like Feidor's blade, followed by the elbow across his face that put him down: afterwards he remembers nothing for a while.

Zoe will have to forgive him as he continues past her event.

In the Pronoia Invitational, Feidor beat him as a result of giving up. In the funeral games of Victoria Braun, he fought with everything he had. Having held his own for most of the bout, the Tiger powered on like a machine, never seeming to lose steam or precision. Leo reached in as far as he could, but in the end he was simply out-classed.

He stopped competing in pankration for a long while after that loss. In fact, he stopped doing much of anything, slipping into a dark rut much like the labyrinth of which PK initially delivered him.

His father had left a few years prior. Though it didn't come as a surprise given his distance already at home, Leo refused to accept any explanation much less touch on the subject whatsoever. He could never understand why he resented a man he was never close to in the first place.

Whatever the emotion, he poured it into sport; powerlifting, extra hours on the blade. Then, Beren invited him to a PK training.

As with most athletic interests, he excelled quickly, besting most his age and weight within a matter of months, including Beren: though he and his friend often avoided each other for pride's sake.

His success, however, did not extend beyond the walls of recreational fanatics at the Gym: sparring, gym bouts, local competitions, yet in his ego's mind he was ready for national contention.

Man was that a mistake.

The crowd's applause to his rear signifies a victor in the spear throwing and a beginning to the final event.

Leo looks at his hands and clenches them into fists. He stares at them for a second, then lets them fall. He knows that even at his best he never contended with a descendant of Vince Yeerum.

Did Alex just want me to get my ass kicked?

He wonders as to the real significance of the Yeerum family beginning from Generation 6. Vince killing Silas, two more showing up years later to participate in funeral games of prominent citizens. He thinks of Vince in mental purgatory. More than fighting he desires to talk with this young Yeerum and make some sense out of everything.

The crowd murmurs. It parts a distance away for the first contestant in the final event. Given the chatter Leo does not have to guess who.

When the fighter becomes visible, the expression that didn't daunt Leo the first time sends chills over his skin. The bronze face of cruel intent, eyes on the scent for blood. The tight braids around his head hang like chains and the Tiger tattoo on his arm nearly comes alive.

The young man scans the crowd as if in search of someone. When he stops on Leo, Leo finds he's unable to maintain his customary stare down in the face of a challenger. The Tiger pays it no mind, however, and moves on.

Leo keeps his head down.

I can't win.

All the lust and false illusions that motivated him as a teenager abandon him for a second chance.

He feels the call to combat, yet defeat prevents him: the Black Lion without claws.

Only then does the notion of not fighting at all enter his mind. Though slightly ashamed, he questions whether deferring would really make him a coward.

As he wrestles his pride, his sister Khloe passes a table nearby. Not normally interested in where she goes or doesn't, her semi-apprehensive look provides him a welcome excuse to prolonging his decision on the bout. Her eyes appear focused on a particular destination. Looking ahead, Leo sees what it is.

The typical flash of bitterness races through his body. It spreads much like a natural reaction to an allergy. Before it penetrates too deep, however, it meets with the hard walls of his brother's words.

A check on his feelings over his father marks a first time sensation. This even more so as it arose from the unconscious level. For as much as Leo tries to suppress it, he cannot move beyond the fact that, despite not wanting to believe Alexi, he knows his brother told him the truth.

Looking on the upcoming encounter between Khloe and Aeschylus, he endeavors to imagine his father through the picture Alexi painted: receiving his daughter with a smile and open arms, chatting amicably on how she gets on, never using a phrase like "how have you been?"

They instead hug dryly, exchange a few words, then Khloe moves on.

Alexi's picture dissipates into thin smoke. To Leo's surprise, however, he doesn't follow suit with his sister. Something he can't pinpoint motivates him to wait and watch.

A moment later his father's head turns toward the wake of his daughter. His face, normally so artistically cool and cavalier, shows humility of the kind that sees her go rather than watches her leave. Seconds pass and the hard outer skin sheds to expose the raw form of softness that in fact fits more naturally. By the time Khloe passes out of sight, it is the tender father of Alexi who remains.

God damn he was right.

The image manifest before him corresponds perfectly to the man residing in Alexi's memory: a doting face, loving eyes; an air of stability and concern that shows he cares more for his daughter than himself.

Leo thinks if only he'd known such a man, to feel the affection Alexi felt, perhaps he might have loved him. He nearly envies his brother. And yet, such love makes him realize how much harder it must have been for him to let their father go.

Leo himself reacted in a powerful way over a person he barely claimed to like much less love. Given a solid bond, the break would've been excruciating and the pieces shattered.

Both pieces.

Leo watches his father lower his head. Little by little he re-dons his protective shell. Once the vibrant musician of Alexi's father turns back into the aging bachelor of Leo's, he goes on his way.

He's afraid.

Leo imagines him pouring over the sickly body of his flesh and blood, letting go of his best friend, a deeper break than the hardest femur...

He's afraid to love us.

Leo confirms his eyes just witnessed what his mind registered in the scene over Khloe.

"He actually might though," says Leo to himself. "I'll be damned."

Hollers rise over the grounds from the circle of the human boxing ring: a challenger has entered to face the Tiger. All thoughts of the fight, however, have subsided in light of what he now struggles to understand.

He considers how openly he scorned his father over the years: not welcoming him in the house, never answering his pings. His spitting in the face of affection hidden so close to the surface must have tormented the old guitarist to no end. The weight of hoarding love you fear to unload, all the while trying to convince yourself it's the only way. The effort earns the hate of your kids, which you soon accept as your lot. Punishment for a broken man, like cursing a lame child for not running.

Leo allows himself to be drawn in his father's direction. Just a step, then another. Soon he is several steps. He goes on with nothing prepared to say, and no way prepared to act.

At the point his father might catch sight of him, however, a strong hand takes his arm. Leo turns with a ready reproach before he sees who grabbed him.

"Statesman Braun," he says, backing down his tone.

"Hi, Leonidas. Could I ask you a favor? Find Beren and tell him I need to speak with him."

"Uh, yeah, actually I was..."

"I would appreciate it," says Statesman Braun, gripping him tighter, "it's urgent."

The intensity of Bouko's poised insistence gets Leo's attention. It also reminds him that when Statesman Braun asked him this the first time, he did not resist. In fact, in his eagerness to prove himself, he used it as a pretext to take Beren's place.

Now again put in the moment, he has made a different choice, and while that may save him from harm, it could potentially leave Beren to face the Yeerum fighter and end up just as hurt or worse.

Leo glances in his father's direction before answering. "Ok, I'll get him."

"Thank you, son," says Statesman Braun, releasing his arm.

Knowing exactly where to go, Leo sifts through the mourners on his way to the ring. It proves a bit more difficult than he anticipated: in this time, he is not yet The Maurileho. Passing through he takes a few glances to each side in hopes of spotting his mother or Anastasia, but they are nowhere to be found.

Beren is, however, and has just finished wrapping his hands when Leo arrives.

"Ready for this, buddy?" says Beren on high adrenaline. "This guy looks mean, but I got him."

The Tiger's gaze bores into Beren. Something deeper than competitive spirit, something motivated by more than glory. Something that tells Leo he found who he was looking for.

"Listen, your Dad sent me to get you."

Beren makes a bothered face. "What for?"

"I don't know but he said it was urgent."

"Urgent? Just tell him I'll be over after the event."

"I don't know, man, he seemed pretty serious."

"So am I," says Beren, throwing a few shadow punches. "Tell him you didn't find me then."

A Braun family member Leo doesn't recognize checks the ring area. He then confirms the Yeerum fighter's participation then converses with Coach P who will referee. He will confirm Beren next.

"Maybe we should let this one go," says Leo.

"What?"

Leo knows he has violated a bro code but also what it will mean if he doesn't.

"We don't know what this guy can do, or anything about him."

Beren glances over as his opponent performs his ritualistic set of forms. Sharp precision complemented by a painter's grace.

"Alright so he dances before a fight. Bottom line, he can punch, I can punch; he can kick, I can kick."

"But..."

"You know what, fine," says Beren exasperated. "Tell my Dad I'll be right over. I'll need to tell my uncle to find someone else."

Leo hesitates, unwilling to accept his friend's sudden change of attitude.

"What? Hurry, they'll need a new contestant asap," says Beren.

Once Beren heads for his uncle Leo goes. Although doubtful, he again thinks of his own father, not knowing how much time he has left to see him.

Leo informs Statesman Braun of his son's statements, and although doubtful as well, seems very relieved.

The renewed commotion indicates the bout has started. Leo looks back to make sure Beren kept his word, but is unable to gain a clear view of the action from his vantage point. He considers going back, but decides to trust his friend.

Moving on he scans the area he initially spotted his father, but he's already gone.

He then moves to the side closest to Lake Maquari. There he spots a group of men he recognizes to be local musicians convening in a chat circle. A black ponytail down the back of a taller one signals the one he wants.

Leo approaches, again mustering his nerve to say what he's not yet found the words for. Within a few seconds he's within arm's reach. As he's about to tap his father on the shoulder, a gasp passes over the crowd.

The lake side angle affords a clearer path of vision to the ring. When Leo looks he sees a young man covering a bloodied face. When his hands drop, Leo realizes it's Beren.

Even at a distance the cut appears long and deep over his left eye.

The same spot over Leo's own eye begins to tingle.

Oh no.

He peels off, shoving through people who remain too engrossed by the spectacle to mind being pushed.

In the ring the Tiger taunts his prey. Cajoling and waving him in. He dares Beren to re-engage.

Coach P places a hand on Beren's shoulder, but he swats it away.

He's taking the bait.

"Yield, Beren, just yield," shouts Leo through the spectators.

Before anyone can intervene Beren launches an attack of well-timed combinations sending the Tiger backpedaling. Mourners shout "Victoria" as his inspiration. Leo even allows himself to hope as the Tiger seems incapable of countering through the barrage.

Apparently Beren does too, risking some wider shots despite the blood flowing into his eye.

Then, in a flash, it's all over.

Quick as lightning the Tiger sets and fires a straight right to Beren's neck: stopping him in his tracks.

The shouts cease with Beren standing limp in front of his opponent.

No more than a punch, and he gasps for air.

No more, and the young spirited teen crumbles over.

Dead.

Leo hears no sound as the crowd erupts. He decks the coach dashing to his best friend's side where he takes up his lifeless hand.

"Beren, get up."

Blood trickles from the side of his mouth. It flows freer mixing with a layer of sweat and stains the once golden hair characteristic of his legacy. He makes no response when Leo shakes him: simply stares at the sky.

"Get up!" says Leo pounding on his chest.

Shieldsmen escort the Tiger away from the commotion, not as a means of detainment, but protection. The great kickboxer looks down on his victim one last time, just as venomous as before the fight. Before turning back he catches Leo's eye glaring up at him and a sinister grin crosses his lips.

Leo ignites. He charges with the agility of a giant cat: so fast he avoids the notice of the Shields and, he thinks, the Tiger. Yet before he can even consider a move, a hard roundhouse kick to the chest thrusts him to the ground.

Though he pops up like a spring, Shieldsmen seize him before he can pursue any further. The resistance, however, drives Leo into an even greater frenzy, requiring more hands to subdue him.

Finally, one of the Shields draws a shock stick and shoots him full of electricity.

Lying next to his friend Leo's will rages against the paralysis.
He wants the world to change, the planet to reverse.
All he manages is a mind-filling scream.

CHAPTER 13 – THE STYX

"**B**eren!"

The name makes a soft echo through the recesses of Leo's mind. It calls him away, growing fainter in the distance. When the last sound fades, his fingers register the sensation of stone under his nails.

He jolts upright.

Anastasia sits to his side though he barely notices. His focus lies elsewhere. From the look on his face he might still be facing the Tiger.

"You," says Leo, scrambling to his feet. He doesn't take his eyes off his grandfather as he rises. "You knew that would happen, you knew he would die!"

Leo dares to grab the cuffs of Alex's polo. "What are you!?"

Alex, with temperate ease, takes his index finger and digs at the base of Leo's neck, sending him effortlessly to the ground.

"Even if I did, you're here, and Beren's fine."

The distant flames of the Phlegethon mark them outside the Pit of Tartaros.

Leo gets up and dusts off his pride. "So I saved him by fighting in real life? Is that the point of all this?"

"Maybe. But did you save your mother?"

The questions seems off point from the person who's been delaying them reaching her: and if the funeral games of Victoria Braun was about Beren...

"No..., I don't know. She looked fine to me...helping you out," he directs at Anastasia.

"Not all damage is physical, Leo," says Alex.

The emotional distress he finally recognized in his father comes to mind. The love and torment hidden just under the skin. The emptiness and frustration burning in the chest. The same distress he might acknowledge in himself during the years following his father's departure.

"There is one thing you're not too late to save, though," says Alex.

A flash of his mother stranded on the banks of the Styx crosses his mind. He has a feeling, however, that Alex refers more to the life waiting for him back in Eulimnos.

"My Dad," says Leo.

Alex tilts his head: not so much in acknowledgement as to invite Leo to consider the point further himself. He then turns and moves off. A second later Silas appears from an unknown direction and the two meet.

"We're ready, General."

Alex nods and they depart in the direction Silas came.

"Come on little brother, we're taking a boat ride," says Alexi.

The idea of crossing the River of Fire by boat seems like suicide to Leo, even accompanied by a Blessed. Noting their surroundings, however, he sees they are actually moving away from the Phlegethon. The area, while similar in its rigid terrain, is not the same as where they crossed given the absence of the gates on the high walls.

"Where are we, Staj?" says Leo as Anastasia comes up beside him.

"On the far side of Tartaros, south of the gates."

Up ahead, a narrower branch of the River of Fire intercepts with another river of no particular distinction. Leo wonders if it may be an extension of the Lethe. Beyond seems to lead into nothing.

A long, sturdy boat rests on the bank with two sets of oars to take them there.

"All aboard the Styx Express," says Alexi. He takes his seat in the middle. He then proceeds to bounce his knees over a ride on a dark river in the gloom of Tartaros.

"This is the Styx?" says Leo.

"Yes," says Silas, settling in. "Now take the oars and don't break rhythm."

Nerves pour through Leo's belly: finally the right path. Finally the chance to make good on his promise and the opportunity Menoitios granted him. For all he's pressed reaching his mother, however, no plan on what to actually do has occurred to him.

"This used to be the river gods swore oaths on," says Alex, taking his place at the head. "Any libation of the Styx was binding, unless you wanted to be sick and outcast for ten years."

Silas moves them into place and gives the signal for Leo to kick off.

The rear position Leo occupies affords a wide view of the vast river. Roughly equal in size to the Pronoian, something in the density of its waters lends it a far mightier presence than the familiar current flowing under the Portland Bridge. As they approach the intersection with the River of Fire, Leo hopes that strength will indeed hold up.

Leo once again starts feeling the growing heat emanating from the flames. He keeps position though, and does not turn. As the heat intensifies his body tenses and his eyes fix to the rear.

Soon the plain waters of the Styx become colored with the reflection of fire. When it seems as though they might be engulfed themselves, Leo feels the heat subside and flames abate. The mystical current forms a comfortable passageway and before long the Phlegethon drifts further and further away. Once the glare of the fire recedes Leo looks off into the distance and the towering bronze fortress of the great Pit appears no bigger than a small hill in Appalachia.

The rowing calms Leo's mind onto his mother and Alex's point of consideration. When Leo really acknowledges it, he was the one who suffered the physical and mental anguish following the fight: both for the loss, and the continued absence of his father. It never occurred he meant so much during the time he was in their lives. It wasn't reasonable to love someone who didn't show love back, though his mother would note how unreasonable that is.

He can't get over how such a force could exist. A force to undermine the very base of our choices, leaving us and all those connected completely vulnerable.

Completely vulnerable.

The answer hangs on the tip of his tongue and also seated opposite.

Anastasia, resting her chin in her hands, pretends not to notice Leo's thought process.

"Do you remember," says Leo, "after Victoria Braun's funeral games, if Mom seemed off or anything?"

Anastasia lifts up her head. "I remember you being off."

"But do you remember Mom. I know you guys were close, a lot more than I thought actually."

The droplets from the oars fall heavier, splashing through the expanse as though amplified with acoustics. Tartaros far beyond sight, as well as anything to all sides of the boat, the trickles become a soothing, yet slightly eerie background.

"You're not the only reason I came here, Leo."

Leo colors a bit. He looks down to avoid her seeing. Though he would assume she speaks of her father, he imagines she would be more direct if referring to him.

"What do you mean?" he says.

"That time was hard for her, when your father left. But not as much over him,…as over you."

His eyebrows furrow at taking her meaning. "Didn't she love my Dad?"

"Yes…," she stops as if she was going to say something but recants. It makes Leo think of the Generation 6 photo of their parents in each other's arms. He wonders if she's known something all these years but hasn't told him.

"But she loved you more," she finishes.

Hearing statements like that fortify him against the weight of doubt which bombards, if not a plan, his resolve.

He thinks how deeply he fell into the old adage of 'not knowing what you have until it's gone' in never expressing the love he now feels for his mother throughout her life. Not having made this gesture makes him seem like such a small person. In any case, with one chance, he would reach her and tell all.

A renewed sense of purpose flows through Leo's limbs.

"Rhythm," shouts Silas from the other end in response to the quickening pace.

Leo relaxes, but turns around and stares across the boat.

He then reconsiders Anastasia's words. It may be true his mother loved him more than Aeschylus, yet it was Aeschylus she lost.

"But if that's the case," he says, "what was the big deal? I was still around."

Anastasia rolls her eyes halfway. "You were physically around, sometimes. And just that: when she saw how everything affected you, she blamed herself: like she should've tried harder with your Dad, not let him go so easily. For your sake…"

The statement lingers in the air. When it settles, the wind whistles away from under Leo's sails. His shoulders slouch and eyes drop under the weight of the charge.

"Rhythm," yells Silas again.

He shakes his head ignoring the rebuke.

"That's what Alex meant, wasn't it? When he talked about other kinds of damage." Leo nearly stops rowing. "And that's just it," he continues, "when I think about it now, it's like everything I did just came back on her."

Anastasia looks on Leo long and tender. She then scoots him to the side and takes one of his oars. Between strokes she brushes his left leg.

"She knew you didn't mean it. You just couldn't see."

By this time the men have struck up their own conversation to the rear. The debate on which of the Gemellan Cities breeds the best bladesmen. The chatter places a screen of privacy over Leo and Anastasia.

"She was the closest thing I had to a Mother the last few years," says Anastasia. She doesn't quite look at Leo, but shifts a few inches closer. "My own was long gone. We filled each other's voids, I guess."

Leo takes in her words. He recalls watching them at the archery event and how they interacted. His mother seemed just as, if not more, fulfilled at helping Anastasia than Anastasia did at being helped. Leo considers how his pride often shunned the same help she offered him. He exhales deeply. "I'm glad you were there for her, like you are now. I always saw you as more of a sister than Khloe."

"A sister?" she says.

Leo turns his head and looks at Anastasia. Anastasia, though she doesn't turn away, lowers her eyes onto Leo's neck as she tends to do at times.

Being near her feels so natural, and when he allows it, even soothing. Perhaps all those years as friends planted deeper roots than he thought; roots he now fears to uproot by taking the wrong step.

"Yeah, well, I guess."

She meets his eyes for a split second before looking down again.

"And now?"

The thumping in both their chests threatens the placidity of the Styx's current. Anastasia closes up ever so slightly as though having bared a part of her body she's not used to baring. Leo looks on her with much of the same thought.

No words can be conjured between them. Given the density of their stares, however, a lot more than one passes inwardly.

Anastasia risks lifting her eyes and catches Leo's waiting. Little at first, they soon grow larger in each other's perception until that's all they see. Then, they lower like drapes of silk.

"Rhythm!" bellows Silas.

They pull away frazzled, returning to the oars double time. A chuckle from Alexi adds to the embarrassment.

"So, Mom, yeah," says Leo, "great girl."

Anastasia stares ahead. A smile crosses her lips, the lower of which she bites with her teeth.

A few minutes pass in silence. The hard, barren landscape has not changed much since leaving Tartaros. Droplets continue falling from the oars, and the oars continue rowing in sync.

Anastasia peeks into the water. No faces. Just a dark swirl like someone dipped their ink.

She touches the surface with the tip of her finger and pulls back from the bitter cold. A disturbance in the dark substance follows the line of her reach but quickly settles back into a swirl. She then holds the finger in front of her face and the water dries nearly instantly.

"I wonder what Beren and Zoe would say if they could see this," she says.

The mention of Beren forces Leo to remind himself his friend is okay. The harsh image of his fall, however, remains strong in his mind, as well as the despair that followed.

"I'd just like to see them at all," says Leo.

Anastasia drops her hand and looks curiously on Leo. "What happened exactly?"

He makes an uneasy face before answering. "That Yeerum, the guy who gave me this," he says pointing to his scar, "he killed Beren with one punch; hit him right in the throat."

"Oh gosh," says Anastasia, covering her mouth.

"I just get this feeling it wasn't random either. That guy was out for blood, and he had his eye on Beren."

"Beren's safe, Alex said so."

"Is he though?"

That Yeerums seek out his social circle does not settle well with Leo. Their lethal skill, coupled with the fact no one seems to know anything about them or where they come from puts Leo on his guard even a world away.

"A Yeerum killed your father, another scarred me; another, real or not, went after Beren. Not to mention the one at my Mom's games who was probably after you for all I..."

Leo stops as though pegged in the head by some hard object. He sits straight up, eyes focused on something distant.

"What's wrong?" says Anastasia.

He slightly squints. "You feel that?"

She tries focusing too but doesn't appear to arrive at anything.

"Thinking about Beren like that, I...I think something's going on with him."

A sense of urgency returns to his gut. The urgency to reach his mother. This combines with the fear that Beren and Zoe might already have done so.

"I can't know unless I sleep."

Leo drops his oar and scrambles in a circle trying to figure out some makeshift bed. He ends up sitting back in his place. He then digs his palms into the sides of his temples and leans forward.

"No," says a voice from the other side of the boat.

Alex makes his way past Alexi then brushes by Leo and Anastasia. He sits down across from them.

"No more of that, Leo. Seeing the world out of time isn't in sleep. It's in you." Leo makes to protest but Alex waives him off, "And it's time you embrace that."

All the years of denial accumulate in that moment: childhood fantasies, teenage daydreams, lucid dreams in the Underworld. Seeing things he wasn't present to see, and knowing things he'd rather have left in the unknown.

Despite its questionable credibility, the impossible pales next to an experience like the Underworld: floating on mythical rivers, reviving dead relatives, and most of all, nearly kissing Anastasia.

When Leo really acknowledges it, it was never a case of believing or not, just overcoming the will not to.

"Ok, Alex,...we'll try this your way," says Leo. He adjusts his position to face his grandfather more directly. "Now what do I do?"

Alex smiles with pride and leans in closer to his wayward grandson. "First, you have to be really in tune with what you want to see."

Leo envisions his lifeless friend falling to the ground: the face of the Tiger, the stare at the sky. Emotion he felt again pours through him as if he were still there. It spreads to the point that even if he wanted to shift focus he would not be able.

"That must be why I sense Beren."

Alex scoots closer. "Keep that. Whatever it is, don't lose it. You'll need it to tap into the source."

"What the hell's the source?" says Leo, nearly breaking concentration.

"Easy...it's what connects you to the divine. The imprint on every soul that will show us our way back. We all carry a sliver."

"I might have got the crumbs."

Alex holds up a hand to check him. He lowers it slowly to ensure Leo's silence.

"That's why it's easier in sleep. When you sleep your mind's relaxed, and all the barriers you put up when you're awake come down; doubt, disbelief, even reason."

It sounds reasonable to Leo, so with a final tilt of the head, he closes his eyes. He inhales deeply, and tries focusing on Beren in happier times: watching the aether shower on Portland Bridge, earning the rank of Corporal in the Guard: winning the torch race in the last Festival of Prometheus.

While these memories bring him pleasure, they serve only as pleasant thoughts. They carry him no higher to the supposed "source" Alex intends.

Leo opens his eyes. He takes a sharp breath and rests his elbows on his knees.

Alex looks on him, and he just shakes his head. The great General then considers for a moment. "Maybe the river would help," he says.

"The river?"

"There's power in the Styx, how else do you think Achilles became invincible except at the heels."

"But that's a..."

"Myth? Tell me about the myth of Leonidas Maquari, a young man who loses his mother and goes into the Underworld to save her."

A lack of retort concedes the point. Stories that to Leo were mere fabrications of creativity and folklore suddenly don't sound as crazy when he imagines how others would view his own.

"Besides, says Alex, "a visual would help. Annie, if you wouldn't mind."

Anastasia takes the oars while Leo and Alex slide to the edge of the boat. "So, you see yourself," says Alex.

Leo's reflection nods.

"Now, see only yourself. Let everything else go, forget you're here. It's just you, and my voice."

Alex pauses. "Now concentrate on Beren, don't force it, feel it, let him in."

This time Leo opts for a different route, drawing first on the visions of Beren and Zoe from the moment he "died." These moments seem more welcoming of his presence and start him on a gentle highlight reel of the two of them writing his legacy, and Zoe finding his mother's bow. Though still all in his head, he nearly forgets he stares at his own image in the water.

It then brings him to the point of Beren's own "death" at the hands of the Tiger. This sensation pulls him further away from the Underworld to the point he can almost feel his friend's blood and sweat under his fingertips.

The helplessness churns in his stomach, enticing him to reach out further. He gives in to this enticement. In doing so he extends beyond the means of his physical being until there remains nothing left of the body to extend.

Nonetheless, he goes further. He taps into something new, something primordial and motivated by pure instinct. His will to connect to his friend is gone. He has submitted to "its" will: the Zen, his crumbs of the source.

He now is Beren.

The quality easily invokes the premonition he felt earlier. In short time the dark waters of the Styx swirl around his reflection and transform into Beren's. Little shows, but enough to see his friend browsing the last contents Leo viewed before leaving the house for his mother's funeral games.

Oh no.

In Leo's disturbed mental state leading up to his intended eulogy, he paid no mind to what he left on or open when he exited the house to cart the empty funeral pyre along Lake Maquari.

Beren has discovered as much through his curiosity. After all he's browsed, he now looks on the document Leo last opened with his virtecran.

The image in the water smears and shudders. This happens in part from Beren's shock over what he's found, but mostly in response to Leo watching all his hopes slip away. His desperate attempt to save his mother. Her likely condemnation to the Plains of Asphodel or something worse. And all his fault.

Mom.

The water swirls into a blur, but not before Zoe enters carrying the picture of Generation 6. She flashes it to Beren who barely notices she carries anything. Beren, rather, directs her attention quite insistently to the screen in bright array. Her reaction is much the same as his.

The vision then disappears leaving the still mental frame of the two rushing out the room.

CHAPTER 14 – CERBERUS

"**O**h shit," says Leo, pulling his head away quickly. "Oh shit!" "We got to get moving: now."

Practically tearing the oars from Anastasia, Leo rows as if competing in a race. "Rhythm, Silas," he says sharply.

"What's going on?" says Anastasia.

"They found her."

The question of Pandora's whereabouts has loomed for some time, mostly for Anastasia who hasn't dared to put it to him directly. She now stares at her lifelong companion with a mix of fear and curiosity over what that could mean.

For Leo the thought anyone would find his mother's body never occurred to him. This he remembers as he towed the empty funeral pyre along Lake Maquari: only half in his wits to face the crowd, and half in his courage to do what he planned.

That Beren, however, would follow his traces, break his passcode, and understand everything his documents imply now screams true in a very sobering way.

"We need to get there before they burn her body or it's too late."

Silas perks up at his last two words. His disquiet betrays a bit more on the matter than he has shown thus far. Anastasia catches his eye, and seems relieved Leo does not.

Guilt weighs on the desperate son more than ever when he thinks of the state of his mother's conscience should she pass before he makes amends. He grinds his teeth thinking how, even in death, his actions end up her detriment.

"Leo," says Anastasia. She looks on him and hesitates. She then moves closer little by little until her lips pause by his ear.

"Where was she, Leo?"

His expression doesn't change. It remains fixed on his strokes and the nothingness behind him. For a moment it appears he won't answer.

"There's a bunker at the house," he finally says. "Hidden. Even I didn't know exactly how to get in. Inside there's a giant freezer. Beren found the blueprints and passcode."

She opens her mouth to chance a follow up question but decides better. Leo nonetheless feels the weight of her stare, and feigns not seeing her in his periphery. Anastasia finally looks down and exhales.

"The body would have to de-thaw," she states. "That should give us some time."

The speed of the boat indicates not everyone shares in this optimism.

Salt marsh grasses begin rising near the bank. They grow thicker and thicker as they pass. In fast time the area is replete in an array of full brush.

Ahead, behind Leo's view, a change in their path becomes apparent. Alexi grows curious and attempts to stand. When he does though, he knocks the boat dangerously off-balance.

"Don't be standing or we'll end up capsizing," barks Leo. Alexi obeys but keeps an inquiring head turned around. Leo, though a strong swimmer, looks on the waters and acknowledges its sheer force, mystical or not.

"Um, Leo..." says Alexi.

"Not now, man."

"You might want to listen to your brother," says Alex.

Before Leo can turn, Silas swerves to avoid a patch of reeds protruding high out of the water.

"Slow down, Leonidas," says Silas.

Leo heeds the Captain and sets to sifting the water. The boat soon comes to a halt. He then turns to see what's caused all the commotion.

"What the hell?"

A maze of sedge and dark algae spread across the river. This is complemented by more grass and reeds. Though nothing terribly menacing, crossing the Phlegethon seemed a less daunting task.

"The Stygian Marsh," says Anastasia.

The name rings a bell. It also tells Leo they are indeed close.

"Well we'll have to get through it," says Leo.

"Do you see a way through?" says Alex offhand.

The boat rocks when Leo stands. He searches desperately, and answers Alex's question by the look on his face.

"Our only option is to dock on the left bank," says Silas.

"The left bank? It's the right we need."

"Then I hope you can swim," says Silas, adjusting their direction.

The fire in Leo's chest seethes as they backtrack. The right bank seems to drift miles for every inch they move. Finally plopping back down, he takes up an oar and jerks it into place.

"Relax, Leo," says Alex. "You really didn't think it would be that easy, did you? Remember whose realm you're in."

No other creatures or serious land obstacles have presented themselves as great obstructions after Menoitios and the White Lion. The real fight has come from within. Regardless, the notion of not passing freely did not occur after crossing the River of Fire, certainly accompanied by one of the Blessed to boot.

They dock. Leo takes a heavy step onto the rock floor. He snatches up his guard, places his hands on his knees, and looks out over the marsh.

The motion of Beren's choice to dig for answers grows more pressing in his mind. Every second draws closer to his friends completing the burial rites. Every second, and his mother's life, likely along with his own, draw nearer to condemnation.

To balance the premonition he focuses on a different one: the one that called him west from the Isles of the Blessed. The one easiest to access and hardest to let go; the one he'd go to hell and back for.

He sifts through the web of his mind for the primal state, the part that existed before his own consciousness. It reaches to him like a distant dream.

He primes for the tender lure he felt on the Island. The feel of comfort. The feel of home. The nurturing hand meddled in a nest of despondency.

After one successful attempt with the aid of the Styx, the connection to his mother tunes in gracefully.

Having made it, however, his eyes widen in a way anything but graceful. He loses his breath, and his guard nearly drops straight from his hand.

Oh no.

He rises hurriedly and turns towards his comrades helping Alexi off the boat. He catches Anastasia for a split second, much like he did from the eulogy podium back in Eulimnos. This time though, he doesn't say goodbye. With no further change of expression, he sprints away far wide of the marsh.

"Leo, wait," says Anastasia, but his powerful legs have already taken him well into the distance. "Come on, before he does something stupid," she says to the rest.

She turns to go when Alex calls her name.

"We have to hurry," she says, swinging her arms around. "I've seen that look on him before."

"Take this," says Alex.

The "why" catches in her throat as he hands her the white Les Paul electric guitar. Alex offers no explanation to the question he perceives, nor do he or the others seem pressured to follow.

Anastasia looks to her father. The burly Captain looks back on his sweet daughter willing to suffer any blade for her, shoulder any world, but he now painfully resigns. In this moment he must trust. "Go, Annie."

She lingers on him another instant, then runs. She runs for love, for justice. The whip of terror stings her every stride, pushing her against the mortal threat of losing the last thing in the above world she truly cherishes.

The terrain bordering the marsh becomes more jagged the further they go. Boulders and sharp indents riddle their way into a hazardous and confusing path. Though far apart still, they remain within an arrow's shot of distance.

Leo arrives to a break in the landscape. Its gape and convenience makes it appear to be a gateway to the center of the marsh. Fixing on it, he rounds the corner.

As if running into a brick wall, however, a horrific sight sends him plummeting to the ground.

The back of a monstrous beast, colored of Tartarean walls, watches patiently over the marsh on hind legs. At the sound of the sudden noise, the serpent in place of its tail twitches and coils in menacing patterns.

Leo's feet scrape the ground rapidly as he scrambles back the way he came. This provokes the beast further to lift its head, which turns out to be three. Around its mane, snakes hiss and lick the air at the scent of an intruder.

Then, before Leo can even stand, the great Hound of Hell twists in fury and lunges forward.

Leo watches as a trio of razor sharp teeth open in slow motion, propel in the blur of a snakebite, and clamp on the throat of the air inches from his nose.

Adamant chains locked around the middle neck restrain it from going any further.

The putrid breath nauseates Leo. Though knows he should run, the frenzy in the hound's eyes makes him believe only night exists.

The hound then opens its massive jaws. Instead of biting, though, it releases a deafening bark even the deadest of souls would hear.

Leo covers his ears, and in the interim is somewhat able to regain his wits. He then scurries behind the high cavernous boulder at the turn of the corner.

His chest swells to the point of pain for his mother in both body and spirit: the thawing corpse in the hands of his friends, and the rotting soul on the banks of the Styx. And now such a formidable obstacle standing like a mountain in his way of reaching her: its icy jaws to be regarded as real as anything his mind might interpret.

The notion he could actually die does not frighten him as much as it happening before making it past. He thinks of his noble intentions sprinting away from his companions a few minutes before. This following his vision of seeing the lonely and distraught woman on the other side of the Styx: condemned to wander, never know peace, and all because of him.

Leo sinks down, back to the wall and bangs his head against it. Though he knows he could not likely defeat such a creature by feat of arms, all that remains is forward or back. He also knows the only way back *is* forward.

Steeling himself, Leo draws his blade. For a moment he sits with it eyes closed, unignited, trying to calm the storm inside his chest.

Cerberus snarls, and follows with a violent tug on the chain sending bits of rock to the ground.

As if in reaction the blade shines forth in colors of red, black, and blue. A moderate hum accompanies it, swelling back and forth between low and mid tones. Those tones never manifest into a chorus, only continue shifting as if lost in despair.

Leo lets out a deep breath. He uses the blade's tip to get to his feet. He then fastens his guard, and walks slowly out from behind the wall.

The hound reacts in a fury, sending forth another series of barks. When it sees its mortal opponent not backing down it bares its teeth in anticipation of the building clash.

Leo looks it over warily. He fixes his stance thinking only a cut to one of the necks might avail him. He eyes the middle one, tightens his face, then steps off as if about to leap from a cliff.

No sooner though, does a firm hand catch his wrist and twist him to the ground.

The blade gets tossed to the side and retrieved by Anastasia a few feet from the jaws of the beast's leftmost head. She then grabs Leo by the cuff of his remaining shirt and practically drags him to the side. Leo complies, too shocked to resist.

"You can't do this," she says, pressing him against the wall.

"I have to, I can't go back."

"You'll die though."

"My Mom needs me," he says, trying to break free.

"But *I* need *you*."

Leo stops struggling. The snarls for his blood drown in the background.

A tiny seed buried deep long ago finally draws the strength to flower. The sun on its pedal blinds Leo at first, but quickly adjusts to serve the purpose it was always meant to.

Anastasia grips him tighter. Tears well in her eyes to the point they may burst. Her regard bores deep into the other side of the young man before her, straining her lips to the point of trembling.

Finally, she relaxes her hands, and a tear falls freely.

"Leo, I love you."

The words fall like a morning mist. They gently coat the surface and manage to reflect all colors of the spectrum in even the darkest of places.

As they seep into Leo's pores, a distant sense tells him his mother has stopped roaming.

"I know you want to save her," Anastasia goes on. She again grips tightly, "but don't make me have to save you."

Leo knows he should say something, but as soon as he opens his mouth a sharp rock tears through the air. He ducks quickly and pulls Anastasia's head under his chest. The rock barely misses. It strikes a few feet to their right and shoots off into the expanse.

He releases Anastasia and chances a peak around the boulder. His face drops. "The chains," he says, lifting up his guard, "he's ripping them from the ground."

The heavy tugs to the throat have placated the beast into a circling trot, yet it doesn't fail to notice Leo.

"Listen, Staj, if we can't take him by force then what? And where the hell is Alex?"

According to myth, only mighty Heracles was able to overpower the great beast by brute strength. Sent by King Eurystheus on one of his twelve labors, the old god Hades granted him permission to take the Hound, only without use of his iconic club or bow. This Heracles accomplished by submitting the beast in a choke hold.

On another occasion Aeneas, with the help of the witch Sybil, fed him honey cake laced with sedatives that allowed them to gently pass.

And Orpheus...

Anastasia gasps and begins to squint, not able to spit out what's apparently filled her head.

The chains clanking behind them indicates Cerberus has recovered from its temporary shock.

Leo waves Anastasia in rapidly to coax whatever advice she might have.

"The guitar," she finally says.

Leo's jaw drops. "The guitar? What am I gonna do with that; serenade him to sleep?"

"Yes! When Orpheus came for his wife, he moved everyone so much with his music they let him pass, even Cerberus."

The mention of its name rouses the Hound's intent back on the intruders. The clanking becomes more rapid and low growls begin to trickle along the ground.

"How do you move a beast?" says Leo with a quick glance, "he won't even know what you're saying."

"Then don't use words, use feelings." She half slaps, half places her hand over his heart. "Even animals can feel."

Cerberus bellows another bark and thrashes against the chains. This produces an even louder crack against the rocks. Spittle flies from his mouth in all directions, discoloring any place it falls like seething acid.

Leo looks to Anastasia, wanting to trust her with all his fiber, but the sight of an old guitar doesn't convince him to drop his weapons.

"Leo, one more and he'll be loose!"

Anastasia grabs the top of the guard then slides her hand down over his.

Leo feels her warmth more than ever in a place so absent of life. Her blue eyes bring him to the banks of Lake Maquari and remind him how water should look: her hair carries the rays of the Promethean sun and shines even in the vacuum of Erebos.

That she makes no motion to fight, holds her ground in the face of horrific death: that she stands at his side with no mind to flee shows Leo her trust is already placed. And if she loves him enough to believe...

Leo's hands relax around his guard and blade. Anastasia wastes no time in taking them and pushing the guitar into his chest.

Leo again glances at his invincible opponent and shakes his head. "This thing barely makes sound."

"Then you make the sound. Remember where you are. Find her." Anastasia leans up and kisses Leo on the cheek.

Find me.

For any lack of sound, the short imperative sings louder than ever.

Leo draws a deep breath and turns recalling the note his mother left when she died.

Use your illusion.

He's long wrestled over the meaning of that scribbled phrase. Since the moment he found it only two ideas have occurred to him: a reference to a Pre-Reckoning album his mother owned, and an allusion to the peculiar ability his mother supposedly knew nothing about: seeing life out of time.

As he stands before Cerberus with a guitar strapped around his neck, he finally deciphers that in order to find her, the album and the ability are one and the same.

"November Rain": her favorite song.

"The solo," he whispers to himself, noting the most beautiful part of the song without words.

The great beast howls, announcing its carnal intent with three harmonizing voices creating a slight dissonance at the taper. Six eyes bore into Leo over the insolence of his defiance. Leo stares back with a steady beating heart and pulls a pick from his pocket.

The hairs of the Hound rise on its arched back from the energy it musters to discharge its attack.

Leo does likewise channeling all his power inward. His mind brings him to a time he'd since dismissed as a bad dream: the hours on the floor next to his mother's dead body as she sit in the position he found her. Shock envenoming, head against the armrest gazing into the same rays that fell on his mother's lifeless eyes. Weariness moving him into fetal position. Hunger the only instinct reminding him he had to let go.

"Let go," says a soft inner voice.

Leo slowly blinks the connection down through his body, out to the guitar, and steps forward.

Cerberus launches its fury at the same instant.

"Leo!"

The chain snaps as Leo strikes the first string.

The note soars through the Underworld in a way no amplifier could produce: like a burst of pure majesty sprinkling ambrosia on a barren desert: so magnificent even the flesh-ripping Hound hesitates its attack.

In the space between Leo's ears the solo sounds replete with drums, orchestra, piano and bass. It carries him home, again to the sight of his mother staring lifeless in her chair. He stands before her: her eyes invite him. When he accepts, they pull him in:

Pandora Maquari stands amongst a group of friends in Lyceum; a streak of blue through her strawberry blond hanging over a collared top. She smiles full of life as they watch a wrestling match: one wrestler in particular.

A blond haired young man moves off the mat making quick eye contact. She follows.

Next they're riding together in his manually driven, pre-Reckoning model car. Top down, both heads of long hair flap in the wind. Pandora's no longer carries the streak. The man inserts a large silver disk of "Use Your Illusion" in a thin slot, setting it to track 9. She shakes her head but smiles when he looks up. It is Silas Wildyn who smiles back and says he loves her.

Pandora dreams of a little boy with hair in his eyes. She gently brushes it away with the tips of her fingers. The boy then leans his head into her bosom as son to mother.

At a local venue she becomes acquainted with a musician named Aeschylus. He is tall with curly chestnut colored hair, and the lead guitarist of Serelin's Secret.

That night, the little boy returns with a guitar.

She and Silas begin learning about the Urn. They sit shoulder to shoulder late into the night reading through old texts: she in scrubs, he in Guard uniform. When one face gets too serious, the other distracts it with a kiss, yet on they read. Soon they spend more time with Alex and Emrick than cruising in the car.

The boy appears again. Older, but looks nothing like Anastasia's father. Pandora wonders, and begins to grow sad.

As her faith in Generation 6 gets stronger, the boy comes to her more often, giving her the idea that someday he would be important to the Search. Though her love for Silas also strengthens, he inspires no visions.

With heavy heart she visits Emrick Wildyn. When the middle-aged Mantis confirms his son would not be the boy's father, her cup of *vin chaud* spills to the floor and into her hands she sobs.

She meets her great love on the lakefront bench and clings to the burly wrestler as though holding onto life itself. Wrenching clumps of his hair, she cries the news into his shoulder. Silas takes the sacrifice with a hard, teary eyed face, but gives no hint of the slightest reproach to her reason.

In their final embrace, he gifts her the music disk from the car with a photo of Generation 6 in the pocket.

The image of Silas and Pandora then morphs into Leo and Anastasia. Leo sees through her perspective the way his mother looked up at them from her bed the night after the Festival.

Finally, she closes her eyes.

Alex, Alexi, and Silas arrive to watch Leo bending high on the neck of his guitar. The notes sing as though coming from Leo's voice itself. They pierce the rocks to all sides and ascend to heights unknown.

Cerberus maintains a steady watch on Leo but stays its ground. The hairs on its back have flattened, the tension in its limbs relaxed, and slowly but surely its belly begins to drop.

The deceased move calmly to the right of the Great Hound which takes no notice. Silas regards Leo a long moment. He then claps his hands behind his back, and lowers his head.

Alex slowly shuts his eyes.

Tears seep from the corner of Leo's eyelids as he brings the solo through its final section. The emotion motivating his fingers focuses on his mother and all he's learned. The emotion streaming down his cheeks focuses on all he's cost: down to her sacrificing the love of her life.

Just then a light appears at the base of his neck: a flicker at first, slowly manifesting into a glow. It clarifies at every note and soon becomes a solid gleam.

What was only thought the spot of a birthmark takes form in the characters A and γ: the alpha and gamma of the classic alphabet.

The letters intensify as the solo nears its end. Blood feeding the muscles on Leo's forearm engorge the veins from choking the neck so vigorously. His fingers, however, still produce the most graceful of sounds.

On the final note, Leo lifts his arm. The light bursts forth in the ecstasy of climax. A blinding array ensues, showering the barren wasteland in a blanket of white.

Then, all is quiet.

Anastasia runs out as the A γ settles back into a faint birthmark. He barely seems to notice when she takes his arm, but pulls her in nonetheless.

Her arms seem to wrap around a pillow in place of a pillar: giving, and non-resistant. Her ear to his chest rises to the beat of steady breaths.

Something wet brushes her ankle. When she looks down she finds mighty Cerberus lying prostrate with its front paws forward. Its tongue retracts after another lick, and its eyes show a ring of chestnut brown around the pupil. Without the personification of the "Death-Daemon of Night," it appears nothing more than an overgrown, mutated puppy that's spent too many years in solitude.

Anastasia dares to approach. She slides her feet carefully over while not releasing Leo who puts up no opposition. The Hound doesn't rustle, only follows her with a look of foreign curiosity that tickles its instincts into second guessing its nature.

She extends a hand, cautious, yet steady. The snakes around its mane remain settled: a few lick the air, but none seem threatened.

The moment arrives when soft, warm flesh touches upon the cool, coarse bridge of the Hound's nose. Anastasia runs her fingertips over the fine hairs creating a buildup of friction that sounds like it might shock her if she pets too rapidly.

Cerberus doesn't respond but to allow her affection. Anastasia smiles, and begins to withdraw her hand when a final lick catches her on the way. It slobbers mythological saliva down her arm that she hesitates to wipe off on her clothes.

She giggles looking back at Leo, indicating she won't mind having to buy a new shirt.

Leo, however, does not remove his eyes from the direction of the marsh. The now clear path to his destination causes him more fear than any monster. Monsters are tangible, even if only in the mind. Victory and defeat he understands.

Yet standing over the vicious Hellhound has beaten him worse than any other, and still he'd rather be going to face Feidor.

Alex walks up and nods approvingly at his grandson.

"It's time to go. Your Mom's waiting." He starts past Cerberus.

Anastasia tugs Leo's hand but he doesn't move. She turns and sees the direction of his stare. She then takes his other hand and starts drawing closer when her father appears behind him.

Silas looks into the back of Leo's head, then down. He sighs placing a firm hand on Leo's shoulder.

"It's alright, son," he says.

Leo doesn't shrug, nor retort. He simply leers at the hand, throws the guitar over his shoulder, and walks off eyes to the ground.

Anastasia considers following but her father shakes his head. Just then Alexi joins.

"Boy, that was some solo, huh?" he says, ever more animated.

"Yeah," says Anastasia, still watching Leo, "some solo."

Silas continues on. Anastasia stays a minute longer to satisfy Alexi's curiosity over the tamed Hell Hound. They approach the beast together, but Alexi doesn't tame himself when he shoots out an eager arm causing Cerberus to rustle and its mane to hiss.

"Easy, Alexi," says Anastasia, putting herself between and demonstrating how she gently puts the Hound at ease.

"Well, I can't exactly die twice."

The group continues toward the ferry each in their own thoughts. Anastasia and Alexi bring up the rear. The rest walk at separate intervals to Alex's lead.

The reeds soon return below Leo's feet, but they might as well be clouds for all he notices, for all he feels under the weight of his guitar and guard: he's nothing.

Clouds might serve better indeed to lift him away, back in time to truly relive the moments Alex offered him as a glimpse: to fix it all, to not even exist; maybe then his mother would've had the life she deserved, and a death she embraced with open arms on her way to rosy fields and loving groves.

A pleasant fiction in the reality of Erebos and the Stygian Marshes.

The group congregates by the Styx. At the edge of the water a scraggly man holding a pole waits in a skiff. He wears a tunic-like garment, a pointed hat, and a face indicating he's none too pleased to see them.

"Well, well, there's a new lot! Two living to boot. Company have we, General? Seems the Master lets anyone in these days," he says. The crooked nosed boatman looks Leo and Anastasia up and down sharply.

"Kharon." Alex bows, "They are here to see my daughter."

"Ah, of course, like a petting zoo. No rush. That one won't be goin' anywhere. I say, you might've done her the favor of a proper burial before you come visiting," says Kharon scratching his filthy beard.

"It will be done soon," says Alex.

Leo says nothing, his feet still on the clouds.

"And she'll be appreciating it I'm sure. In the meantime though, I'll be taking my danake as is due."

One of the coins offered as payment for passage across the marsh. The other being the obolus coin. Funeral custom dictates it be placed in the mouth of the deceased for Kharon to remove it. He now holds out his hand eagerly.

"They're with me," says Alex.

The old daimon scrunches his hollow face and retracts his hand into a loose fist. His ageless eyes lower and bear into Alex.

"In my day, the dead stayed dead," he says, grinding his teeth. Turning to Leo and Anastasia he flicks his head for them to board. The others follow, and the boat starts gliding on no prompt but Kharon settling in the rear.

EUCATASTROPHE: THE RETURNS

CHAPTER 15 – THE ELM OF FALSE DREAMS

Despite being the first to step on the boat, Leo tends toward the back near the dirty garments of Kharon. Somehow the stench of algae and sewage seems a better fit for company than any of his companions, or himself even.

Anastasia takes his hand from the seat at his side. He wonders if he'd swim back if she didn't. Otherwise, he avoids all thoughts and sight of the river. He much prefers the floor, which he uses as a hole in the sand while the storm passes in and around him.

Nonetheless, he feels every inch they move like a distance of ten feet. The steady progress of the boat drives on like the inexorable flight of an arrow closing in on prey, and the Black Lion the mouse.

The boat maneuvers smoothly by the navigation of Kharon's pole. It cuts an easy path through the sedge and tall reeds that spread like a labyrinth around them. For its briskness, however, nothing shows on its black sails. Indeed, they hang so flat and dreary as if never having hoped for any wind.

A rustle amongst the passengers shakes the boat from its dream. Anastasia squeezes Leo's hand. She, along with the rest, adjusts her position forward in a fixed gaze.

Leo, however, doesn't follow suit. A growing bubble of disquiet expands in his chest. Knowing there's something ahead to see, and likely what it is, makes him plant his eyes to the floor even harder.

Alone on the approaching shore, a young woman awaits. Her strawberry blonde hair flows over a sleeveless top: it is interrupted only by a blue strand resting on her shoulder. Sturdy hands rest at the sides of form fitted jeans. She glows more radiant the closer they get.

The presence she omits touches Leo's instincts the way it first did from afar on the Isles of the Blessed. Only now it is louder, more poignant, and in the simplicity he felt it as a child. A part of it calms his anxiety, a part of it amplifies.

He draws a deep breath as the boat skids to a stop on the jagged bank. Alex is the first to step off.

"Dora," he says hopping onto the ground. He takes a moment and regards his daughter in the prime of her youth. He then places his hands on her shoulders and pulls her in for a deep embrace.

"Hi, Daddy," says Pandora. She lights up like a little girl who hasn't seen her father all day, at a time when a day feels like a year. Burying her head into his protective arms she doesn't seem to pay any mind to his looking her age or pre-Reckoning attire. From the look on her face, though, she more than recognizes his essence.

"Mom!" says the next person off the boat.

Pandora lifts her head from her father's chest. She almost needs him to keep her up, however, as she lays eyes on the son torn from her nearly three decades ago.

"Oh, Alexi."

The healthier than ever adolescent races into his mother. They squeeze each other with the force deprived them in life. Alexi has never looked so alive, as if the Plains of Asphodel fade more and more by the second.

Pandora shuts her eyes tightly and grabs fistfuls of Alexi's shirt. Her grip is just as much affectionate as it is guarding.

"Oh my boy,...my brave little boy."

Though Alexi doesn't cry, his skin glows richer than ever. The twinge of wholeness that settles in his eyes shows full cognizance of the sentient and unbreakable bond between mother and child.

"See Mom," he says staring off over the Styx, "we're all back together, like we never left."

Pandora chokes out a giggle and wipes the side of her face.

The boat waddles as a heavy footstep meets the dry ground. No other sound breaks the peaceful silence or loving embrace for a few seconds more. Finally, a "Hey, Dora," escapes the man's lips.

Pandora's eyelids release the tension. They then slowly open in the direction of the strong voice she once called home.

Familiarity clings to the pages of an old photo album before they realize they no longer need it. As the due of their sacrifice comes full circle, it transports them through the moments of moving on to a place of simplicity they never left.

The moment begs for epic words, for all the years apart have meant and all the ones to come will mean.

Pandora lightly guides her oldest son to her side and with a faint smile says, "hey."

Silas curls the corner of his mouth and steps forward. Standing before his beloved, he places his thick fingers on each of her temples and pulls her forehead into his lips.

"Mom!?" says Alexi from below.

Pandora makes a girlish laugh and quickly gives her confused son the same type of kiss.

"It's ok, honey, it's a long story. We have time."

Alexi calculates the husky captain with moderate scrutiny. He then looks to Anastasia stepping off the boat, and slides himself back into his mother's side.

Anastasia wastes no time bursting onto her surrogate mother.

"Staj," says Pandora kissing her on the cheek, "thank you. Thank you so much."

Anastasia hugs tighter.

"No, thank you, Mom."

They release, and regard each other with a true sense of fondness and admiration.

Pandora's free hand remains clasped in Anastasia's. They breathe the relief of successfully reuniting, yet sigh the regret of soon having to part again. Anastasia places her other hand on top of Pandora's and draws it into the left side of her chest. They then embrace again.

Amongst such tender scenes, however, one remains aloof of the picture.

All turn to the battered young man in blood stained jeans and barely a rag to call a shirt.

He stands one foot on land and one foot in the water, head down as an extinguished flame; his silence speaks as though his allotment of words has run out.

Pandora steps away from the rest. She pauses at intervals to see if he will acknowledge her, looking on her mighty son as a baby dove with a broken wing.

She continues approaching until directly before him: still trying to catch his eye. When he doesn't offer it, she brushes the hair out of his face like the little boy she saw in her dream. The boy she knew would be him.

The touch of her hand releases the dam, and Leo collapses into his mother's shoulder. His weapons crash to the ground like a fallen warrior: his tears beg all the forgiveness his words won't express.

"I knew you'd find your way," says Pandora stroking his dark curls.

Leo remains tucked in as though hiding emotion from his classmates in primary school. The muscles over his body tense trying to suppress the shudders. When the fit finally assuages, he hastily wipes the right side of his cheek.

"You're here because of me," he says as much for his mother as for himself to hear aloud.

Pandora draws a deep breath. "Yes, but not the way you think."

The white guitar lying on the soiled ground recalls to Leo's mind the little boy holding a similar one in his mother's vision. The gentle hand that wiped the curly hair with such tender grace, eventually a discolored stub of mangled digits.

Leo draws his head up, shirking at the memory. He has a difficult time thinking about all this in any other way.

"It wasn't fair," he says, raising his eyes, "more now even." He glances at Silas then looks away. "I felt you guiding me through. I just had to get you out of here."

Pandora looks on her son with a sad smile, then embraces him again much tighter than before. Leo has never felt such vitality in her. Her fully functional fingers grip into his back with pronounced strength.

While Leo relishes the moment in his mother's arms, a peak at a disdainful Kharon standing primly on his skiff reminds him they are not out of the tree yet.

"Come on," says Leo breaking, "we got to get home before Beren burns your body."

Leo leans down and scoops up his guard and attached blade. The guitar he throws around his neck and slides to his hip.

Grabbing his mother's hand, he makes to turn, but the vitality he felt a moment before returns as she resists to follow.

He turns sharply at the tug. "What are you doing? Come on, we gotta go."

"Honey." She places her other hand over his and draws him in. "It won't be Beren: because it has to be you."

The resolve on Leo's face melts into an enigma of understanding. He tries to comprehend, but the words remain hanging in the air between them.

"You have to be the one to finish it," she says more poignantly. "Leo, I can't go with you."

The force of Leo's limbs nearly abandons him. He never imagined his mother's body burning, much less him the one to burn it. The finality carries a sobering chill to the fact she just said she wouldn't be going.

He then thinks of all she's suffered: at his hands, his father's, the omegas', the Fates', the sun, the moon.... That she refuse another chance to live after enduring such a death sends Leo in spirals. That she should refuse him, without his making amends...

"What are you talking about?" says Leo, scraping at loose dirt. "Of course you can go back. Menoitios said..."

"Honey," says Pandora. She looks over her shoulder at her beloved son, her dear father, and her dearest Silas. "I am home."

Leo looks after her. A slight glare enters his eyes at the others come to take her away. He then squeezes her wrists with flailing energy, "But you told me to find you, to see the way. Emrick said only I could save you. So you have to come home: I got nothing left."

Leo grabs both her arms but cannot find the strength to fight. Pandora waits patiently, then draws his head into her chest. Tears seep over the damaged skin of his scar and wet the barren ground below.

"I don't regret my choices," she says in an even tone, "and now it's time for you to make your own."

The charge falls against thick layers of dependence. Harder he clings to his silent anchor, the one who's formed the basis of his existence from the time he was born to the time she now dies: taken for granted, uncomplaining. Feeling her slip away feels like losing the very feet on which he stands. A part of him wishes to die along with her. Another part seems like it already has.

He holds his mother tighter, wrenching every bit of feeling to carry with him when it's gone.

A hand rests on top of his. The gentle heat of the palm soothes the desperation in his grip: the reassurance of its connection provides an anchor of its own.

Pandora senses it too and shows greater relief than her son. Moving her lips close to Leo's ear she whispers, "and you're already off to a good start."

Leo looks up. The two women of his life never looked more beautiful side by side: vibrant colored eyes, lustrous hair over fair complexions. For a moment he forgets which one is which. Nonetheless, enjoined as three brings him to the pinnacle of what love's had to offer: the fullness, the joy, the security. He nearly smiles even.

As with all precious moments though, they come and must go so that we knew they were ever precious. The end stares Leo in the face, and leaves nothing for it but to resign to the fact that only in the end could they ever be joined again. As for now, only one would stay.

Pandora passes Leo's free hand into Anastasia's, and withdraws her own.

"I know you'll make me proud," she says in sincere delight of the pair before her. "I love you always."

With that she hugs them both.

Leo again says the words without speaking. He locks on to his mother as though trying to memorize every line, wondering if he'd do just as well to stay "dead" to the real world and live out his days with his deceased friends and family: pre-Reckoning chats with Alex, duels with Silas, Alexi's quirks, Anastasia's laughter, and time; time to make amends, time to be the son he never was in life.

The fantasy of it all nearly sweeps him away. Though as he stands before the relatives assembled before him and considers their paths to where they are, perhaps death is a privilege he's not yet earned.

He thinks of Vince Yeerum and the place his conscience led him, and imagines it would only be worse in his own current state. Finding his mother and repenting is not enough to cleanse him. Only in life would he find that opportunity. As Alex aptly said, he was not one of them.

So with two separate roads to follow, he packs away the treasure his mother's left him, and sends a promise in return.

Always.

Pandora nods, understanding fully.

Before turning to the others she catches Anastasia's eye. She gives her a sincere half smile.

"I will," says Anastasia blushing.

Pandora nods again in confident relief.

"I know."

Silas walks up and steps around his daughter. He extends a hand toward Leo. Leo takes it and Silas puts him in a bone crunching handshake. The Captain looks into the young kladimans making the same supplicating request.

"Yes...sir," Leo quickly grunts through the discomfort.

Silas grunts in acknowledgement. Having made the point, he allows for a slight curl at the side of his mouth.

He then takes his daughter aside. A bit removed and alone, they hold each other close and exchange hushed words.

Meanwhile, Leo bids farewell to the Maquaris.

"Be good, little brother," says Alexi, reaching up to drape an arm around Leo's thick neck. "And keep playing like Dad."

Leo smirks. "Or maybe I'll let him play like me."

The remark pleases Alexi, yet he takes a distant look. Leo imagines he would like to be the one returning to play with their father again.

No words of consolation come to mind, nor any to help understand how something so loved by one could have been so loathed by the other.

Leo pulls his big brother in. The muscles on his forearm chisel from the force of his clasp. Through it he says it all: thanking Alexi for supplying the other side of the coin, and promising he would somehow find the will to play for them both.

When they part, Alexi studies his brother for a minute. Nothing scrutinizing, just a fresh look on a person he should have known his entire life.

Alex follows his grandson with a fond smile. Before reaching Leo, he adjusts the rim of his intersecting "NY" cap at a slight angle, then offers a hand. Leo makes to shake it when Alex claps his palm and slides his hand up to the fingertips. Hooking the ends, he pulls Leo in with a one-armed hug.

Leo checks his hand upon releasing to make sure it's still there.

"Oh," says Alex chuckling, "you guys don't do that anymore? We used to call it a pound."

Leo hesitates. "Uh, no, sorry, we don't...'pound' anymore."

Alex adjusts his cap again. "Well, you get the point."

Neither go on with anything to say. Alexi keeps Anastasia busy to the side with his fond goodbyes. Silas and Pandora keep busy doing much of the opposite.

Leo and Alex regard one another as if staring through a window in time.

"Well," says Leo after a while, "guess the guitar worked out."

Alex grins at the veiled small talk. "You're welcome."

"And," Leo begins, putting his hands in his filthy pockets. "... thanks."

The others start coming back before Alex can acknowledge, but Leo sees his meaning was understood.

Pandora moves to her father's side and Silas to hers. Alexi quickly nuzzles his way and turns his back into his mother's arms.

Anastasia rejoins Leo in front of their family.

"When you get back," says Alex to both, "go see that old bat Emrick. Tell him I haven't forgiven him for outliving me this long."

"Okay," says Anastasia giggling.

"He's going to have some things for you too; make sure you get there."

Leo lowers his head in assent. "We will."

As the moment of parting arrives, all hold their breaths to delay. The positive energy disperses into the air, the heartwarming chatter absorbs into the rocks.

Leo surveys the group. He's about to deliver his final words to his mother when her hand shoots up to her chest. She bends over wide eyed yet more from foreign sensation than pain.

Leo springs forward catching her. "Mom."

An armor piercing cackle rings through the expanse. It comes from the skiff docked by the Styx.

"Told you, didn't I?" says Kharon pointing a bony finger, "mighta done er' the favor of a proper burial."

The urge to slice the daimon's rancorous head from his shoulders nearly overwhelms Leo until a look from his mother steadies him.

He immediately channels the energy he's built up into the feel of his mother's skin. Closing his eyes, he reaches for her essence. Her energy soon combines with his to give a clear picture of the source of her ailment.

Beren.

Leo opens his eyes and looks deep into his mother's.

"It's Beren and Zoe. They're completing the rite."

A look of resignation crosses Pandora's brow. She parts her lips to speak.

"I love you, Mom," Leo interjects. Pulling her in he kisses her forehead and jumps to his feet.

He quickly looks to Alex on how to proceed.

"Get to the Elm tree straight ahead," says Alex, consistent and collected. "Anastasia will know what to do."

With a final glance at his mother, he races off with Anastasia closely behind.

The giant Elm looms not far before them. Its qualities closely resemble the tree in the lake, as does its luscious bloom in defiance of its grim surroundings. They halt before its trunk.

"Are you ready?" says Anastasia.

Leo takes her hand, "yeah, hurry."

"Hold on tight."

Anastasia kneels before the Elm and touches its base. A white glow forms around her fingers then at the back of her neck. Underneath a part in her hair the Classic letter M as in "Mu" signals to Leo who really brought them into the Underworld.

Back by the river the four deceased stand huddled in a group. Alexi, deep in his mother's arms, waves a farewell goodbye as high as he can manage.

Leo looks back one last time amidst the growing shine. To his great surprise, he sees the White Lion perched on a distant crag high behind his family. It shows no aggression, and remains as calm as Cerberus following the solo.

As their eyes meet, Leo perceives a lively blue in place of the hollow dark. The color appears the exact same as Alex's aether blade: it even carries something of its soothing nature. Leo turns away feeling a strange connection of sorts to his monstrous pursuer.

The light of the tree intensifies. Leo quickly returns his brother's wave as the pull downward into the tree intensifies likewise. It gets stronger before he even has a chance to wave again.

A split second later both pull and light culminate, causing Leo to fight against the traction and squint through the brightness. It nearly prevents him from seeing the blurred silhouette of his family altogether.

Yet in one final effort, he pushes himself to his limits. He keeps hold of Anastasia on one end and extends his head as high as possible on the other. Through the blurriest of images he manages to see his mother reach across her chest, take Silas' hand, and rest her head on his shoulder.

With that his body relaxes, and he submits.

ΔΔΔ

Leo's eyes readjust to find dozens more staring up at him. The faces don't register, only a white array of garment. It covers an area of green the sun seems to reach.

His first breath savors of cool breeze mingled with the richness of aquatic life. Pores long since shut greedily consume the warmth hitting the back of his neck. The vastness of the rainbowed sky welcomes him home with open arms.

Before he tries to make sense of his living dream, he searches for any sign of what he thinks might have been his dormant one.

The slight panic puts his surroundings out of focus. Scanning the field from left to right, white and flesh mix to form a faceless melee. The warm sensations of Eulimnos become muddled with the cold and damp of the Underworld: the bright sun with the blinding light of Anastasia's neck.

Leo raises his palms to his temples and turns his head. Closing his eyes at least interrupts the confusion brought by what now appears to be the real in front of him. Opening them, a slight movement to his rear catches his attention.

Down by the lake, bow in hand, Anastasia wiggles her fingers discreetly in front of her chest. It takes a moment for Leo to realize it's even her, much less the reason for the weapon.

She stands in a ready position. With a cloth wrapped arrow notched on the string, she keeps it over an open flame as if waiting for a sign to ignite and release.

Leo finds the reason floating nearby on the clear water: the funeral pyre he built with his friends on the night they found him alone outside: the night before his mother's games. He remembers carting it along the water's edge the next day: empty. Glancing into the current one, however, he sees it's quite the opposite.

The whole of the Underworld moves into a shade of doubt as he looks down to find himself once again at the eulogy podium. The same place he revealed his decision to find his mother through the depths of the lake. The mourners looked up at him as they do now: and as then he begins to lose his grip on what *now* is.

The confusion of sleep or awake, dream or reality sinks its slobbery fangs into his mind. It yanks him side to side to the point he considers jumping into the lake again just to prove he did it the first time.

He hunches over, hanging on to the podium by the tips of his fingers. He shakes his head to weed through the barrage of Underworld images passing through in rapid array. The only clarity he manages is the constant in each slide.

In a desperate glance he looks back to Anastasia. He searches for any indication in his loyal companion of her acknowledging what he wants to believe as true. A sliver of proof that would validate a trip through wonderland with their deceased relatives: a ration of credibility on the closeness that became.

Anastasia remains, still at the ready. She watches him with the same measure of concern she might have as the old friend from down the way: curious, moderately affectionate, and certainly not out of this world.

Leo fights the flailing sensation by focusing his remaining energy on hers. Instantly his memories tune to the moments most prevalent from the current time he questions from before: her following him into the Underworld, sleeping placidly in the grove, embracing after Feidor, saying "I love you," holding his hand to bring him home.

The feeling resonates to the point he cannot help giving her the look he sought. He tries to check himself, but she's already caught it. The exposure leaves him preferring the crowd of faces.

Then, to his surprise, she more than reciprocates.

A gentle relief crosses her brow. Her eyes take on the tender blue of Lake Maquari. She cocks her head to the side, and through the light blonde strands falling before her face her squint of happiness shoots a burning arrow of its own.

The open affection breathes life back into Leo: affection he might have felt but she never would have shown had they not experienced the Underworld.

Leo's mind eases into a clear lens of all around him. The festival grounds, the marble houses on the hill, strewn equipment from the funeral games, his own home behind the trees to the left.

The familiarity makes it easier to spot Beren and Zoe, holding their victor's prizes conspicuously side by side for others to judge their comparative worth; Khloe standing arms crossed wondering what's taking him so long; and his father, Aeschylus, hands in pockets to the rear, yet not out of sight of his daughter.

The pieces fall into place, confirming all that happened the way it should have.

So with a click on the podium's audio, Leo sets to the task laid upon him:

"Hi," he begins, for lack of a more appropriate introduction. "Good to see everyone, actually."

Mourners wait with anticipation over what words Leo might have crafted for such a speech, if he was able to craft any at all.

Leo clears his throat. The elated surge of being home begins to wane. A late autumn breeze skimming the water from the opposite side of the lake sends a sobering chill over his skin. Whether or not he believes the Underworld and its bittersweet end are true, his mother is dead, and no amount of dreaming will change that.

He does his best to gather his thoughts. "Sorry I wasn't here for the games, but...I had to figure out why I'm here at all."

He poses the question as a passing notion. The "why," however, sails far into the distance of Leo's past even before the time he stayed home to tend to his mother: the young adolescent learning guitar, the Lycean competing for kladimans glory. When he aims at his own choices, the "why" drifts off into nowhere.

Yet for the first time, he swallows his pride, and redirects it outward away from himself. Not much to his surprise does it find a happy home in the choices of another.

Relaxing his thick shoulders, he exhales and he continues the eulogy:

"I'm here because a lady named Pandora Maquari isn't."

The scenes from Cerberus flash through his mind: the love for Silas, the dream of a little boy, the trip to see Emrick. Then, letting it all go for that boy who now stands the broken down young man with nothing to credit himself but the vain epithet of The Maurileho.

"I'm here because of love I never earned; sacrifice I never recognized."

He lowers his head a bit.

"I could spend the rest of my life regretting all the hurt I caused her, everything I took for granted, all the more I could have done to get her back, and it still wouldn't be enough."

A pause captures the grip of silence holding the mourners in place. Leo's words trail behind him in a reflective tone, as if only meant to be heard in the quiet corners of privacy.

Staring down at the podium, he loses sense of time. Fallen leaves rustle across the grass of the festival grounds. A mourning dove coos. Finally, he lifts his head and makes a slight nod.

"But I won't," he says. "She doesn't want that."

He catches his use of the present tense. He realizes he as yet feels her essence on the banks of the Styx, waiting to pass. Pandora's warming sensation moves over him but he knows it's time for her to go.

"The only thing I can do for her now is live: live for who she was, and who she'd want me to be.

That's why I'm here."

Mourners stay silent at hearing such words from the Maurileho. Zoe makes him a sad smile.

As he descends the podium, a lone clapper triggers an avalanche of applause. It comes from the direction of Aeschylus.

Leo, however, pays it no mind.

Stepping into Lake Maquari, he positions the pyre to send it off. In it his mother rests peacefully in regal dress surrounded by scores of roses symbolic of her new home. The makeup hides her withered features to depict a healthier woman ten years younger. To Leo's eyes, however, only the fresh faced 20-year-old with the blue streaked hair remains.

Leo pulls a coin from his pocket and places it in her cold mouth.

"It's done," he whispers.

He caresses the hand in the tissued area with the missing fingers. He feels their touch on his forehead once more as she would brush his hair away. This time, he brushes hers.

Then, with one last gentle squeeze of her hand, he gives her body over to the lake. A gentle shove sends the pyre moving. It glides as if floating on air in fixed course.

Once several yards out, Anastasia ignites the tip of her notched arrow. The flame of Prometheus burns bright in the cool Meton afternoon. She holds it before her for everyone to see, but keeps her own eyes only on Leo.

The pyre maintains a consistent drift as though guided by the lake itself. Once at a fair distance, Leo exchanges looks between his mother and Anastasia. Then, he only looks on Anastasia. With a slight hesitation he gives her the nod.

Be happy, Mom.

Anastasia makes a sad smile back. She then eyes her beloved target, and draws. While holding a little longer than customary, she releases a perfect shot and the pyre sets to flame.

The crowd shuffles to witness the beauty of a soul passing on through the fire, through Prometheus. None better than the eagle flying above. It passes slowly in delight of its overhead view. Once past the rising smoke it descends and takes its place on the boulder above the elm.

The flames burn away any remaining preoccupation Leo might have had over his mother's death. This doesn't include her loss, but any notion of a bad ending leading to something worse. This proves especially true when he fixes on the image of the lovely, vivacious woman running through fields with her love at her side.

He imagines a love so precious would be worth holding on to even to the stormy depths of Tartaros.

With that idea he looks over at Anastasia. She remains facing the pyre. Her bleached blonde tussles about in the breeze. With the bow hanging at her side, and the purity of white covering her body, she has never seemed more fierce and beautiful all at once.

Leo sets to a discreet walk so as not to disturb her precious persona. He sees nothing but her along the way. Once at her side and she still hasn't noticed, he takes hold of her bow hand and swings the weapon to the side. Her body opens in welcome surprise. Leo then wraps his hand around the back of her neck, looks her in the eyes, and kisses her for the first time.

His hand grips tighter to squeeze any remaining doubt. His lips press harder to purge any remaining fear. When all is gone, all that remains is them.

The love that now flows freely between them sows roots Leo swears to always cherish so long as they continue to grow; lakes or fields.

In the crowd, Beren and Zoe exchange bewildered looks.

"Did we miss something?"

CHAPTER 16 – THE PORTLAND BRIDGE

Lake Maquari reflects the last trickles of smoke on its shimmering plane. The pyre simmers to a cool burn, and ashes dance on a light breeze.

Throughout this time, Leo has held to his mother's essence as if she were standing next to him holding his hand. Imagining her happiness only amplified the warming sensation. As the rite completes, however, and the remains of her worldly body pass on to Prometheus, Leo now feels that essence within him extinguish.

He inhales as though the only one drawing from that air. Those around him seem displaced. Somehow, trapped in the world he left when he ran into the lake, in a past they haven't lived, free of the time Leo feels lasted weeks.

To keep his feet on the ground, however, he needs only look left, and his anchor holds him fast.

"You ok?" says Anastasia with a squeeze of his hand.

"Yeah," says Leo. "I'm just trying to get a grip on all this."

"You and me both." Anastasia notices the odd looks of people witnessing them together: those who don't know she confessed her love under threat of being torn from existence by a giant three-headed dog. Everyone, in other words.

Anastasia looks down at her hand locked in Leo's and nearly mirrors their odd expressions. She keeps staring as though she might wake up at any second: as if life were the real dream.

After a few times pinching herself in the side, however, the lakes and houses of Eulimnos still stand as always. The hills and polis of Prometheum follow to indicate that whichever side of the butterfly is awake, she is right at home.

Mourners have been approaching little by little to pay their respects and take leave. Many Leo recognized as family of his mother's former patients and old colleagues from her job. Several of his own acquaintances from the gymnasium presented themselves as well.

Some, however, he did not know. These ranged from the fine and erudite to the rough and tumble. With no more time but for a quick response, however, he took away the notion there was much of his mother's story about which he was unaware.

A break in the flow allows Leo to turn back on Lake Maquari where he appreciates his greatest condolence. Serene simplicity in its waters, void of human protocol: a constant companion throughout his life and often a preferred one. Some say it dates back years before the Reckoning, some say it was born of the Reckoning itself. Either way, it comes to no surprise it would house the magic of the Underwater Elm as a portal to the Underworld.

For a moment he forgets his circumstances. He begins to drift off in the peace of the lake. When he's about to lose himself completely a sharp tensing of Anastasia's body draws him out.

The direction of her look obviates his question. Approaching from the right, a dark muscular form looks on them with a firm gaze. His hair is tied back in braids, and down his arm he bears a tattoo of a fearsome tiger.

The kickboxer, now known to them as a Yeerum, walks up still holding his victor's prize. Though distinct in facial complexion from the fighter who scarred Leo, he clearly shares the strong, fluid body movements of his bloodline; the movements of Vince.

The young man extends a calloused hand. "Condolences," he says, making eye contact with Leo.

Leo carefully releases Anastasia's hand to correspond the steady grip. He then nods but doesn't lower his eyes. As he looks on, he finds himself slightly mesmerized by the light blue contrast to mocha skin. The voice also departs from the hard physique in a cool easy tone.

Letting go Leo notices the scar tissue on top of the Tiger's knuckles and immediately throws up his guard again. He recalls on three occasions their destructive force as weapons: his own scar, Coach P's brutal beating, and the most recent plunging into Beren's throat.

Vince's descendant senses the discomfort and averts to Anastasia. He looks on her as though recognizing a face from an old photo, not being too surprised, or disappointed. Anastasia breaks from the hypnotizing gaze edging closer to Leo's side.

The Yeerum glances back at Leo. "Is this your wife?" he asks.

A light rouge flushes over Anastasia's face, darkening when Leo doesn't respond.

"This is Anastasia...Anastasia Wildyn," Leo finally says.

"Oh," says the young fighter in a falling tone. His near perfect posture falters a bit at hearing her identity. He nods in acknowledgment of making her acquaintance but does not commit to making eye contact again.

Leo waits for Anastasia's subsequent reaction to the awkwardness of confronting someone so alike to Vince Yeerum: a feeling somehow reflecting the renewed void of her father.

For as much as he waits, however, none seems to surface. If anything, she looks on him with a slight sense of pity, much as she eventually looked on Vince.

Leo imagines whatever void there was, Silas himself filled in the Underworld: even then as he does now, if not with his presence, his love. Furthermore, for such lethal fighting skills Leo can sense no malice, apparent or distant in the humble young man towering before him.

The Tiger finally builds up the nerve to face Anastasia again and makes out an "I...," before something over Anastasia's shoulder catches his eye. His expression grows dark in response, almost as he would face an opponent trying to do him harm.

"I...have to go," he coldly mutters. "I'm sorry for your loss," he directs at no one, - shuffling off.

Leo is about to comment on the oddity of the situation when Anastasia pulls away. "What's your name?" she calls after him.

The great kickboxer stops about a dozen yards away and turns his head.

"Sage."

Before she can say another word he is off, and Statesman Braun is standing before them.

"Hello, Leonidas. Anastasia."

Beren's father lingers on the latter a trice longer. His gaze, though light, penetrates to guilt unknown by the observed. Anastasia looks away.

"A fine eulogy, son," he says to Leo. "Your mother would have been proud."

"Thank you, sir. I'm sure she is."

He turns deliberately back to Anastasia. "Your father, Silas, would have appreciated it too."

The tension communicated on the part of the old statesman reminds Leo of the urgency he pressed in "requesting" that Leo find Beren before the match with the Tiger at Victoria Braun's games. Perhaps he feared a vengeful tactic for having been the one to kill Vince Yeerum in Silas' defense. Perhaps he now takes offense to Anastasia fraternizing with the enemy.

"Well," says Anastasia after a pause, "they're finally together at least."

Statesman Braun raises an eyebrow to "finally."

The surprise reminds Leo most remain unaware they know about Generation 6. Indeed, Leo now sees Bouko Braun in an entirely different light: the clear-headed Polity leader to the idealistic crusader in reverse order.

"Yes, well, what's in store now then?" says Statesman Braun, reverting to his typical diplomatic tone.

Leo assumes the question posed offhand, yet now posed becomes a serious question on point. To even think of it exposes a lack of purpose left by the absence of a sick mother to care for, and a dead one to save. Yet daring to overcome it exposes something much worse.

The smoldering pyre drifts further and further out of sight. The last remnant and cut of thread cling to Leo like the thin wisp of smoke struggling to trail Pandora's rest. Leo finds he's unable to answer Statesman Braun's question.

"Just move on with whatever I find," Leo spits out.

"Very good," says Statesman Braun, eying them back and forth. "We'll see each other soon then." With a quick nod he retires.

Leo and Anastasia exchange glances once he's gone. The question, however, still lingers in Leo's mind. Of all the doubts over Generation 6, the "Search," etc, the only one directly lingering is the task Alex set for them to visit Emrick. The last remaining loose-end from the Underworld. Leo knows only then will this chapter in his life be closed, if it's even meant to be closed.

He and Anastasia continue attending to guests for some time. Eventually only a few dozen remain.

"I wonder why Beren and Zoe haven't come to stand with us," says Anastasia.

Leo shakes his head and smirks. "Probably the same reason we haven't gone to stand with them."

In all their years as friends, the group of four have always stayed platonic, so far as anyone would acknowledge; and as such forms their dynamic. Leo worries what dissonance a couple would bring.

Scanning the field for them, Leo spots his father instead engaged in hopeful conversation with Khloe and her family. Watching him hug one of his granddaughters Leo imagines him hugging Alexi, and even himself as the child from his mother's visions. The brutal pain of losing a best friend, as Aeschylus did Alexi, flashes through his mind as he held Beren in his arms. This is a wound that would never have healed.

Anastasia takes Leo's arm and leans up toward his ear, "The one thing you can save." She quotes Alex's words in Tartaros. "Maybe it's time."

Leo considers, then nods in a different direction. "You might take your own advice there."

Seated at a banquet table, withered hands laying on the armrests, Emrick Wildyn patiently awaits his granddaughter's reaction to seeing him.

When she doesn't scowl or turn away he ventures a gentle smile, which she returns.

"I'll be back," she says, sliding her hand from Leo.

For so many years she blamed Emrick for the death of her father. She always thought the peculiar, aged mantis as living by two faces: one the sweet, doting, grand paternal figure, and the other the cult guiding fanatic, luring people like her father in with monsters like Vince Yeerum. This is, or so she thought.

Knowing and understanding her father now as a young woman, however, she feels drawn to follow a similar path; follow her own beliefs, by her own will: fight and potentially sacrifice for a cause she believes in: like the burly Captain now enjoying the fruits of his patience.

As the old man before her draws nearer she sees her father in him clearer than ever. She imagines the Captain as a one hundred-year-old eagerly awaiting his grandchild and feeling ever so proud of his own. Then she imagines him only remembering his own through his grandchild.

Regarding Emrick she realizes she wasn't the only one to lose.

"Ah, Little Orphan Annie, all grown up," he beams. "It's been quite some time."

Her grandfather's apparent lack of sensitivity dampers her own a bit.

"Hi, Grandpa: and I'm not an orphan you know," she says as much to herself as to him.

With a dead father and an absent mother, the term does not seem that far from the truth. Indeed, the idea of returning home to her mother after such a beautiful time with her father seems like moving into Tartaros from Elysium. Yet she recalls peering into the stars on their way to the Plains of Asphodel when the world of Prometheum thought she and Leo were dead; the condition of her mother over her loss. She recalls her father's parting words and remembers being an orphan is not an option.

Emrick chuckles and waves a slow, dismissing hand.

"OH it's just an old radio pr...never mind."

A silence follows where although they've broken the ice, no one's planned what to do beyond that. Anastasia stands jittering, in part from nothing to say and in part from projecting scenarios of what she might expect from an inevitable re-encounter with her mother. Emrick sits observing her jittering.

"So, I must say," says the old man, tip toeing a bit. "Leonidas failed to mention anything, uh, different between you two when he came to visit me."

The allusion to her very public show of affection makes her even more jittery, yet in an elated sort of way. She blushes despite herself.

"Oh, uh, yeah: it's complicated."

Emrick slaps his bony knee. "Makes me wonder what my son would think to know...," he pauses.

Anastasia stops jittering. "Know what?"

"It's complicated," says the old man with a grin.

Anastasia smirks, not so much at her grandfather's humor as to her father's interaction with Leo through the course of the Underworld: a flurry of snide remarks, healthy blows, awkward secrets, and tolerant understandings.

She reflects, "I think he would be overprotective at first, but come around once he sees the person inside Leo, the person he could be."

Emrick doesn't contradict. "He was always a tough egg to crack. But once you did he was fiercely loyal."

Oh Daddy.

"I know."

A white bushy eyebrow raises at this. "Indeed, you seem to know a lot for someone who was very young when she lost her father."

His tone reminds her of Alex when he was probing something from Leo. She also notes the fact she is talking to a mantis nearly impossible to deceive. And even if she could, would she want to?

More important than anything he is her last remaining family who wants anything to do with her. He is the something she *can* save. As for the other, she will try her best.

She sighs looking down on the old friend of Alex. Though not terribly inclined to so quickly disclose her story of the Underworld, she takes a seat next to him.

"You'll never believe what happened."

△△△

Watching Anastasia move toward someone she's ignored for years inspires Leo in his own task. He justifies buying time with concern, but once granddaughter and grandfather have both smiled he sees he need not be in either case. Armed with that push, he steps off.

Twice already he has attempted to engage his father and twice has been interrupted. He cannot hope for the same luck a third time, much less in the "real world."

Once he comes within the distance of several yards, Khloe walks off, and he pauses. He'd hoped to use her and his nieces as a buffer. His father then assumes the discreet, forlorn expression Leo witnessed before when he watched his daughter leaving.

Leo resumes: mind still blank: feet still moving.

When a few paces away no lightning bolts strike he decides there is nothing for it but to say the word.

"Dad."

Aeschylus stays facing the other way. A look of discomfort flashes across his face as though having heard a voice inside his head.

"Dad," says Leo a little louder.

Aeschylus turns, eyes a little wider than usual.

"Oh, Leo, uh, hi," he says.

The encounter marks the first time in several years they've come face to face. The time shows in Aeschylus. His once lush brown hair has grown spotted in color and lies thin on his shoulders. The wrinkles on his face correspond to the anguish written everywhere else.

"Hi, Dad," says Leo trying not to scare him away.

Aeschylus indeed looks as though he might bolt anytime. His eyes remain wide, body tense. His mouth scrambles for anything his tongue can manage to form.

"That eulogy, it, it was nice," he says, combing his hair with the back with his hand.

The gesture transports Leo to an even stranger place than the Underworld: a time, for a time, when their house lived in relative harmony. As a young boy his father would return home for the day and remove his gray top hat. He would then smile at him and Khloe while putting his hair back.

Later as a teenager, Leo took a knife to that hat and burned it.

"Thanks. Glad you got to hear it," says Leo. He notes his father never replaced the hat.

Aeschylus takes heart from his son being glad over anything. "I also got to hear you at the Prometheia," he says with more enthusiasm. "Your mother's song; you won even."

Leo nearly laughs. He remembers the only reason he played was to spite his father who had preceded him.

"Yeah, I guess I did."

A short silence follows sending Aeschylus back to scrambling. His discomfort rubs off a little on Leo, who realizes he'll have to make more of an effort than just short answers.

"I saw you with Khloe's kids; they seem to like you," says Leo.

Aeschylus calms a bit and nods nostalgically. "They're so big now. I really like playing with them, when Khloe lets me."

Leo doesn't have to tap into his father's past to imagine the joy he felt playing with Alexi, nor what he'd give to play with him again. Perhaps he sees his granddaughters as a means to recapture some of those moments with regards to his son. And with regards to Leo and Khloe, a clean slate.

Another silence follows. This one a bit heavier. Leo searches for any banal piece of small talk he can think of, but decides it's better to end the reunion before resorting to the weather.

"Well...thanks for coming out,...for Mom," says Leo. He places his hands in his pockets. "I'm sure she appreciates it."

Aeschylus mirrors by running his hand through his hair again. "Right, yeah, I'm..." he begins to say. "I guess I'll be seeing yah."

Leo shakes his head. He considers a handshake, but turns instead. Before actually moving off, however, he looks back on the old musician.

"Listen," he says contemplating his words. "Maybe we could... jam sometime..., if you felt like stopping over."

The proposition revives something in Aeschylus.

"Oh yeah, sounds great. I would say I'd give you another lesson, but you'd probably be the one to give it to me now."

The compliment recalls his brother's farewell from a time a few minutes away and a place a world in the past. He visualizes the image Alexi painted of their father in the Plains of Asphodel: the kind, loving man who valued his family above all. Though Leo cannot yet look on his father with those eyes, he wonders what parts he may have missed due to his own anger. What he can do, however, is fight to remember his father's story, and at least allow himself the opportunity to save whatever is left of that man from so many years ago, and perhaps some of the boy Leo was as well.

With this in mind Leo considers his father's statement next to his brother's words. A note of amusement crosses his face and he curls the side of his mouth. "I'll see what I can do." He then reaches out and offers his hand. "Thanks for coming."

Aeschylus regards the hand held before him, then slowly lifts his own to accept his son.

"See you soon, then."

The handshake flushes a fair amount of tension wrenched in over time. The open air soothes and alleviates. Eulimnos beckons a welcome home and safe return.

This time, when they part, Leo is the one who looks after the other.

A few minutes later, after a small amount of searching, Leo finds Anastasia in tete-a-tete with her grandfather. He wonders at their appearing in such confidence and concludes there must indeed be something in the Eulimnan air that day. A part of him also wonders what two estranged people might have to talk about besides the weather, and worries what she might reveal so soon.

"Ah, Leonidas," says Emrick raising his cane in greeting.

"Mr. Wildyn,...or, Emrick," says Leo cautiously.

The old man makes a pleasantly amused smile. "So," he says sliding in his seat, "did you find what you were looking for?"

Leo takes a sidelong glance at Anastasia. She avoids his eyes at first, then innocently shrugs.

"In a way, yeah."

Emrick snickers. "Well I hope to hear more about it. I'll make sure to have more *vin chaud* for when you visit tomorrow." He rises to leave.

Leo offers an arm but is waved off.

"Bye, Annie. Thanks for the chat."

"See you tomorrow, Grandpa."

Leo means to inquire over the "see you, Grandpa" he thought he'd never hear and the "tomorrow" she's apparently filled with plans when two familiar faces appear at a distance. A head above the rest they move intently, tittering over a piece of knowledge only they seem privy to. They avoid eye contact with the pair they approach.

"Time to face the music," Leo says.

Anastasia spots them and braces herself at his side.

Leo thinks of all he's seen them do that they will never know of: all they have said of him he will never forget; all he might have lost should even one have fallen away.

A second later the group of four comes face to face. They stand reunited after what seems like an eternity to two. For a moment they do nothing but stare.

While both pairs have reasons for oddness, Beren and Zoe hide it less. They regard their friends standing together with feigned straightness. They then look at each other, snort, and burst out laughing.

Though awkward, open laughter gives a much better vibe than cached behavior. Indeed, after witnessing so much sadness in them over their loss, Leo almost feels happy he and Anastasia can now provide them with some amusement.

"Ok ok, what are you guys playing at here," says Beren catching his breath.

"Nice to see you too," says Leo.

"Nice to see us?" says Zoe. "You make it sound like we weren't just together earlier today...you know...when you guys weren't hooking up in front of everybody. Or at all, rather."

When the expected retort doesn't come, Beren and Zoe check themselves of their fun. When the maturity chiseled on Leo and Anastasia's faces from the long of the Underworld shows in place of the shy girl and angst-ridden boy from next door, it stifles them altogether.

"I guess we did miss something," says Zoe, slightly taken aback.

Leo considers how odd it must really seem to see a pair of friends you've known all your life become lovers in a matter of hours. In that light, he nearly feels the same even given the time of the whole experience that brought them there.

He makes a small laugh, "Yeah, you could say that."

The small line forming behind Beren and Zoe grows more antsy over the prolonged "condolences" the four seem to be sharing. Leo sees their catch-up will have to wait.

"Listen," he says, "there's a lot you guys need to know. Let's meet up at the bridge later after we get this cleaned up."

The earnest tone catches their tongues yet they nod in agreement.

"We'll give you a hand with this, then we can go over together," says Beren.

"Alright," says Leo. "Just go ahead and join them, Staj, I'll deal with the rest of these people I don't know."

Anastasia goes along while Leo sees off the few remaining mourners. Though strangers aside from a few random neighbors he's not spoken to for years, none strike him as anything peculiar. For the most part they make their ceremonial bow, utter their rehearsed words, and go on their merry way. Leo is about to go on his own when a final mourner approaches.
estate

The man's unnatural fluidity of motion sets Leo's mind askew. The pure white ruffle atop his head reminds Leo of the western Appalachian summits in winter. Combining hair and movement, however, Leo gets the sensation of seeing another drifting spirit of the Underworld, like Vince, or his brother.

A closer look reveals no spirit to his relief. Just an elderly individual utilizing Nubas Technology to carry him along in the absence of legs.

An upgrade from the old Nubas' cyberficial limbs which functioned well for amputees but applied too much pressure for fragile hip joints, the Model 3000 transports them along itself a few inches from the ground. Many say it works better than real legs. But for the cost, people might sacrifice their own voluntarily.

Most people, that is.

Leo almost finds it resentful the ease in which the frail man approaches. To think of all his mother had to endure for refusing the procedure; her only excuse not to dip into the family estate she held so sacred.

When he stops Leo takes note of a strange dot on his forehead. Red in color, it appears to be a complimentary point atop a tall gaunt frame embellished with oval glasses. His skin is dark like the Tiger's, but not of the same shade.

"Good afternoon," the man says in soft, accented Americana. He offers a flecked, bony hand.

"Hi," says Leo, hesitant to touch him.

His skin is cold and clammy and shows signs of discoloration. His light brown eyes, though slightly bloodshot, carry a soothing effect as they patiently take in Leo.

A note of familiarity rings in the back of Leo's mind. He begins to reciprocate the searching look of the person he thinks he recognizes in front of him. Before he finds his answer, though, the crippled man finds his first.

"Mmmmmm, there you are, Dora," says the man, relieved.

"Excuse m...?"

"Keep your word, Leonidas," he says. He takes Leo's forearm with surprising strength, then looks down at his missing legs. "We owe her so much."

The man lifts his head and tilts back for a clearer view of Leo through his spectacles, then floats away without another word.

A shot to Leo's shoulder draws his attention away before he can make out where the man went.

"Hey buddy, you got this wrapped up?" says Beren half-sensitively.

Leo takes another look in the direction the man departed.

"Yeah, let's get out of here. Actually, no." He continues thinking of the final mourner and what possible connection he could have to the family. "I gotta get something at the house. I'll be back."

"Ooooo...k. We're almost done and we'll be ready to head out."

Leo waves his acknowledgement as he rushes off in the midst of his latest thought.

Clean-up does not require much more than collecting the items Khloe brought over for display of her mother's life; slide pics, bubble vids, personal belongings to serve as memorabilia. The funeral services tend to the rest.

Once they've finished their part, Khloe thanks them gladly and is sure to note the absence of her brother's helping hand.

Before they part ways Khloe motions Anastasia aside. A slight jitter accompanies Anastasia's step as she wonders what Leo's sister could have to treat with her in private.

Once alone Khloe reaches into her handbag and pulls out a metallic object attached to leather.

"Here, why don't you have this, Staj," says Khloe offering it.

Anastasia curiously accepts an old model of archery release for the compound bow: the ones that used a basic latch and trigger system.

"I know it's probably not much compared to that magnetic thing you have, but this was my Mom's before she stopped shooting."

Indeed, she finds the initials "PS" etched into the palm. This of course dating to the time Leo's mom went by Pandora Serelin.

Fingering the beautifully tarnished areas of the release, Anastasia smiles through choked back tears.

"Thanks, Khloe."

Leo returns a short time later with a guitar on his back and no further explanation of his trip to the house. None ask, and after a full day, none feel like the short walk to the tram that would take them to the bridge. As such, they opt for an M-Coach.

Leo walks over to a small parking lot on the far side of the festival grounds. There stands a roadside console into which he taps coordinates. Within a matter of minutes a compact, neon green four-seater glides down the road's solar plaques.

Upon arriving two automated doors pop open to reveal a circular set of blue cushions. The four file in and they close. A command prompt then requests a destination.

"Portland Bridge," says Leo.

The calculations process and the coach moves off. It glides so lightly over the plaques people rarely sense any movement.

Conversation stays casual along the way, commenting mainly on highlights from the day's games. Leo and Anastasia are only of half mind; otherwise preoccupied with how best to tell their friends they had just spent an unaccounted-for afternoon in the Underworld with their dead relatives whom they reached through a tree.

In short time they near the western outskirts of Prometheum. With the lake region a ways back, the landscape comes together to the potential of denser growth. Consequently the balding trees and barren brush envelop them to both sides to the point even sunlight barely makes it through. With fewer and fewer residences, nature creates them a narrow pass out of civilization.

A few stray leaves glide off the contour of the coach. Many are fallen brown kicked up from the wind in the road. Others yet retain their varied color from the trees, doing their best to cling to autumn's last breath.

The soothing sounds of the Pronoian River reach their ears as they arrive at the border of their city-state. Above stands one of the few pre-Reckoning style feats of architecture left in Prometheum.

The Portland Bridge, put out of use well before the Reckoning, serves as the gateway to the Lands Beyond. That it "serves," it rather represents, for the "port" between "lands" seldom anyone uses.

Its recognition originates from the attacks on Prometheum by a "tribe" now known as Pronoia. These dissenters from the

Promethean polity hierarchy unleashed wave after wave on the bridge in order to access the territory for claim.

The Sacred Rains cleansed this lust, and after mutual inspiration a peace treaty was effected on that very bridge between Alexander Maquari and Petr Drugov. The two civilizations even went so far as to adopt a common divinity.

Today, however, mostly young people frequent it for their recreational activities.

"You bring those Hoff's?" says Beren, stepping out of the M-Coach.

"Yeah here," says Leo. He passes over a frigo of lager.

"I'll get this one," says Zoe regarding the screen displaying the coach fare, which is barely anything. A blue laser scans the retina of her eye and projects her image in a bubble to the right.

"Citizen Zoe Qwynshing, confirm," a smooth female voice commands.

"Confirm."

The voice recognition accepts her confirmation and the coach moves off.

The grand structure looms just ahead. Its traditional look combined with its coarse weathered surface gives it both a majestic and eerie feel. Underneath the late afternoon sun, its breadth casts a long dark shade on the water below.

All the darker for Leo: the thick pillars of chalky stone just as well be high walls of bronze: the flowing river below a current of fire.

The alluring fire...

Two fingers snap in front of his face. "Earth to Leo," says Zoe.

Anastasia interjects before Zoe can provoke further.

"Hey," she says, placing herself close to his face. "Come on"

Leo's pupils readjust to the light.

"I..."

"I know," she whispers. She takes his hand and pulls him along.

Zoe watches them move off hand in hand. She puts on a face as though catching two squirrels in the process of mating.

For Beren, a cat and dog.

The four make their way onto the loose stone topping the bridge. They then align themselves with the rusted tracks of the old-style steam locomotives. Beren uses the beer to balance himself on top.

Once above the roar of the river they find a manhole that leads down to the interior chambers.

Beren leads, followed by Zoe.

Anastasia sets a foot on the ladder when she notices Leo standing a few yards off. He looks down into one of the historical plaques, rather focused on whatever he watches.

These plaques, published by the Heritage Department, typically appear in the form of short documentaries highlighting a relevant event from history. On this occasion, the bridge.

Anastasia walks up behind Leo and looks over his shoulder. Scenes of fierce combat unravel on the very place they stand. The captions and narrator spit out description as fast as the blades clashing on screen.

"It's Alex," says Leo, taken in by the actions of the featured soldier.

The camera follows a man wearing a dragon scaled helmet with a thin red visor. From the mouth pours artificial flame that seems to correspond with the breathing.

His movements are quick, extremely agile, and matched only by the skill of his opponent.

"How do you know it's him?"

"There's a bluish hue to the blade," Leo points. "Blue: that's Alex's color; that's Alex's aether blade."

Anastasia moves around Leo for a better look. "The one he gave you on the Isles of the Blessed?"

"Yeah. Only my color was darker."

"It was," says Anastasia, sounding hopeful.

Leo glances sidelong at her optimism, then leans closer to the screen. "Can you hear it?"

Anastasia follows suite, and from her brightened look has recognized the familiar choral patterns ringing off Alex's blade.

Her face grows quizzical. "You know what's odd," she says, "I can hear the other one's too."

Leo shifts his focus to Alex's opponent and indeed perceives emanating sound and color.

A part of him feels disappointed in no longer being able to call his grandfather's blade truly unique.

A closer look at the man piques his curiosity.

"Hey, does that guy's helmet look like it's lined with...shark te..."

"Ho! You want me to drink all these myself?" shouts Beren poking his neck up from the manhole.

"What?" says Leo looking around for the voice. "Oh yeah," he says, spotting Beren below, "we're coming. Just had to see something." Looking back he sees the man in the shark toothed helmet has passed out of view.

"Since when are you the heritage type?" says Beren ducking back under.

In one final look at the screen, an Alexander Maquari not very much older than the one in the Underworld removes his helmet to bask in the rain. Although Leo has seen old reel and photos of his grandfather before, the association he now has makes the historical significance all the more keen, and the personal even keener.

The two of them make their way down the manhole to find their friends have not waited. Leo gives Anastasia a hoist from the stoned floor of the base compartment to the gradually smaller ones that lead upward. His strength under her weight nearly sends her flying through.

After a few minutes crawling they reach the middle of the bridge where Beren and Zoe have already set up.

"Grab a Hoff," says Beren, sliding them the frigo.

The micro freezer almost collides with Leo's head as he emerges from the previous compartment, earning Beren a reproachful glare. After all that's happened recently though, his old friend has never had a better idea. So he taps the front sensor twice and eagerly accepts the two ice cold lagers that slide out. Once Anastasia has hers it signals they can all now open.

"Bout time," says Beren. He pops one open with his thumb. He starts to bring the bottle to his mouth when Zoe slaps his arm causing him to spill a few drops on his shirt. Beren responds by trying to pinch her ear but Zoe catches his finger and bends it back.

"Alright alright alright!" says Beren, submitting to his pride. "Anyway." He rubs his knuckle. "Here's to great friends," he hails, raising his bottle. "And a great lady." The final toast he adds at Leo. "We'll miss her, but we'll all see her again someday."

The tone merits a silent pause before clinking their drinks and tipping them back.

Leo sips a second longer than the others. He wonders if he could ever believe in himself enough to see his mother again, in his own life or death. Anastasia simply rests her head on his shoulder and strokes his arm.

Despite the moment, the gesture provokes a swell of discomfort in such close proximity. Zoe betrays a suppressed giggle while Beren takes a hearty swig. He then resorts to searching for the cap from his Hoff.

All Hoffman Lager Tops contain a notable moment in sports history. Many date back well before the time of the Reckoning. Some collect them for trivia, others to make into drinking games.

"Babe...Ruth," Beren begins reading. "Babe Ruth calls his shot at the 1932 World Series." He pauses to consider. "Never heard of him." Beren flicks the cap aside. "Gimme one of Feidor at the Pronoia Invitational slicing through that guy's guard."

The name startles Leo thinking about his hypothetical rematch with Feidor in Tartaros. Even more so, however, the shark toothed helmet from the historical plaque on the bridge.

Zoe slaps Beren in the gut. She likely assumes Leo's reaction due to his scar.

"Oh yeah, sorry," says Beren, taking another sip.

After another awkward silence Zoe sends a leering glare at Anastasia locked on Leo's powerful arm. She then sets down her drink a little harder than she has to. The clink of glass on concrete reverberates throughout the compartments.

"Ok you guys, I think we've waited long enough," she says, claiming everyone's attention. "So what is it exactly we need to know? And why are you guys like hooking up in front of everybody!?" She utters this last bit using her hands to draw an outline of them seated together.

Anastasia edges closer to Leo to hide her blush. Leo, in spite of overcoming the bout of uneasiness in exposing himself to his friends, doesn't seek to immediately explain himself. Maintaining a straight face, he looks at both his comrades and takes another sip of his Hoffman's.

"Listen," says Leo, setting down his drink, "a lot of what we tell you you're not gonna buy. But you need to know: and not just because of this," he says tilting his head at Anastasia, "but because it involves you too."

Beren shuffles forward and rests his weight back on one hand. "Ok, now you got me curious."

"Since it's all pretty much out of this world, I'll start with the physical evidence."

"Evidence?" says Zoe.

With that Leo draws the picture of Generation 6 from his mother's closet. He takes a look on it himself, then hands it to Zoe. He sits back to let it sink in.

"Is that..." says Beren.

"My Mom?" says Zoe.

"My Dad?"

"With your Mom," they say together with regards to Pandora.

"If only that were it," says Leo.

Beren snags the picture and flips it over. "When's this from?"

"2049," says Leo.

"2049?"

Zoe snags the photo back. She sets to re-examining it with this new knowledge. Her look reads as though seeing the people in it for the first time. Her look holds as she fingers the fraying at the photo's edges, also a possible first with regards to the old-style laminate photos.

"That's just the tip of the spearhead, man," says Leo. "You guys might as well open fresh ones."

Beren shakes his head and pulls the frigo between him and Zoe. Once with new drinks, they position themselves for story time.

"So it all started when I went to see Emrick."

"The crazy Mantis?" Beren interjects.

Slap.

"Oh, sorry," says Beren to Anastasia. He rubs his arm from the back of Zoe's hand.

"Anyway," Leo continues, "he tells me of this tree, a tree that crosses realms..."

Over the next hour Leo recounts his journey to the Underworld. He makes no attempt at an epic tale but is careful to present it whole in all its characters, creatures, and uncoverings. By the time he finishes his friends have adjusted position several times and left just as many empty bottles.

For a few moments no one speaks.

"Ok so let me see if I got this straight," says Beren. He positions his hands as if trying to solve a math problem in the air. "You hid your mother's body, jumped through an underwater tree, hung out with your dead relatives, fought an omega, fought *Feidor* - again - but not really; crossed a river of fire, played a guitar solo to get passed a three headed monster, and found your Mom as a hot 20 year old?"

Slap.

"Sorry. But once you were back, you ended up at the same time as when you left, so none of it actually happened?"

Hearing it summarized objectively makes it seem even more complicated than a math problem. As such, Leo hesitates. "It did. And it didn't," he says attempting to balance his own confusion.

"Right. Got it. Most of all though, you're telling me you were meant to find some magical Urn, and use it to complete the Apocalypse!?"

From math to physics. This statement of Beren's hits harder than the first. Leo seeks refuge in Anastasia's cool and confirming face, reminding him that not only does she fully believe, but that the mission was never only Leo's to begin with.

"Not just me. Us. You saw the picture."

The incredulity weighs on the foundation of material proof. Beren and Zoe exchange glances.

Anastasia then scoots toward them and assumes a like position. She requests to see the picture. Zoe slowly passes it over and she sets to look.

Much of what Leo has recounted Anastasia has either been part of or already heard about secondhand, but not all. The details he acquired from his visions she had not yet known about, nor had she seen the photo.

"Alright so what's it gonna take, killing a dragon?" says Beren. Both he and Zoe fight back smirks.

While Leo does not appreciate the sarcasm he would have spit out in even higher proportion, he understands his friends' reaction to his outlandish charge. This despite the photo which doesn't prove much anyway. Having lived it himself he barely believes it happened.

"The truth is we have no idea," says Leo. "I'm not even sure your parents would know. The only person who does is Emrick Wildyn, and we were told to see him."

"By who, Alexander Maquari?" says Zoe, unable to resist a gentle quip.

"Actually, yeah."

Seeing Leo is serious, they refrain from any further remarks. Beren, however, casts Zoe a knowing look. She nods in return.

"Leo, sweetie" she begins carefully, "we know you sometimes tend to...zone off a bit: maybe you just had a lucid dream, with everything that's happened?"

"It wasn't a dream," says Anastasia, cutting in sharply, "I was there too."

That they would attribute the tale to his peculiarity doesn't surprise Leo. In any case, he withheld specifics of any special "abilities" to avoid the story becoming overwhelming. As such, there was no mention of "seeing" his friends mourn and finding his mother's body.

They offer no response to Anastasia's interpolation.

"Listen," Anastasia says in a calmer tone, "I know it sounds crazy, but just come with us to see my grandfather, hear him out, then choose what you want to do."

Beren looks to Zoe. He shrugs his left shoulder. Zoe responds with one of her half smiles.

"Sure, Staj, we'll go," says Beren.

"But...," says Zoe, pointing a finger in the air, "there's still a leeeeeeeeeeeeetle part of the story you've, uh, conveniently forgotten to tell us."

Both Leo and Anastasia wait for the follow up: Leo with a blank stare, Anastasia with a coy blush.

"The love story, hello!? You guys are like, totally together."

That type of explanation escapes Leo's faculties to tell, so he just keeps staring and wonders how it happened himself. Anastasia allows her blush to flow free. Seeing Leo incapable of such a topic, she picks up his silence. "I guess," she says. She glances at Leo again. "I guess I finally opened up, mainly because I had to."

"What do you mean?" says Zoe, inching closer.

"This one wanted to fight Cerberus."

"What!?"

Leo exits the conversation to allow tell of her grand confession of love in the face of death: all the better told in pure, unadulterated, girl talk.

He grabs his acoustic guitar and slides to the edge. His feet hang over the river flowing far below. After strumming a few chords, Beren joins him, tugging the frigo behind.

"What's the matter buddy, too mushy for yah?" says Beren handing Leo another Hoffman's.

"Yeah, and I lived it," says Leo. He takes the bottle and pops the top.

A guy silence follows where they think certain thoughts too "guy" to say to the other. Particularly, knowing Beren's undisclosed romantic side, that the story was certainly not too mushy for him. Beren, dying to get the scoop from Leo, will save face and get it out of Zoe later.

"Anything good?" says Beren opting for the bro talk on beer.

Leo flips over his bottle cap.

"Vince Lombardi wins the first Super Bowl with the Green Bay Packers."

He flicks the cap with his thumb over to Beren who snags it out of the air.

"That name Lombardi rings a bell," says Beren. "I wonder where Green Bay was."

"I think a place in the central part of the continent," says Leo. He nods toward the opposite river bank. "Why don't you go find out," he adds.

Beren shakes his head and lets out a laugh. "Oh man, you remember that game?"

Tease the Fates is a common game for adolescents and teens in Prometheum; to cross the bridge into the Lands Beyond to see who is willing to go furthest and stay longest.

"I remember you getting lost and pissing yourself," says Leo.

"Whatever, asshole" says Beren looking away to sip his beer.

Leo quickly realizes the hypocrisy of his statement. How often did he cling to Alex for both guidance and protection through the long of the Underworld. Leo quickly adjusts his tone.

"Those things you heard and *thought* you saw were probably just the Hunting Tribes messing with you," he says.

When Beren doesn't reply, Leo catches him staring off a bit. He then recalls Beren's description of what happened: finding himself isolated under the impending new moon. The darkness seeming to reveal more activity than the light. Hard breaths and strange colors, then finally a familiar face.

"You looked pretty spooked when I found you," says Leo.

After Beren had been gone much longer than usual, the others ventured on to utilize the last bit of sun light. When that faded with no sign of Beren, Zoe suggested they go back to tell Statesman Braun. Anastasia complied; Leo knew a search team would take too long to prepare and execute, especially if Beren were hurt. So he told the girls he would stay. Once they left, however, he continued in deeper.

"How did you ever find me anyway?" says Beren.

Leo began by merely searching a wide area. As despair set in, however, his eyes became of less use. Beren occupied his thoughts more and more, until he became Leo's full presence of mind.

Then, much like tapping into Beren's consciousness on the river Styx, a connection of sorts was made: an image, flashing before his eyes, a lovely bed of ferns amidst a break in a canopy. Desperation led him to accept the vision far quicker than otherwise. He stepped off immediately, trusting his instinct for the direction.

Moving through the dark woods he kept close hold of the mental picture. He then sensed a colorful scene of twilight sky overlooking a valley. Knowing well Beren's partiality for this type of beauty, he concluded Beren must be near that location.

Passing through the bed of ferns he followed a clear path to an opening in the trees. Just past was the overlook. He paused, scanning with his feelings.

The presence of a third party alerted him. He turned quickly, but nothing was there. Looking back along the ground, though, he finds his friend unconscious a few yards down the decline.

"I don't know," says Leo in response to Beren's question. "Guess I got lucky."

"I was the one who got lucky, man," says Beren. "I don't know what would've happened if you hadn't stepped up."

If I hadn't stepped up.

Leo remembers not stepping up at Alex's simulation of Victoria Braun's funeral games. He remembers Beren falling from the Tiger's punch to the throat. That time, however, unlike the Lands Beyond, he did not get up.

A body tumbling into them interrupts the moment.

"Alright, bitchesssss, time for some pics!" says Zoe. Practically laying over Beren and Leo she pulls up the camera icon on her wrist pad. She sets the coordinates to inverse mode then projects the range in front where it will take the shot.

The lens appears a few feet out over the river. The girls take their places, and the picture snaps before much warning to the guys.

The image portrays a timeless and familiar grouping: Leo straight faced holding his guitar; Beren making an honest yet toothless smile; Anastasia with a squint; and Zoe puckering for the spotlight.

The rest of the evening unravels with much of the same. Leo dedicating himself to the soundtrack, Anastasia dividing her attention between the music and conversation, Beren making sure everyone has a fresh Hoffman's, including the occasional tuber passing by below; Zoe getting into everything, and capturing it all on file.

Eyelids eventually grow heavier as the frigo grows lighter. Leo strums softly with his pick, then starts plucking with his fingers. Soon after he sets the guitar aside altogether.

"Night cap, buddy?" says Beren, already handing him a bottle.

"Yeah I guess. I feel like I've been up for a week."

"You have been," whispers Anastasia.

"I could probably get going after this one," says Zoe taking a sip.

"No!" says Anastasia. "We can't miss the aether shower."

"Well, if it's even aether," says Beren.

"It is," says Anastasia, "and it's nice to listen to." She casts Leo a supplicating glance.

"Alright, I'll wait with you."

The rest get comfortable and don't say otherwise.

Leo feels too drained to offer an opinion on the Night's Chorus. Some say the Sacred Rains altered the atmosphere, charging greater levels of aether into the earth's sky. When this excess aether discharges, it is supposedly responsible for the faint choral harmony people tend to perceive.

Others believe the Rains opened a portal straight to the omegas, and that what you hear is the voice of Prometheus himself.

As for Leo, it was always much of the same. Now having felt the phenomena in his very hand, however, things were certainly not the same. Not only can he attest to the sound and color of his grandfather's weapon, that its power can actually manifest something as tangible as a blade makes him wonder about its true limitations with the right manipulation. Nonetheless, for the moment he can at least accept aether being as real as his experience in the Underworld, however much that may be.

The sky soon consumes what remains of the day's colors. As the darkness sets in, the waxing moon presses. The stars add the final touch for any would be spectators.

A silence falls that seems to stifle even the sound of the river. Then, a gentle hum.

Leo shakes his head and takes a swig of his drink. "Well, there it is," he says.

"There what is?" says Beren.

"You didn't hear it? The Night's Chorus."

Beren glances at Zoe, "I didn't hear a thing."

Zoe shrugs in agreement.

"I heard it," says Anastasia.

Beren and Zoe smile at her as though recognizing her consideration for Leo as a mourner and her boyfriend.

A second hum.

"There it is again," says Leo trying to prove a point.

Anastasia appears comforted while the others struggle with their senses.

More notes follow in a series of slow, legato, phrases. Louder to Leo's ears, yet still the others don't react.

Finally, when the sound has doubled from it first being heard, a trickle of neon colored plasma drips in the sky.

"Oh I heard that one," says Zoe.

Leo wonders whether somehow his experiences have sensitized him to the sounds. Too tired to pay it further mind, he closes his eyes and allows himself to be absorbed by the music.

Anastasia curls up and rests her head on his chest. She watches more droplets fall in an assortment of colors: nothing solid, everything in between. Then, she too gives in to the weariness of her journey.

CHAPTER 17 – CARAS MAKARION

Cool mist glistens on the paling greens of the river bank as the rosy fingers of Eos spreads her morning dew. Thick droplets cling for dear life until released in a shower by the dismount of a Red Heron. Gliding just over the water's ripple, the flow of white noise seems to carry it.

Anastasia wakes to its call.

She runs her tongue over dry lips as the crispness of the late Autumn air follows the great bird's path.

Zoe rustles, but quickly re-snuggles around Anastasia's waist; Beren does likewise with his arms around the frigo.

The movement rouses Leo, whose eyes open with the back of his head bumping the chamber wall. Taking in the scene before him, he fears he never really returned to Eulimnos and that Alex has just sent him to relive another moment in his life. Apprehension seizes him. He wonders what else he could have done to harm his mother.

Anastasia turns her head up. "You ok?"

She places a hand over his. The warmth relaxes him a bit. The gesture also confirms something she never would have done in a memory of the past.

"We'll go home soon," she says, "as soon as these sleepyheads get moving."

Home: somehow, after living there his entire life, it feels like something totally different. With no one there waiting, it feels like nothing more than a house.

"Wow," says Zoe rubbing her head, "we totally passed out here." Wiping the sleep from her eyes she takes a closer look, "some harder than others. Wake up, lunk," she says, slapping Beren's leg.

Beren watches the ball leave Babe Ruth's bat and fly higher and higher until...it meets Zoe's hungover face at the climax. He moans his disappointment and pushes her away.

With everybody up they gather their things. The weight of a half-sober morning alleviates any desire to chat, so they make their way back to the road in silence. A few yards away Beren walks ahead toward the M-Coach console.

"I got this one," he says, tapping commands.

Leo worries a coach might get him to the house too quickly. He looks down the path ahead which suddenly appears much longer without the prospect of a vehicle. He finds it's a prospect he much prefers.

"I think I'll walk it today," he says.

Anastasia looks up at him, then to the others. "You guys go ahead. We'll see you at my grandfather's, yeah?"

Beren stops punching and puts on an anxious face. "Can't we meet at the station?"

Slap.

"What, you afraid the old Mantis has a giant three-headed dog guarding his estate?" says Zoe who avoids Leo's glance. "What time?" she asks Anastasia.

"How about 15:00."

"Ooooooooooook then, I'll send you a ping with the times."

The four friends exchange hugs and shakes, then make to part.

"Don't say anything to your parents before we see Emrick," says Leo after them.

Beren and Zoe hesitate. Seeing the look on Leo's face, though, they apparently forgo their questions. Anastasia takes Leo's hand, waves once more at their friends, and they go.

Leo, for all his intentions, finds walking a bit less appealing accompanied by lingering Hoffman's. He notices Anastasia's step to be a bit slower too. So when she veers off and steers him toward the Rail station, he doesn't resist.

Once aboard, he finds he does not regret that decision at all. The drone of the passing tracks comforts and abates the mounting distress of his new situation. Anastasia checks on him now and then, but does nothing except to make sure he hasn't forgotten her hand.

They arrive at the Lake Maquari stop and descend the hazy morning. Leo looks towards the direction of his house, and pauses.

"I'm just going to get some clothes and I'll be there," says Anastasia.

"Ok," says Leo. He remains still, unsure how to treat their parting. Though his feelings haven't changed, the magic and passion of the Underworld have given way to the cool blandness of their own.

When Anastasia takes the initiative, however, he tastes Elysium once more. The sweetness in the air, the juice of its fruits, the warmth of its sun: all in just a peck.

He refrains from licking his lips until reaching the kitchen side door of his house. For a moment he stands in the doorway. The cocoon of Anastasia's kiss guards him from the sting of uneasiness he feared to return to. He even takes a moment to look right into the master bedroom. Not wanting to burst his bubble too quickly though, he heads for the basement.

He has full intention on changing and washing up when he lies on his couch. He has even fuller intention of only resting his eyes when he lays back his head.

A few hours later he wakes to light feet on the staircase.

"Time to get up sleepyhead," says Anastasia. She descends wearing a transparent cotton top over a tight purple blouse.

Leo rests his head back down.

"Come on, we have to meet Beren and Zoe at the tram station."

"How long have you been here?"

"A while."

"And your Mom?"

Anastasia breaks eye contact. "She was still...asleep."

Her manner indicates much of the usual at the Wildyn residence. As such, it reminds Leo he wasn't the only one to leave someone to the Underworld. His own condition dims in light of this, then brightens in its company.

"Alright," he says. He hoists his legs onto the floor and kicks off. Walking past, he squeezes her inner arm. "Just give me like ten minutes."

In the bathroom Leo reaches for the gel he decides he doesn't feel like using. Instead, he takes in his reflection much the same as he did leaning over the water at Silas' grove.

He almost finds it odd to see his scars again. Even reliving those moments as fictional had him nearly believing they would be erased along with the person he was before he met Alex: whoever that was, and whoever it became.

The glare in the mirror reminds him of the shimmer on Silas' pond. The more he stares the more it ripples. It almost feels like falling in.

The wound Menoitios delivered his chin throbs as it did when he knelt by the water. Once again Leo presses on it. Though his finger rests on clear, uncorrupt skin, the ache increases at his touch.

Impossible.

He digs harder and harder to deny the growing pain which makes it only cry in protest. When his eyes can no longer hold any more water, he stops.

A drop falls onto the marble counter and rolls down the sink. He leans his head over and blinks out the other. He then lifts his pant leg and checks the spot he sliced himself with the aether blade. Again clear skin, again real pain, though nothing like the impact of blunt force from an omega's war hammer. The same goes for the long scratch down his back from the White Lion on the Isles of the Blessed.

He looks back at himself in the mirror. He wonders how much of the body and how much of the mind was vested in the Underworld. Both in one place or the other makes it easier to accept. Now back in Eulimnos, he feels as though half remained and half returned, or somehow got caught in between. The impossible and the real, all blending together.

With that he figures he best shower before he finds Vince Yeerum floating in his bedroom.

ΔΔΔ

Leo and Anastasia catch the next tram after a quick lunch of leftover *bourguignon* stew over rice. The short trip passes much nicer after food and rest. Beren and Zoe flag them down on the Skyview station platform looking equally refreshed.

They depart together, continuing down the road away from the tram. After several minutes they turn onto the path leading up the incline to the estate. Once past Hellebore Creek, the house comes into view.

"A little overdue for a trim," says Beren commenting on the severely overgrown brush layering the manor.

"Woooooh let's see how much landscaping you're doing when you're a hundred years old," says Zoe.

Leo runs his hand along the drying brush lining the path. Looking up at the manor he recalls thinking much the same as Beren when he saw it for the first time again last trip. Now from another mental angle, however, he sees the vines and greens complimenting nicely the vanilla white of the hard exterior: almost as if it were designed to form that way to make a camouflage of sorts.

Leo enters the covered walkway first. In contrast to the rest of the property, he notices a significant change in its upkeep. He looks back to Beren. "You might be surprised," he says with regards to the landscaping comment.

The walls before heavily vined now clearly display the guarded history it's kept for so many years: Hector and Achilles, Orpheus and Cerberus, Zeus and Prometheus. Leo stops at the mural of Alex overlooking what would become Eulimnos.

The view, however, appears slightly different; not that the image has changed so much as his perception strengthened. The position from which Alex views the lake looks very familiar. In fact, it looks very much like...

"Oh my gosh," says Zoe from behind.

"What?" says Leo.

"You gotta be kidding me," says Beren, fingering a place on the wall for closer inspection.

Leo takes another look at Alex's location then walks over behind them.

He reacts nearly the same to what they see.

In a cavernous setting shrouded in darkness, a young man faces a three-headed monster. In his hand he holds a guitar and points to the sky with the same intensity as the beast growls. Although his back is turned, no one has to guess who it is.

"Leo," says Anastasia brightening. "It's you!"

"But how the hell," says Leo. He approaches cautiously. He too runs his finger down the wall, yet more so to ascertain what could have produced an image only two living should know about in such vivid detail.

"Curious, isn't it?" says a raspy voice from down the corridor.

"Grandpa," says Anastasia.

"Were you beginning to doubt it really happened?" says Emrick.

A closer look at the mural shows four smaller figures witnessing the events. To Leo's rear a blonde female stands carefully yet firm behind part of a boulder. To the right, three stoic faces watch attentively: Alex, Silas, and Alexi.

"I guess, but...did you put this up after Staj told you about it?"

The old man's face wrinkles in amusement.

"I'm a mantis, not a painter; and that is no painting."

"Then what is it?"

Slow steps move down the corridor. "Oh, just an old concoction a witch friend conjured up."

"A witch?" says Zoe.

Beren turns for another look at the mural. He focuses particularly on the white glow coming from the base of Leo's neck.

"So everything he said," says Beren, "is true."

Emrick lends an ear.

"The Underworld, the Urn, Generation 6?"

Emrick's eyes begin to squint like his granddaughter's.

"Let's go inside."

Beren hesitates before reacting to Emrick's invitation. When he does move, he glances at the back of Leo's head. Leo then recalls he left some of the more peculiar details of their journey out of his recounting on the bridge. As such, he imagines his friend to be feeling quite peculiar himself at the moment.

The four friends follow the elderly pace through the wooden doors and into the lobby. Leo notices the room brighter than his previous visit, but sees no interior lights.

"The solar shingles shine some light in if you let them. So it makes a lighted shade," says Anastasia, taking Leo's arm.

"For years this estate has been used for spiritual study," says Emrick. "As an extension of the Academy." He stops in front of the grand staircase. "But it wasn't always for that."

The taps from Emrick's cane ring through the hollow space as he walks around then under the staircase. In a short, dark, closet-like space he taps an unmarked spot on the wall prompting a retinal scan. They all note a difference in texture on the surface compared to the glossy finish of the walls in the lobby. Upon confirming his identity a door size slot unhinges and opens for them to pass. Anastasia follows first, then the others.

Inside Emrick taps a line of candles that sheds soft light on another series of mural images. These scenes, however, seem to run as one. On them they depict a large, muscular creature in the likes of Menoitios. It pours liquid from an ornate jar onto the clouds. What falls below, however, is not water.

"Is this supposed to be the Sacred Rains?" says Zoe.

"But where's the rain?" says Beren. "There's just a bunch of Classic letters falling on our heads. But then..."

Leo follows the pattern lining the wall and stops toward the center. He notes how the letters drench the people as though it were really rain. Noting one in particular, he glances curiously at Anastasia.

"That symbol there," he says, nodding upwards. "The 'Mu.' I've seen it on you, Staj; like, *from* you."

Anastasia regards the mural and gently rubs the back of her neck.

"What do you mean *from* her?" says Zoe.

"The tree. It's how we got into the Underworld."

"What's that have to do with the letter?"

"It started shining on the back of her neck when she touched it."

"Ooooo—k."

Though Leo has twice witnessed this magic, seeing its origins is another magic unto itself. He then considers the mural Beren pointed out. All of a sudden he feels strange thinking how long he's carried a mystical letter embedded in his own neck.

He too touches the spot. Although his fingertips find only skin, underneath seems to tickle further into the depths of his mind.

That any "letter" got there at all surprises him. Being born several decades after the Sacred Rains would make it impossible to happen as the image depicted. Running things through to their logical conclusion then, he could only have inherited it at birth. This unsettles him even more. It again reminds him of all his mother *chose* to endure for his sake: the pain, the loss, all for an ungrateful child.

Until this point Emrick has remained aloof of the conversation, allowing the young people to reason through the phenomena themselves. He takes time observing each one: their behavior and reactions to the new world they've entered.

"Let's move on," he says. "Perhaps a little more convincing will do before I show you what you need to see."

They continue to the end of the hall where a wooden barrier confronts them. It stands more or less the entire height and breadth of the corridor. All look for an outline of a hidden door but find nothing but bark and stub.

"Is there a retinal scan," says Zoe.

"This door doesn't open by conventional keys," says Emrick.

"Can you open it, Grandpa?"

Emrick considers a moment then steps to the side.

"Yes. But today you will."

When Anastasia doesn't yelp the "what!?" they were expecting, Beren and Zoe nearly do it for her.

"Well, Leo's already been painted by a witch, so why not, let's see what she's got," says Beren making way.

"We're going back already?" says Leo toward Emrick.

"In a manner of speaking."

"But there's nothing to do there except visit, and I doubt Menoitios is in the mood for that," says Leo. He rubs his chin where the fearsome omega struck him.

"For all you traveled, you only saw a fraction of 'there.' Keep in mind as well you only ended up where you did because that was where Staj intended."

Leo fathoms the notion there might be other parts to the Underworld, or what they call the Underworld, that he or anyone hasn't seen. He wonders how much his own pre-conception influenced the dark, mystical world that shaped before his eyes when they arrived on the banks of the Lethe. Was Elysium beautiful, Asphodel plain, and Tartaros gloomy because they were in their own existence? Or the existence he brought with...

Even in the so-called "real world," do all eyes see the same?

As Anastasia approaches to perform her task, Leo questions what could ever have made him see her as anything but beautiful.

Her gentle hand touches the wood and he notices her nails painted red. He cannot recall whether the color is a new or old one.

The skin on her arm flows soft and smooth. Its color appears so pristine it might have been painted by a brush.

And her eyes...:in the dimly lit passageway they seem to glow an even more radiant blue as she concentrates; much like the color of her father's grove. Underneath the brightness of her bleached blonde hair, she is as her own sea and sun to whatever absence of life.

Her classical character again sparks on the back of her neck. He imagines it's a spectacle that would never get old. Curious of his friends' reaction though, Leo reverts his attention to Beren and Zoe as the process begins.

Both pairs of eyes remain locked on the "Mu" shining ever greater from their shy, petite friend. When the shift in gravity hits, those same eyes widen along with their tensing bodies. Zoe wrenches her grip on Beren's wrist to the point of choked veins but he doesn't seem to register any discomfort.

Quickly, however, they fall to the allure of the light like flies to a flame. It calms them, draws them in. Little by little their eyes droop. Then, they are gone.

ΔΔΔ

The five appear in a room made from rock under cover of modern amenities. Emrick sits in a reading chair and pulls an old-fashioned paper cigarette from a small red and white cardboard box. He then strikes a match, takes a puff, and ashes in a small black tray.

The others regard him strangely; non-vaporized smoking is uncommon in Prometheum, much less by an elderly.

"Tobacco," says Emrick, pulling on the brown and white stick. "Old habit, pre-Reckoning thing. Used to think it made me look like the Marlboro Man."

"Who?" says no one in particular.

"Oh...right..., never mind. Care to try?"

Everyone politely declines. They then go peeking around the room they aren't quite sure isn't a dream brought on by a white light coming from their friend's head.

Beren moves left past Emrick's chair and stops before two flags on the wall. The one is black and white and contains the acronyms "POW" and "MIA." The image underneath shows a large head of a man with a watchtower in the background. The last bit reads "YOU ARE NOT FORGOTTEN." Beren stares at the image for some time before moving on the next.

The other begins with a series of stars boxed off in a blue rectangle on the top left. From this extends long lines of red and white stripes. Beren runs his hand along one, then looks back to the POW flag.

Zoe occupies herself with a shelf of vinyl disks. Each rests inside a decomposing sleeve measuring about a foot in diameter. She draws one of a dark pyramid traversed by colors of the rainbow to one side, and a pale ray to the other. She finds the sleeve itself to be empty. The disk she sees placed on a square, rigid machine with a rotating arm resting to the side. At its tip a needle hangs down. Zoe leans her face in close and slowly moves her fingertip toward it. At the point of contact a loud blast sounds from a speaker nearby. Zoe jumps and immediately looks to Emrick. The old man just smiles and puffs in return.

Leo goes past the smoking mantis and overhears Anastasia posing rhetorical questions as to the debatable health benefits of tobacco for the elderly. He moves through a small kitchen with basic items such as knives and old heating devices. What really interests him, however, are the walls: or rather, the encasing structure to whatever encasement they would classify as their current shelter.

"This rock," he says looking over the walls and ceiling, "it's just like those passageways by the River Lethe."

Emrick observes Leo's remark and takes another puff.

Leo presses against the wall with his fingertips. Though he never felt around the passageways, it feels familiar nonetheless. He allows the cool dampness to move up his bones. Further it travels until it demands his full attention. His focus turns inward.

A sensation flits around his head like the erratic pattern of a bat. His own energies touch upon another and ricochet back. The sensation forces him outside his normal flux of mental process.

He shakes his head hard. "We're definitely not in our realm anymore," he says, catching the bat with a chopstick.

While somewhat engaged, and mainly for good measure, he reaches out for his mother. On one hand it surprises him to not make an immediate connection; on the other hand it's exactly what he expected. In the end, what was once a burning flame he now only senses as a residue of embers.

"So that little light show thingy she just did," says Zoe, "took us to what?, the Underworld?!"

Leo lowers both his hand and head from the wall. He exhales. "A part of it I guess." He glances at Emrick, then Anastasia. "She's a key."

"Alright then," says Zoe shaking her head up and down. "Why not."

Beren crosses his sinewy arms. "Well if she's a key, what the heck are you?"

The question sends Leo for a loop. Though he acknowledges his gift more and more, the notion he could "be" anything never occurred to him. He quickly looks away.

"What do you mean?" he says.

"The same thing was happening to you in the mural, but the light made a "gamma"."

Leo recalls the feeling of elation at the climax of his solo. The moment of taming the great beast: the moment he learned of his mother having sacrificed Silas for his sake.

He figures to deny something that's always lain just under the surface of their friendship would be pointless in circumstances such as these. His friends' strange regards when he would drift off did not escape his notice growing up. In any case, in that his "gamma" led him to his mother and the truth, he can no longer consider it worth hiding.

"I have these...visions sometimes," he says nonetheless with effort. "Whatever that makes me."

None of his friends comment, but Anastasia tries catching his eye with her smile.

"I might have something that helps," says Emrick. He sets down his smoke for his cane. He then walks them into a side chamber a bit past the kitchen. Inside they find tall rows of print literary volumes apparently arranged in alphabetical order.

"Yooooo, paper books," says Zoe, fascinated by the classic binding. "These have got to be ancient."

Emrick places his hand on an old style numeric safe set amongst the shelves. A knob in the center receives the coordinates in a series of alternating turns. He then removes a volume riddled with stains, uneven pages, and line breaks.

"I've been waiting a long time to give this to you," says Emrick. He approaches Leo holding the book carefully. "But I always had faith you'd come around."

Leo accepts the gift just as carefully as it's offered. He slowly runs his hand over the hardcover which feels like a soft leather of sorts. A large "M" adorns it, complimented by an array of classical letter inscriptions.

"What is this?" says Leo. He flips to a random page.

"The memoirs of Alexander Maquari."

Certainly not what Leo had in mind when his grandfather instructed him to see Emrick. Oddly enough though, it comforts him to hold something of his grandfather's in his hands again, something of Alex's, something of Alex. And yet, he doesn't see how memoirs of a relative's past will help him figure out his own present and future.

"But..." he starts to say.

"Read it, then come back with your questions. I have files of it for the rest of you."

"We have to read it too?" says Zoe.

Emrick nods.

They curiously crowd around Leo for a glimpse at the book that will explain why they are living in a fantasy novel.

"Now before you go, I have some things for you," says Emrick. He exits to another room.

The four look up from the book and after Emrick. They then look to each other before moving off. The statement reminds Leo of the things Alex had for him on the Isles of the Blessed.

They walk back into the living/kitchen area and down the hall to the left. They pass a display of old style picture frames, but in the dim light Leo does not catch the faces therein. Emrick then stops before a sturdy door and places his hand on a screen in the center. A red light flashes. Once it registers his identity, the door creaks open.

Inside an assortment of weapons adorns the room to all sides. So many, in fact, it appears to be an armory of sorts. As

Leo takes a closer look, however, he quickly realizes it's not just any armory.

Beren and Zoe run to the transparent cabinets like children in a candy shop.

"Look at these blades," says Beren. He eyes a pair of matching ones hung crossways. "You know, they kinda look like..."

"Your father's?" says Emrick. "They are."

He looks closer. "What?" Indeed, the hilt carries his father's signature double "B," one looped through the other.

"Anything familiar for you Zoe?" says Emrick.

"Actually, y..."

As her hand touches the cabinet door a puff of air interrupts her sentence. At the same moment the door becomes unhinged. Zoe steps away as though having accidentally broken into a bank vault.

"Relax, Zoe," says Emrick. He too touches the cabinet, opening the airtight sealants in other parts. "Have a look."

She hesitates a moment at his consent. Then with a smile and eager eyes she dives in and sets to handling a series of gold laced maolances.

Beren does likewise with his father's. He makes a few short strokes in the air, testing the weight and ergonomics: the Twin Blades of Braun. He then stops with a curious look at another pair.

"Check this out," he says. He takes up two empty hilts laying on a velvet strip at the bottom of the unit. "These blades aren't finished."

Zoe runs her fingers over the bladeless ends.

"Those aren't normal blades," says Leo reaching for what he believes to be Alex's section. He grabs what he once thought to be a long slab of white stone. Clearing his mind the blade manifests in a dark shade of purple. It harmonizes the divine song of the night which Leo hears clearer than ever.

"They're aether blades," says Leo, letting it dissipate.

"Aether? This just gets weirder and weirder," says Zoe.

As they bombard Leo with questions, Anastasia wanders over to a different set of weapons; a serrated xiphos blade, along with its aether form, next to a collection of archery equipment.

"You know your family's taste," says Emrick walking up behind. Anastasia smiles remembering her father's movements while training Leo in Elysium.

"That blade was mine," he says. He points to the serrated one with a sand colored hilt. "Then my son's; now, it's yours."

Anastasia's smile turns into an open mouth of surprise. Emrick takes over her former gesture and reaches up a slow arm toward the blade. With surprising strength he takes it in hand. He examines the pristine steel and hilt embroidered with the "W" of their namesake. He then presents it to his granddaughter.

Anastasia accepts mainly to relieve Emrick of the weight. She then fumbles needing him to relieve her of nearly slicing herself in half.

"But I'm not a bladeswoman," says Anastasia, recouping.

"It can't hurt to know a bit if you're in tight corners." The old mantis offers the hilt in a more formal gesture. "And I'm sure I know somebody who would be more than willing to teach you," he adds with a wink, creasing a thick white eyebrow.

Anastasia finds odd the notion of wielding a deadly tool on someone she loves.

She takes a moment and watches her friends scrutinize her love over his uncanny ability. The muscles on Leo's forearm ripple as he manipulates the unignited hilt. While some would find that attractive, she prefers the grisliness of his scars: his weakness over his power; the side he caches to the side he flaunts: the side only she can truly claim to know and call her own. Such a treasure, invaluable, even at the chance of learning blade from the Maurileho himself.

Anastasia grins, "I'm sure Beren could show me a few moves." Just said wrangles the hilt of the aether blade like a flashlight low on solar power. His efforts in trying to get it to react only frustrating him more.

Emrick raises the other eyebrow at the spectacle, "suit yourself."

He replaces the blade and moves to the next cabinet. "In the meantime, perhaps *this* would give you more to sink your teeth into."

Emrick lifts down a stringless bow in a silky platinum finish. The limbs, instead of holding a straight diagonal, curve slightly at the lip. On the inner part of the top one reads "P.M, 55'".

Anastasia's mouth again drops. "This was Mom, I mean, Pandora's; I can't accept it."

"Annie," says Emrick, stepping closer. "I know she'd want you to have it; and so would he."

Anastasia glances at Leo still struggling with Beren and Zoe. Yet she also realizes Emrick could be talking about her father. Either way, those are wishes she'd be happy to honor.

"Besides," Emrick continues, "I'll bet you never seen an aether bow before have you?"

Anastasia cracks a smile despite herself, then takes the bow with confidence. She holds it out to allow her hand to adjust to the grip, and her arm to react to the weight. She checks the sights by fixing on a random point to her right.

The bow utilizes the slightly obsolete yet not unheard of Zero Tech Tapping sight. Once aimed on a target, one simply locks in the calibration by tapping a button on the grip. Anastasia does so around a vase depicting Odysseus with his own bow. The clever king, just returned from Troy, enacts his revenge on the brazen suitors of Penelope. A crosshair appears across his chest.

Emrick catches her eager eye. "Go ahead."

Barely the words escape his mouth when a flash shoots from the top of the bow to the bottom. The string pulsates in shades of passion red to tender rose. A faint harmony of tranquil breeze fills the air.

Zoe, at this point the one trying to work the aether blade, tosses it back to Leo and darts over to Anastasia. The two guys look at each other, then Beren catches sight of the bow and follows. Leo strolls behind.

Beren and Zoe wait the whole of a second before they start in on Anastasia. Before any of their rambling can be comprehended, however, Emrick holds up his hand to speak.

"There will be time for answers later."

Beren and Zoe make to protest, but the vibrant blue from the ancient man's eye tames them into a calm submission.

"I'm sure you're all wondering what the point of all this is," he says, still looking at Beren and Zoe. "What Leonidas told you about Generation 6, so much as he knows, is true."

Emrick pauses and adjusts his position to address them collectively. He then decides a tall stool would be of better order.

"This place we've come," he says. He waves his cane side to side, "Was known as the Hub: headquarters, of sorts."

The old man again adjusts to place the bulk of his weight on his right side and off his crippled left. He winces slightly in settling.

"Your parents believed in the Search," he goes on. "They are of the Awakened, and so are you." He makes sure the "you" applies to all four.

Beren and Zoe put on the blankest of stares.

"Take them the aether arms, and they will know it's time for a talk."

No one can muster a "but," and even if they could, Emrick's tone was of no mind to explain any further today.

"Now if you'll excuse me," says Emrick, tediously positioning himself to stand, "I think I'll have to cut our little rendezvous short for today."

Anastasia scurries over in reaction to her grandfather's struggle. She takes Emrick under his left arm to support placing his feet on the ground. Leo steps in afterward but Emrick waives him off.

"I'm alright now," he says. He stays close to his granddaughter who does not let go.

As they move off, Leo sees Anastasia walking arm in arm again with her father, and Emrick with his son: a surrogate tie for both to latch on to. As one they each seem to carry the part of Silas the other lost. As one Silas walks among them.

The others grab their weapons and file back to the entrance. From the inside, an infused pattern of roots makes up the lining on the wall as opposed to the bark from above. This time, Emrick himself steps forth.

Both Leo's limbs are immediately seized: one the gentle hand of Anastasia: the other the zealous grip of Zoe. The process then unfolds much the same. Before the light becomes too blinding, however, the character on Emrick's neck strikes Leo as something slightly different from what he saw on Anastasia's.

Back in the muraled corridor they again pass by the dramatic scenes of near and distant history. Beren and Zoe pay it little mind, now with their new colorful magic blades. Leo, however, pauses on his own image in front of Cerberus. He regards the gamma Beren found so fascinating. His eyes scan its shape shining from his neck, 'γ'. He wonders what characters his friends will have, seeing as how Emrick counts them as one of the Awakened as well.

He then looks on the guitar that saved them from being eaten in three parts. Such a fine playing gift from Alex, he couldn't understand why it was gifted at all at first. Nonetheless, for such a sound it produced on the banks of the Styx, it might as well been dipped in aether too. He hopes to track it down if he could ever learn where Alex left behind his personal belongings.

Ahead Beren pushes open the thick, wooden door leading to the lobby. Zoe follows with Anastasia leading Emrick. Leo takes one last look as they wait in the doorway then brings up the rear.

As he takes hold of the door to close, a small engraving catches his eye to the left of the palm reader: "A. W. M., 2030."

"A-W-M," Leo whispers.

Alexander William Maquari.

"Hey," Leo flicks his chin diagonally. "Why are my grandfather's initials on the door?"

Emrick raises both eyebrows. "He put them there," he replies matter-of-factly. "Before he built the house."

That Alex would have built a small mansion over a portal to where people smoke tobacco and talk about the apocalypse doesn't surprise Leo at all: much less that he might have dropped an "oh yeah, I forgot to mention..."

"So this was...*his* house?" says Leo.

As he recalls, Alex, or Grandpa as he was known then, certainly spent a lot of time at the estate. As far as he knew, however, he maintained living space elsewhere.

Regardless, if the place were indeed his grandfather's, then it would have necessarily passed to his mother. His mother is gone.

"But that would mean..."

"That's right," says Emrick. He holds out his hands in a serving motion. "It's yours."

Leo moves his eyes over the immense, and strange, property just lopped at his feet.

"Freakin' Alex."

Emrick bellows a laugh. "Just give me a month's notice if you decide to evict me. Otherwise, I'm a good roommate."

"What?"

"Never mind."

CHAPTER 18 – MORNING JAM

The train drops them early evening at Lake Maquari. During the ride many looks came their way over their fascination with fancy blade grips. Many looks, until passengers saw they sat with the Maurileho. Amongst the friends the trip passed in silence.

"I don't know about you guys," says Zoe twirling in a lazy circle as she walks, "but I've had enough freak for one day." She quickly pecks everyone on the cheek. "I'll see yah later."

With that she pivots left onto a path bordering the southwestern part of the lake.

"I'm gonna get going too," says Beren. He hugs Anastasia and does the same, one armed, with Leo. He then heads for the pedestrian bridge straight ahead.

Anastasia turns to Leo, taking a second before she speaks. "I guess I better check on my Mom again." She tends towards the direction of her house.

"Uh, yeah sure, I'll see yah." As though observing a form of etiquette more than following a lead of passion, Leo leans down to peck her on the lips. Anastasia waits until he's about to pull away then pulls him in again by the sides of his head. Their eyes open wide at the same time. Leo's are left the same as she giggles off.

Dusk lights his way through the Festival Grounds on a course he could run in the dark. The colored sky begins to assume a shady hue in preparation for Night's Chariot dragging its blanket of stars. The reflection gleams off Lake Maquari.

Leo arrives at the front door and reluctantly offers his thumb. The house opens, but doesn't welcome. Despite all the comforts inside that would aid after a long day, he decides staying out seems cozier.

Pulling the door shut he walks into the yard. He plops down on his mother's bench by the apple tree and rests his thick arms over the back. He attempts to distract his attention onto the beauty of the lake. With no disturbance, the water appears like a mirror uprooted from the ground. It reminds him of all the memories captured in the Lethe.

He finds his way to the eagle's boulder where the Torment of Prometheus rests its wings. He feels drawn: perhaps to its durability in isolation, or its peace in solitude.

His mind carries him below to the bough of the tree where he re-enters the Underworld in what seems an entirely different part of his life. As the pictures of his experience flash in real time, however, he realizes he's merely flipped a page: a page that ends up right where it started; on his mother's bench.

He shakes his head away.

He tries looking forward, to the next day, the next hour, but that page remains blank. Which page he likes less he doesn't know. For now, the current one will have to do.

An alternate distraction presents itself in the form of a capital "M" staring up at his side. The memoirs Emrick assigned him to read. He runs a finger over the letter as a child would feel for curiosity.

He almost envies Anastasia not having to learn about her grandfather from a book: not secondhand. Nonetheless, it wasn't like he benefited from the great Alexander Maquari when the General was alive anyway.

Oddly enough, he misses his grandfather from death more than when he knew him as "grandpa." He misses Alex.

Leo's hand resting on the cover suddenly makes Alex seem not so far away. So lifting the heavy volume, he splits the pages at a random spot.

Lines and lines of penned text spread across the sheets. It flows in an array too monotone to draw any interest. A few more pass, and still the same.

He then comes across a heavily scribbled section entitled "Seeds of the Reckoning." This does not, however, appear to be the original title. Discerning the effaced letters one by one it reads: "College Life." Though he knows college was a form of the Academy, he never heard an expression to imply a particular lifestyle associated with it.

He continues on through a series of unfamiliar events when he comes to a heading that recalls something from Emrick's: "9/11."

The date etched on the mural of the two towers. The Ruins of New York, before they were ruins: Alex and Emrick's birthplace.

Though history never much interested Leo, the intrigue of reading a first-hand account of something only taught in Peedabooks sways him to go on.

The entry follows:

"9/11/2001,

I'm on my way to my Gen Ed American Gov class when I hear one of my brother's talking about the Twin Towers being destroyed.

"What's going on?" I say.

"A fuckin plane just hit the World Trade Center."

I was like, "Yeah, ok man."

He looks at me and he's not playing around.

"Yo, why would I lie about that?" he says. "Look at the news."

I found a bunch of people already gathered around the small TV at the Student Center. What I saw looked like a scene from Black Hawk Down. My buddy wasn't lying. A replay shows this plane crashing into the top of the building. It looked like a toy on TV. Then there was all this smoke. A few minutes later, it collapsed like an avalanche. That's all I had time for.

During class I tried to think if I knew anyone who worked there. I didn't really. Then I heard the second tower had been hit and gone down too.

At that point I started feeling uneasy in my gut. It started happening again, and I didn't need the TV anymore to see what was going on. Screams, chaos, fear; the firefighters.

The firefighters.

Then, nothing.

I thought of my mother. I thought of being at school in PA. I thought of feeling helpless.

My father was dead.

AWM."

Leo stops reading at that final bit. He'd never heard much of his great grandfather. Alex himself being so old during his lifetime, he never imagined his grandfather having parents of his own.

Furthermore, to read about an event in the first person that now only exists in history feels quite strange: especially knowing the person at the age he wrote it eighty years after it happened. Leo decides to browse for something less heavy.

A page of hand drawn pictures seems relieving. At first nothing but a tapestry of shapes forms to his perception. Once he weeds through the strokes of the painter's hand, however, it could have been a picture from his own mind.

It's the Underworld; a map he can follow from his entrance near the Lethe over to the Isles of the Blessed: across the fields of Elysium to the Plains of Asphodel: then, from the Pit of Tartaros to the far side of the Styx. It brings him joy to see the place he found his mother. That is, until he sees the place he left her.

The Elm of False Dreams.

"False dreams?"

Doubt again bombards the wall of confidence Leo had so tediously begun to build. A footnote to the page explains that dreams passing through that particular tree are random and non-prophetic.

Random and non-prophetic.

Leo slams the volume shut with a loud clap.

For all he struggled in the Underworld not to dismiss his experience as a dream or extended vision: and now only to learn it would have been "false" anyway.

He tries to anchor himself on Alex's advice not to dwell beyond the subjectivity of reality.

"Reality is what you believe to be true," ring his grandfather's words from Elysium.

The simplicity of the statement almost insults him. In following its logic, if he believes it happened, then it's real. The only problem is the "believe" and "real" part.

At most he can gamble on a handful of modals. He thinks it may have happened, so he might think it could have.

While that lazy half-truth brings him a grain of intellectual respite, to lack the full leads to greater torment over the risk of dishonoring his mother. To not believe what he saw would be to discredit all that motivated her in life. To just not believe would undermine all she left in death.

Damn.

He rests his head back and attempts to bore out the logical mishmash by rubbing his temples with his palms. The technique proves surprisingly soothing, so he relaxes and closes his eyes.

He wonders how long he can stay on the bench; how long having nowhere to go would allow it. Tending to his mother at the end of her life was at least something to tend to, though he regrets to acknowledge how much he begrudged it at times. After that remains Generation 6 which he'd like to begrudge. Beyond, he finds no purpose: only the bench.

Just then a pair of hands pushes back his curls and begins rubbing the sides of his head where he left off. The contact assuages so deeply he wouldn't care if it were Feidor giving the massage. More and more, the bench seems the right choice.

"Better?" says Anastasia after a minute.

Leo finally opens his eyes. "I'm good."

She walks around and sits to his left: not too close, just enough to mark her presence.

Though Leo's eyes remain open, the absence of his stare would indicate anything but attentiveness. Anastasia observes him carefully. Then, she leans over and takes the memoir off his lap.

"You started reading?" she says opening the front cover.

Leo flops his head to her side. "A bit yeah."

She continues flipping through but doesn't stop to look at any page. Reaching the end in a few more turns, she shuts and rests it on her own lap. "Find anything interesting?"

Leo to this point has kept the same position since she arrived: leaning back like trying to sink into a recliner, but actually chained to a rock.

"You could say that."

Anastasia waits.

Several seconds pass and he still avoids direct eye contact. At this point the last bit of color has faded from the sky. Ancient Nyx with his aureole of dark mists has spread his veil across the heavens. The stars have then proceeded to assume their rightful places.

Leo continues staring forward as though there were something to see over the dark lake. Finally, he brings his arms up and wraps them around his chest.

"How is it you never doubt, Staj?" he asks, still looking ahead.

The question doesn't elicit an immediate response, even from a firm believer like her. She breaks from watching Leo and assumes his focal point over the water. She too stops over the area of the boulder. For a while she considers the place they would escape to as children, swimming side by side until eventually Leo would swim past. This the place that would also become their escape to the Underworld. Like Leo, she eventually finds her way back to the bench, and onto him. She then scoots over and opens her body in his direction.

"I follow my heart," she says close to his face.

Leo lowers his eyes onto his folded arms.

"I don't need to have everything justified. I don't need to be able to see, touch, or even understand something to know it's real."

The sense of liberty in her clear verbalization of something so elusive creates envy he cannot avoid. He opens his mind, and tries to let it in, but everything gets jammed in the doorway.

He sighs in defeat.

"I just can't believe that way," he says. "I jus..."

The word falls on lips hard pressed against his. The intensity shocks him, but quickly takes him out of mind to a place he knows nothing. A place where his pores brim with a power too immense to explain, and too sweet to bother.

Anastasia pulls away, but stays close enough to feel her breath on his chin.

"When you can explain that, you let me know."

The blue of her eyes swirls him into a trance of barely hearing what she says. If he didn't know any better he would think them jewels glowing in another realm. Indeed, when she lays her head into his shoulder, Eulimnos could be a realm all to themselves.

The aether shower begins a short time later. Leo however, finds himself to be the only spectator. He cracks a smile.

Anastasia's head snaps up as though she heard his thought. Eyelids half shut, she fights off the day's activities. The next time they shut completely Leo swings his arm under her legs and scoops her up like a little kitten.

She comes to halfway across the yard. She doesn't startle or lose balance, but wraps her arms around Leo's neck anyway.

"Wow," she says with a tired smile. "I feel like a princess."

Leo grins. "I missed my workout today."

Inside he lays her on his silver couch. While its size could easily accommodate two, he opts to sit on the floor below her head.

Anastasia wraps herself in the old wool blanket and settles deeper into the cushions.

"And your Mom?" Leo asks.

She frowns. Her eyes drop for a second and she props herself on her elbow. "In one of her...moods."

"She won't care you're not back?"

"She didn't notice I was gone last night. I doubt she will tonight either."

Leo understands more and more why Anastasia attached herself to his own mother. He imagines the reason to be the same for him. He only regrets that it took her dying to realize it, because in life the thought never occurred.

The fact makes it hard to understand why his mother ever attached herself to him. What had he done besides defy and act for himself: what had he sacrificed apart from a few months when her terminal health gave him no other moral option: what had he been for her aside from a prophetic vision validated by a senile old man. Perhaps the answer lies in Anastasia's faith: unexplainable.

Generation 6 is and would be his last chance to make right over his mother. It would also be his initial chance to put someone else first in his new life.

The doubt arising from the Elm of False Dreams, the temptation to fall back into his cushion of agnosticism, all stem from the supposed "beliefs" he's held so dear for as long as he remembers. Yet if asked what those beliefs actually consist of, he wouldn't be able to put the simplest into a phrase. In the end, they are just more doubts: ones of which he's used as excuses for his own convenience.

He stands abruptly. "You know what?" he says in no particular direction.

He starts pacing but doesn't finish his utterance.

Anastasia doesn't ask "what?". She instead sits up and tucks her thin strands of blonde behind her ears.

"My Mom would notice if I weren't home." He continues pacing. "And be on my ass about it no matter how much I bitched and complained."

He finally stops and faces Anastasia. His shoulders relax, and his body stands on lighter feet. He stuffs all but his thumbs into the pockets of his Amines.

"I'm going to see this through," he says. "Generation 6."

Anastasia smiles and watches eagerly. If a moment before she was tired, she now brims with excitement.

The enthusiasm, however, checks Leo on his hasty declaration. He quickly looks down. He realizes he's taken his first step onto the abyss with nothing but faith and goodwill underneath. Such footing falls on empty ground: faith and goodwill never having been his strong suits. He finds it's nowhere near time to step off completely.

He makes a labored nod and looks up at her again. "Or at least give it a chance."

Despite the emendation Anastasia's smile doesn't fade. In fact, it grows tenderer.

This softer encouragement imbues the opposite effect in her smile. No pressure, just support. This time, he nods easily with his head held higher.

"I owe her that much," he says.

The assertion resonates through the room. It rounds the corner where Leo played with his toys as an innocent child, and on to the area where he played his guitar as a bitter teen. The rest absorbs into the son of Pandora Maquari.

Leo settles back into his spot on the floor and rests his elbows on his knees. He looks up at Anastasia who props her cushion into place. She regards him a moment, then runs a finger down the length of his scars.

"Oh, my Leo."

With that she closes her eyes.

Leo considers going upstairs to his actual bedroom, but can't imagine anywhere being more comfortable than the hard floor he's on.

ΔΔΔ

The morning air pours in through the secuscreens of the fenestrators left open overnight. The chill wakes Leo from his propped position on the floor. As he rouses, he's unsure whether the cold or the giant goosebumps popping up on his arms were the cause of his interrupted sleep. When the last goosebump reaches the end of his arm, he sticks up a drowsy head and looks about. He's surprised to find both the couch and his hand empty, having expected both to be occupied by Anastasia.

Rising, he wraps his hands around his meaty arms. He moves to close the fenestrators straight away. He then stretches his obliques with a face of discomfort, reconsidering the definition of comfortable he settled on the night before.

Anastasia comes down a few minutes later carrying a Tempe cup. Its contents contain water, and is set to lukewarm.

"Thought you might have left," says Leo.

"No I was just..." she says pointing back up the stairs.

It wouldn't surprise him if she'd taken some time alone amongst his mother's things. He wonders what she'd gain from that exactly, and if doing the same would benefit him. Nonetheless, alone means alone, so Leo does not press for any more.

"So I guess the food's ready then?" he says quickly to interrupt her stuttering. "First one up and all."

"Oh I think that's the last one up." She folds her arms and rests her weight on her back leg.

Her sweet resistance fills him more than any breakfast he might have eaten by himself. Though he typically ate that meal alone, knowing there was always someone upstairs like his mother or even Khloe made it a matter of choice rather than necessity. The latter proves much scarier than he thought. Anastasia's presence proves much less intrusive than he'd care to admit.

"Fine, you win this time," says Leo. "But you might end up regretting it." He snags her water and steals a sip as he passes by.

They start up the stairs when the welcoming chime rings from the basement door. Nobody reacts as though it had malfunctioned, yet they wait and listen. After a few seconds, it chimes again.

"Who could that be?" says Anastasia.

"I don't know. Khloe wouldn't chime at that door."

"And Beren and Zoe wouldn't chime."

Leo descends thinking it might be some melodramatic mourner. Someone who wanted the private audience of a house call so he'd remember how much they cared when *they* die.

When he opens the door though, it is quite a different mourner, and one he'd not forget.

"Dad."

Aeschylus Serelin stands in the doorway wearing a guitar on his back and an uneasiness on his face. In his left hand he holds a bag of freshly brewed Pronoian tea from Daphne's. The other hand rubs over the top portion of his wrinkled forehead. His legs jitter to the point it's unclear whether he'll enter or flee.

"Leo, uh, hi. I hope this isn't too early, or soon or anything... but I thought I'd take you up on that jam session...if you can of course. I brought breakfast," he adds, holding up the bag.

Though Leo extended the invitation in what he believed to be sincerity, a part of him hoped his father would procrastinate for a long time, if ever come altogether. What's more, a chat on neutral ground greatly differs from seeing him in the home where all the hurt began.

He looks back at Anastasia, already scrambling for excuses in his mind.

She descends. With a look of compassion she keeps Leo's eye as she makes her way towards him. At his side, she strokes the back of his hand then wraps herself tightly in his arm. A tender smile adds the cherry.

Sweet resistance.

Leo turns back to his father and nods. Sooner or later their open engagement would come to pass. At least if he accepts for today he wouldn't have to face the awkwardness of their encounter alone: and he would also get out of making breakfast.

"Alright, yeah, come in."

Despite the promising vibes and signal to advance, Aeschylus hesitates at the doorway. His rheumy eyes look over the top of the frame. His veiny hand remains in limbo between his forehead and side. Finally, with a quick glance at Leo waiting, he lifts a heavy foot over the threshold.

"Wow," he says, taking his first breath. "It's been a while."

He looks over the room as if all the energy of its past fell on him at once. Slow, weary eyes move about, stopping at times on certain places. They even stop on places where there is apparently nothing. Once they find the music area, though, they don't roam any longer.

"I thought you might be down here...you and Staj." Aeschylus looks up and hands Anastasia the bag. "There's some black tea and brioche for all of us."

"Thanks," says Anastasia, setting it on the table. She begins unloading its contents and shoots Leo a knowing glare. This Leo deflects with the pretext of accepting his drink. He looks back on her once she's handed Aeschylus his.

The aged, lonely man paces a few rounds not quite knowing where to settle. He sips his tea sporadically and with a slightly louder slurp than the silence would normally allow. The studio equipment again and again draws his attention.

Leo sips his drink as quietly as possible to avoid slurping what he doesn't have words for. The more words that escape him, the more frequent his sips become. He soon alternates each sip with one of his own knowing looks at Anastasia. This time she deflects.

All the while, however, his father's glances toward the music area do not escape him. A twinge of ire moves over his body, followed by a thought of audacity. He catches himself before too much manifests on his face. What manifests on Anastasia's face, though, indicates he didn't catch himself enough.

He looks down into his cup. He then takes a long sip which ends up burning his tongue. The pain proves a pleasant distraction. He sips again.

Though he never imagined his relationship with his father would mend overnight, he sees he will have to give himself as much time as he figured on giving Aeschylus. Places like the music area where they spent so much time turn out to be more detached and sensitive after so many years of animosity. Nonetheless, it is also the place Alexi took some of his greatest joy and fondest memories. Leo fights hard to cling to that.

At this point Aeschylus begins sensing the discomfort. His sips too become more frequent, and his right hand returns to rubbing his forehead. Just as it seems he will stand to leave, Leo stands first.

The scarred, young guitarist makes no comment as he maneuvers around the DC sound system. He then reaches behind, and pulls out an object long since stowed away.

"Here," he says to Aeschylus, "your stool."

The old musician stares not only at the object, but at Leo placing it in the arrangement they played together so many times when he was a boy; when Alexi was a boy. His hand falls slowly to his side.

Leo makes to grab his own guitar but stops. Both his brows furrow inward in suspicion. He then pulls out a black and gold guitar case he doesn't remember even owning.

He sets it on his stool cautiously and stands by observing. No particular insignia draws his attention but for a sticker of opposite facing pre-Reckoning guns with roses wrapped around them. The roses at least remind him of Elysium. In any case, with nothing else for it he starts unlatching the drawbolt closures. When he opens the top, his eyes grow wide and bright.

Aeschylus, seeing the astonishment in Leo's eyes, carefully moves toward him to get a better look. His eyes widen even further. "A Les Paul Custom!," he says in the face of the pre-Reckoning vestige. "That's quite the antique."

Leo racks his brain trying to find an explanation as to how that guitar could have made it all the way from the Underworld to the house. When he catches the grin on Anastasia's face, however, he realizes he need look no more. A smile of gratitude crosses his lips.

"Come to think of it," Aeschylus continues, "it reminds me a lot of your grandfather's."

"It was," says Leo. "Ale...Grandpa gave it to me."

This time it's eyebrows up. The lines on Aeschylus' leathery forehead crease as he mulls over the ivory finish and pearl-laced fretboard. He cocks his head to the side and murmurs an anachronistic "hmm".

"Well, no one better for it," he says. "For him to give that up he must have really believed in your potential."

"He did," says Anastasia, setting down her Thermacup. "And so do I. Jelly or neufchatel?"

"It's jam," say father and son together. Leo looks away but not enough to suppress the break of a laugh.

"Whatever you guys say," says Anastasia. She proceeds to dipping the knife, then just goes ahead and takes the first one for herself.

Aeschylus grins but doesn't direct it at Leo. He instead pulls out his guitar and kicks off with a fancy pentatonic lick from the high end of a scale to the low. Leo perks up, and immediately matches it note for note at shredding speed.

Aeschylus cocks to the side once more. "Looks like you'll be teaching me now," he says. He continues into a chord progression with a proud smile.

With no special focus or visions of any kind, Leo feels his brother's contentment from far in the depths of the Underworld. He finds it odd he would accept such a feeling. He imagines he does in what Anastasia calls the basis of her faith.

The basement room then fills with the sounds of a second guitar not heard for so many years. Leo looks back on his father strumming away to his humble statement, deferring to his son's lead. Leo answers with a smile and a thought:

Or maybe not.

And so the morning passes in relative harmony: balancing the discord of a father he couldn't fathom, and the girl he couldn't see.

End of Book 1

EPILOGUE

A virtecran scrolls the latest news posts of the *Time's Current*. High in an office overlooking Pronoia, a ringed, female hand taps on a lead story. The ring contains the Classic letter "v." The story is titled: "Daughter of General Maquari Passes into the Flame."

"Eulimnos, Prometheum (14:22),

"Dozens of mourners gathered to witness the funeral games of Pandora Maquari: daughter of renowned Reckoning General, the late Alexander Maquari.

Events were a mix of excitement and emotion as participants and spectators rallied the contests.

Leonidas Maquari, twenty one years of age and son of the deceased, followed the games with a heartfelt eulogy:

Q SoundBits = "The only thing I can do for her now is live: live for who she was, and who she'd want me to be. That's why I'm here."

Local thespian and close of friend of Leonidas, Zoe Qwynshing comments:

"Yeah, who knows where that came from. Then he starts tongue rolling his best friend!"

Said young woman, Anastasia Wildyn, closed the day by igniting the pyre. This with the bow she used to win the marksmanship category earlier.

Pandora Maquari worked several years as a home care infirmary. She is survived by Leonidas, and daughter Khloe Mahning of Prometheum Proper. A son, Alexi Serelin, precedes her in death."

A call notification pops up over the time and date: 14:33, 13/16/80.

Muzak rings, and the elegant woman considers the caller. "Accept," she commands.

The sound stops.

"Hello, Bouko. I thought you might call," she says casually.

"Goetia," says Statesman Braun. "We have a problem."

She saunters to the window with her back to the call. Coolly lifting her hand she regards the dark marble ring in front of her face. A pale white light flashes through the "v," then calms.

"No," she says, lowering her hand. "Just a boy."

BOOKS IN THIS SERIES

GENERATION VI

Generation VI is a futuristic tale set in the city-state of Prometheum. It follows Leo Maquari as he struggles to come of age after his mother's death. A trip to the Underworld sets him on a mission to save her, but leaves him on a journey to discover the secrets of the world above.

The Underworld

His mother's dying wish is impossible: "Find me."

Leo Maquari never really believed Prometheus brought civilization back from the brink of extinction. But when his mother passes, restless dreams plague him, warning him of the torments that await her if he can't bring her spirit peace. Guided by visions he's long denied, he descends into the Underworld, where primordial monsters roam, deceased relatives live, and long-buried secrets come to light. But the deeper Leo travels, the clearer it becomes that his greatest trial is not death itself, but what awaits him on the surface.

The Road To Pronoia

BEFORE GLORY COMES THE RECKONING

Still shaken by his journey through the Underworld, Leo Maquari sets out across a post-apocalyptic world on a quest that could change the fate of mankind. Along the way lies Pronoia, the home of a famous gladiatorial-style tournament that offers glory, distraction, and danger in equal measure.
But the road is long, lands are hostile, and ancient powers stir where civilization thins. Haunted by visions, rivaled by a legendary warrior, and hunted by forces older than the gods, Leo must decide whether destiny is something to fulfill—or to defy.

ACKNOWLEDGEMENT

I'D LIKE TO END by recognizing certain individuals who played a significant part in this journey. I'll start by thanking Professor Tom Philipose, formerly of St. John's University. He took me on as a budding writer and molded me into someone dedicated to a lifelong craft.

I'd also like to thank Matt Zazzarino, formerly of St. John's University as well. He and I worked together on this project for quite some time. As an editor, he had all the qualities I could ask for: patience, objectivity, and great critique. I believed we enjoyed a solid connection throughout, and the project would never have turned out the way it did without his help.

Finally, I'd like to thank my readers. I'm grateful to all for the opportunity to share this important piece of my imagination. I welcome you to the world of Generation VI, and hope you'll stay tuned, because there is more to come.

PRAISE FOR AUTHOR

AN AMAZING AND CAPTIVATING READ. A triumph of the author's imagination. I hope to see more works from Jeff Wimperis in the future. 5 Stars.

- WORLD ECONOMY

ABOUT THE AUTHOR

Jeff Wimperis

Jeff Wimperis is an American writer out of the Pocono region of Pennsylvania. Prior to his debut novel, Generation VI, he published several short stories and poems of speculative fiction.

When not writing, you can typically find him working on a new guitar piece for his YouTube channel, teaching ESL at a local college, or watching a good boxing match on DAZN.

He is currently working on the third book of the Generation VI series. This will be the final chapter in the original trilogy, and take Leo and friends to the grand finale in their quest for the Urn.

www.ingramcontent.com/pod-product-compliance
Lightning Source LLC
Chambersburg PA
CBHW030634260626
47157CB00007B/2328